the COLDEST PASSION

the
COLDEST
PASSION

VICTORIA LUM

Cover Design Copyright © 2023 Y'All That Graphic
Editing by Becca Mysoor, Grace Bradley, and Amy Briggs
Proofreading by Virginia Tesi Carey
Formatting by Elaine York of Allusion Publishing
www.allusionpublishing.com

Author's Note: Please note this story may contain
areas that may be sensitive to some readers.
For a list of potential areas of sensitive content, please visit:
https://www.victorialum.com/sensitive-content-information

To anyone whose life has touched grief or tragedy,
may your heart find a new rhythm,
and may you find your light again.

If it wasn't for my daughter, I probably wouldn't be alive. It's a thought I've kept from everyone around me.

They don't suspect. I'd never let them suspect.

No one wants to peer beyond the veil and see the demons within. It's easier to embrace my façade of charm and smiles.

"Turtles! Daddy, come look!" She points excitedly at two large, brown turtles in their enclosures. They lie there like rocks, camouflaged by their surroundings. I don't understand her obsession with them.

The Los Angeles Zoo is a little gem nestled slightly north of downtown LA. Its grounds are not as big as the more famous and affluent zoos around the area like the San Diego Zoo, but the size is just big enough for you to take your little children on a fun trip without tiring them or yourself out. The weather is in the high eighties as we begin to officially enter the summer season, which is almost all year round in LA. The crowds are thankfully not very large today, so it's easier for me to keep track of my energetic kindergartener. Small graces.

"I see... Those are enormous turtles. Let's see what they're called." I hoist her up on my shoulders to read the sign. "They're called the Aldabra tortoise. They have a long lifespan and can live up to one hundred fifty years. These turtles are from Africa, which is very far away. They like to eat small plants and grasses."

"They do look very old and wrinkly...and they have many spots, a little bit like Grandma. I can't wait to tell Ms. Chapman on Monday. I bet she loves turtles too."

My breath catches in my throat at the mention of Liz, her kindergarten teacher, and my best friend, James's sister.

No, I'm not going to think about her today.

Lucy tugs my hair, eliciting a grimace from me. "Daddy. Daddy, look at me."

"Gentle fingers, Lucy, don't pull on people's hair. That's not very nice. Use your words."

She stares down at me, a little pout on her cute lips. "Are you very old, Daddy? Like the turtles?"

I chuckle. "I'm thirty-six. Not as old as the turtles, but a lot older than you." I stare up at her little face, cataloging the blue eyes, Abby's eyes, the smooth, silky face with a bit of baby fat, the adorable button nose, and the dimples, courtesy of me. *What did I ever do to deserve this little angel in my life?*

Lucy's pout turns into a frown. "That's very old." She pauses, her lips quivering, and whispers, "Will you die, Daddy? Like Mommy?"

The chaos around me blurs into the background, leaving me with the sound of the blood rushing in my veins. My grip on her tightens as pain flashes through my body akin to a lightning strike, adding to the constant, dull ache in my chest. "Someday, Lucy, but not for a very, very long time. Daddy is still very young, so don't you worry about a thing." I swallow the lump in my throat as I fight to keep my composure.

"I love you, Daddy."

I swing her down from my shoulders and hold her tight against me, blinking away the moisture gathering in my eyes. She's so tall now. Not a baby anymore. My chest twists in wistfulness. I take in a whiff of her hair, the sweet, unique scent only your flesh-and-blood can provide, settling my frayed nerves. My hands tremble as I pat her back. "I love you so much too, pumpkin. To the sun, the stars, the moon and back, until the end of time."

I pray she doesn't ask me any more questions.

Abby was young, too.

Thankfully, at least one thing is on my side, and she suddenly perks up, the somber mood seemingly forgotten, and announces, "I want to see giraffes and kangaroos. They're my favorite."

I've given up trying to make sense of the mind of a five-year-old. Their favorites shift constantly. It's like channel surfing on television—everything looks good, but nothing enticing enough to stick and hold your interest. Shaking my head, I set her down and amble toward the giraffe enclosure, sidestepping families with strollers, little kids running around, personnel buzzing by in golf carts, and small groups of tourists with their color-coordinated T-shirts. My phone vibrates in the pocket of my jeans.

"This is Parker."

"Wellington, where are you? It's so loud in the background. Are you at the zoo? Man, your last name is too long."

"You know, you can just call me by my first name. Not everyone has a two-syllable last name like you, Chapman. I'll have you know, I'm a descendant of royalty."

"Don't let that get into your head. It's already big enough," James snarks.

"You're such an ass—"

"Daddy, you used a bad word!" Lucy pulls my shirt and gives me a glare, or her best imitation of one. Children shriek in the crowd around us, and I hold the phone closer to my ear.

"Sorry, honey. I need to remember next time." I give her hand a little squeeze. "What happens when we make a mistake?"

She grins and exclaims, "We say sorry and try again."

"Daddy will try to do better next time."

She beams, apparently mollified. *Thank God.* The strangest things trigger her tantrums these days.

"Is that Lucy? Tell her I said hi. Jess and I miss her a lot. She can come over anytime." The baritone voice on the line reminds me

James is still there. "Not you though, you can't come over anytime, but feel free to drop off Lucy."

James and I have a love-hate relationship according to him. I'm sure it started when his wife went on a date with me before he got his shit together and won her over. Somehow, he found it in his "forgiving" soul to relinquish the past and be friends with me. Or maybe it's because I'm a fun person to hang out with most of the time provided you don't peek into the inner workings of my mind.

"Uncle James is a meanie. Let's not be like him when you grow up," I announce loudly, earning a lot of giggling from my little pipsqueak.

"Why are we still friends, Parker?"

"I don't know. I have so many great qualities, I can't just choose one. My sparkling personality? My good looks? My dimples? Because your wife likes me?"

"You're so lucky I know you aren't serious, because any sideways glance at Jess and you're done, jackass."

I burst out laughing, and the ache in my chest temporarily lightens a smidge. "Chill, man. You're so easy to rile up. Anyway, I *am* at the zoo with Lucy. What's up?" We reach the giraffe enclosure and I nudge through the small group of people gathered there and secure a prime front-row viewing spot for Lucy. The tall, graceful animals are peacefully munching on the green leaves of the trees, ignoring the surrounding chaos.

"Just wanted to see if you're still alive. Missed you at our NBA finals night party last weekend. Game one started off great. The team is having a solid season this year." Rustling sounds filter in from the background followed by a small murmur, "Sleep a little bit more, sweetheart."

"If only you could see my face. I'm gagging right now. You're still in bed? And I know you love me despite what you say because you're calling me first thing in the morning with your hot wife sleeping next to you."

"I don't have kids, so I get to sleep in...and I'm getting up right now."

"Anyway, last weekend was a shitshow at work because of the homeless shelter project, so I had to go into the office. Trust me, I wanted to be there. I did watch the highlights later but count me in for game two."

"You going to Emily's birthday next Saturday, right? Jess wanted me to confirm with you." More rustling and clicking as James is most likely walking to the kitchen to fix a cup of coffee for Jess. These two are so in love it's borderline nauseating.

"I'll be there. Cindy will watch Lucy that night."

"Sounds great. Got to go." He disconnects the call just as Lucy is pulling on my sleeve.

"Daddy, Daddy...Daddy!"

I look down at the sole reason for my existence. "Yes, pumpkin?"

Lucy jumps up and down. "They're so cute! Look, they're eating leaves...like a salad!" She flashes those adorable dimples at me and continues, "That tall one is daddy giraffe, the little one is baby giraffe, and the medium one is...mommy giraffe." Her lower lip wobbles toward the end.

My heart clenches at her forlorn expression, her nose a little pink as if she's on the verge of tears. I grit my teeth and force out a reassuring smile. "Yes, a whole family of giraffes. They're very happy, just like us."

"I wish Mommy is still here. I wish I have a mommy."

How do you explain to a child life is not all roses and sunshine? Good people don't always have happy endings? People you love can suddenly disappear...just like that, with no rhyme or reason? I wish this job didn't fall on me. I'd much rather break the news Santa Claus isn't real.

I squat down at her eye level and brush a few golden strands from her smooth face, now pink from the heat. "I wish that too, Lucy. She may not be here with us, but she's watching down on us, okay?" I give her a quick peck and start tickling her, a sure way of redirecting her attention. She screeches in laughter and attempts to return the favor, giggling when she sees me squirming dramatically and making a fool out of myself.

"Daddy, you're silly!"

"And you're silly Daddy's equally silly daughter." I hoist her back on my shoulders. "Come on, let's see some other animals."

I let out a deep sigh of relief at the joy on her face, even though it doesn't fully alleviate the ache in my chest.

Nothing ever does.

I've gotten used to not breathing fully, not sleeping peacefully. This is what a combustible cocktail of grief, anger, and self-loathing will do to you. My own personal IV, sending the bitter brew to my system around the clock, like a bad trip on drugs which never ends.

Two hours later, we've visited kangaroos, tigers, bears, all sorts of birds, and we're both ready to go home. A short, quiet drive later, we arrive back at our two-story, five-bedroom contemporary home I designed as one of my first projects when I started my architecture and design firm with my partner ten years ago. Growing up poor, my mom and I always moved from apartment to apartment, wherever the cheapest rent was. Mom struggled to raise me as a single mother after my dad passed away when he was forty from lung cancer. She worked two blue-collar jobs to keep the electricity on and put food on the table.

I always dreamed of living in a beautiful home with my family. I'd go to work each day and come back to a happy wife, with kids running around the backyard or swimming in the pool. The house would be messy, the laundry thrown over the sofa, a husky chasing a calico cat all over the place, and the home would be chaotic and noisy, but full of love. Instead, I'm handed the harshness of reality. Now, this family only comprises the two of us and the house is too quiet, like the life has been sucked out of it, leaving a structure beautiful in appearance, but soulless.

Perhaps art imitates life.

I fix a quick blue-box macaroni and cheese for Lucy, who is thankfully on her best behavior today and reheat some leftover frozen lasagna from last night. The dishes pile up in the sink. I make a mental note to load them in the dishwasher after dinner. Cindy can put them away when she returns tomorrow. I scarf down the meal, the food tasteless on my tongue, and turn on *Spot and Lola* for Lucy. A happy, animated family of corgi dogs materializes on the screen, and Lucy is instantly mesmerized. Why is it children's entertainment always shows a set of happy parents? Don't they know life doesn't always work that way? I clench my jaw and start loading the dishwasher as my phone rings.

"Hey, Cindy, did you enjoy your night off? Miss us already?" She has been our nanny for the last two years, an absolute godsend, helping me keep the ship somewhat afloat. Lucy loves her.

"Parker, I just want to let you know I got a new job as a secretary for a law firm. The hours and benefits are great. It was just too good of an opportunity to pass up. Unfortunately, I found out today they want me to start as soon as possible, but I was able to push it out for a week. I'll be back tomorrow, and we can talk more but I didn't want to delay telling you the news any longer."

My heart drops. Where the fuck am I going to find childcare with this short notice? Lucy is starting summer vacation in one week and I still have my full-time job. Mom and Rick, my stepdad, are in Portland, and he's still working, so she can't come down here to help for such a long period of time. I exhale forcefully, my mind searching for solutions to this dilemma.

"Is there anything I can do to make you stay? A raise? More vacation days?" My foot taps a nervous rhythm on the floor.

"I…" She sighs, which isn't a good sign, and continues, "I'm sorry. It aligns with what I want to do in the future. I know this puts you in a tough position."

I crack my neck in an audible snap, relieving some of the pressure gathering there. I sigh in resignment. "It's okay. Thank you for letting me know. Let's get dinner together on your last day to celebrate your new job."

Another person Lucy loves leaving her out of the blue.

Lucy giggles from the living room as I slide down the kitchen counter into a sitting position, my hands still wet from pre-rinsing the dishes. I close my eyes, pinpricks of pain flashing in my head, a sure sign a migraine is around the corner.

I'm so tired, but I must keep going...for Lucy.
After all, I killed her mom.

"**M**s. Chapman, Marcus said you don't need to fall in love and get married to have babies. But Mommy and Daddy said that's how babies are made." Kiera scrunches her nose at me on the playground at the last recess and snack time before dismissal. Marcus stands next to her, his arms crossed and face smug, but still adorable in the way only five-year-olds can pull off. Summer is in full swing, with the scorching heat rising to almost one hundred degrees as the sun turns the playground into a veritable oven. The kids are still running around the asphalt in glee, sweat dripping off their faces, and shirts plastered to their backs. It seems not much can dim the spirits of kindergarteners.

"Well, that's true. Some people have babies and aren't married." I need to tread carefully or else I may start a heated debate between the parents and the administration, which I certainly don't need.

"But then, how are babies made? Can you let me know? I'm very curious." A small crowd has gathered now, and the voice which has just spoken is Lucy, Parker's very adorable daughter.

Parker.

That man irks me in a way no man ever has before. I'd like to believe I'm an easy person to get along with. My friends always gush about how thoughtful and sweet I am. But this man, for some inexplicable reason, has hated me since the moment he met me last year. I still remember the day as if it occurred yesterday.

Jess and her sister, Emily, met me at a Greek restaurant for a girls' lunch and Parker ran into us. He was the first person Jess swiped right on when she joined *InstaConnect* before she and James finally got together. He was the most drop-dead gorgeous man I had ever seen, at least, from his online profile, but nothing could've prepared me for seeing him up close in person. The thick head of golden-brown hair, with streaks of blond, like he spent time in the salon, but is most likely a result of excellent genetics. The piercing green eyes, mysterious, and always seeming like they're holding secrets. The strong jaw, reminiscent of the Greek sculptures in museums. Those dimples, which he uses to his best advantage. The imposing, tall figure. Those corded muscles flexing with every movement he makes.

"Hi! I'm Liz, Jess's friend in every sense of the word." I grin, staring at the gorgeous man in front of me, a bit nervous for some unknown reason. I extend my hand toward him.

Parker looks away from the other girls. "Liz, nice to meet—"

His expression freezes as he clasps my hand in his, his emerald eyes darkening in something akin to shock as unidentified emotions flash in his gaze. A muscle twitches in his cheek as he swallows, his Adam's apple bobbing up and down his muscular neck.

I freeze, my smile slipping under the intensity of his stare. Parker squeezes my hand tighter. I wince. "Ouch. You have a strong grip there."

Parker snaps out of his trance and drops my hand as if he has touched molten lava. He tugs at his collar as a dark flush creeps up his neck.

"Sorry about that," he replies, clearly flustered.

He drags his hands through his thick hair, his eyes darting away but quickly returning to me. He shifts his body as if uncomfortable.

He turns to Jess. "It's great seeing you, Jess. I'm sure we'll talk soon." Parker's eyes flicker to me again, intense emotions brimming in his gaze. Then he promptly turns away and strides out of the restaurant.

If that isn't dislike at first sight, I don't know what is. It's like I contracted the plague and he refused to come within ten feet of me. Despite him being best friends with my brother, he's made every effort to avoid joint events when I'm present. Or in the unfortunate circumstance when we have to be at the same place at the same time, like Jess's and James's wedding, he'll pretend I don't exist.

I don't understand. And as an educator, I despise things I can't figure out. It's akin to the boxes not lining up exactly the way you want them to when you prepare PowerPoint presentations.

Extremely annoying. A scab I want to pick at.

"Ms. Chapman!"

The gaggle of kids snaps me out from my trip down memory lane. Where were we?

"How are babies made, Ms. Chapman? I really want to know." This time, it's Marcus voicing the all-important question with Lucy, Kiera, and a few other classmates nodding vigorously like bobbleheads in a bumpy car ride.

They really don't pay me enough for this. Why is it educators of our future leaders get paid abysmally while—I'll get off my mental soapbox.

I lean down and glance around quickly as if I'm telling them a secret. The children crowd closer. "Well, you see...this is a big secret, but a baby is made from two small cells from a man and a woman. A cell is a very teeny tiny piece from our bodies."

"But where do these pieces come from? How does it all work?"

Riiiiiiiiiing.

Literally saved by the bell.

"Okay, kids, time to line up and go home. Have fun during your summer vacation! I'll miss you all so, so much."

The children shriek with joy and proceed to line up in their usual spots. Melanie Chan, a fellow kindergarten teacher who shares my classroom, sidles up to me, her straight hair tied in her signature ponytail, a look rivaling a certain famous starlet. "Cells, huh?"

"You heard that? Why didn't you come over and save me?"

She snorts, her warm, brown eyes dancing. "No way I'm touching that subject with a ten-foot pole."

"You're no help whatsoever." I bite my cheek to keep from smiling. "You're coming tonight, right?"

"Wouldn't miss it for the world. I can't believe I finally get to meet your girlfriends. I feel like I know them already from the stories you tell me."

"They'll love you. Especially Ems. She's a firecracker." We walk to the front of the lines and begin leading the children to the lunch tables where the parents pick up the younger students.

The pickup area is chaotic in the best way. Crowds of children sitting in little groups at the tables with their backpacks and lunch bags in tow gesturing excitedly at each other. Parents filtering in, some looking frazzled, carrying younger siblings in their arms, others with beaming smiles on their faces. Children leaping into their parent's embrace. Screeches of joy, bubbly laughter, and excited chatter as kids anticipate the beginning of summer vacation tomorrow. I survey the area, my hands smoothing my navy-blue sundress, which folks have told me brings out the blue in my eyes.

"Who are you looking for?"

"Huh?" I ask, puzzled at Melanie's strange observation. It's almost a routine now, my eyes sweeping the tables in front of me, not wanting to miss anything...or anyone.

"You're scanning the area like a soldier stationed on a lookout, searching for enemies."

A familiar young brunette dressed in a white tank top and distressed jeans pushes through the crowd, waving her hand at the children sitting at our closest table.

"Cindy!" Lucy pauses before turning and sprinting toward me. "Bye, Ms. Chapman. I'll miss you." I give her a big hug and she happily scrambles over to her nanny.

I let out a breath and bite my bottom lip.

Of course, *he* won't come to pick her up himself. He never does.

"Earth to Liz. Earth to Liz."

"Sorry, woolgathering a bit there." I plop down on one of the empty benches and wait for the rest of the parents to pick up their children. "Don't be silly. I was just making sure I recognize who the kids are going home with."

Melanie narrows her eyes. "Right." She follows her scrutiny with a cock of an eyebrow.

Point completely taken.

• • •

"Liz, thanks for hosting girls' night this week!" Emily, known to her friends as Ems, squeals as she wraps me up in her signature koala hug. This petite firecracker, small but very mighty, gives the best hugs, but we always joke because of her size, they're better described as koala hugs than bear hugs.

"Of course! We take turns hosting, but sorry you guys have to cramp into this small space." I'm renting a studio apartment in the northern part of Pasadena, a beautiful city nestled in the base of the Foothill Mountains just north of downtown LA. Rent is exorbitant and with my measly salary, I can only afford a tiny place but at least I don't have to share it with anyone. It's my dream to someday own a home of my own. At least then, I'll be building equity instead of throwing money into the ocean month after month. In the meantime, I try to make do with the cramped quarters. I decorated the living room walls with colorful photos of friends and family, and art prints I purchased from flea markets. My navy-blue linen sofa may be small, but I dress it up with velvety cushions and throw blankets. Two sunshine-yellow, structured bean bags serve as additional seating.

"No worries. My little shoebox of an apartment is only marginally bigger, but I wouldn't trade it for anything." Emily lives in a high-rise in downtown LA to be closer to her clients and to be in the heart of the city where she can easily attend various events and gatherings. She's a prominent image consultant at a renowned public relations firm whose clients include a plethora of athletes, executives, celebrities, and politicians in the media hub of the country.

"Thanks for bringing wine. Jess and my coworker, Melanie, are already here. Jess brought pasta from Luciano's. Go get situated." I take the two bottles from her hands and head to the kitchenette to fetch some glasses.

"Sis! So glad you can make it this week. We missed you last week at my place," Emily exclaims, and I know she's gesturing animatedly as she talks. "Ooo, hi, I'm Emily, Jess's younger sister. You can call me Ems. You must be Melanie?"

Carrying a tray with four glasses of wine to the living room, I introduce Melanie to the group. "This is Melanie, my work-wife. We teach the same class together. Melanie, here are the infamous Kingsley sisters, Jess and Emily."

"I feel like I know you girls already! Liz talks about you all the time." Melanie grins, helping me set the glasses on the circular marble coffee table. "I'm so *honored* to be invited tonight. Liz has been dangling the invite in front of me for weeks. I've had to do classroom cleanings, supply restocks, and many unspeakable things in order to be here." She sighs dramatically and shakes her head, sending her long ponytail into the air.

"I like her," Emily concludes, her eyes twinkling. I roll my eyes at the two of them. I knew they'd hit it off.

"I love your top. The bright yellow really pops against your black jeans," Jess says softly, her hazel eyes gentle as she admires Melanie's bright-colored top.

"Aww, thank you. You girls look terrific too. I've seen photos from Liz, but they don't do the two of you justice."

"Well, flattery will get you *everywhere* with me." Emily beams, her hands brushing over her brown fishtail braid. "I've worked hard to cultivate an image, and it's nice to be recognized." She's always a chic dresser, and today is no exception.

I return to the kitchen to bring out some plates and utensils so the girls can serve themselves. Luciano's is Jess's favorite Italian restaurant near where she and James live in Manhattan Beach. The aroma of creamy alfredo sauce, pesto, and tangy tomatoes fill the space as I open the oven, where Jess was warming the pastas earlier. Today's selection includes simple angel hair pasta with shrimp and vine-ripened tomato sauce, freshly made pesto garlic chicken linguine, and creamy spaghetti carbonara with a hint of truffle. And breadsticks. Always the breadsticks.

"Girls, dinner is ready," I holler at the gathering in the living room.

The girls descend on the pastas and breadsticks like vultures, serving themselves with generous helpings of food, and we settle in place at my small, circular dining table next to the kitchenette. My heart warms as I see Jess heap the spaghetti onto her plate—two years ago, she had a really severe anxiety attack which landed her in the hospital. She was worried about everything, from her changing relationship with her best friend, my brother, and her weight. In these last two years, she worked extremely hard to deal with her condition in a healthier way and I really admire her for her bravery and perseverance.

"So, what are your plans now that you guys are off for the summer?" Jess inquires as she ties up her luscious black hair into a low ponytail.

I sigh, poking at my pasta. "Find a job. I put a few feelers out there...a tutoring position here and there, a temp spot in an office, just waiting to hear back. I may apply to a few more positions later this week. I need the money if I ever want to have any hope of purchasing my own place." I look down at my plate, thankful this meal is not on me. Luciano's isn't cheap.

"We'll ask around as well...maybe not in our industries but will see if our friends have part-time gigs in line with what you're looking for," Jess volunteers. She and James both work with numbers and that's definitely not my strong suit.

"Thanks. I really appreciate it." I shrug. It is what it is. Sometimes, I have to take one step at a time and hope things will work out for the better. "In the meantime, I might spend more time on my family genealogy project."

"How's it going?" Jess asks.

I drink a sip of water and reply, "The results have been very interesting. I'm getting close to tracing our ancestors to the eighteenth century. Genetic Genie, the online company I'm using, has been sending me a lot of information about my extended relatives. I'm actually connecting with some of them."

"Wow. That sounds awesome. Keep us posted on the progress." Jess looks at her sister. "Maybe we'll do something like that one day and see what we find."

"What about you, Melanie?" Emily chimes in before she takes a sip of her wine.

Melanie perks up. "I got my dream job...aside from being a teacher, of course." She leans in and pauses for dramatic effect. "I'm going to be working at Pendleton Books as one of their sales associates! It has always been my dream to work at a bookstore and be surrounded by the new-book smell."

"Ooo, is there an employee discount?" I waggle my brows at her.

"Definitely, just let me know what you want to get." She looks at the other girls. "And that applies to both of you too."

Emily's eyes crinkle at the corners as Jess and I give each other a high-five. Our bookshelves are going to be stocked with romance novels. Book boyfriends for the win.

"How's the dating life, Ems?" I take a break from the carb overload. So satisfying, but I know I'll regret it later when the food coma hits.

"The usual. There's a new guy I'm hanging out with these days. But you know me, I don't do serious. Date them, then dump them."

"Month one?" Jess raises her brows at her sister. Emily subscribes to the short-term dating theory of enjoy the honeymoon period for around three to four months and jump ship before the seas get rough. She attributes her dating style to their parents' cordial and indifferent relationship.

"Yep. Mason is pretty chill and embraces a very zen lifestyle, which is kind of nice, given how intense my job can get, especially when dealing with celebrities and such."

"Don't you want to eventually settle down? Find your soulmate, have kids, live the American dream?" I polish off the rest of my plate, tempted to lick the sauce off, but that would be uncouth. Jess gives me an imperceptible nod at my question.

Emily shakes her head, her chocolate-brown eyes dimming. "I don't think it's in the cards for me, and I'm totally okay with that." She shrugs nonchalantly, but her knuckles are white around the stem of the wineglass in her hands. She flashes a smile which doesn't quite reach her eyes and turns toward Melanie. "So, Melanie, what about you? Seeing anyone special?"

"Nope. *InstaConnect* has been dry lately." She picks up her remaining breadstick and purses her lips. "But I'm still young. Maybe I'll meet someone at the bookstore the old-fashioned way this summer. Wouldn't that be a scene from the movies?"

I nod. It would be the perfect meet-cute. I imagine walking into my favorite place on earth, a bookstore filled to the brim with books from all genres, the smell of freshly ground coffee intermixed with newly cut paper, the quiet, soft jazz playing in the background, and the soft hum of readers, excitedly discussing their purchases. I'd walk straight to the rainbow-colored bookshelves of the romance section and gingerly pick out books with covers catching my eye or books from my to-be-read list, courtesy of social media recommendations.

As I'd turn around with my hands full of literary goodness, someone would bump into me. My pile of books would fly out of my hands and scatter to the ground in a loud clatter. I'd bend down to pick them up and a strong, masculine hand and a whiff of amber would catch my attention. My gaze would slowly trail up. Time would slow to a standstill as everything fades to the background until I'd almost reach his face. This is it, my soulmate, my perfect man, my prince in real life, coming to rescue me from this boring, proverbial provincial life.

"Liz, earth to Liz." Melanie swipes her hands in front of my face, jolting me awake from my perfect meet-cute, a scene only seen in movies and rarely in reality. Darn it—I didn't even get to imagine his face.

If only life imitated art.

"Sorry, I was daydreaming about meeting my perfect man in the bookstore." I sigh, a small smile gracing my face. "It'd be so wonderful."

Melanie shakes her head. "I tell you, what you're looking for doesn't exist. Fairytale princes are fictional characters. Swoony heroes only exist in literature and movies. Real life is messy and definitely not a fairytale."

"That's not true. My parents are an example of the fairytale coming to life. Thirty-seven years of marriage and still going strong," I reply wistfully, images of my loving parents filling my mind. Mom and Dad dancing during the countdown every New Year's Eve as the clock strikes midnight. Them giving each other long hugs and kisses when they thought no one was looking. Dad whispering sweet nothings into Mom's ear, turning her face crimson and him winking at me when he catches me looking. "I want what they have. The fairytale."

"I admire your dream, Liz, I really do, and I hope you find your special someone even if he's not who you were envisioning. Have you gone on *InstaConnect* lately? I hope it's working better for you than it is for me."

I take out my phone and frown at the heart-shaped icon. I despise the app and everything it represents, finding love in the form of transactions, so commercial, so superficial, so unromantic. "I've saved several profiles, but I'm not so sure about them."

Emily jumps out of her seat with the energy of a child on Christmas morning and reaches across the table as Jess tries to unsuccessfully pull her back. She snatches the phone out of my hands. "Let me see!"

I wave Jess off as she looks at me apologetically. "Let her have at it. Can't wait to hear her analysis."

Emily grins gleefully as she swipes on my phone. "Let's see... Anderson Cook, chef...oooh dating a chef has its advantages, thirty-five, great smile, what's wrong with him?"

"Aside from the obvious issue of a chef with the last name Cook, he says he works sixteen-hour days at the restaurant—when will I see him?"

"You'll make it work if you guys like each other," Jess adds.

"Fine, fine, moving on. Brian Chang, half-Chinese...just like us! I like him already." Emily squints at the screen. "What's he wearing? It's atrocious."

I finish my food and monotone my reply, "I'm assuming you're looking at the one photo with a weird clash of the neon colors? Yes, fashion sense is definitely an issue with him, but it's not my main problem. If you keep reading, it says he loves meeting people and going out."

"What's wrong with that?" Melanie interjects, a frown marring her features.

"I like people, but I don't *love* people. I can totally see this being an issue later on with him going out every weekend and me staying home."

"Okaaaay..." Skepticism laces Emily's voice as she continues, "Moving on. Greg Van Doren. He—"

"Hates jazz with a passion. I love jazz. We're going to argue about music choices on our future cross-country road trip." My eyes feel heavy as the food coma hits. I shouldn't have eaten the second serving of breadsticks. But the garlic goodness, who can pass it up?

"Aaron—"

"Likes video games, but doesn't like to read." My eyes snap open. "*Who* doesn't like reading? There are worlds out there waiting for us to discover." Melanie and Jess nod vehemently at my answer. At least I'm blessed with reader friends in my real life.

Emily looks up from the phone. "Liz, these are your only saved profiles. You aren't giving anyone a chance."

I drink a few large gulps of wine and the buzz quickly settles in for what'll probably be a painful conversation. "It's not that I don't want to give anyone a chance. It's just no one gives me goosebumps, the strike-by-lightning feeling. I want to be one of those 'one true pairings' we root for in TV shows and romance novels. Finding someone who gives me butterflies, doesn't have baggage or hang-ups, who clicks with me, and has similar interests as me... that's not asking for too much, right? I know I'm no spring chicken, but I don't want to settle. I'd rather be single than settle."

"Hear, hear." Melanie raises her glass at me for a toast. "And you're not *that* old, Liz. You're only thirty-four. That's nothing in modern times."

"Just make sure you don't swipe left too easily. Sometimes, the right person is in front of you without you knowing. Don't be one of those online missed connections people." Jess glows pink from the wine, a phenomenon she told me is called the "Asian glow," which she thinks is embarrassing but I think is cute.

The night passes by in a blur of gossip, jokes, more wine, and laughter. Emily invites Melanie to her birthday gathering next weekend. After the girls head home, I bury myself in a pink fluffy blanket and curl into a ball on my couch. Turning on my small flatscreen, I eagerly scroll to the latest episode of the popular Asian television drama, *Fated for You*. Darn Melanie for getting me hooked on this addictive show where every single episode ends on a cliffhanger. Even though I don't understand a thing they say, my eyes are getting a workout as I follow the story with the subtitles. I'm mesmerized by how the hero loves this plucky girl-next-door heroine even when she makes all sorts of silly mistakes, loses her job, gets herself locked in a public toilet, and has the most horrific sense of style, but he gets her. Just the way she is. A deep ache settles in my chest as I lose myself in the show, living vicariously through the fictional characters, resigning myself to the idea maybe I'll never find what I'm looking for.

This perfect man...loving the very imperfect me.

The way love should be.

Speaking of which, *should* is an interesting word, because what *should* happen, pretty much guarantees it doesn't, and I hope, in my case, love will work out for me.

My right thumb rubs my left ring finger as I wait for the elevators to open to Olive and Salt, the popular new restaurant on the top floor of the Kensington Hotel in downtown LA. A nervous tic, or so they say. The tan line is almost imperceptible now to the naked eye but feels very much noticeable every second of the day, an invisible brand keeping me tethered to the past.

A past I can't outrun. A past which feels very much like the present.

The doors open with a *ding,* and I'm met with a cacophony of sounds in the popular restaurant. Groups of people huddle around the reception area dressed in trendy attire befitting of the establishment and waiting to be seated. Chefs are yelling instructions to sous chefs in the large, industrial open kitchen. Servers juggle multiple plates of deliciousness in a balancing act rivaling the best circus performers. The restaurant is lit up with multiple dark-grained wood pendant lights with exposed lightbulbs. Excitement and happiness permeate the air.

I survey the space, searching for my friends. A woman in a miniskirt and halter top stands by the receptionist's desk and gives me a once-over. She bites her lip, a clear invitation in her eyes. I stiffen and glance away.

I feel abos-fuckin-lutely...nothing.

My chest has a gaping hole where my heart is supposed to be. And apparently, my dick is malfunctioning as well, which is nothing new to me in the last few years.

Resuming my search, my eyes rove the crowded restaurant once again and I finally spot Emily with James, Jess, and another person I haven't met yet, already seated at the far corner table by the windows. I crack my knuckles and steel myself for another performance. *Dial in the grump, no one wants to see him. Be charming, Parker. It's what they expect of you. Happiness. That's what they're looking for.*

Navigating my way around the small tables, each packed to the brim with patrons, I rearrange my face into a broad smile, making sure I crinkle my eyes for a dash of sincerity. "Emily, happy birthday! What are you now? Twenty-two, twenty-three?" I wink at her.

Emily's eyes twinkle with mirth as she attempts to keep a straight face. "You're too charming for your own good, Parker, but thank you. And you know I'm twenty-eight now. My goal is by the time I reach your age, I'll have everything together just like you do, Mr. Charismatic, Successful, Architect of the Year."

Guilt slices through me at her compliment. *No, you don't want to become me.* Swallowing the thick emotion, I grin and clasp my hand dramatically to my chest, feigning shock. "Well, thank you. That's high praise coming from you. And you look radiant and are doing well in *your* life, and that's what counts. Twenty-eight is still young by the way."

"Seriously, Parker. First you try to charm my wife, then you try to charm her sister?" James utters in mock anger beside Jess, who's shaking with laughter.

I shrug nonchalantly and reply, "This charm is natural and doesn't require any effort to turn on, unlike someone who's wound up so tightly. I still don't know why Jess chose you." Emily snickers in the background as James harrumphs in faux displeasure, drawing Jess in for a kiss that's borderline indecent as if to prove a point.

"Hi, I'm Parker." I flash a smile at the only person at the table I don't know.

"I'm Melanie. Nice to meet you." She waves enthusiastically before she takes a sip of water.

I retrieve a small package from my pocket and hand it to Emily. "Here you go, birthday girl." It's a bit warm in the packed restaurant, so I take off my casual suit jacket, roll up the sleeves of my blue, button-down shirt, and sit down at one of the remaining spots at the table.

"Thanks, Parker, you didn't have to. I'm so excited about tonight! It's been so long since we all got together for dinner and dancing." She puts my gift aside and looks up. "Speaking of everyone, where's Liz?"

"She's running late, she had an interview for a summer job—speak of the devil, there she is. Liz, over here!" Jess tucks a few strands of her long hair behind her ears as she peers behind me.

My stomach flips and I take a sip of ice water, the mere seconds buying me some time to brace myself and prepare for the inevitable. Taking a fortifying breath, I slowly turn around.

Liz, the person I make every effort to avoid despite being the sister of my best friend, slowly makes her way over to the table. Her golden-brown hair is pinned casually on top of her head with loose ringlets framing her heart-shaped face. Her tan, slim-fit, off the shoulder dress clings to her every curve, molding over the generous swells of her breasts, narrowing around her slim waist, and flaring out at her round, luscious hips. She doesn't notice the dozens of eyes trailing her as she passes by the other male diners. She breaks into an infectious, wide smile when she sees us and sashays between patrons as she eagerly makes her way to our table.

A riot of emotions fills me, a convoluted mess, as I try to figure out what to respond to first—the burn of anger deep in my chest, the heated discomfort of blood rushing south, my body inappropriately and inconveniently waking up to her sinful figure, the spark of amusement at her overt happiness, or finally, the clawing sensation in my gut I can only describe as guilt. Liz stops in her tracks when she sees me, a deer in the headlights, her beautiful blue eyes widening as she realizes the only remaining chair at the table is next to mine. Those eyes, so familiar yet foreign to me, haunt me in my dreams. I clench my fists, letting my fingernails dig into the soft flesh of my palm, look away, and quickly turn back around in my seat.

"Hi, guys, sorry I'm late. I was at an interview for a temp job downtown and had to change before I came here. It ran a little long because they were behind. Happy birthday, Ems! Here's your present."

I sense her presence behind me, and the hairs on the back of my neck prickle to attention. She gingerly sits next to me, careful and measured in her movements as if she's somehow fearful of me. A light scent of vanilla wafts to my nose. My body stills, all nerve endings alert, as I glance at her from the corner of my eye.

"Hi, Parker," she whispers, her sweet voice wavering toward the end.

I'm tempted to ignore her, but it would be too obvious. I poke at the ice cubes in my cup with my straw. "Liz." I muster a half smile. Barely. It's either this or be cold to her. *And you know she doesn't deserve that from you, Parker.*

"Right," she murmurs before focusing her attention beyond me to the rest of the group.

"So, Parker." James's voice draws my attention away from Liz. "Cindy is watching Lucy tonight?"

I groan, rubbing my hands over my face. "No, Cindy quit. Her last day was yesterday. My neighbor is doing me a favor and watching Lucy tonight. His kid is Lucy's best friend, so it's like an extended playdate." I cock my brow at Emily. "I'm only doing this for you, birthday girl. I don't go out at night and shirk my fatherly duties just for anyone."

"Oh sheesh," James mutters and rolls his eyes as I cackle at his irritation.

"What are you going to do with childcare, then?" Jess asks, concerned.

"I don't know. I've contacted a few agencies and am waiting for interviews to be set up. I may take a few days off of work or hire a temporary sitter while I figure things out. Worse comes to worst, I'll ask my mom to come down for a week to buy me more time. I just can't ask her to stay long term since Rick is still up there."

The waiters take our entrée orders and the servers come by with appetizers soon thereafter. Everyone settles into their seats and digs into an array of tapas, consisting of specialty breads, cold cuts, ceviche, and other appetizers.

"Liz, how did the job interview go today?" Melanie washes down a bite of her food with some fruity concoction, probably half made of sugar.

Liz sighs next to me, her normally chirpy tone deflating. "I don't think it's the right fit. They only want three hours every other day and I want a full-time job, or at least something that pays decently." She shifts around in her seat and takes a sip of water. "It's okay. Things always work out. I'll find something." I sneak a glance at her as she grins and reaches in front of me for the bread basket. Her shoulder lightly grazes my face and I sharply inhale, her sweet scent invading my nostrils. I close my eyes, not wanting to focus on her slender neck in front of me, to resist the temptation to bite into the alluring, soft skin there. To punish. To mark it up. *Fuck. Don't think this way.*

But sometimes logic can't override emotions.

And my emotions are a mess when it comes to her.

She jolts away, as if realizing how close we are. "Sorry, just trying to get the bread." My eyes snap open and I take in her flushed appearance, the pulse on her neck fluttering rapidly, snaring my attention. *I wonder what other things can put that expression on her face—fuck. Shit. Stop that train of thought.*

"I know this isn't ideal, but my friend owns a gentlemen's club in downtown. They need waitresses for their evening shifts. I hear the tips are really good and they provide security for the girls, so it's pretty safe. You may just need to deal with some unruly customers every so often and some unsavory comments. If you're interested, let me know," Melanie offers with a slight grimace.

Liz groans and taps her dainty fingers on the table. "At this rate, I may need to take the job, if anything, for the money."

The blood roars in my ears at the thought of Liz, in her voluptuous glory, wearing some ridiculous outfit, serving up drinks in a place where other men will ogle her tits and ass. My hands curl tightly around the wineglass and heat rises in my chest. I want to snap the stem in half.

Rage.

Why the fuck do I care, anyway? I couldn't care less what she does on her own time.

Just as I was about to interject, James asks, "Liz, why don't you nanny for Parker instead? He just lost his childcare and Lucy already loves you. That way, Parker has three months to look for a suitable replacement."

I nod mindlessly as anything sounds better than the image of Liz in a skimpy outfit at a club.

Hold on. What? Fuck no. No, no, this is a bad idea.

"What?" Liz asks, echoing the question in my mind, and I whip my face in her direction just in time to witness the astonishment embedded in her features.

Jess's gaze flickers between us, her hazel eyes shrewd as if figuring out the answer to a question no one asked. At her scrutiny, my eyes drop to the wineglass in my hand. She chimes in, "That sounds like a great idea. Liz, you love Lucy, and I'm sure Parker will be a good boss." She turns to me, her elegant brows arched in question. "Right, Parker?"

Silence fills the table as everyone awaits my answer, but I find the only opinion I care about is the person next to me. "Is that what you want, Liz?" My gaze slowly trails over to the maddening woman next to me.

She looks up at me from under her lashes, her hands toying with the salad fork. "I...I'm okay with the arrangement if you are."

"Fine."

"Great! It's settled then. Good news for the both of you, and an excellent beginning to my birthday celebration." Emily claps her hands as the entrees arrive. Clinking and clattering of silverware fill the air as we all dig into our meals. My perfectly cooked filet mignon melts in my mouth and I almost moan out load. It has been so long, too long, since I've gone out to eat a well-prepared dinner without Lucy in tow. I'd almost forgotten what this feels like.

"Thank you, Parker." Liz's voice pulls me back into the present, immediately souring my appetite.

"No need."

"But you didn't need to. I know you don't—"

I grit my teeth and am hit with a sudden urge to rinse the aftertaste of the steak from my mouth. *Calm the fuck down.* I drink a sip of ice water, the chill a warm welcome to the fire building in my chest.

"I said...no need to thank me." I struggle to keep my voice even. Setting the glass down with a light *thump,* I watch the condensation seep into the tablecloth. *Deep breaths, Parker. Don't be an asshole.*

She clams up and resumes eating. I push my steak away, my appetite gone, and drink a few gulps of some variety of red wine in my glass. It might be grape juice for all I care.

"So, Parker, how's *InstaConnect* going for you?" Emily asks from her seat. "After you went out on the one date with my sister," she sneaks a glance at Jess and continues, "did you go on others?"

I rub the back of neck as warmth creeps up my face. "No, I haven't gotten into it." Out of the corner of my eye, I see Liz pausing, with her fork suspended in the air. Ignoring her, I continue, "Not sure if I'm ready to date yet. Too many things going on and too little time."

"But you should make time for it if that's what you want—"

"Melanie, did you tell Jess about the television drama you recommended to me?" Liz asks, interrupting Emily's interrogation, her tone a complete one-eighty from a few seconds ago.

Melanie gasps and slaps her palm on her forehead. "Oh yes! I forgot!" She rubs her hands together with excitement surely mirroring her students. "So, the drama is called *Fated for You* and it's the most addictive piece of television I've *ever* watched. And I know my television shows. This drama deserves to be nominated for all the swoony goodness."

Liz squeals eagerly. "Let me, let me. So, it's about this billionaire, who of course, is a bit cocky and very handsome, but he's really lonely deep inside. He has all these hot girls throwing themselves at him twenty-four-seven, but does he want any of them?"

"Don't tell me, he *doesn't* because he's allergic to hot girls," James deadpans as Jess elbows him and motions for Liz to continue.

"No, he doesn't want any of them, and *not* because he's allergic." Liz scowls at her brother. James, at this time, has given up on all attempts to appear serious. He closes his eyes and slaps a palm on his forehead with a groan as she continues, "Anyway, none of them spark anything in him and one day, he was returning home from dinner and was caught in the rain without an umbrella—"

James holds his palm up. "Hold on, why would he be walking in the first place? The dude is a billionaire, shouldn't he have a driver?"

I observe the woman next to me, noticing the blush settling in her clear complexion, her blue eyes sparkling with life and laughter. Liz ignores James as she gestures with both hands, her body practically vibrating with positive energy. *So much fucking positivity it's almost toxic. But oh so alluring. You just don't want to admit it.* "He meets our plucky heroine, a normal office worker. She's the complete opposite of him, frumpy to his sophistication, naïve to his jadedness, and an all-around klutz."

"Let me guess, they fall in love because love conquers all. The end."

"James! It's really good, don't hate it until you watch it." Liz pouts.

"I've seen it. It's crack," Emily agrees.

"Masterpiece. It's a *masterpiece*," Melanie chimes in.

James waves his white napkin in the air. "A smart man always knows when to back down, especially when his opponents are four beautiful women." He looks at Jess with his heart in his eyes, and says softly, "I'll watch it with you later, sweetheart. This seems right up your alley." My chest spasms in a flash of pain as I look at the two lovebirds. *I could've had that with Abby, maybe, if we had more time.* Could have, should have—the two phrases are frequent flyers in the airline of my daily inner dialogue. I massage the invisible soreness, the pressure a temporary salve to a permanent wound. Clenching my fists, I struggle to regulate my breathing as my sadness quickly morphs into anger.

So much fucking anger.

"Are you okay?" Liz taps me on the shoulder.

"I. Am. Fine," I mutter under my breath, not looking at her, as I struggle to control my emotions. *Funny you should ask that. You, of all people.* I bite the inside of my cheek to keep from lashing out. Balling up my napkin, I place it on the table, the slight tremor of my hand betraying the roiling inferno inside of me. I stand. "Excuse me, guys, I need to use the bathroom."

I spin around and stride away without a backward glance. *Fuck, you should've controlled yourself better.*

After I finish my business in the bathroom and wash my hands, I splash some cold water onto my face in an attempt to reset the madness threatening to break free from within. I catalog my haggard appearance in the mirror. I see the same golden-brown hair, shorn shorter at the sides and haphazardly arranged on top, the same green eyes appear dull to me, but no one seems to notice, the faint lines around my eyes, a five o'clock shadow. By all appearances, I resemble the Parker Wellington from three years ago before Abby passed, but the changes are there, the shadows under my eyes, the dimples rarely making an appearance unless in public.

I can do this. Fake it until you make it.

Taking a deep breath, I practice my usual smile. Still very convincing. I can do this.

I toss a paper towel in the trash can and open the door, preparing myself to face my friends again.

Liz stands in front of the door in her fiery glory, blocking my exit. She's vibrating with anger, her normally calm blue eyes darkening with intensity, her tempting lips flattening as she glares at me, tapping her feet on the ground.

"Are you going to move? This is the men's room. The women's room is next door."

She steps closer as I flatten my back against the closed bathroom door. Stabbing her index finger at my chest, she asks, "What's the problem with you? Do you have an issue with me?" She seems so small to my six-foot-one-inch frame, and yet, when she's angry, standing up for herself, she's *glorious*.

Breathtaking.

If only things were different.

"What are you talking about? I don't have time for this." I make a move to sidestep her.

She pivots, her eyes flashing in anger as her she raises her voice. "I've *never* done anything to you. *Anything*. What did I ever do to deserve this treatment from you? How *dare* you make someone who has been anything but nice to you feel this way?"

I snort. If she only knew what she did. How my life has fallen apart because of her. How I'm a ghost of my former self because of her. How I'm just a walking corpse, waiting for my time to run out in this world.

All because of her.

Don't blame other people for your shit, Parker. You know it's not true.

"Move, Liz. I don't have time for this crap."

Instead of backing down, this appears to inflame her even further, and she resumes stabbing at my chest again. "Answer me, Parker. What did I ever do to you?"

Predatory instincts stir inside me as molten lava rushes through my veins. I grab her fingers mid-stab, and her eyes flare at the expression on my face.

"*Don't* test me, Liz. Trust me, you *don't* want to test me."

Our breathing grows ragged in the narrow hallway as I war with an impulse to either strangle her or to kiss her senseless. *What the fuck?* I settle for clutching her fingers tightly in mine, my roughness against her softness, the moment stretching long enough to give her a small glimpse beyond the veil into the darkness. Her lips part as she takes in quick breaths. The fluttering in her neck becomes more pronounced, beckoning me like a beacon in the night. I swallow the lump in my throat and sidestep her successfully this time, leaving her frozen in position, and stride toward the dining area.

"Why did you offer me the nanny job if you hate me so much?" A slight tremor appears at the end of her question.

The naked vulnerability in her voice halts me in my steps.

"Fuck if I know."

And, deep down, I really *don't* want to know.

I'm fuming. So much I can barely keep a straight face for the rest of the dinner, sitting next to this Grade A, mercurial asshole. At this point, I don't even want to work for him. I'd much rather dress in a sexy outfit and be ogled by hundreds of men than be confined in a house with him. *This is Ems's special day. Don't ruin it for her. After dinner, when we go to the club, you don't need to hang out with him. Only for a little longer now, you can do this, Liz.* After I return from the bathroom hallway showdown, Parker acts as if nothing ever happened at all. He jokes with everyone at the table, throws out his signature wink here and there, flashes those annoying dimples, and just turns on the charm.

This man has issues, deep-seated problems. How do they not see it?

The rest of the dinner thankfully passes by uneventfully and cordially. I ignore the maddening man next to me and he does the same.

Emily announces as we walk on quiet streets after our wonderful meal, "All right, Steven got us a VIP booth at Ambrosia, the popular new club down the street, opened by the famous Fleur Entertainment, which for those of you not in the know, is the large

Big Apple entertainment and hospitality powerhouse. Steven said it was a birthday present for me. He knows the execs at Fleur, and they hooked us up. My little brother is finally good for something."

Steven is the third and youngest of the Kingsley siblings. He's twenty-five and lives in New York City, working his way up the ranks at a prominent investment banking firm. A certifiable workaholic and, as he calls himself, "a man with distinguishable tastes when it comes to food," he's as equally picky about his romantic relationships as his siblings. The Kingsley siblings all have different romantic hang-ups and with Steven, I've never seen him date anyone and not from the lack of opportunity, either. I was hoping he'd be able to visit this weekend for his sister's birthday, but it seems like the timing didn't work out.

A crowd begins to form in front of a shiny new high-rise built as part of the downtown gentrification and reform a few years ago. The exterior of the building is mainly made of floor-to-ceiling windows, towering silver beams, and in front of the door stand two bouncers, who could probably be extras on *Mighty Wrestle-a-thon*, securing the entrance of the nightclub. The line curls around the building as excited chatter fills the air. Fleur is known for their sophisticated hotels, restaurants, entertainment venues, and nightclubs, and they have a variety of establishments ranging from hip and trendy places such as Ambrosia, to exclusive and invite-only, high-end establishments such as the Orchid in Manhattan.

Emily walks to the front of the line, her shoulder-length brown hair gleaming in the moonlight, wearing a slinky silver sequin outfit, which draws attention to her. She reaches the towering bouncer and beckons for him to dip down so she can whisper to him. A few moments of murmuring later, he laughs and waves us in. Emily swings around, flashes us a peace sign, and we follow her in.

The thundering beats to what no doubt is a popular hip-hop song nearly shatter my eardrums the moment we step inside the club. Not my normal scene, but I'll make the best out of it. The décor of the club is impressive, with glass pillars featuring dancers and gymnasts performing to the music, aerial artists flying across the air with wires, multiple strobe lights sweeping around the room, allowing for the place to be dimly lit but also dark enough to offer some mystery and privacy. A large bar lit up with neon under lights surrounds one of the multiple dance floors and a glass staircase leads to a second floor where the VIP booths and dance floor reside.

We settle in the plush leather seating of a private VIP booth on the second floor. It's a little calmer up here, but still very noisy. I sit next to James with Jess and the girls on the other side of me. Liquid refreshments, that's what we need. I grab the gold-leaf-encrusted menu on the table and peruse the selection.

"Haven't been to a club in forever, huh?" James murmurs to Parker, who's sitting on the other side of him. My ears can't help but eavesdrop on their conversation.

"Abby used to love clubs, being a free spirit like she was. I was always the one who preferred to stay home." I sneak a glance at them and see Parker rubbing his ring finger again, something he seems to do often in the few times we were in the same place together. "So, yes, it's been a few years." He rarely talks about his late wife who passed away three years ago.

James clasps a hand on his shoulder in reassurance. They've grown close as friends after Parker bowed out of pursuing Jess and instead helped them get together. "The club has comped drinks for us tonight. I'll drop you off if you get drunk. Let loose a little. It's not often you have a chance to come out and be yourself without responsibilities. Relax. Take the edge off."

Parker chuckles. "I'm doing fine, but thanks." He suddenly glances over and the smile slips off his face as he catches me staring at him. I quickly look away, my face heating, but am thankful it's so dim in here. "I may just take you up on it," he murmurs.

"Hi, guys, I'm Josh and I'm your concierge tonight. What would you like to drink?"

"What do you recommend, Josh?" I smile at the gorgeous man standing next to our table, who may be one of the many struggling actors in LA. His carefully trimmed curly hair, mischievous eyes, and mega-watt smile instantly brighten up my night.

"Depends on what you're looking for tonight. All of your drinks are on the house. If you want classics, we have top-shelf bourbon and whiskey here, and some of them are from signature reserves. If you're in the mood for cocktails, our Manhattan, Sex on the Beach, and Midori Sour are pretty popular here." He gives me a wink and a grin. "We can pretty much make anything you want. Our bartenders are all exclusively trained in New York."

Melanie leans over and shouts over the music, "Why don't we order one of each and we can all try a sip to see if we like it?"

"Like a cocktail flight! I love that idea." The night is getting better as we go, free drinks, girlfriends, who can complain? "Jess, you game?"

"Sure, I have a designated driver today, so I'm going to party it up with you girls."

I grin, looking up at the smiling Josh, who's already scribbling down our orders. He returns his gaze back to me and leans a little closer. "Since it's your first time here, let me let you in on a little secret. We have a private terrace out here we usually reserve for special guests, but no one booked it for tonight, so I can probably show you...I mean, you guys, if you like."

Melanie waves her hands in the air and mouths to me, *"He's flirting with you. Go for it."* She waggles her brows and nods enthusiastically. As much as I love the attention from a good-looking guy, he's way too young for me and completely not what I'm looking for. I open my mouth to respond.

"We're fine over here, and James and I'll take two bourbons from the reserve." Parker's normally gravelly voice takes on a clipped edge.

Whatever Josh saw on Parker's face has him backing away a smidge. With a muted smile, he nods and walks away.

"I wanted to see the terrace, Parker," Emily bemoans.

"I'm an architect—I've seen all the drawings of major buildings and developments filed with the city. That terrace is nothing to write home about." *What a liar and buzzkill.* He smiles slyly at her, showcasing one of his annoyingly charming dimples. "You want to see a beautiful terrace? I'll invite you over to my place and you'll see what an architect's gardens look like." He follows that with another wink. I fight the urge to roll my eyes at his surface-level charm.

The drinks arrive quickly, and Josh sets down a tray of hard liquor shots we didn't order and a small cake with sparklers on it. "Happy birthday from the house."

Emily squeals as we all sing "Happy Birthday" to her. She almost cries tears of joy and has Josh take a group photo of us. "I'm going to send this to Steven. He's getting the biggest hug from me the next time I see him." She taps on her phone and seconds later, my cell chimes with an incoming text in the Kingsley and Chapman clan chat group.

Emily: Steven, you're so awesome. I wish you were here but this birthday is so much fun. Here's a pic of us. Miss you.

A few seconds later, Steven replies. He doesn't sleep much and is most likely still at work.

Steven: Glad you're enjoying my gift. Say hi to the guys for me.

I stand up and propose a toast with the shots. "Ems, thanks for being the best friend and sister-in-law a girl can ask for. I love you and happy birthday again! Here's to many, many more birthdays with you. I hope all your dreams come true."

"Hear, hear," Melanie exclaims, and Jess gives her sister a big kiss on her cheek. Even the normally stoic James is grinning.

We down the shots in rapid succession. "Wow, what did they put in this? This is not the cheap, watered-down stuff." Jess grimaces, chasing the shot with a large gulp of ice water.

Liquid fire burns through my veins as the buzz settles in quickly. Warm tingles spread through my body, and my mind turns to mush. My head bobs to the strong beats of the hip-hop music blaring on the dance floor. I'm ready to let loose and enjoy the beginning of my summer vacation and whatever it holds for me.

"Let's dance!" Melanie drags us girls out onto the dance floor.

We swing our hands in the air to the sound of the music, letting our bodies take over. Jess and Ems are the best dancers out of all of us with their ballet dancing background. Melanie bops her head around, oblivious to the rhythm, happy in her own world. The strobe lights flash to each rhythmic beat as the crowd goes wild. I close my eyes and let the music wash over me, surrounded by my most favorite people in the world. I relish the euphoria flooding through my veins.

Soon, two guys who appear to be our age come up to us. "You girls look like you're having fun. Can we join the party?" the tall brown-haired one asks.

"Sure, the more the merrier!" Emily hollers back over the loud music.

James mysteriously materializes next to Jess and slides his hands over her stomach, anchoring her to him possessively. The brown-haired guy takes Emily's hands and spins her toward him. Melanie giggles as his blond friend wraps his arms around her waist and whispers something in her ear. I'm left dancing by myself, which I don't mind and frankly prefer. I can never be relaxed enough to dance with strangers in close proximity.

I shut my eyes, losing myself in the haze of the alcohol, the emotions of the song, and the loud, yet intimate environment. My troubles and worries disappear into the night and all I'm focused on are the sensations in my body. A moment later, a new song plays over the speakers, a song I recognize from a long time ago, "Body Party" by Ciara. The seductive beats and lyrics send shivers through my body. I sway to the rhythm and gently open my eyes. James and Jess have proceeded to half-dancing, half-kissing on the dance floor, oblivious to the entire world. My heart pangs with envy, wanting what they have. The other girls seem to be having fun with their temporary dates, laughing and whispering to each other. I push away the transient melancholy. *Better to find the right man than to settle.*

The buzz of the alcohol intensifies, and I bring my hands to my neck, feeling the heated flesh and the rapid pulse there. I continue rocking my body to the music, living in my own world, when suddenly, the hairs on my neck stand at attention as I sense the heavy weight of someone's stare on me. My eyes sweep around the room, searching for the source of the unease, noting nothing unusual until my gaze flits over to our table.

I see Parker, sitting by himself, his aristocratic nose and sharp jawline prominent in the ambient lighting. His piercing eyes threaten to laser me on the spot as he tracks the movement of my hands. His public persona is wiped away and replaced with a smoldering expression. *Danger.* My mind warns me but I suddenly find myself unable to move under his scrutiny. He grips his glass tightly as he holds my stare, neither of us backing down or looking away. Heat rises in my body at the intensity on his face, his burning gaze pinning me to the spot, casting a spotlight only visible to the two of us.

I don't know what comes over me, if it's the liquid courage, if I'm a glutton for punishment, or if I just want to piss him off frankly. This time I cave to the madness. I keep my eyes on his glittering gaze as I begin swaying to the song again, my body taking over my mind.

My hands slowly slide down my neck and skim over the tops of my breasts, lingering on the smooth skin, now warm to the touch.

His eyes flare in the dim lighting and as the sweeping spotlight hits the table, I notice his hand shaking as he brings his glass to his lips. The hatred in his gaze slowly melts into something far more dangerous.

My fingers trail over my breasts, which are now full and tender to the touch. I lightly cup and massage the curves, relishing in the tingles the motion generates.

I bite my bottom lip to contain a moan and continue to gyrate to the music as the crowds fade from view, leaving me alone...with him. A man who is completely infuriating and mysterious, waving all the red flags in the world, and all but bellowing at me to stay away. But somehow, I can't. I seem to be drawn to him for inexplicable reasons.

The two of us, alone in our spheres of loneliness, surrounded by hordes of people, yet blind and deaf to them.

Parker's eyes follow my hands as they make their way down to my stomach, his jaw locking as his face darkens with each passing second of my private dance for him. I swing my hips and dip my body low before swiftly flipping my head and upper body back up and slowly straightening to a standing position. He slams his glass down on the table and clenches his hands in tight fists. His eyes trail up my body as if he's slowly undressing me in public. My breathing shortens and molten heat rushes to my core as if I feel every caress from his eyes. His penetrating stare holds mine and renders me immobile on the dance floor once again.

Thump. The music swells to a crescendo.

Thump. I breathe in a ragged breath, my breasts heaving with exertion.

Thump. The stark hunger in his gaze threatens to set us both aflame.

I feel exposed and vulnerable.

House music replaces the sensual song from a moment ago and I blink rapidly, my hands on my thudding heart, feeling like I just completed a marathon.

What just happened? You hate him, Liz, remember? He's an asshole.

My breath catches as I break his hold on me. I suddenly feel very claustrophobic. "I'm going to go to the restroom, girls."

"You want me to come with you?" Jess inquires.

I wave my hand as I walk away. "Don't worry about it. You guys have fun. I'll be right back."

I rush to the bathroom on the far side of the second floor with the desperation of a woman running to catch the last bus of the night. Slamming my back against the cool tile wall, I lock the door behind me. My pulse is still galloping, and I can't even blame the shots anymore. I wash my hands with icy-cold water, hoping to calm my nerves as I take in my flushed appearance. My carefully pinned curls are slowly unraveling. I remove the bobby pins and shake them out, letting the loose waves fall past my shoulders. My lips are plump, probably from when I bit on them earlier. I look like someone who has been ravished in the dark.

Except nothing happened. Absolutely nothing.

Nothing can happen because he's the exact opposite of what I'm looking for. Parker runs hot and cold, with enough baggage to rival any A-lister celebrity's actual luggage when traveling. He is not anyone's ideal boyfriend material.

But the spark, the elusive spark you've been searching for all these years. One missing in every man I've ever come across.

Until now.

So inconvenient and inappropriate.

No. It's the alcohol and the animosity. Strong feelings can sometimes elicit powerful reactions. That has to be it.

I shake out my arms and legs and roll my shoulders as the strange tension slowly dissipates. *Better. Much better.* Taking a deep breath, I open the door to return to my friends.

"Hey, gorgeous. I saw you dancing out there just now. You're so sexy." A tall, wiry banker-type of man waits for me outside of the bathroom, leering at me.

Unease circles my gut as I look around. The hallway is dim and unusually quiet. I should've taken up Jess's offer to come with me. "Thanks." I give him a shaky smile as I brush past him, eager to leave.

He grabs my wrist in a tight grip. "Hold on a second. You were aching for it on the dance floor. I could see it." He tugs me to him, and I smell a powerful stench of whiskey on his breath as he draws me close. "Come on, I can satisfy you tonight."

I struggle in his arms and raise my voice, trying not to let my panic show through. "Let go of me this instant. I'm not interested."

"You're so cute, baby. You're just playing hard to get. Come on, girl, I know what you need. You looked so hot for it out there. I can give it to you. All night long." His grip is bruising my wrist and I try to tug free to no avail. Just as I'm about to give his feet a hard stomp with my stilettos, followed by a swift kick in the balls, a familiar gravelly voice bellows in the background.

"Drop her hand and back off. She said no."

Parker.

I sense his presence as he prowls over in measured steps.

"Who the fuck are you? Mind your own business," the sleaze-bag grounds out, his earlier bravado disappearing quickly as Parker approaches me.

"If you don't drop her hand right now and back away, I *will* physically remove it from your body." I hear a crack, akin to someone cracking their neck or their knuckles. "Trust me, I'll enjoy every moment of it because I'm aching for a fight," he growls.

Sleazebag looks behind me as his pallor turns green and he quickly releases me and scurries away. The wimpy bastard.

I let out a shaky breath. I know it was a close one. If Parker wasn't here, things could've gone south very quickly. I rub my red wrist, wincing in pain. There'll no doubt be a bruise there tomorrow against my pale skin.

"What the fuck were you thinking? Can you do anything right? Is your sole existence to destroy other people's lives and, quite possibly, your very own?"

I snap my head up and find Parker in front of me. His emerald eyes, normally crinkled at the corners to everyone except me, are now eerily cold and intense. If there's such a thing as an icy inferno, his expression would be it. Anger boils inside me and just as I'm about to give him an enormous piece of my mind, he grabs my wrist and smooths his thumb over the red marks, his calluses rough against my tender skin. His touch awakens every nerve ending on my body, and I suddenly find myself speechless. The pain in my wrist is replaced by something else...something headier. Goosebumps form on my skin as he lightly circles the tender flesh, his gentle touch completely at odds with the harshness of his face. He takes a few steps toward me, backing me to the door, a complete reversal of our encounter earlier in the evening.

"Why you?" he whispers as his forehead dips toward mine. My eyes flutter closed as I'm ensnared by the rioting emotions within us. The hallway is quiet except for the muted music from the dance floor and the sounds of our ragged breathing. With my every inhale, my breasts graze the solid wall of his chest. "What do you want from me?" he rasps as his forehead touches mine. Notes of amber and bergamot waft to my nose. His unique scent.

The panic and fear from earlier dissolve, replaced with a scorching intensity so thick I can almost taste it. My eyes snap open as his forehead lifts from mine and I find his forest-green eyes glinting in the dim light, his pupils blown. He is standing so close to me, a few centimeters more and we'll be flush against each other.

Sometimes, the shortest distance feels the longest.

I hold my breath as my mind blanks, unable to remember the thousand logical reasons why I should step away or the millions of red flags warning me to stay away. Parker releases his grip on my hand as he trails his fingertips lightly up my arms before stopping at my neck, eliciting shivers in their wake. Helpless to resist the blazing fire burning me from within, I lean against his touch, inadvertently baring my racing pulse to him. His large palm encircles the column of my neck, his thumb stroking the sensitized skin there.

"So fragile yet so strong at the same time," he whispers, his eyes on my thundering pulse, "so innocent yet so guilty, all wrapped up in one fucking tempting package." His riddles make no sense, but he pays me no heed. *I should run. A normal person would run away.* But I find I can't move, and somehow I want to prolong this moment with him.

He cages me in with his other hand as his fingers continue stroking my fluttering pulse, the lightness of his touch at odds with the burning intensity in his eyes. All my senses are on fire as I thirst for something I cannot name. My tongue slips out to wet my parched lips and his eyes zero in on the movement, naked desire swimming in his gaze. A moan catches in my throat and my nipples prickle to attention, aching for this strong, virile man before me.

Nothing makes sense.

He stares at the hard nubs protruding from my dress, tempting him, beckoning him, provoking him. *Touch me.* "Fuck," he groans as his breathing becomes heavier. A muscle tics in his jaw as he vibrates with tension, and I wait for the inevitable to happen... for him...to just...snap.

But he doesn't.

He lets go of me and steps away slowly, his eyes finally returning to my face. A mask of indifference replaces his ravenous expression mere seconds ago.

"Jess asked me to look for you," he said, his voice emotionless and aloof, as if the last few minutes were figments of my imagination. Only a slight tremor in his hands gives him away. At my silence, he continues, "You coming?"

He turns his back on me and walks away for the second time tonight.

Parker

Traffic slows to a snail's crawl on the 110 freeway in the light rain. Can people fucking drive? It's not even pouring out and Angelenos are acting like a hurricane has hit our shores. I see people rolling down their windows to point at something in the distant horizon. Squinting my eyes at the commotion, I finally spot it. A double rainbow and not the half-assed ones you usually see, but two full, vibrant concoctions Lucy would probably appreciate.

Fucking rainbows. People are slowing down the traffic for fucking rainbows. My phone chimes with an incoming text:

Liz: Parker, I'll cut to the chase. I don't think I can be a nanny for you. Frankly, I don't think you want me to, anyway.

Shit. *What did you think was going to happen, dumbass? She'll take your craziness lying down? Especially after Saturday night?* My cock stirs for the first time in years at the thought of her sensual tease on the dance floor. God, the way she moved her body.

All for me. Just. For. Me.

Fuck. Life just likes to throw curveballs at me. Kick a man while he's down.

The snail's crawl is now at a standstill. I resist the urge to honk as a call comes in on my Bluetooth.

"Honey, I've been thinking about your situation. Are you sure you don't need help with Lucy now that Cindy quit?"

"Mom, we're fine. I got her a temporary sitter for now, but a friend's sister is willing to help out for a few months." *If I can change her mind.*

I hear the range hood turn on as my mom is most likely puttering around in her little kitchen. "Are you sure? I spoke with Rick, and he said he's fine with me coming down to help you for a bit until you find a replacement." Mom has lived a hard life working two manual-labor-intensive jobs to raise me and put me through school. As a result, she has a bad hip and back, and watching a kindergartener around the clock will be tough on her old wounds.

"Yes, I'm sure."

"Is your friend's sister trustworthy? Experienced?" I almost laugh at the question. I'm the one who's not trustworthy. Especially around her.

"She's actually Lucy's kindergarten teacher who happens to be looking for a summer job. Lucy loves her, so I think it'll be a good fit." For Lucy. Anything for Lucy. Even if it means I have to leash the monster within me, even more so than I have been doing these days.

"Son...I'm worried about you."

I sigh, rubbing my fingers around my temples at the soreness gathering there. There's a type of weariness no amount of sleep can erase, not that I'm sleeping much these days.

"I'm fine, Mom."

Clanging of pots and pans come across the line. "You may be able to fool everyone, but you aren't fooling me. You've been burning the candle at both ends. When I visited you two months ago, I could tell. You don't really have a life outside of Lucy. Parker..." she sighs, "you're still young. Don't throw your life away because of what happened with Abby."

"Mom!" I shout, gripping the steering wheel before counting to three and starting again. I force myself to calm down. "I'm sorry for raising my voice. You'll just have to trust me. I'm fine."

"Are you still going to the therapist? Please tell me you are."

I groan, itching to end this conversation, but not wanting to hurt her feelings. "I am. In fact, I'm heading over to see her right now." I exhale forcefully. "Look, I really am okay...and I have to go, safe driving and all."

"Love you, honey. Please let me know if I can help. What I want more than anything in the world is for the spark to return to my son's eyes."

"Love you too, Mom."

I disconnect the call as I gaze at the rainbows in front of me, wishing I could feel an iota of wonder or joy—anything other than the numbness and darkness swirling within.

. . .

"How was your week, Parker?" the salt-and-peppered-haired woman with shrewd brown eyes and horn-rimmed glasses sitting across from me inquires, with a notebook on her lap and a ballpoint pen in her hand.

"Things are fine, Marybeth."

"Walk me through this past week, then."

I lean back in the smooth leather chair in the small office, a monthly routine I'm following more for the sake of telling my mom I'm still seeing a therapist. "Nothing special, really. I took Lucy to the zoo. She enjoyed the animals." I try a grin, making sure it's wide enough so my dimples are showing.

She smiles at the mention of my daughter. "That sounds wonderful. I'm glad you had some time for fun activities with her." She pauses and scrutinizes me.

Click. She presses the top of her pen once.

Click. Click. Two more times.

The watch on my wrist ticks, sounding like the deafening chimes of Big Ben in the quietness of the room.

My grin falters as she leans back in her recliner and crosses her legs. She tilts her head to the side and resumes our staring contest.

I hate shrinks. They don't behave like normal people.

"Why are you here, Parker?"

"Because my family thought it was a good idea for me to see a therapist after the death of my wife." More so because of the one time when Mom visited a year and a half ago, she found me passed out on the bed, piss-ass drunk after punching a hole in the bedroom wall. Lucy was apparently crying and by my bedside, but I didn't hear her.

I fucking failed the one person who depends on me the most.

It was also the anniversary of Abby's death.

Mom insisted I get help or she'd move in with me permanently. At the time, James had been mentioning how Marybeth Connors was helping Jess with her anxiety issues, so I secretly looked her up and gave her a call. So, here we are.

"Do you think you need to be here?"

No, I don't think so. Talking about my feelings isn't going to help shit.

It's hopeless.

"I think it doesn't hurt to try." I shrug, trying nonchalance for a change.

She sits up as she scribbles something on the notepad in front of her. I wish I could see what she's writing down. Is it something along the lines of "This is a fucking piece of shit who's wasting my time?" She sets her pen down and leans in, her hands clasped on top of the notepad. The staring contest begins anew.

Click. Click. Click.

More clicking of the ballpoint pen.

I want to take the pen and chuck it out the window.

Rubbing the back of my head, I sit up. I let out some air I was holding in. "Lucy's nanny put in her notice last week. My friend's sister is going to help for a few months." *Here, a bone for you.*

Marybeth tilts her head to the other side and murmurs, "That must have been stressful, losing childcare. How does Lucy feel about the situation?"

"She's sad Cindy is leaving as she's grown very attached to her since Abby..." I clear my throat, failing to dispel the lump that has formed there. "But Liz is her kindergarten teacher, whom she also loves. So, it's the ideal situation for her." I chuckle, hoping my face looks like one of relief.

She nods. "What about for you? How do you feel about Liz and the situation?"

My smile freezes in place.

That's the million-dollar question. One I don't want to answer. I shift in my seat, the blue tie around my neck feeling like a choke-hold, slowly cutting off the remaining air filtering to my lungs, the bare minimum keeping me sane. Fuck, I need to get back to work. The homeless shelter project that's almost done, the proposals, the meetings.

Responsibilities.

"What's your top emotion right now when you think about Liz and the situation?"

I take the bottle of water she offered me at the beginning of the session, uncap the lid, and take a sip, hoping the coolness can quiet the burning fire brewing in my gut.

Anger.

"Shit, Abby. Do you need to fucking go right now? We're in the middle of an important conversation about our marriage." I pace around the living room, tugging my hair.

Abby throws her cell phone and wallet in her tote, her blonde hair flying behind her as she hurries around the room in search of something.

"Dammit, where are my keys?"

"Abby, are you listening to me? You never listen. Do I even matter to you anymore? Why are you rushing off to see a stranger instead of staying to talk to your husband? I've tried to be patient with you and empathize with your need to find your biological family, but it has become an obsession...one that has taken so much of your time and energy. You don't even have time to spend with your daughter anymore, not to mention me. Can't you see she needs you? Can't you get your head out of the clouds and put your family ahead of your needs for once?"

She pauses as she looks at me, her deep blue eyes flashing in anger. "What do you mean, do you matter to me? You know you do. You know how much I gave up—"

I thump my hand on the wall, my fists curling tight as I struggle to rein in my frustration. Thank goodness Lucy is at daycare. "What? When we got pregnant? We decided to keep the baby together, right? We decided to get married, right? I didn't force you to do anything."

"Ugh. You just don't understand." She swings around and tosses the cushions on the floor, finally finding the keys hidden underneath the blanket on the sofa.

"Explain it to me, then. Tell me why you can't spend more time with your daughter when she obviously wants to play with you. Tell me why seeing this stranger who has canceled on you before is more important than talking to your husband, the father of your child. Tell me why you're dropping all the plans we've made for tonight because a stranger is suddenly free to meet up."

Abby stops by the door and turns around, her face mottled and red. "Why would you understand? You have a family. Your parents love you. You knew who they were. How would you understand wanting to find out more about where you came from?"

"We are your family! We love you. We have been here this entire time," I thunder. "Don't we matter anymore?"

Tears gather in her eyes, but she remains silent. The last remnants of my heart pulverize under the weight of her stare.

She turns around and leaves, slamming the door behind her. Seconds later, a flash of lightning and a loud roar of thunder reverberates through the room.

I wish we weren't married anymore.

My cell phone buzzes, no doubt another incoming message. My eyes refocus, and I find Marybeth staring intently at me. Remembering her question, I smile and answer, my voice steady and sure, "Relief. I feel relief. Liz will be a good caretaker for Lucy."

Liar.

Parker: I want to apologize for Saturday. I had some issues I was dealing with, and I shouldn't have taken it out on you. Will you reconsider? If not for me, then for Lucy? I know I probably don't, and shouldn't, matter to you, but Lucy needs you. Please.

I stare at the text message on my phone, my earlier anger slowly dissipating. In my fury toward Parker, I forgot there was a child involved. Darling, sweet Lucy, with her bubbly personality, who lost her mom three years ago. My heart clenches at the thought of the little girl growing up without her mother's love. *Maybe it was an off day for him. He's rude, sure, but he was never like...that in the past, in the handful of times I've breathed in the same air as him.*

Sure, keep telling yourself that.

Riiiiiing. My phone blares to life, shocking me out of the should-I/shouldn't-I mental spiral I'm about to embark on.

"Hey, Jess, how are you?" I set my phone on speaker as I rummage through my closet for an overnight bag. *Maybe a few nights wouldn't hurt. Just to test things out. Lucy needs you, Liz. Suck it up. Be a wo-man. If it doesn't work out, you can always leave.*

"Liz! I'm doing fine. I just want to call to see how things are going with you."

"Ugh. It's going okay. My car broke down this morning so I have to get it fixed...which is more money I need to spend that I don't have. Now, why can't money rain from the skies?"

Jess chuckles at my description. "Oh man, I'm so sorry. Let me know if you need me to give you a ride anywhere in the meantime. Speaking of money, I'm just checking in on you since I didn't get to talk to you privately on Saturday. I was thinking more about it the last two days and was wondering...are you okay with James and I volunteering you to be Parker's nanny? I just realized how we might've put you in a weird position. Maybe you don't want to for whatever reason, and we put you on the spot. Maybe we should've—"

"Jess. You're rambling again." Aha! My old duffel bag from grad school is still there. Pulling it from the depths of my closet, I dust it off and check to make sure the zippers still work. "Don't sweat it, my dear. I know why you guys thought of me when the opportunity came up."

"Are you sure? The vibes between the two of you have been rather...odd."

Tell me about it. "I'll be honest with you. I'm really, *really* tempted to turn him down because he's just not that nice to me... but please don't tell James that. They get along so well, and I don't want to get in between them. But Parker's not someone I'll volunteer to hang out with unless it's absolutely necessary." *And apparently when buzzed and high on music.* "But then, I think about poor little Lucy...and I really want to be there for her. She's the sweetest kid. It's so hard to imagine half of her DNA is his."

Jess laughs at my unflattering assessment of Parker. "Oh man, Liz. Remind me not to get on your bad side." The sound of car keys clinking and a car's ignition roaring to life comes through the phone. "I'm off to visit a client and my audit team there. I just want to make sure you're okay. Talk soon."

"Thanks for calling. Go get them, Ms. Auditor."

Okay. No wishy-washy behavior. Let's do this.

Liz: Apology temporarily accepted. Whether or not it remains permanent is up to you. When do you want me to move in? I'm willing to test this out for a day or two. But I don't have a car right now. My car broke down and I need to take it to the shop next week.

My fingers hover above the send button. Somehow, the small text message seems significant, as if I'm standing in front of a fork in the road and this small action will propel me to a path I can't return from.

Ridiculous.

Squeezing my eyes shut, I hit send.

A few seconds later, his response comes through:

Parker: I'll pick you up tomorrow afternoon at four. Will also help get your car fixed as well. The least I can do. Thank you.

Thump. Thump. Thump. My heart thuds rapidly for no apparent reason. I hope I haven't made a mistake I'll come to regret later on.

• • •

I pace back and forth on the sidewalk in front of my apartment at three forty-five p.m. I can't seem to stay still. I filled my duffle bag with a few basic changes of clothes, a sleep shirt, a pair of fuzzy slippers, and some toiletries. It'll be an easy getaway bag if things go south. Droplets of sweat gather at the base of my neck as I attempt to fan myself with my hands. The temperatures are hovering around one hundred degrees today, and the skies are unblemished, without a single cloud in sight. The blazing sun slow cooks every living thing in its path, including me.

Standing underneath the shade of a large oak tree, I berate myself for not waiting indoors. *This is not a job interview. You don't need to be early, for goodness' sake.* I hum a few songs under my breath as I scroll through social media, admiring a few aesthetic posts from my favorite bookish influencers. I check the time again. 3:47 p.m. My legs tap against the tree trunk in a nervous rhythm. A few more reels. 3:50 p.m.

Just as I'm about to start pacing again, I hear the hum of a quiet, expensive car engine parking next to me on the street. A dark-blue luxury sedan with tinted windows. The driver's door opens and out steps a version of Parker that's pulled from the deepest depths of my fantasies. Dressed in a dark-gray, slim-cut suit with a crisp, white shirt, and a navy-blue tie, the sunlight reflecting the golden threads of his tousled hair, the sharp jaw perpetually covered in the slightest bit of scruff, Parker walks toward me, his eyes hidden under a pair of dark aviators. This is the *GQ* Parker we don't get to see often.

"Liz." His voice is raspy from apparent disuse. Clearing his throat, he tries again. "Liz, thank you for doing this."

My face heats up from the sun I'm sure, and I reply, "Don't worry about it. Just don't make me regret it. Where's Lucy?"

"I still have a sitter for today since I had to go into the office for most of the day. But I figured it'll be better if I come get you earlier while the sitter is still here, so you can get settled in the house without worrying about watching Lucy from the get-go. The sitter typically leaves before dinner, so we should have a few hours for you to get situated."

He points to the duffle bag baking under the sun on the front steps of the apartment. "Yours?"

I nod as he retrieves the bag and opens the passenger car door for me. "Thanks."

Putting my bag in the backseat, he slides into the driver's seat and comments, "That's a light bag you got there. You sure you have everything you need?"

I buckle my seatbelt. "You're on probation, so I don't think I need to pack for a few months yet. I reserve the right to jump ship at any moment. I'm only doing this for Lucy...and definitely not for you."

He snorts, a dimple appearing on his face as he drives away. *I wish I could see his eyes and know what he's thinking.*

The drive is quiet. Too quiet, courtesy of the wonderful high-end soundproofing of expensive vehicles, something I don't have the luxury of experiencing very often with my public school teacher's salary. I fiddle with my seatbelt and shift in my seat. The leather seats are usually very comfortable but now feel stiff against my body. Parker taps his fingers against the steering wheel as he rolls his neck. Instead of relaxing, he appears to be more rigid than he was a few seconds ago.

"Ugh." I give up and reach for the touchscreen and dials. "Do you mind if I turn on the radio?"

"Be my guest. Just press that button over there."

A news station comes on. I snort. Of course. What a complete bore. Shaking my head, I flip to a popular soft rock and pop music station which usually plays songs from the last decade.

It's decided today is officially Mess with Liz Day.

The sensual lyrics of Ciara's "Body Party" blast out from the wonderful surround sound speakers, every word and beat crisp and clear in the small confines of the car. *Is it too much to hope he doesn't remember what happened on Saturday?*

My fingers freeze as my skin warms up in mortification. I finagle with the controls, accidentally clicking on another button on the panel. Now the radio station dial has disappeared and another display of menus is in its place. *Shit. Shit. Shit. Where's that radio station dial, damn it!*

Ciara's sexy voice croons over the radio and, unlike Saturday night, this time, I'm completely sober and in full possession of all of my senses. Memories of my embarrassing private show flash through my mind. His intense green eyes. His sole focus on me. The tingles and the aching want in my core. His fingers caressing my neck. My thighs clench automatically and my eyes dart to him, desperate for something, for anything.

Parker's hands are glued to the steering wheel in a death grip, his knuckles white against the dark leather. A dark flush creeps up his neck and a muscle twitches in his cheek. Without looking away from the road, he slowly slides my desperate fingers away from the screen, his touch jolting me in what I hope is static electricity. A few seconds later, the music changes to a lovely jazz piece.

Beads of sweat gather on my forehead as my breathing slowly returns to normal. After clearing my throat, I ask, "What are you looking for me to help you with as Lucy's nanny? Besides the usual childcare?" *There, nothing happened. Moving on.*

His Adam's apple bobs as he swallows, and he replies, his gravelly voice a tinge deeper than usual, "Childcare will be great. I have her schedule written out at home for you. She usually wakes up around eight in the morning and goes to sleep by seven at night. If you have time and can help out with cooking, that'll be great. Fewer takeouts and freezer meals are probably better for her. She goes to ballet camp for half days on Tuesdays and Thursdays, and you may need to take her to playdates. Until your car is fixed, you can borrow one of mine." He turns his head toward me, my face reflecting in his sunglasses, and murmurs, "Hope that's okay with you."

Duties, responsibilities, work assignments. This I can handle. "Fine with me."

Soon, we pull up to the most stunning contemporary, two-story house I've ever seen. Dark wood paneling and large glass panels form the walls of the structure, with straight lines and sharp edges breaking the house into multiple levels, most likely for functionality and aesthetic purposes. Skylights can be seen from the sloping roof, and I think I spot a lovely second-story terrace garden. Towering, well-trimmed hedges surround the perimeter, providing privacy to its occupants. Parker opens the door to the three-car garage and parks his sedan next to a black SUV. This place looks like a page out of *Modern Architectural Digest.*

"Wait until you see the inside."

I jolt at his voice coming from outside my window. Apparently, my jaw has been hanging open for the past minute as I analyze every beautiful detail of his home. Even the garage is fully completed with real walls, floor-to-ceiling built-in shelving, and industrial pendant lights, giving the space a warm glow. *Who has pendant lights in the garage?* Parker shakes his head at my astonished expression and slides the aviators off his face, storing them in his suit pocket. His beautiful, emerald eyes, with flecks of gold, are sparkling with amusement. He opens the door for me.

"You and Lucy live here?" I gasp, my awe betrayed in my voice. I'm in love. With the house, that is, and I haven't even been inside.

He slams the door shut and carries my duffel bag inside. "I do own an architectural firm. What were you expecting, me to live in a dump?"

"I knew you had your firm, but I just never expected you to be...good at what you do." *Ouch, Liz, you're better than this.* I apparently can't seem to find my inner niceness when I'm around him.

We enter a brightly lit hallway into another bright room—the main living room would be my best guess. The floors are made from sturdy, tan, light-grained wood. Framed black-and-white photography decorates the white walls. Ansel Adams, perhaps? The large skylight and the floor-to-ceiling windows of sliding panels bring in natural light to the space. A sizeable dove-gray sectional sits in the center of the living room across from a clear glass fireplace. In the middle of the room is a white wool rug with a circular marble coffee table. A flatscreen television hangs from the ceiling—apparently, this is one of those smart homes with retractable television sets. The house is breathtaking...but a bit cold for a family. I notice a curious lack of family portraits and knickknacks.

Beyond the wall of windows is an oasis of greenery and trees, completely at odds with the native southern California desert shrubbery. I reflect back on Parker's arrogant consideration of Ambrosia's terrace. Maybe there's something to the source of his cockiness.

"Living room, kitchen, office, gym, and playroom are downstairs. Two of these rooms are technically extra bedrooms when guests come over, but for now, we repurpose them for other uses. The bedrooms are upstairs. I'll show them to you later." He beckons me over to follow him as he strides past a large chef's kitchen complete with a black marble island, crystal pendant lights, a wall of stainless-steel appliances...and even a pizza oven. He heads to a hallway with two closed doors. Television sounds emanate from one of the rooms.

Parker slowly opens the door. A teenager sits on a light-pink sofa, surfing on her phone while Lucy's eyes are glued to the television, oblivious to our arrival.

"Lucy, look who's here." He breaks into the warmest, widest smile I've ever seen from him. His shoulders marginally relax from their normally stiff posture as he hunches down and spreads his arms open for his daughter.

"Daddy, you're home early!" Lucy careens into Parker's embrace as he chuckles at her enthusiasm. My heart skips a beat at the affectionate scene before me. Lucy's gaze flickers up and finally spots me at the doorway. She quickly climbs out of her father's hug and flies into my arms. "Ms. Chapman!"

"Hi, Lucy. I've missed you a lot, and it's only been one week." I ruffle her golden curls, which are arranged in her usual low ponytail. I look around the room, finally noticing the neat shelves with toy baskets and a few large toy boxes lined up along the walls. There's a small table with two chairs and some art supplies that are also precisely stacked and ordered in small buckets. This house is so pristine...even the playroom is clean. "Wow, Lucy, you have a lot of fun toys and things to do in this room."

Lucy looks down at her feet. "It's not that much fun when no one plays with me." She kicks her feet on the soft cream carpet.

"Well, how about if Ms. Chapman plays with you? And because you're such a good girl, I'll even let you call me by my first name when we're not at school, okay?" I lean in and pretend to whisper the world's biggest secret to her. "You can call me Lizzy, but don't tell your friends at school."

Lucy giggles and nods vigorously. "Pinkie promise." She extends her little finger to me, and I hook mine around hers, laughing at her exuberance. I sigh in relief, my lips tipping up in a smile. It's the right thing to come, to be here for Lucy. My gaze flickers up to the silent man, who a moment ago was talking to the babysitter, only to find him standing a few feet away from us, staring at me, the earlier happiness seemingly drained from his face. Tensed shoulders. Locked jaw. Eyes burning with indecipherable emotions. I tilt my face to the side and frown.

Realizing I'm observing him, he wipes his face clean of any discernable reactions. "Lucy, would you like for Lizzy," he tilts his head, giving me a pointed look, "to be your nanny this summer?"

Lucy shrieks and claps her hands. "And stay here with us?"

I take her hand and give it a squeeze. "Yes. Like a giant sleepover—what do you say?"

"I love it!" She bounces around the room, her positive energy infectious. "This is the best day ever! Come with me. I'll show you my room." She tugs my hand and drags me out the door.

"I'm making us dinner. Lucy, dinner in thirty minutes, okay?" Parker hollers behind us.

"Okay!" Lucy leads me to a spiral, glass staircase with the same light-grain wooden steps as the rest of the house and opens the first door to the right on the second floor. "Here's my room."

Lucy's room is a wonderland of various shades of blue, with white clouds painted on the ceiling, a princess bed with all the frills and lace, complete with a large, white fluffy beanbag, and another floor-to-ceiling window overlooking the back gardens. Wallpaper with rainbows and hearts is showing signs of wear. A tall bookshelf lined with various princess dolls and stuffed animals sits in one corner. In the opposite corner is a smaller bookshelf with an assortment of picture books and toys. This whimsical room looks completely out of place with the rest of the house.

"Your room is beautiful. So many colors and is very fit for a princess like you."

Lucy giggles. "I call it my princess room too. Our house used to be more colorful, but Daddy cleaned the house and bought a lot of new decorations a long time ago. But he let me keep my room like this." She blinks her ocean-blue eyes at me as she plays with a fidget spinner. "Mommy decorated this room for me when she was still here...but I don't really remember her anymore... I wish I do."

"Oh, sweetie. Come here." My eyes sting as I try to blink away the tears threatening to spill out. I clear my throat and ask, "Why don't you show me your favorite book? We can read for a little bit while your daddy makes us dinner."

She immediately perks up—a quality unique to young children I'm extremely jealous of—and rushes off to pick the thickest book from her bookshelf and hands it to me. *Twenty Princess Bedtime Stories*, of course. We sit on the beanbag, and I begin reading the story of Princess Mirabella and her adventures with her fairytale prince, a wonderful classic. This is how it starts, the dreams of romance, love, and happily ever afters.

Three stories in, Lucy begins to doze off and the days' worth of tension catches up to me. Just as I am about to nod off myself, Parker opens the door.

"Dinner's ready," he announces...cordially. That's a start. Maybe this will work.

I wake up a grumpy Lucy and we trudge to a black, circular dining table next to the kitchen. Three plates of chicken nuggets and steamed broccoli await us, with a side of ketchup. I furrow my brows, directing a pointed look at Parker and he returns my stare with an arch of a brow.

"Chicken nuggets again? I don't like chicken nuggets. I hate them!" Lucy pounds her hands on the table and pushes her plate away. A sleepy child is as bad as a hormonal teenager. Or is it the other way around?

"Lucy! What did I teach you about manners? And Daddy's busy today. I didn't have time to make anything else or to get take out."

"You're always busy! I hate chicken nuggets and I'm not going to lie, Daddy." Lucy rubs her eyes and returns a fierce glare at her father, who from all appearances looks like he's about to blow a gasket. *Uh oh, Lucy is about to have a meltdown.* I recognize these signs from overtired kids at school.

"You will eat that meal, or you won't eat anything at all tonight!" he hollers at her, his face mottled with anger.

"I hate you! Why can't we have normal food like the other kids in class? Why do we always have chicken nuggets and pizza? Why can't we be like other families, Daddy?"

Parker freezes, his hands gripping the fork in front of him as he struggles visibly to take a calming breath...and failing. "Lucy Wellington—"

"Hey, sweetie." I take both of Lucy's hands. "Look at me. What did we practice in class? When we are upset, what do we do?" I give her a little squeeze and a reassuring smile.

She scrunches up her nose and replies, "We take a deep breath."

"And if one deep breath doesn't work?"

"We take another one."

"Okay, let's do that together, shall we?" I exaggerate a deep inhale. "Breathe in...one...two...three." I exhale loudly, "And now breathe out like you're a fire-breathing dragon!" Lucy closes her eyes and follows my instructions. "Again. Now breathe out like...a unicorn blowing bubbles underwater."

Her eyes fly open, and she scrunches up her adorable little eyebrows. "That's silly, Lizzy. Unicorns don't live underwater."

My eyes widen dramatically. "What? They don't?"

"Silly Lizzy."

I squeeze her shoulder. "Feel better now?" She nods. "So, tell me why you don't want to eat the chicken nuggets. We have chicken nuggets at school too, and you eat them just fine."

"Daddy's chicken nuggets taste like cardboard. They don't taste like the ones from school." Considering school lunches are definitely not gourmet, it says a lot about Parker's cooking...or reheating skills in this case. I gingerly pick one up and take a small bite. *Oh my gosh, she's right. This is complete shit. It's so overdone it may as well be cardboard.*

Forcing myself to swallow, I take a sip of water, washing the atrocity down my throat. "Well...they do taste *interesting*. But Lucy, your daddy worked hard to prepare this for you. If you don't like something, next time, you can tell him why with your words. We don't yell at each other. That's not polite and not a kind thing to do. Your daddy loves you and we need to treat those we love with kindness. When you yell, you hurt your daddy's feelings. He'll be sad."

"He yelled at me too! Very loudly. It was very scary."

"And that's not right of him, either. I'll talk to him." I lower my face to her level. "So, what do we do when we hurt someone's feelings by saying mean words?"

She mumbles, "We say sorry." Lucy gets off her chair and runs toward Parker, wrapping her little arms around his waist. "Daddy, I'm sorry. I love you, but your food tastes horrible...and that's not a mean word. I'm just being honest."

Parker lifts Lucy up onto his lap and buries his face into her neck, his thick hair falling over his forehead. "Daddy's sorry too." He glances at me and mouths, *thank you*, his previous icy demeanor warming up slightly. The temperature has moved from frigid to tepid.

Progress. Perhaps this may work.

I get up from the table. "Why don't I see what we have in the kitchen? I'll make us something that doesn't taste like cardboard—what do you say, Lucy?"

She exclaims her approval as my shoulders shake in amusement. How did this man survive all these years? If only Steven were here—he'd be so appalled. He has the most sophisticated palate of our friend group.

A quick dinner of spaghetti and meat sauce later, which Lucy happily gobbles up, Parker gets her ready for bed and tucks her in. He trudges downstairs as I'm putting the last plate away. I sense his towering presence before I see him. He leans against the wall, silent and still as a statue.

I glance at him, my breath catching in my throat. If I thought *GQ* Parker was pulled from the deepest recesses of my mind, well, nothing has prepared me for casual, at-home Parker. His hair is wet, most likely from a shower, and his bangs cover part of his face. He scrolls his phone as he brushes his hair back, tousling it just so, and an unruly lock falls back in front of his face. He has shaved, the dim pendant light illuminating every angle of his jawline that's sharp enough to cut glass. Parker is clad in a thin, sleeveless shirt. He crosses his arms, showcasing the sinewy muscles and strong biceps clearly familiar with the gym. A small tattoo—a phrase of some sort—wraps around one of his biceps. His gray sweatpants hang low on his hips, with a sliver of skin peeking through between his shirt and the waistband. All muscle and no fat from what I can see. My mouth salivates with an irrational desire to tease the strip of skin there.

"You done there?" His low voice sends tingles throughout my body.

Startled, I nearly drop the plate in my hand. "What do you mean?"

"The plate. You've been holding it for the past minute."

Flustered, I quickly turn around and return the plate to its proper place. "Done now." I toss a towel at him as I walk past him. "Next time, I cook, you clean."

I almost round the corner before his voice stops me. "So, there's a next time?"

"For now."

• • •

I settle on my queen-size platform bed with a sigh of contentment. There are benefits to this arrangement. For once, I get to take an actual bath instead of rinsing off the day in my tiny shower in the shoe closet that's my studio apartment. The guest room on the second floor is spacious, with more floor-to-ceiling windows and a large balcony overlooking the luscious gardens and swimming pool in the backyard. There's an ensuite with a jet tub *and* a shower, double vanities, and a walk-in closet probably the size of my bathroom at home. The room is decorated in a neutral palette of pale lavender and gray bedding, white walls, and blackout curtains, which close with a press of a button. If I lived here, I wouldn't need to stay in a five-star hotel when I travel because nothing else would compare.

Taking out my phone, I find several missed messages.

Emily: So, how did day one go? Is his terrace as nice as he makes it out to be? Can't believe we haven't been to his place yet.

Jess: Did you survive unscathed?

Emily: What do you mean unscathed? Is there drama? How can anyone have drama with Parker?

Melanie: You know, I thought I felt a vibe on Saturday.

Jess: Oh no, Melanie, you did it. You used the word vibe. Emily loves all things "vibey" and now she'll never let this go.

Emily: What vibe? Tell me!

Melanie: Trust me, there's something there. In fact, I bet you five dollars.

Emily: *Gasp* That obvious? Omigosh, I'm so in. You're on.

Groaning, I debate what to tell them and ultimately decide less is more in this situation. I snap a photo of my beautiful room and send it to them.

Liz: I'm alive and very much doing well. See for yourself. I think I'll just live here forever and never move out. And there's no vibe going on whatsoever. At all. Zero. Zilch.

Melanie: The lady doth protest too much.

Liz: Stop quoting Shakespeare. We're not at school anymore.

Seeing no three dots appear, I tap on the Genetic Genie app to do some online family tree perusal. Two messages await me in my inbox. I rub my hands together and click open the first one.

Hi Liz, Thanks for using Genetic Genie. Here's a discount for future services...

Ugh, spam. I click on the next one.

Thanks for the message, Liz. I'm definitely happy you reached out. Always down to find long lost relatives to see if my penchant for pineapples and anchovies on my pizza is inherited! I always knew grandma had a sister she lost touch with. Where are you located?

Your second cousin (is that right?), Kim

I like Kim already; she has a sense of humor. I quickly type out a response:

I'm in California. Where are you located?

I open up the Excel spreadsheet I use to keep track of the family tree and relatives I've found on Genetic Genie these past five years and whom I still need to follow up with. I've painstakingly cultivated a long list of potential relatives and have contacted them one by one to see if they're interested in connecting. The app doesn't share detailed genetic information showing how close the relation is, other than indicating a general genetic match, unless both parties consent to it. I hum to myself as I go through the names and notes on the spreadsheet.

Peter Chapman: Check. Third cousin, twice removed. Lives in the UK.

Gabby Martinez: Check. Second cousin. Lives in Canada and loves hockey (no surprise there).

Bob Jones: Ghosted me. Maybe not interested. Can send a follow-up in a month.

Gail McIntire: Ghosted me. A fun person to talk to but no show at meetup. Followed up, but no response, most likely not interested or changed her mind. But will see, hoping she'll reach out soon.

Kim Chapman: Check. Second cousin. In-progress conversation.

The list goes on and on. Honestly, what started as a nerdy endeavor has blossomed into a wonderful project which allows me to connect with so many people around the world. I can't wait to complete this undertaking and present the family tree, with photos, notes, and stories, to my parents for their upcoming wedding anniversary in a few months. By then, hopefully, I'll be out of Parker's hair and be several thousand dollars richer.

Parker. The enigma. A chameleon.

I search his name on social media apps and sites and peruse the photos he made public. Simple headshots for the most part, of which a few are familiar, because I saw them before on the *InstaConnect* profile Jess showed me when she was single. A few professional photos. Two photos of him and Lucy. No photos with friends. No photos of his late wife or his parents.

A complete mystery. My hands itch to pick at the invisible scab there.

CHAPTER 7

Liz

"**G**oodnight, sweetie," I whisper to Lucy as I tuck her into her princess bed. I've been here for two weeks now, and we have established a good rhythm. Our days are spent doing a variety of activities ranging from mini-lessons on reading and simple math to playtime in the sun, trips to the park, and splashing in the backyard pool. She's doing well in her ballet lessons and is always eager to show off the new moves she's learning at camp. She's so adorable, she makes my heart melt.

Lucy yawns, her eyes already half-closed. "'Night, Lizzy. See you tomorrow."

I lean in and kiss her softly on her forehead before closing the door behind me. The house is quiet as I head downstairs. Parker is most likely in his office again, where he usually is every night after doing the dishes. As promised, he got my car fixed and insisted on covering the expenses, saying my car is a work necessity.

Things between us have calmed down a bit, no longer as volatile as the night in the club two weeks ago. He's still an enigma—his moods waffling between curt and charming as if he can't even figure out how he wants to act, as if he's bearing a huge burden only visible to him, but somehow, there are moments when he forgets.

Those are the moments when he is charming…the very moments when I get flutters in his presence. It seems like my heart is drawn to this very much unavailable man…someone who is everything I'm not looking for and yet a person I'm infinitely curious about. I can't shake the feeling there's so much more to him than what meets the eye. And I want to unpeel those layers one by one…to get to the center and see what he's hiding. My fingers ache to smooth the ragged edges, the ruffled feathers, to dress his wounds and make it all better. Apparently, I'm a modern Florence Nightingale.

Shaking my head, I grab a bottle of water from the fridge and head to the backyard, which is quickly becoming one of my favorite places in his home. He has outdone himself with this oasis, a mini-retreat in the middle of a bustling city. Taking a deep breath, I smell the sweet scent of wildflowers, light but not overpowering. The sound of crickets accompanies me as I settle into my favorite oval lounge chair, the soft cushions molding around my body perfectly. The night breeze is just right, not too brisk, but cool enough to chase away the heat from the day. I set my water bottle on the table next to me and close my eyes, enjoying the peaceful quiet.

A few moments later, I feel a weight upon me, the sharp focus of someone's attention. Blinking my eyes open, I scan my surroundings, finding Parker leaning against a wooden column near the back patio. His body is a statement of coiled tension, a dichotomy to the casualness in the rolled-up sleeves of his dress shirt and his otherwise relaxed attire, but he looks like a panther lying in the wait, ready to pounce at the most opportune moment. The muscles in his forearm flex in the dim light as his fingers grip the tumbler he's holding tightly. He's staring at me—his green eyes are dark under the wispy light of the moon. Slowly, he lifts his cup to his lips and takes a sip, the muscles in his corded throat rippling with each swallow.

"Holy shit, you scared me. How long have you been standing there? Couldn't you have made your presence known?" I scramble up into a sitting position, my heart thumping against my rib cage. The earlier ease of the evening dissipates rapidly as my pulse picks up.

He slowly uncurls himself from the column and saunters over, his steps appearing light but measured at the same time. "I've been here this entire time. You just didn't notice me. And I didn't want to interrupt you as you were obviously enjoying a quiet moment to yourself."

"Oh."

"Oh indeed." He chuckles, his deep voice sending shivers down my body, as he sits down in a recliner next to me. It appears I may be getting the charming version of him tonight. A small breeze carries his scent of bergamot and amber to me. A smell I find myself liking...perhaps a little too much.

"You don't have to work tonight?"

"I do. It never ends, but I find myself wanting a break."

"We all need to rest and relax sometimes. You have to take care of yourself first in order to take care of the people around you," I murmur, glancing at his pensive profile from the corner of my eye.

He hums noncommittally as he stares at the stars in the clear night sky. "Do you believe the theory that the dead are up there watching over us?" His voice is so soft, I could barely hear him.

The thudding of my heart becomes more noticeable as I turn to face him. A heaviness cloaks his figure as he keeps his face turned upward toward the night sky.

"I'd like to think so. The people who loved us never truly leaves us. Maybe they're not in the stars, but they're around us." I swallow the lump in my throat as I watch him bite into his bottom lip, unleashing a savagery it doesn't deserve. I want to tug the plump lip from his teeth, to soothe the bite marks I'd no doubt find there.

My heart clenches involuntarily as I war with an internal desire to walk over to him, to wrap this lonely man in my arms. Perhaps that's my downfall—I can't resist helping a wounded animal and that's who Parker is...or at least the Parker I've observed in the last two weeks. A wounded man, hiding behind a tough metal armor, wielding the swords of anger and coldness around him like a weapon, scaring anyone who dares to creep too closely.

Parker snorts derisively. "If that's the case, I'm sure she's up there laughing at me. At what a fuck up I've become." He sits up and leans forward in his chair, clasping his hands in front of him. His head hangs low as he stares at the floor.

"Y-You're trying your best. Don't be so hard on yourself," I murmur, not knowing how to respond. I'm guessing he's referring to his late wife, but I don't want to pry and ruin this rare moment when he's letting me get close to him without his shield and weapons between us.

He turns his face to me, his eyes intense in the moonlight. "You don't know what I did." He chuckles mirthlessly as if he is a punchline to his own joke. "You don't know *anything*," he mutters under his breath. Parker swallows audibly, his Adam's apple bobbing in his throat. He turns his head back toward the floor again. "I shouldn't even be talking to you about this...least of all, you."

His words are cryptic. Nonsensical. But the anguish in his voice draws me in. "Parker, I know you and I haven't interacted on the best terms before I started staying here, but...I can tell you're trying your best to be a good father to Lucy, to be a kind friend to my brother, and I'm sure you're diligent at work or else you couldn't have achieved all of this." I gesture to the house and the backyard and continue, "So, whatever it is you're feeling, I hope you know it isn't true. I may not know you well, but at least I know this...you're trying your best, and that's all that matters in life sometimes." My hands ache with a desire to smooth out the tense muscles on his back.

Parker stills, and I can't even see his frame move as he breathes. Suddenly, his shoulders shudder and he takes in one ragged breath. And another. As if he's getting in gulps of oxygen after holding his breath underwater for too long. Slowly, he faces me again, his eyes glittering with unsaid emotions, his teeth gnawing at his bottom lip again. His nostrils flare as he pins me with his stare and his hand clenches into a tight fist on his lap. Slowly he stands, his eyes never leaving my face.

He swallows. "You make it so *hard* for me to..." he begins, his voice gravelly.

"For you to what?" I whisper.

He begins to take a step toward me as I lean forward, drawn by his magnetized gaze. He stops himself mid-step and shakes his head, suddenly backing away. "Nothing." He lets out another deep chuckle. Another one without any trace of humor in it. "Nothing at all." Parker backs away a few more steps toward the sliding glass doors. Before he steps in, he murmurs, "Thank you, Liz. Thank you...for everything." He enters the house and closes the door behind him.

The night is quiet except for the sound of the blood rushing in my ears. I clasp my hand to my chest, rubbing the invisible ache there.

CHAPTER 8

Parker

"No, we're not taking on the project." I stare outside the window of my office, my hands in my pockets, observing the three-car pile-up from the distance. Flashes of red and blue lights. Tiny dots of black-and-white patrol cars.

I can't really hear the sirens from up here. A small blessing.

What time is it? I tilt my wrist and look at my watch. Three-thirty. Two more hours before the end of the day.

"But Parker, the profit margin is lucrative. They pretty much offered to give us a blank check to work on their project. We'll be plastered in the front pages of every magazine." The voice belonging to my partner, Dylan Jones, emanates from the flatscreen on the wall opposite the window, drawing me away from the commotion below. We met in college and grad school at Cornell and decided to branch out and start our firm five years after graduation. We haven't looked back ever since and now we are one of the premier, award-winning boutique architectural and design firms on both coasts. He's based at our New York branch while I head up our LA headquarters.

"It's blood money, Dylan. You know that. Elias Kent's businesses are shady and constantly being investigated for all sorts of illegitimate activities. There's a reason why he's giving us carte blanche, because no one will take the job." I level a stare at my partner and friend.

Dylan rubs his eyes and leans back in his leather chair, his shoulders slumping in defeat. "Ugh, I know. Why is it so difficult? The project is just so enticing. To be able to create a campus rivaling the largest tech companies, with no financial restrictions." He sighs heavily and glances at me with resignation in his slate-colored eyes. The weariness in his voice extends beyond work stress. Something else is going on, but he's being closed-lipped about it. We technically should be in our prime right now, but somehow, both of us seem to be surrounded by a dark aura we can't shake.

"I know." I pace around the office floor, my eyes flickering back to the windows. "Stuff of dreams."

"You're right though, Parker. Once you get in bed with the mob, you probably can't get back out easily. Not worth it." He runs his fingers through his short, black hair before clasping his hands in front of him. "So, how are things going on your side? The homeless shelters are coming along?"

My lips quirk up in a smile. The county has enlisted our services in designing a series of homeless shelters throughout the downtown and surrounding areas. While this isn't one of our most lucrative projects, this is one of the few projects I've still retained a personal connection to. All the other jobs have been relegated to dollars, cents, and profit margins for me, a means to an end. A means to survive. Somewhere along the way, I lost the passion to create beauty, to innovate, and to design for the future.

I press a button on my phone to ring up my secretary, but it goes to voicemail. "Give me a second, Dylan. I'm going to get the files."

Opening the door, I survey the bustling office. Our firm, Wellington and Jones LLP, encompasses three floors in a downtown LA high rise. The office is open concept, with floor-to-ceiling glass walls for offices and decorated with sustainable materials such as bamboo and reclaimed timber, soothing green and brown colors, reminiscent of the great outdoors. Warm lighting glows from the ceiling and desk lamps while natural sunlight streams in from the windows. Colleagues working on various models and sketches huddle at tables, seemingly engrossed in their projects. Muted conversations. The slide of file cabinets opening and shutting. A quiet, comfortable hum serves as the background. It's my home away from home, but ever since Abby passed, this is the only place where I feel remotely myself.

My eyes snag on my secretary walking briskly toward me. "Betsy, can you bring in the latest binder for New Beginnings?"

"Yes, sir."

I head back inside my office and walk to my desk, my fingers trailing the smooth mahogany of the table. "Betsy is bringing in the binder and I can take a look at the latest drawings and the actuals versus budget." I stare at Dylan, who is currently leaning back in his chair with his eyes closed. "It's pretty much done. Construction is at the tail end right now. We only had to make a few changes to the drawings at the last minute, but everything is coming together...finally. Our design team also did a good job with the interiors."

"I'm happy for you, Parker. Maybe this gives you some closure. Contributing back to society...I know that's important to you." His eyes flicker open as warmth bleeds into the grays of his irises.

Betsy knocks and drops off the thick binder on my desk before excusing herself and closing the door behind her. I open the binder and turn to the page I'm looking for. "It looks like we're right on target with the estimates and they may ask us to work on other community projects afterward. I think it's a win." I flip back to the first page and admire the latest drawings and photos of the center. "Regina McDonald New Beginnings Centers," I murmur more to myself than to Dylan. "Mom will be so happy."

"I'm sure she's proud of you and will be touched once she finds out you named the shelters after her. It's the perfect circle, someone who has utilized shelter services as a child and growing up to later design better places for those in need." I hear a chime from his laptop. "Hey, I have to go to my next meeting. Talk soon."

"Thanks, Dylan. I'll keep you posted."

My cell phone beeps with an incoming message.

James: I can't believe you're finally inviting the gang to your house. Two years. Seriously. Are you a secret superhero and live in a bat cave no one can visit?

I scoff and type back.

Parker: You've been to my place before. I just haven't invited everyone else. But then, no one has really complained before.

James: Deep clean, Parker. You've built up this image of your place being some magical paradise, and now the girls are expecting nothing less than perfection. Hope it lives up to their expectations. I mean, it'd be kind of sad if the house of one of the "Top 10 Architectural Bachelors of LA" is a mess.

I snort, sensing his sarcasm all the way over here. I type in a quick response.

Parker: Please, they'll be nothing short of impressed.

James: We'll see. Btw, Steven is bringing a colleague. You okay with that, right?

Parker: Yeah, he texted me about it earlier. Sounds good.

I shake my head and check the time before I pocket my phone. Three forty-five. Fuck. Since when do I care so much about going home on time? Irritation washes over me and I tug at the red-striped tie around my neck, needing air. I walk back over to the windows. More patrol cars line up on the street, looking like tiny zebras from where I stand. The swirling lights of the ambulance and firetrucks add to the ruckus as they arrive on the scene. A sizeable crowd has gathered around the intersection and traffic piles up. Faint sounds of car horns and sirens filter their way up to the office. I can't seem to tear my gaze away from the turmoil below.

Buzz buzz.

"Coming. One second."

I stare at the messy living room and tug at my hair. I hurry to straighten up the cushions on the sofa and pick up the throw blanket from the floor. Papers are scattered on the wooden floor and coffee table. I haven't cleaned up since my fight with Abby. She fucking hung up on me when I called her on the phone after she darted out the door. So, instead of being a responsible adult and straightening up the house, I spent the last three hours in good company—three bottles of craft beer and Chinese takeout of lo mein and kung pao chicken. Toys are scattered throughout the living room, courtesy of Lucy. The place looks like a tornado went through it.

Buzz buuzzzzz.

Screw it. Who cares if people think this place is a mess? I scamper toward the sound, nearly tripping over a few wooden alphabet blocks on the rug. I throw open the door in a rush as the buzzing sound of our doorbell begins anew.

Flashing crimson and blue lights temporarily blind me. Neighbors peek their heads out of their windows. The brief blare of sirens is suddenly silenced as an officer most likely accidentally presses a button in the patrol car parked in front of my house. Rain. So much rain, pouring down like an act of God, forming deep puddles of water in my front yard.

They say you know precisely the moment your life changes. The air smells different. Time moves at a slower pace. Your hearing is amplified. Your senses come alive.

Dread coils in my stomach as I turn to the officer standing before me. My heart pounds against my rib cage. I stare at his collar, dark navy blue, the corners crisp but soaked through from the rain, not wanting to meet his gaze, and see the truth in his eyes.

"Are you Parker Wellington?" a gruff, nasal voice asks.

I nod, suddenly speechless, nausea churning in my gut. Decorum dictates I should meet his eyes. I slowly drag my gaze up to his and my breath catches in my throat as I see sympathy reflecting back at me.

I know what he's going to say.

No. Please.

I start to shake my head, the sound of my heartbeats thrumming in my ears. "No," I mutter. "No, no, no."

He clasps his hand on my shoulder. "I'm sorry, sir. Your wife has been involved in an accident..."

I don't hear the rest of his sentence as I gasp for air, white flecks dotting my vision, and I hurl the contents of my dinner into the bushes nearby.

The faint sound of sirens snaps me out of my trip down memory lane. My heart races a mile a minute as I draw in one ragged breath after another. Placing my palms on the glass, which is warm from the sunlight, I shut my eyes as beads of sweat gather on my forehead.

I can't breathe.

Twisting my body around, I suck in mouthfuls of oxygen as nausea roils in my stomach, threatening to relieve the remnants from lunch a few hours ago. Irrational panic fills me and my hands turn clammy.

Home.

I need to go home.

I snatch my suit jacket from my chair, stuff my laptop into my briefcase, and head out of the office.

· · ·

"Lizzy! The floor is lava. You aren't supposed to walk on it!" Lucy shrieks, her excitement palpable.

Thump. Thump. Thump. "Fine, let's start over. The sofa is the mountain and aaaaaahhhh the volcano is erupting! The floor is lava! We need to run." Liz lets out a deep gurgle, doing a poor imitation of what I presume is the cataclysmic event happening in my living room.

More happy screeches. Giggles and laughter. My chest slowly warms, the previous chill abating, and I walk quietly down the hallway toward them. Colorful pillows and cushions litter the floor. Blankets and comforters hauled from the bedrooms are now strewn about. Even the bean bag from Lucy's room is making an appearance in front of the fireplace. The living room is a veritable pigsty.

I've never seen anything more beautiful in my life.

I softly pad across the hardwood floors, wanting to witness the scene firsthand before they notice me. Liz is standing on a pile of bedsheets she pulled from God knows where while Lucy is cushion jumping in an attempt to reach her. Liz has been with us for a month already and with each passing day, I'm more and more eager to come home on time, to see what image of domestic bliss awaits me, to bask in the warmth of her presence.

Even though I know I'll be under the scrutiny of a pair of beautiful eyes who see too much, who seem to understand me too well. But I find myself not wanting to hide as much from her...despite the anger and guilt that threaten to overtake me whenever I steal these glimpses of joy. Despite me knowing this deepening connection between us is a bad idea—something I should stop in its tracks. But sometimes, my wants battle against my shoulds and lately, the wants have been surfacing as the victor with these moments of happiness being the spoils of war.

Memories to file away for later when the darkness and loneliness creep back in.

"This is too hard, Lizzy. My legs are too short. I can't reach the blankets," Lucy complains as she attempts a leap from her pink cushion, but pulling back at the last minute.

Liz laughs and tosses her head back, her golden tresses flying behind her in wild abandon. Her blue eyes radiate joy. She throws her arms up in the air, highlighting her enticing figure, currently clad in a simple gray tank top and a pair of pink sweats. She emotes with her entire body.

Her eyes. The unique sapphire is both familiar and unfamiliar at the same time.

Her sweet voice, the dulcet tones are capable of warming the coldest of souls.

Her laugh, a sound I ache to hear again, to hear it directed at me.

Her.

I can't look away.

I'm the moth drawn to the burning flame, knowing I'm soaring toward my death, yet helpless to resist the lure.

"Take a leap, Lucy! If we fail, we just try again and don't give up."

Lucy huffs and puffs out her little chest. Her hair is fashioned into two intricate braids, complete with two little bow barrettes. She bends her knees and leaps off her cushion.

I hold my breath.

Liz snatches her from mid-air, wrapping her arms around her as both of them collapse on the pile of blankets, giggling and shrieking.

"I did it! Did you see it, Lizzy? I was brave."

"I did! We survived the eruption. We are safe...*forever*!" Lucy cackles as Liz embarks on a tickle battle. After a minute or two of happy screaming, Liz snuggles Lucy close to her chest and presses kisses into her hair.

My racing heart slows down and thuds, slow and steady, as if it's finally awakening from a long slumber. Flutters gather in my gut. Warmth spreads from the hollow in my chest to my extremities as I take in the beautiful picture before me. I find my lips tilting up into a grin, a genuine one this time. Leaning against the wall, I catalog every detail, from the splotchy patches on Lucy's face to the way Liz's strands reflect burnt gold under the sun. I memorize every sound, wanting to sear this image into my brain and to hold on to this feeling before I'm dragged back into the real world.

Liz ruffles Lucy's hair in affection and Lucy scowls. "My braids. Don't mess them up, Lizzy."

Liz snickers and replies, "If I mess them up, I'll just re-braid them for you." She wraps her arms around the wiggling Lucy, eliciting more laughter. Glancing up, her eyes rove across the room before snapping back, her body freezing when she finds me standing there. Her smile arrests on her face as her entire body stills.

I flinch, her expression dragging me back into my reality, as forgotten thoughts and emotions, albeit temporarily, flood my synapses. *What am I doing?* The tension in my muscles that briefly abated comes coiling back like a tsunami, obliterating my previous good mood. The flutters in my gut morph into clawing guilt. The heat in my chest burns, and the flames of anger threaten to make a resurgence. It's like my body no longer knows how to react around her anymore and it feels anything and everything, all too much, all at once.

"You're back," she murmurs, her voice echoing in my ears. Her dulcet, beautiful voice.

I ball my hands into fists and smooth my face into a polite veneer. The least I can do. *She doesn't deserve this from you. She's as much of a victim as you are.* The nagging voice of my conscience is more incessant these days, but I shove it away even though deep down, I know it's the truth. It's easier to hold on to the anger, to latch on to the pain. I don't deserve to be happy, to be free of its shackles. We stare at each other, unidentifiable emotions swirling in the deep-blue pools of her eyes. She furrows her brows.

"Daddy!" Lucy disentangles herself from Liz and launches herself at me. "Lizzy and I were playing 'the floor is lava' and I just made the biggest leap..."

I bury my face in her braids, her flowery scent instantly calming my rattled nerves. Liz tentatively walks over to us. "Are you okay?" she murmurs.

My eyes flicker to her gaze, now shining with concern. I feel naked. Exposed. I swallow the pins and needles in my throat and respond, my voice rusty, "What do you mean? I'm fine. Don't read too much into everything when nothing is wrong."

Her hand reaches out as if to touch me, but she pulls it back immediately, catching herself just in time. "I just thought...your shoulders tense up when you're stressed." She shakes her head and looks down at her feet, chuckling softly. "What am I talking about?" Biting down on her plush, pink lip, she shifts on her feet.

I force myself to relax my clenched muscles, the mounting ache there surprising me. I guess I never noticed the pain as it's always there. Lucy slides down my body and happily bounds over to the living room to resume her obstacle course of faux lava and rocks. I straighten up and tug off the tie around my neck.

Clearing my throat, I reply, "Things are fine. Don't worry." I nod at Lucy, who is happily jumping on the sofa at the current moment. "How are things today?"

Liz wrings her hands, her feet tapping in an incessant rhythm, as nervous energy emanates from her entire being. Despite my forced relaxation, the tension is still palpable between us. "Things are great. We did some reading this morning and practiced simple math...adding and subtracting small numbers. Now, we're taking a wiggle break before TV time." She twists and pulls at her fingers. "I was just about to prepare din—"

Unbidden, I reach out and clasp her hands in mine, my large palms engulfing hers, wanting to soothe her jitters. Her fidgeting stops as she stares at our interlinked hands. Her face flushes a pretty pink. My rough hands, cut up multiple times in my early days in modeling class, relish in the silky softness of her skin. I immediately release my grip on her and recoil, disgusted with myself, yet wanting to reach back out to her at the same time. *Control yourself, Parker. This is so inappropriate on so many levels.*

I step back until there's a safe distance between us, my breathing quickening despite the lack of exertion. "Thank you for your help. I'll change and watch Lucy while you cook."

I give her a curt nod and escape to my bedroom, shutting the door behind me. Sliding down to the floor in a sitting position, I rake my hands through my hair and pound my fist on the floor, the temporary pain a soothing balm and distraction to my convoluted soul.

Get a grip. Get a damn grip. You don't deserve her. You don't deserve to be happy. Remember what you did? Remember her role in it? Closing my eyes, I breathe through my nose, exhale through my mouth. Once I feel I have my wits about me, I shrug out of my business attire and change into a T-shirt and a pair of workout shorts. Maybe I'll hit the home gym after dinner tonight and work off the rioting emotions inside me.

I clamber down the stairs, finding Lucy in front of the television, surrounded by an array of cushions and blankets, watching *Spot and Lola* again, her favorite cartoon of late. I sit down next to her and ask, "Why do you wrap yourself up like that? Are you cold?"

She shakes her head, her eyes still glued to the screen. "No, but the volcano eruption is over now, and we're in the ice age, so it's very cold...pretend cold."

I gasp in mock horror. "You don't say? Then Daddy is freezing his butt off right now, uh oh."

She whips her head at me and groans dramatically, "Oh no! Daddy can't freeze. You need to take care of me." She slides over to my side and wraps one of her blankets around me, cocooning us to the best of her abilities. "I love you, Daddy. Us against the world."

A sharp pain slashes through me as I curl my arms around her. Lucy deserves so much more than I can give her. She deserves a happy family, a mom, and a dad who isn't hanging on by a thread.

And who do you have to blame for that, Parker?

Lucy burrows herself deeper into my side as we watch the ruckus the little brown dog and her sister whip up. She giggles at their antics. "Daddy, watch this part!"

"Sure, pumpkin." I rub my hand around her shoulders and blink away the moisture in my eyes. "I love you, too," I whisper into her hair.

One episode of *Spot and Lola* later, Liz hollers from the kitchen, "Wash up, dinner is ready!"

I turn off the television and carry Lucy to the bathroom, where we wash our hands to the tune of "Happy Birthday," a trick she learned from school to ensure she is thorough in her cleansing. Lucy scampers to the dining table and climbs onto her chair, her eyes wide with surprise.

"Is that *lasagna*, Lizzy? It's my favorite."

Liz winks at her. "Yes, sweetie pie. I know. You always seem to love it at school. Wait until you try Lizzy's lasagna. It's really yummy."

She hands me a plate of lasagna and settles into her seat. Lucy digs into her food with unmatched enthusiasm, smearing tomato sauce all over her chin. I cut a small piece to try and nearly groan with pleasure when the tart tomato sauce and the savory juices from the ground beef hit my palate. It's been so long since I've had home-cooked meals consistently. Too long.

"Really? How long?"

I look up, finding Liz's big blue eyes on me, her mouth quirking to the side. I must have spoken my thought out loud. Patting my mouth with a napkin, I reply, "Meals at home of this caliber? Three years. Since Abby…" I look down at my plate before continuing, "But even then, she didn't like to cook, but at least she made edible food, unlike me."

"I see." Her heart-shaped face is pensive as she searches my face for an appropriate response.

I swallow another bite of the lasagna and hand Lucy a glass of water. "She tried her best with us…but sometimes you can't fit a round peg in a square hole. I guess I just didn't see it at the time." I set my utensils down and find myself rubbing my ring finger again, staring at the faint line there.

"Mommy didn't like to cook, Daddy?" Lucy interjects, curiosity in her clear-blue eyes.

"No, she didn't, pumpkin. But she still cooked better than Daddy."

"Daddy's food doesn't taste good," she agrees.

"Well, if you like the lasagna, I can cook it more for you while I'm here." Liz's warm voice draws my attention back to her. She smiles, a genuine smile showcasing her pearly whites, with such warmth in her gaze.

At me.

The smile is an arrow straight into my heart. Whether it's a Cupid's arrow or a fatal one, that's to be determined. Or perhaps they are one and the same. I grip my napkin tightly in my fist. This is the second time this smile is directed at me, the first time being the day we met, when the wind literally got knocked out of my chest.

I don't deserve it.

I don't deserve her forgiveness for my mercurial moods.

I hate how my mind cannot decide between dislike and affection when it comes to her. And frankly, if I were to be completely honest with myself, I think the dislike is quickly fading into the background and replaced with something I don't dare name.

Something I can't let myself name. I hold on to the last vestiges of anger as if it were my last lifeline.

My eyes shift away, and I bite my tongue, relishing in the pinch of pain. Well-deserved punishment for what a mess I am.

"Thank you," I murmur, finishing the last bits of my dinner. "So, you've been here for a month now—have you fully adjusted? Anything Lucy and I can do to make things easier for you?"

She shakes her head and pats her lips with her napkin. "No, we have a good routine now. Things are going pretty well, actually," she murmurs, her eyes flickering up at me before darting away, "surprisingly so."

I bite my cheek, a small grin threatening to appear on my face. As long as I don't think about what happened in the past, during these temporary moments of amnesia, I've enjoyed having her around. It's like a breath of fresh air has been let inside the house. It's like the sun has started shining after months and months of gloomy rainstorms.

"Daddy, why don't we have pictures of Mommy in the house?" Lucy asks nonchalantly as she pokes her lasagna with her fork, spearing only the pasta but missing the meat sauce completely.

My knife and fork clatter to the table, my temporary good mood disappearing. My mind races for an appropriate answer to appease her. I feel the warmth rushing to my face and the prickle of Liz's attention on me, as she patiently waits for me to answer Lucy. *Because I can't look at Abby and not think about why she died. Because every night when I fall asleep, the last thing I see is her angry face, and I can't bear to see her in the daytime. Because I don't need any more reminders of why I can't live with myself and how I took your mom away from you, pumpkin.*

"Daddy?"

"Hey, Lucy, do you want ice cream after dinner? You've been so good today. I think you deserve a treat. What do you say?" Liz claps her hands together in overt excitement as she steals a glance at me with sympathy in those arresting blue eyes.

Those familiar blue eyes.

The warmth of gratefulness collides with the twist of anger triggered by her sympathy, and I drink a gulp of ice water, attempting to short-circuit my system which is already miswired, with no hope of returning to normal. Liz furrows her brows at my expression. She always sees too much—too much for her own good. *Don't try to figure this whiplash out. I can't escape it—I'll just drag you down with me.*

Slowly pushing out of my chair, I stand up. My hands grip my plate as I clean up the table, not looking at her, but attuned to her every moment, her every breath. I carry the dishes back into the kitchen, escaping my feelings toward her, which are getting murkier with each passing day.

Liz puts Lucy to bed, and she trudges downstairs, catching me as I was about to head into the office. "Parker." She places her hand on my arm, then snatches it away, but the burning sensation where her palm met my forearm lingers. "Do you have a second? Can we have a chat about Lucy?"

Unease curls in my gut as I nod. I hope everything is okay. Leading her into the office, I beckon her to sit in the chair in front of my desk as I take a seat in my leather chair, ready to finish some work I brought home earlier.

She shakes her head, but instead opts to stand in the doorway. Twisting her hands, she takes a deep breath and says, "Lucy is a sweetheart as we both know...but sometimes when we play, she mentions missing her mom. I know it's normal for any child who has experienced a death of a parent, but I thought I should let you know."

My chest tightens as heat rises in my body. *It's all my fault.* The pang of guilt makes a reappearance, accompanied by the familiar and heady burn of anger.

Rubbing my eyebrows, I stare at the keyboard in front of me. "I-I'm trying my best here." I exhale a ragged breath. "Is there anything I should do more of?"

She plods closer, her footsteps light on the ground. Hints of vanilla waft through the air. I glance up and find myself staring at her dazzling blue eyes, which are looking at me in sympathy.

"No," she murmurs as she places her hand on mine, the warmth spreading throughout my body, "I can see you're trying your best. I told you the same two weeks ago and I stand by the assessment. But I wouldn't be doing my job if I don't tell you what's going on. I think it's completely normal for her to feel this way at times. I'll be thinking of fun activities to do with her and perhaps you can come with us for some of them...like the upcoming Orange County Fair, or maybe when we go to the bookstore tomorrow. Spending more time with her precious daddy can't hurt." She squeezes my hand and starts letting go.

I grip her tightly, not wanting to sever our connection. She gasps, staring at our joined hands, her face flushing a pretty pink. Tingles spread from where we touch, and my nerves come alive. Warmth rushes through my body as blood flows south. I take a ragged breath as I smooth my thumb over the back of her soft hand. Reluctantly, I let go of her and murmur, my voice husky, "I'll take the day off tomorrow and go to the bookstore with you two. Thank you for letting me know and doing such a good job of watching her."

She swallows, her tongue slipping out and wetting her lips. Her luscious lips. Stepping back slowly, she says, "You're welcome. It's the least I can do. If I notice anything unusual, I'll let you know." With that, she steps out of the office as if someone were chasing her, taking her warmth with her. My chest spasms with conflicting emotions.

Vitriol—what used to be easy when it comes to her—is now replaced with a heady dose of something I don't want to imagine or think about.

Something I can't contemplate. Not now, not ever.

Because she and I, we're destined to be, at best, passing ships in the night.

CHAPTER 9

Liz

"**H**ey, guys! So happy to see the three of you here today," Melanie exclaims, a broad smile on her face, as we step into the bright interior of Pendleton Books, one of the last indie-owned bookstores in the Pasadena area. The store, with its towering shelves and tables filled with colorful books from around the world, is one of my favorite places to visit whenever I have free time. Quiet chatter from groups of people fills the place. There appears to be some sort of author event happening today. My heart twists at the thought of physical bookstores potentially disappearing in the future as the world moves toward e-commerce. Nothing can replace the feeling of stepping into this small slice of heaven, being surrounded by thousands of untold stories, waiting to be discovered.

I bring her in for a brief hug. "Well, we decided it will be a nice little trip for us to visit Lizzy's favorite store." I nod to Lucy, who's grinning at us. "And I told Lucy my good friend works here and can get us books at a discount."

"Shh." She looks around surreptitiously. "Let's not go around advertising that, shall we?" Melanie glances at the imposing man behind me who's standing there like a bodyguard, surveying the place and no doubt wondering what he has gotten himself into. "Hey, Parker! Nice to see you again."

Parker flashes one of his award-winning smiles at her, the grin not quite reaching his eyes. His social smile. "Hey, Melanie. Hope we aren't bothering you too much while you're working."

Melanie waves her hand in dismissal. "No way. It's a bit crowded today since we have an event, but it's not like I need to give you guys a tour or something. Just come find me when you're ready to make some purchases. I'll ring you guys up." She glances behind us, and her eyes widen. "Okay, looks like I'm needed for a little mishap in the graphic novels section." Walking away, she looks back and hollers, "Come find me later, okay? And Parker, thanks for the invite for tomorrow! I can't wait to visit your grand architectural wonder." She smirks before turning around and heading over to an aisle where it appears a good number of books have toppled off the shelves. Shaking my head at her shrinking figure, I inhale deeply, taking in the wonderful smell of new books. The crisp, slightly sweet scent, unexplainable, yet addictive all the same.

"You know why bookstores smell so good? Books are made of organic compounds, such as your usual paper, ink, the glue binding them together. Almost all paper contains a compound called lignin, a relative to vanillin, which, as you probably guess, is where vanilla comes from." Parker's husky murmur combines with the irresistible scent in a lethal combination. I shiver. He chuckles softly at my reaction as if knowing how his presence affects me.

I tug Lucy with me as we head toward the children's section. "How do you know this stuff? From your news radio?"

"This might baffle you, but I'm a pretty smart person."

I snort, the half laughter shaking off the butterflies percolating in my stomach.

He laughs, his voice rich, like a deejay in a late-night radio show. "As an architect, I study the qualities of many organic materials. It's something I've picked up over the years," he explains.

Sneaking a glance at him, I find him staring at me with those piercing green eyes, currently shining with warmth, a look I don't see very often. My heart skips a beat as he smiles at me, his dimples showing. I return his smile tentatively, feeling a bit flustered. He flinches, his expression falling abruptly as if he caught himself doing something he shouldn't be doing. I frown, puzzled at the capriciousness of his moods.

We enter the children's section which is filled with rows and rows of colorful paperback and board books, with comfortable mini chairs and fluffy poufs for little ones to sit on. A few racks of plush animals and toys fill one corner. Kids of all ages are running around the space either playing with the toys or carrying books to the small, round tables placed throughout the area.

Lucy tugs on my hand. "Lizzy, can I go play with the toys? Pretty please?" Her eyes widen as she stares at the veritable wonderland in front of her.

"You can play with one toy and then you should pick out some new books." I glance at Parker, who is staring at us with muted bemusement. "Your daddy will buy any book you like for your bookshelves at home." I grin cheekily at him and wag my brows, teasing a small grin from him. A reward, a token from the relatively lighter-hearted version of him today.

"Really, Daddy? You'll buy me any book I want?"

Parker shakes his head and squats down so he's face level with Lucy. "Yes, pumpkin. I'll buy you your books so Lizzy can read them to you at home...and you can ask her to read you five books before bedtime tonight." His eyes flicker to mine as he arches his brow, his lips twisting up in a small smirk.

I purse my lips. *You evil man.* Knowing Lucy, she'll pick the five biggest books and it'll be an hour of reading and answering her questions about the stories. Lucy squeals as she runs off to the stuffed animal section. Smiling, I gaze after her. This is how a love of books begins. I remember Mom taking me to the bookstore and library when I was young, and I'd marvel at all the beautiful books sitting there, waiting for me to pick them up. My heart twists at the thought of little Lucy not having her mom to take her to these places. I'll do my best to give her a taste of the experiences I had with my mom when I was a child. Lucy now has two toys in her hands, her little face scrunched up as she contemplates which toy to play with first.

I straighten up and turn toward the romance and fiction section on the other side of the store. Twisting my lips to the side, I stare wistfully at the colorful shelves, wondering if I'll have time to check them out before we head back home.

"I'll watch Lucy. Why don't you go browse around?" Parker slides his hands into his pockets as he stares at his daughter with a soft smile on his face.

"You sure?" I can hardly contain the glee in my voice.

He glances at me and tilts his head toward the rainbow shelves. "Go. I got this."

Rubbing my hands together, I walk toward the romance section, my mind reviewing the books I have on my "to be read" list. Too many books, too little time. I stop along the way and admire the new beautiful hardcovers of favorites I've read in the past. I can't help but pick up a few of them. I'll reread them and they'll be part of my collection forever.

I amble down the aisles filled with great love stories, from the sweet and innocent young-adult section with an abundance of coming-of-age tomes to the grittier and darker taboo romances. I'm an equal opportunity romance reader. As long as the plot is enticing and the writing can transport me elsewhere for a little while, I'm a fan. Soft jazz plays in the background as I pull out books catching my eye or new releases I've been aching to get my hands on. Before I know it, I have a thick pile of at least ten books in my arms. Coming to bookstores can be dangerous for my wallet.

Window shopping, you're window shopping, Liz. You'll look at these beauties and flip through them, and then pick only one to take home with you. Even with Melanie's employee discount, I can't afford to buy them all, and plus, where will I store them in my shoebox size apartment? Turning the corner to enter the last aisle, I spot a bright magenta cover, one with an assortment of wildflowers. I've been seeing this book everywhere on social media. I meander over to my target, carefully balancing the stack of books against my chest, and reach out to pluck one volume off the shelf.

The tower of books wobbles against my chest and slides off my arms, landing in a loud thud on the carpeted floor. Groaning,

I stoop low to pick up the fallen books, which are in a disarray around me. "Why do you do this to yourself, Liz? You aren't going to buy all of them, anyway," I mumble under my breath to myself.

A pair of shiny black dress shoes appear in my vision and the scent of amber and bergamot fills the air. Long fingers and corded, muscular forearms reach down and pick the books off of the floor, one by one.

"Are you trying to buy the entire bookstore?" the gravelly, familiar, sardonic voice asks.

My eyes cascade up his body as a sense of déjà vu hits me in the face. The scene I described when the girls were at my place earlier this summer...this is it. Except this time, I see the face clearly. The sharp jawline, the aristocratic nose, the luscious golden-brown hair, the piercing emerald gaze with a teasing glint in the irises, the soft lips tilting up in a small smile.

Butterflies reappear in my stomach as my hand absentmindedly reaches for the closest volume next to my feet. Warm fingers touch mine as Parker retrieves the same book. My breath catches as the zing of electricity zaps through me and I quickly draw my hand back. He inhales sharply and he shudders, a motion so small and brief I almost miss it. Unreadable emotions flicker through his eyes before disappearing. A muscle twitches in his cheek and his gaze darkens as he hands me the last volume. "Here you go."

We stare at each other, the seconds bleeding into minutes, or perhaps the minutes are distilling into mere seconds. Time feels different somehow. The air is charged with tension as my heart flutters in my chest.

"Daddy! You forgot this one." Lucy trots up to us, the bright magenta book in one hand, and a stuffed unicorn in the other.

The moment breaks and we slowly stand up and face the little munchkin, who has the biggest smile on her face. I sneak a glance at Parker, finding him somewhat stiff and tense once again as he stares at his little girl.

"Where are your books, Lucy?" I ask.

"Daddy already gave them to Melanie." She hands me the pink book and points to Parker and me, each of us holding half a dozen books or so. "You have a lot of books, Lizzy. Do they have pictures in them?"

Laughing, I shake my head. "No. Sadly, no pictures in my books. But I can imagine the images in my mind when I read the words. Someday, you'll be able to do the same."

She stares quizzically at me, as if she doesn't believe me. A book without pictures? What blasphemy. "Are you going to buy all of them?"

"No, I'm not. I'm just going to pick one to buy. I have to save money. Maybe next time I'll buy more," I reply as I survey the two stacks of books between Parker and me.

"I want to go to the restroom, Lizzy." Lucy hands Parker her unicorn plushie.

"Okay, let's go, but give me one second. Lizzy is going to pick the lucky book who is coming home with us." My eyes scan through the titles and quickly settle on the magenta volume. The fear of missing out is a real thing. I guess I'll read this one first. "I think we should take the beautiful pink book home. What do you say?"

"I like the pretty book. It has flowers on it," Lucy agrees.

I put the pink book on a small shelf designated for purchases, so patrons don't need to take the goods with them into the bathroom.

"Can you hold these other books for me? The shelf is too small. Once we take care of business, I'll come out and put them away." I turn to Parker, only to find his outstretched arms as if he anticipated my question.

"I got this—I'll put the books back and buy Lucy's items. Go take her to the bathroom. I'll meet you two back in the car." He smiles softly at me.

Flashing him a quick grin, I turn and take Lucy to the restroom. After we finish our business, I retrieve the pink book from the shelf and head toward the counter. Not seeing Melanie in sight and not wanting to disrupt her at work, I quickly pay for the book and head to the car. On the drive home, I text her:

Liz: Didn't see you on our way out. Don't want to bother you at work. We're heading back now. And don't worry, I only got one book at full price. Next time, I'm definitely taking you up on your employee discount.

A few minutes later, my cell phone pings.

Melanie: Drat! Sorry about that. I got called into the back room to do inventory counts. The not so glamorous side of the bookselling business. If you can't find me next time you're here, just send me your list. I'll buy them with my discount online.

Lucy chatters in the background about all the new books we'll read today and I glance at the man beside me, his profile serious as he stares intently at the road, his brows furrowing as if deep in thought.

"Hey," I murmur softly. "Lucy had a lot of fun today. Thanks for coming out with us. You guys will be fine...she'll be fine."

His eyes flicker to me, his jaw clenching before he swallows. With a curt nod, he turns his gaze back to the road. The lighter-hearted Parker is now gone and replaced with the somber version of him. My chest aches at the heaviness emanating from his body. Reflecting on his mood swings in the past, perhaps he was going through some things we weren't aware of. After all, being a widowed, single dad can't be easy.

This man is a mystery wrapped in a beautiful package. A person I'm growing to care more and more for with each passing day, with every brief, accidental touch of our fingers, with the side glances, and moments of quiet conversations. My mind doesn't want to read into these interactions while my heart clamors for more, suddenly insatiable, as if a feast has been placed before me after a long period of fasting. *But he's everything you're not looking for.* The argument is sounding more and more outdated and immaterial—stale bread to be brushed aside and thrown away. *Perhaps the heart wants what it wants. No, let's not get ahead of ourselves.*

That night, after Lucy is in bed and I finish a few chores around the house, I open the door to my bedroom, finding a large paper bag with the Pendleton Books logo on my bed. I gingerly peek inside and gasp in shock. All the books I wanted to purchase but didn't are stacked neatly in the bag. A small piece of paper lies on top:

> Liz,
>
> Consider this an apology from me for being a jackass. Thank you for putting up with me.
>
> Parker
>
> P.S. Life is too short to deprive yourself of the things you love.

The butterflies reappear in my stomach and warmth spreads from deep within me. I clasp the note to my chest.

This man. This alluring, infuriating man.

A mystery.

CHAPTER 10

Parker

"Welcome to my humble abode." I swipe my arms out with flourish as Emily and Melanie enter the white marble foyer near the front door of my home.

"Shut up, Parker. *Shut up*." Emily's eyes widen, akin to Lucy's cartoon characters, as she shoves Melanie in the ribs. Her mouth hangs open as she takes in her surroundings.

"Humble...my ass." Melanie coughs as she glowers at Emily, who is oooh-ing and aaah-ing at everything, leaving the two of us in the proverbial dust.

Emily admires the glass fireplace and peers past the wall of glass into the backyard. "I can't believe we haven't been here before! Parker, how could you? This is unbelievable. No wonder you were turning your nose up at their terrace at Ambrosia."

I shrug, my lips twitching into a teasing grin. "What can I say? I aim to please. And I *never* oversell." I wink as she rolls her eyes at me.

"Hi, girls! Welcome." Liz sweeps into the room, wearing an almost translucent white dress hinting at a black bikini underneath. My blood heats up as I take in every dip and curve, her full breasts swaying, swatches of skin playing peek-a-boo with every step she takes. "You guys bring your swim gear? Parker's pool is amazing." Lucy trails in behind her, clad in a watermelon tankini, her hair tied up in a little bun on top of her head.

Melanie whistles and waggles her brows. "Dang, I didn't know you were hiding all that underneath your clothes." She gestures at Liz's figure, making an hourglass gesture with her hands.

"Oh, shut up." Liz flushes, the rosy tint starting at her cheeks blossoming to her neck and shoulders, disappearing under the V neck of her dress. *I wonder if the rest of her pinkens so easily.* I stuff my hands into the pockets of my cargo shorts as I turn slightly away, adjusting my stiffening cock.

Lucy gasps, "Lizzy! You said a bad word."

"Oh, sorry sweetie. I shouldn't have said that." Liz shoots daggers at Melanie, who is still grinning smugly. "Melanie, please *refrain* from commenting further."

I sidle up to them. "Hi, ladies, are you embarrassing my nanny?" I grin, flashing them my smile as I stand next to Liz.

"Your nanny, huh? Knight in shining armor coming to the rescue?" Melanie muses, her eyes dancing. "I see how it is."

Emily returns to us after taking a quick survey around the room. "Parker, I need you to design my home when I get rich one day."

"You're already rich, Ems," Liz says.

Emily harrumphs. "That's my parents' money, not mine. I'm dirt ass poor." At my arched brow, she amends, "Okay, not dirt ass poor but not rich, anyway."

Liz laughs. "Parker is great at what he does. Not just this home, but you can check out his gardens later. They're spectacular." She glances at me and winks, sending a sharp rush of pleasure through my veins. "I've had the honor of standing next to him a time or two and seeing some of his drawings for the projects he's working on. They're so amazing."

I'm very tempted to take her hand and give it a squeeze. This warm and fuzzy feeling is foreign to me. *Us against the world. Hold on, what the heck are you talking about?* I lightly shake my head, dispelling the insane thoughts in my mind.

Turning back to Emily, I smirk. "I'll design your home for free, just for you." Just then, the doorbell rings. "Must be the others. Help yourself to anything in the kitchen."

I open the door to a scowling James with Jess, Steven, and a tall blond man who resembles a stock photo model for Scandinavian royalty. "Whoa, what's gotten into you? Nice to see you, too."

"Don't get me started. Of all the people *Steven* here decides to bring, he brings *this* clown over there." James storms inside, his broodiness entertaining.

Jess comes up to me and gives me a light hug, her head barely reaching my shoulders. "Thanks for the invite. And don't listen to my jealous husband, he's just pissed Steven's colleague happens to be a guy Mother set me up with one time." She peers around the house, her eyes shining with laughter. "You have a beautiful home, which is no surprise, given your profession." I pin a look at James, whose face is still veiled in a mock scowl. *See? What did I tell you?*

The "clown" in question steps up and hands me a bottle of expensive bourbon, earning my good graces almost immediately. "Thanks for letting me tag along. I'm Charles Vaughn." His tall frame and bearing reflect money, most likely old money. He flashes me a confident smile, his appearance resembling the A-list actors of Hollywood royalty. *This is who Mrs. Kingsley set up Jess with? No wonder James is salty about it.*

"You're welcome. Any friend of Steven's is a friend of mine." I reach out to the youngest of the Kingsley siblings, pulling him into a hug. "Long time no see, Steven. Man, has it been that long? You look different."

Jess and Emily's youngest brother has aged a few years since I saw him last. Instead of the air of a fresh college graduate, he now carries himself with a thread of veritas. His face is more chiseled than when I saw him last, the baby fat long gone and replaced with muscle. His lips twitch up in a sly grin. "You still look the same, Parker. Glad to be back at home."

More shrieking from the living room indicates Jess has reunited with the rest of the girls. I usher the men into the kitchen and pop open a few bottles of craft beer from the refrigerator.

"Cheers for more reunions in the future." We clink our bottles together and I take a sip, savoring the cooling sensation down my throat. Despite the storm clouds threatening to unleash themselves around me at any time, my friends bring in a breath of fresh air, temporarily allowing me to forget, to be the Parker Wellington from three years ago, and I'm grateful for the reprieve.

I turn to James, who is still eyeing Charles from head to toe. "Oh drop it, dude. You're friends with me, and I actually *went* on a date with Jess *and* danced with her at her firm's gala."

Steven shakes in laughter as Charles tips his beer at me in thanks.

James crosses his arms and muses, "I'm just trying to see what Mother saw in him."

Charles raises his hands in surrender. "Probably the Bank of Columbia name and no offense taken." James raises his brow, apparently surprised at the candor. "Look, I was just dropping by to say hello to them when Mrs. Kingsley surprised me with a set-up. Frankly, Jess and I were both equally taken aback, and she made it abundantly clear she wasn't interested from the get-go."

James levels a stare at Charles and apparently decides he passes the assessment. He lifts his beer in his direction, his lips tilting up in a small smile. "I'm apparently cursed to be friends with people who were romantically linked with my wife."

"A bit of a stretch there, drama queen." I snicker, my heart feeling the lightest in days. "So, how do you guys know each other?" I direct my question to Steven and Charles.

"Steven works at Pietra Capital, which is a partner of our bank, so we kept running into each other at functions and events. I'm tagging along on his trip back here because there's a joint investment opportunity we're looking into up in San Fran, so we decided to do a pit stop down south and relax for a few days."

"Finance is a small world in New York. All the big players know each other." Steven brushes his hands through his thick, black hair, which is carefully tousled into an effortless hairstyle. "Where are the girls?"

The house is mostly quiet except for faint laughter coming in from the backyard. "I think they're making use of my backyard oasis. Come on, I'll show you guys around." The group follows me through the living room and out the sliding glass doors to the back.

When I designed this house all those years ago, I asked one of our prominent landscape architects to craft a retreat within the bustling confines of the city, so my family can have a place to enjoy the great outdoors without needing to drive far away to regional or national parks. The architect carefully curated an assortment of drought-resistant plants, shrubbery, and native trees that thrive in the unforgiving dry heat yet carry blooms of beautiful colors. The plants and flowers chosen are mostly perennial, and there are nooks and crannies along the sides of the yard with reclining seats or secluded benches for reading or other relaxing activities. It used to be the one place Abby and I would frequent at the end of the evening, after a long day of work and childcare duties. I hardly come back here anymore.

We follow the excited chatter and sound of splashing water to the far corner of the backyard, where I have an outdoor kitchen and a large, heated infinity pool, complete with a jacuzzi and a waterfall feature. Emily and Melanie are talking while sunbathing on the poolside recliners. Jess is wading in the water and splashing Lucy, who is floating in her pineapple-shaped swim ring. And Liz...well, nothing can prepare me for the sight of Liz.

Her golden-brown hair is plastered to her head as she breaks the surface of the water like a wet dream come to life. Droplets cling to her heart-shaped face, unblemished and smooth as silk as rivulets of water slither down her body, caressing her full tits, which are threatening to break free of the confines of her simple black triangle string bikini. She pushes herself out of the pool and graces us with her tiny waist, a glint of something sparkling in her belly button, fuck—she has a piercing—and the full hips I've imagined so many times but have never seen without clothing other than the scrap of material between her thighs. My hands ache to replace the water, to slowly peel the tiny bikini bottom off her and worship every inch of her. Then I want to mark her up, pinken that skin, make her moan—

No.

I expel a sharp breath from my lungs as my muscles lock in tension. I should look away. I shouldn't be thinking of her like this for so many reasons. Too many reasons. But I can't tear my gaze away. My willpower isn't strong enough. Why fight it anymore? The truth will come out at some point, right? Why not enjoy the heat of the firestorm before it incinerates us? Fuck. Clawing guilt attempts to break through my armor but is overtaken by the scorching heat of lust. Blood rushes to my cock, the uncomfortable pressure causing a red haze in my vision.

Charles whistles next to me, the sound shrill and grating. "Damn, I need to come over to LA more often."

I whip my face toward him and catch his appreciative gaze on Liz. I shouldn't fault him. Any red-blooded male wouldn't be able to look away. But fuck if I don't want to slam my fist into his face right now. *Why do you even care, Parker?* James was right. He is a fucking clown. I clench my hands tightly, my fingernails digging into my palm, and I turn away from him, from the pool, from the one woman I should hate but unfortunately don't, the one person I should stay away from...and a thousand more "shoulds."

"Charles seems to like Liz, huh?" a quiet voice behind me asks.

I release my clenched jaw and attempt to rearrange my features into something more amiable. Angling my face toward Steven, I answer, "Really?" I feign naivety and make a show at searching for the two of them, who are currently standing next to the pool with Liz flushing at something Charles is saying, the pink tinge of her skin sending renewed fire through my veins. *Only I can do that to her.* "I didn't notice."

"They'd make a good couple, don't you think? He's a good man. Even though he comes from a wealthy family, he has none of the snobby air. He's very sharp and successful at what he does."

I hum noncommittally as I reach over to the table next to me to grab a water bottle. Anything to keep my hands occupied. Anything to keep me from walking over there and knocking him into the water. I twist open the cap and guzzle half of its contents in a matter of seconds, trying to put out the raging inferno building within me.

"Maybe I should ask Liz to see if she's interested? What do you think? They look great together."

"What the *fuck*, Steven?" I crush the bottle in my hands, my anger finally snapping. I whip my face toward him, ready to give him a piece of my mind, only to find him smirking at me, his dark-brown eyes twinkling with amusement. He arches his brow.

The damn asshole.

He chuckles, slides on a pair of aviators, and crosses his arms, showcasing the muscles he must have worked hard to gain these past few years. "There we go. What I suspected all along."

"What on earth are you talking about? You have been here all but fifteen minutes."

"The others are idiots if they don't notice how you stare at her."

"I didn't stare at *shit*."

"And I call *bullshit*." He widens his stance and rocks on his heels. "So, if I tell Charles right now Liz is single and ready to mingle, you'll be okay with that?"

I grind my teeth as the irrational burn of jealousy floods through me. "Whatever."

Steven tilts his head to the side, wearing an annoying grin on his face, and calls out, "Hey, Charles!"

Charles and Liz pause their conversation midsentence and look over. I bite the inside of my cheek in an attempt to retain the neutral expression on my face. I clench and unclench my hands. "Don't," I grit out.

Steven barks out a laugh and shakes his head. "Remember, we have a call with the bank in an hour." The fucker.

"Buzzkill, Steven. Can't you see I'm busy right now?" Charles rolls his eyes and turns back to Liz, continuing some god-awful conversation that is putting a blush on her face.

"Since when are you so observant?" I mutter, the tightness in my shoulders loosening a smidge.

"Not a kid anymore. Working in a high-stress field for a few years does wonders for your observation skills." Steven has made a meteoric rise to power pretty much unheard of in his industry in the short tenure he has been there. I'm sure he has picked up many skills along the way. One doesn't swim in shark-infested waters and come out on top without savviness. "Look, I don't know what's going on with you, but whatever it is, tread carefully with Liz. She doesn't have much experience from what my sisters have told me in the past. Don't start anything if you plan to hurt her later."

I won't be starting anything with her if I can help it.

I can't.

And fuck if she didn't hurt me first without knowing. *But it was unintentional*, my conscience whispers, attempting to silence my stubborn mind. The mind that is holding onto the last threads of anger because the repercussions of letting go are unthinkable. Because once I let go, I know I wouldn't be able to help myself... and God help her then.

"Nothing is going to happen." I snap my neck in an audible crack, relieving some of the pressure that has gathered there.

"Whatever you say. As long as you believe it."

The day passes by quickly and soon it's lunch. I ordered some food from a local Mediterranean bistro and everyone helps themselves to a healthy serving of kefka, beef and chicken kabobs, hummus dip, and various appetizers. Liz, now thankfully clad in her coverup, is sitting at my outdoor dining table with the girls, her arms waving animatedly as she communicates with her whole body. Charles makes his way over to the empty seat next to hers and sits down, angling his body toward her and curling his arm around her chair. That man is *this close* to being manhandled by me. I keep my eyes on Charles while I scoop up some food and take a seat across from Liz, who is oblivious to the attention she's receiving from the man beside her. James and Steven sit on the other side of us.

"So, Liz, what do you like to do for fun?" The hoarse voice of the blond Adonis across from the table aggravates me. I take a swig of beer, my appetite suddenly waning.

"I love to read and watch TV. Nothing too exciting." She laughs as she curls a golden lock of hair behind her ear.

"Really? I love reading too. What genre do you typically enjoy?" I fight the urge to roll my eyes at his predictable answer.

"Mainly romance or anything romance-related, including fantasy or thrillers with romantic elements." She dips her head down as if embarrassed and continues, "I'm a sucker for people getting their happily ever afters... I know, I should probably read more classic literature or high-brow books."

Charles turns fully toward her and leans in, his interest clearly displayed in his body language. "Hey, as long as you enjoy it, there's nothing wrong with reading romance. No need to be shy about it. In my opinion, there's something to be learned in any book you enjoy reading, and even if there isn't, if you're entertained by it and it makes you happy, then the book has served its purpose." He reaches over and pats Liz's hand on the table in reassurance.

My eyes focus on the movement, and I clench my jaw. Red haze fills my vision, independent of any rational thought. I zero in on his hand still atop hers, his fingers touching something that isn't his. *But she isn't yours either. She sure as fuck can't be yours.*

"Parker? Parker!" A voice sounding like James breaks through my heated concentration and travels to my ears.

"What?" I snap, my eyes still glued to Charles's hand on Liz.

Conversations stop as everyone stares at me. My face heats up from the inspection by my friends.

"Will everyone fucking stop staring at me?" I hiss, the burning lava in my veins overflowing as the rage I've been bottling inside for so long leaks out in this moment of weakness. "Don't you have something more interesting to do?"

"You okay, man?" James asks softly, his brow furrowing.

I close my eyes and focus on my breathing. Deep breaths in, deep breaths out. Again.

Shit, I'm losing my grip today. They're looking for charming, happy Parker, not the usual, messed-up grump that you are. And certainly not the raging lunatic you are inside. I roll my neck and crack my knuckles, relishing in every satisfying pop as I try to rein in my galloping emotions, which are currently unleashed and sprinting out of the gate.

Deep breaths. I can do this. Everything is fine. Releasing a shuddering exhale, I twist my face up in a grin and proceed with dissecting the meat in front of me. Once I rein in my emotions, I glance up, staring at my friends, who have various levels of concern showing on their faces. "Sorry, I didn't mean to blow up at everyone. I've had a lot on my mind these days and I should've handled it better." Guilt claws into me. They don't deserve my tantrums. They don't deserve to be the victims of my anger...the anger I used to think was toward her but I've come to realize how ridiculous the notion was. "I sincerely apologize. Please, continue eating."

I take a few sips of cold water, giving myself a few seconds to reset, to tamp down the fury always close to rising to the surface. My face heats as I attempt another smile. Everyone resumes eating and chatting as if the last few minutes didn't happen at all. I breathe easier as the tense moment passes and I resume eating. My eyes flicker to Liz, only to find her staring at me.

Liz cocks her head to the side, concern in her blue eyes as she purses her lips. Charles slowly releases her hand. *Finally.*

She frowns, the expression in her eyes seemingly asking, *are you sure you're okay?* I swallow the lump in my throat and look away, not wanting to be unveiled under her stare. My nerves feel too raw, too exposed. Moments pass by and my eyes can't help but flicker back to her to find her still scrutinizing me. I clench my jaw and blink before slightly inclining my head. *I'm fine.* My eyes hold hers in reassurance as she softens her rigid posture and takes a deep breath. She bites on her plump bottom lip. I let out a deep exhale and sit back, my eyes drifting away to the person in front of me. My fists slowly unclench on top of the table.

Charles sits back in his chair and clasps his hands in front of him, his eyes bouncing between the two of us as if he's a spectator to a Wimbledon match. Catching me observing him, he raises a sardonic brow and gives me a pointed look. I return his inspection and silent question with a defiant glare of my own. Charles tilts his head to the side with a knowing smile on his face and turns to Steven to engage him in conversation.

James nudges me and asks, "Hey, are you sure you're okay?"

"I'm fine."

"I mean, the outburst just now...and it's not the first time I've noticed you being super tense. I never wanted to prod and invade your personal space, so to speak, but I can't help but think something is going on and I won't be much of a friend if I don't ask how you're doing."

Swallowing the bite of kebab, which feels dry in my mouth, I reply, "I-I'm fine, really. I have things handled." *No shit you don't.* "Don't worry about me." I chuckle in self-derision. "The life of a widowed, single dad can get stressful sometimes. I hope you'll never understand that."

"Hey, hey. Stop eating for a second."

I pause, turning to look at him and find the familiar blue eyes watching me with concern. "Anytime you need someone to talk to, about anything, or if you just need help looking after Lucy so you can have some alone time...you reach out, okay? Anytime, Parker."

Swallowing the lump in my throat, I nod. I clear my throat. "Thanks, man, that means a lot."

James resumes eating, seemingly appeased with my answer. "So, how are things going with my sister?"

I pause, my knife in midair. "What do you mean? Nothing's going on between us." *Nothing can ever be going on.*

He scrunches his brows. "With her nannying here...for Lucy. What were you thinking about?"

"Never mind. I misunderstood." I quickly recover myself and resume eating, the kebab serving only as sustenance and not for taste anymore. "Things are fine. Lucy loves her. They get along well. I come home to delicious meals each day. Everything's great. Excellent. Can't complain."

Silence fills the air as I wash down my food with another sip of beer. I glance at James out of the corner of my eye only to find him staring at me once again, his blue eyes darkening in scrutiny, as if I'm a complex data set he's analyzing for work, looking for patterns, unveiling the underlying secrets and trends.

"Stop staring at me, dude. You're creeping me out."

"Huh."

"What?" I dab my mouth with my napkin as irritation threatens to lace through in my voice. I attempt to fold the napkin into a neat square, my fingers faltering with the corners. The damn corners always don't line up precisely.

"Huh, can't believe I'm so slow." He scoffs, shaking his head as he resumes his meal.

I pretend I don't hear him.

. . .

"Remind me why we're doing this again?" Steven grumbles as we settle around the coffee table in the living room, taking a respite from the summer heat after a quick dip in the pool. The late-afternoon sun casts a golden-orange glow to the room. Lucy is happily getting some tablet time in her playroom.

"Don't be a buzzkill, *Steven*." Emily shoots a glare at her brother, who is tapping his fingers impatiently on the table. "I told you I'll come prepared with a theme for this get-together. Keep things interesting, you know?"

"Can't wait...I'm absolutely beside myself with anticipation," he drawls with a sardonic lift of his brow.

Emily waves him off and leans in, practically buzzing with excitement. "So, as you all know, the theme of our last few meet-ups has been 'nostalgia.' Last time, we met at Jess and James's place for board games, and the time before that, we played game consoles from the Nineties at my place... You had no idea how much effort it took for me to procure those relics. Well, today's theme is a continuation from 'A Blast from the Past,' which means we'll be playing some games today from middle school and high school."

"What games?" Jess questions. "I don't remember playing anything memorable."

"You were a nerd, always trying to please our parents, so of course you wouldn't know. But don't worry," she leans back, pointing at herself in haughtiness, "I got you."

"Let me guess! Are these going to be in the vein of seven minutes in heaven or spin the bottle or something like that?" Melanie volunteers, eliciting a loud grumble from Steven.

"Bingo! Exactly! But we'll get to that later. There's going to be a twist to the game. Since the game is a not-suitable-for-children, we'll play it after dinner. First, let's start with truth or dare to warm up, then dinnertime, then we regroup for adult games. A special rule to my flair of truth or dare: you can only choose up to five dares in our ten rounds. So, no chickening out and choosing an easy way out. We'll vote at the end, and whoever gives the most surprising answers or performs the best dares wins."

Charles raises his hands. "Hold on, what do we win?"

"Just the glory of being able to gloat that you won."

"That doesn't sound very enticing," James comments, wrapping his arms around Jess, who is currently sitting on the floor sandwiched between his legs.

Liz rubs her hands together gleefully. "I totally got this. Let's get this started." She has changed into a loose, off-the-shoulder T-shirt, which is thankfully less revealing than her swimwear, but no less enticing. The joy lighting up her face used to be abrasive, rubbing against the invisible wounds in the hollow of my chest like the sharpness of newly formed mountain ridges after an earthquake, but lately, the rough edges are softening under the elements. The burn of anger has receded to the background, and more often than not, I find myself forgetting the many reasons I shouldn't be thinking of her this way. Like a drug addict, I'm craving her smile, her melodic laughter, and the crinkle around her eyes when she's excited about something.

"Okay, as the youngest of the gang, you can start, Steven. Go ahead, draw a name from the bowl to find your partner in the first round."

Steven grabs a sheet of paper and snorts. "Ems, what comes around goes around." He waves the paper with her name in the air before folding it back up and tossing it into the bowl. "Truth or dare?"

Emily narrows her eyes and stares at Steven, calculating the best choice forward. "There's no way I'd trust you not to ask something embarrassing. Dare it is."

"All right. That's probably smart. So that's one dare already, four more left. You can't avoid questions forever. I dare you to…" He looks around and continues, "Give my friend Charles over here a kiss."

Emily flushes briefly as she sneaks a glance at Charles, who is giving his best come-hither look. Straightening her back, she strides over to the man. "A Kingsley never backs away from a dare." She grabs Charles by the face and plants an audible kiss on his cheek. Everyone hoots and hollers.

"Cheating. That's totally cheating," Steven grumbles.

"You didn't specify where. So, I'd say it counts," Melanie chimes in, giving a nod of solidarity to Emily, who sits back, the flush on her face melting away to her usual pale complexion.

"Okay, Parker, I got you. Truth or dare?" Emily tilts her head and pins me with her gaze.

"I've nothing to hide," I respond. *You're so full of shit.* "Truth."

Emily gives a sly smile and mutters something like "testing out the vibe," eliciting a shocked gasp from Liz, whose eyes widen in something resembling fear or embarrassment. "Tell me three things you like about Liz."

I sneak a glance at Liz, whose face is as red as Hester Prynne's scarlet letter in Nathaniel Hawthorne's classic. She stares at her hands, as if suddenly finding her fingernails interesting. Blood rushes in my ears as I contemplate my answer. If you asked me a month ago, I may have had a hard time answering because of the perpetual fog of vitriol and guilt impeding my vision. But now…I don't know how I can say anything without causing more questions to be asked later.

Rubbing my hand on my ring finger, I begin. "Liz is a great caretaker to Lucy. She's patient and kind and Lucy loves her." I pause, silently willing Liz to look at me. When she finally looks up, the blue pools of her eyes clear, I continue, "For this, I thank you." She flashes me a brief smile, the flush in her face temporarily lessening. She shifts in her seat and her eyes dart around the table.

"Liz brings joy everywhere she's at." *Even in this prison, giving me occasional reprieves from the invisible bars caging me inside of my mind.* Liz slowly blinks and presses her full lips together before releasing them in an inaudible pop I can somehow hear or *feel* from across the table.

"Finally," I clear my throat, my voice suddenly hoarse, "she has a good heart, and is always willing to forgive and see the best in other people." *Even someone like me. Someone who's the last person in the world to deserve her goodwill.* Liz swallows as she blinks away the sheen gathering in her eyes. She gives me a watery smile.

My heartbeat thunders in my ears. I want to escape this room but also want to drag her into the madness with me.

"I owe you five dollars," Emily utters as she eyes Melanie, who is grinning with smugness. "Steven, give me five bucks, will you?"

"What's going on?" James asks.

"Nothing concerning you, brother-in-law. It's between us girls."

Steven shakes his head and forks over a crisp new bill from his wallet. Emily pushes it over to Melanie with her index finger.

"I knew it! Muahahaha. Thank you...thank you very much." Melanie cackles, pocketing the bill. Liz's flush returns in full vengeance as the rest of us stare at the ladies in apparent confusion.

A few rounds later, it's Melanie's turn. She picks Liz. "Truth or dare, Liz?"

Liz bites on her plump bottom lip, eyebrows pinching in concentration. "Truth."

"Tell us about your best romantic relationship in life so far."

"I..." Liz's face turns crimson as she draws a hand across her face. "I...have never been in a relationship," she whispers, ducking her head slightly, pinning her eyes to the table in front of her.

She's inexperienced. I don't know why it matters to me or why I'm reacting this way. But deep inside this depraved mind of mine,

I want her to be single, even though I'll never have her. Nor should I ever have her.

Melanie gasps in surprise. "Really? Not even one?"

"Okay, next person." Steven hurries the game along as Liz shoots him a grateful glance. He gives her an imperceptible nod in return and hands her the bowl of names. James gets called next, and he chooses a dare, but it seems like the previous topic of conversation hasn't died down among the girls yet. My ears strain to listen to their murmuring while James is performing some stunt involving a certain number of pushups and sit ups.

"Well, I mean, I've dated around, but never found the right person, and just didn't want to be in a relationship...just to be in one," Liz whispers to Melanie.

"And there's nothing wrong with that," Jess chimes in, glancing at Emily, who is studying Liz with interest.

"Hold on...so does this mean you're completely...inexperienced in all areas?" Emily asks softly. She looks around the room and follows up with the smallest of whispers, "Are you a virgin?"

The roaring sound of blood rushing in my ears mutes the noise from the dare. I keep my eyes trained on James, making sure to heckle and cheer as expected, as the implications reverberate within me. *She's a virgin.* There's nothing wrong with having sexual partners in the past, but somehow, the thought of Liz being completely untouched sends heated blood straight to my cock. I bare my teeth in what I hope resembles a dimple-flashing smile of amusement as I tap my fingers on my knees, my hands itching to touch, to possess, to conquer. I want to watch the darkness of my ink spread on the blank sheet of paper that is her with the artist being me.

The things I can show her.

Fuck. You're tainted, Parker. Your tastes run dark. You're embroiled in a web of lies and she's an unwitting participant. Did you already forget the role she played in your current state? Or is your cock ruling your mind now? Did you forget about Abby? I crack my knuckles again and start clapping as James finishes his intense workout-related performance, my mind still reeling from

Liz's revelation. My eyes flit back to Liz as she looks away from Emily, the pink tinge in her cheeks beckoning me. Her blue gaze meets mine and she stills as if ensnared by this magnetic field between us.

A trajectory that will surely lead to our ruin.

CHAPTER 11

Liz

I feel his heated stare on me long after I leave the living room to check in on Lucy. Those glittering green eyes, the smoldering emerald pools I could spend a lifetime swimming in and never reaching the bottom. I shake my head. *This is silly. This is just your inner hopeless romantic trying to read something into a situation which doesn't exist.* I open the door to the playroom to find Lucy curled up on the sofa playing what sounds like *Fruit Bandit.*

"Lucy, sweetie, time to put the tablet away. It's dinnertime. I made your favorite lasagna and also a few casseroles. Afterward, I'll read you a story and we can get ready for bed, okay?"

Lucy sighs, her grubby fingers rubbing her eyes. "It's already dinnertime? But I want to play more."

I gently take the device away from her and set it on the small table nearby. "I know, sweetie, but too much tablet time is bad for your eyes...and your neck. You don't want an ouchie, right?" I snuggle her against me, savoring the heat of her little body against mine. Someday, I want a daughter just like her. "Little children need to eat and sleep to get enough energy to play tomorrow...and to grow! You want to be tall like Lizzy, right? Or maybe you'll be taller than me or your daddy!"

Lucy mumbles against my shirt, "That's silly. I don't want to be taller than Daddy, that'll be too tall."

Laughing, I hold her hand and lead her to the dining table, where she takes a seat. I hurry to the kitchen to take out the dinner I prepared earlier: a simple three-cheese lasagna, an easy cream of mushroom chicken and rice casserole, a batch of chicken pot pies I just reheated in the microwave, and a baked eggplant parmesan. We still have some leftovers from lunch, so there should be enough to keep everyone satiated.

"Wow, quite the domestic goddess, aren't you?"

I turn toward the voice, finding Charles leaning against the marble countertop with an empty glass in his hands. My face heats up at his compliment.

"This is all simple fare really, nothing special. But thank you."

"So, how has it been, working here? Steven told me you're helping Parker out for a few months?" He crosses his legs, seemingly in no hurry to refill his water.

I set the hot plates on the counter and load a few new dishes into the oven for a quick reheat. Double ovens, got to love them. "It's been great. Lucy was in my kindergarten class at school and she's the absolute sweetest kid, so the adjustment isn't bad at all. She isn't hard to take care of, and we get along well." I take out Lucy's plastic dishware and scoop a small slice of lasagna onto her plate. Wafting my hand on top of it, I wait for it to cool down a bit before I bring it out to her.

"And Parker?"

I look up, finding his pale-blue eyes pinned on me, his lips tipping up in a small smile as if he's in on a secret I don't know about. I quickly look away as my heart skips a beat at Parker's name. What was I going to do next? Oh yes, fill up Lucy's cup with juice.

I hurry to the refrigerator to pull out a carton of orange juice and, doing my best to appear nonchalant, I reply, "He's fine. Just fine. He's good friends with my brother."

"And with you?"

My fingers are still on the cap and I wet my lips. "I... We..."

"Is everything fine over here?" a deep, gravelly voice that never fails to make me shiver asks from behind us.

Taking a deep breath, I finish pouring the orange juice into the cup, carefully filling it halfway so Lucy won't be able to easily slosh it and make a mess later. "We're good here. Charles is just keeping me company." I rummage through the drawer for the mermaid utensils Lucy loves.

"Right, I'm sure," Parker mutters, sarcasm bleeding into his voice.

"What?" I ask, puzzled by the strange inflection in his tone.

"Nothing."

I feel his heated presence behind me as the hairs on my neck prickle. His soft footsteps are silent, but imposing at the same time. The warmth radiates from his chest onto my back, seeping through the thin layers of cotton. Hints of amber and bergamot linger in the air as he rests his hand lightly on my hip, the pressure feeling like a brand, his other arm reaching around me to grab Lucy's bowl and utensils.

"Here, let me help you with that," he murmurs, the deep timbre of his voice ghosting over my ear. I tremble.

"T-thank you."

"You're welcome." His voice is husky as the words dissolve into a few low chuckles. I finally turn around and look at him as he slowly backs away, his gaze lingering on mine for a few moments before he turns around and strides out of the kitchen. I stare at his retreating backside, temporarily rendered speechless.

"You were saying?" Charles's voice snaps me out of my trance.

"S-sorry, what was your question?" I pick up a rag and wipe down the countertops, eager to do something with my hands.

He barks out a laugh and twists his lips to the side. "Parker," he repeats.

"Oh. Yes, things are fine. He's my brother's friend. He's a decent employer."

"Riiight." He snorts, finally walking up to the refrigerator to refill his glass with water. "I can recognize when I may be intruding on something." His gaze rests on my face and he continues, "But if things don't work out and you're interested in a personal tour of New York City, you know where to find me." With a wink, he turns around and leaves me standing alone, flustered and confused.

Dinner is a pleasant affair as everyone compliments me on the casseroles and pot pies. Melanie insists she needs the recipe of the tomato parmesan as she reaches for seconds. Lucy dutifully finishes her plate of lasagna and I walk her upstairs to get her ready for bed.

"Can Auntie Jess come up and read a story to me?" The two have apparently bonded since the swimming pool splash fest.

"Sure thing, sweetheart." I brush out her loose curls, her beautiful brownish-blonde hair a shade or two lighter than mine. "Jess, you're requested upstairs," I holler downstairs.

A minute later, Jess pokes her head in the doorway and asks, "What does my princess want?"

"Storytime!" Lucy gathers her blankets around her in bed as she looks up expectantly at Jess.

"All right, just for you, Lucy goosey." Jess settles in next to her for a quick tale of Little Red and her visit to her grandma. I smile at the two of them, curled up in bed. Despite Jess's anxieties about whether or not she can be a good mother due to her constant worrying, I know she'll be a wonderful mother one day. Call it intuition. We quietly walk out of the room, closing the door with a click, and proceed down the stairs.

"Hey, Liz?" The concern bleeding through her voice stops me mid step. I turn around to look at her, finding a small frown on her face.

"Yeah?"

"I...had my suspicions, but now that even Melanie is mentioning it, it's darn near impossible not to notice. Are things okay between you and Parker?"

I let out a deep breath and sit on the wooden step. Jess settles down next to me and patiently waits for my response.

"I...I honestly don't know what's going on. I used to think he hates me, but now...I'm not so sure. One minute he acts like he tolerates me, or even likes me, and the next minute he's cold again. It's messing with my head."

"Seems unlike him too, right?"

"Between the two of us, I've never really experienced the Parker you guys know. There's just something...off about him, like he's somehow hiding something from me. I'm not sure what's going on or how I feel about it." *Or maybe you don't want to dwell on the feelings he elicits in you, because he's all types of wrong for you.*

"To be honest, I don't think he's who he appears on the surface. James doesn't tell me too much so as not to betray his confidence, but from what little he tells me, Parker's life, even before his wife passed, hasn't been easy."

I sneak a glance at her, my heart picking up in rhythm at the thought of learning a little more about him. My enigma. *No, no one is your enigma.*

Jess nods and continues, "He had a tough childhood and grew up poor, but he worked really hard and, of course, dug himself out of the projects to where he is now. From the little I know, his marriage to his wife was a bit troubled as well, especially toward the end, and then she passed, leaving him with a two-year-old. James and I don't like to pressure him to talk to us, but we figured if he needs us, or if he ever wants to talk, we'll be there for him. But I can imagine he's shouldering a lot by himself."

My heart clenches in pain at the thought of the beautiful man carrying the weight of the world on his shoulders. By himself. While trying to keep a smile on his face and be brave for his young daughter. The unspeakable pain and loneliness he must be feeling. All the emotions and trauma bottled up inside with no outlet. Before I got to know him and see past the cold front he puts in front of me, it was easy to dislike him, to call him an asshole and be done with it. But now, having spent more time with him, seeing his love for Lucy, chatting with him at dinner and learning a little bit more about his passion to help the homeless, there's a lot more to him than what's on the surface. I wish... I wish I could take some of the anguish away. The agony I see in his eyes when he thinks no one is looking. The shoulders more often stiff and tensed than relaxed. I wish... I wish I could chase away his monsters somehow.

This complicated, messy man. This person I somehow can't stay away from. The person who is slowly but surely invading the sacred territory of my heart. And I'm helpless to stop it. Logic doesn't seem to matter anymore.

Jess snakes her arm around my shoulder, giving it a soft squeeze. "Well, if anything happens and you need to talk about it, you can always call me. Or, if this doesn't work out and you need a temporary place to stay since I know you had sublet your studio, just let me know. Our home is always open to you."

I bite my lip and pat her hand on my shoulder. "Thanks, Jess."

She gets up and dusts the lint off her pants. "Come on." She nods toward the living room downstairs. "Let's get downstairs before Ems chases after us. Got to get the games started!"

The group has already gathered in the living room again, where Emily and Melanie are pouring what looks to be vodka or some other clear alcohol into shot glasses. Parker and James are in the kitchen, loading the plates and utensils into the dishwasher. Steven and Charles are sprawled out on the sofa, watching a base-ball game on the TV.

"Okay, Lucy is in bed. Ems, what do you have in mind?" I tie my hair into a low ponytail and sit on the rug with Jess, awaiting further instructions.

Emily gives me a sly grin. "This will be so much fun. A total blast from the past."

"Oh boy." Jess sighs. "This is going to be painful."

"Hey, guys, gather here...turn off the TV, because it's time to bring back a classic," Emily announces, her hands miming a drummer playing a set. "Our next game is...seven minutes in heaven!"

The announcement is met with collective groans from every-one except Jess, who looks adorably confused.

"Why does everyone have on that face?"

Charles speaks up. "Hey, not me. I totally don't mind this game." He glances my way and twitches his lips up in a flirtatious smile. "Especially with all the beautiful ladies present."

Parker snorts in derision as he takes a seat on the other side of the coffee table across from me. "This is such a stupid game," he grumbles.

Emily gives him a wink. "Parker, your age is showing." Upon seeing his raised eyebrow, she amends. "Fine, this may be a little... immature, but humor me, I couldn't come up with anything better."

"I'm young at heart, Ems, bring it on," Charles quips, earning a death glare from Parker. The room devolves into chuckles.

"So, since most folks seem to know this game, I will explain the rules for your benefit, Jess," Emily begins. "The rules are simple. I'll draw the first name and that individual will draw another name. Then they'll toss the names back into the bowl for the next round. The two folks chosen will go to the entryway coat closet and stay there for seven minutes."

"That's it? What do you do for seven minutes then?" Jess inquires.

"Well, that's up to the two folks. They can talk, they can sit in silence, they can sing songs, or they can do *anything they want*," Melanie emphasizes the last words with an arch of her brow.

Jess's eyes widen as she picks up the hidden meaning. "But... I'm married. Isn't that a little risqué and inappropriate?"

Emily nods. "I thought about that, so, married people, aka you two, will be able to get a pass. Just drink a shot if you get called...if that's what you want to do."

She looks around the room and seeing no objections, she continues, "Okay, so it seems like we're all on the same page. So, just two house rules. First, no cell phones. Second, the light in the closet remains off. So yes, that means if you choose to go to the closet, you'll be in the dark. Annnnd...in the interest of consent and making sure everyone feels comfortable, any party can opt out at any time and instead take a shot as punishment." Emily concludes her instructions with another swipe of her hands, pointing to the shot glasses lined up on top of the marble table.

I gulp as nervous jitters make their way through my body. I may have played this game once or twice in high school, but as an adult, with *him* here, somehow this feels different, even if going into the closet doesn't mean I need to do anything salacious. I twist my hands and purse my lips, debating my strategy if I get called.

Emily draws the first name and calls out, "James! You're the lucky winner."

James rolls his eyes and mutters a litany of curses under his breath. He draws a name from the bowl. "Melanie."

Melanie cocks her eyebrow at James.

"No offense, Melanie. As a married man, I'm obligated to go to the closet with only one female. And that's my wife. I'm taking the married person pass." He gives Jess a tender smile as she snuggles deeper against his side. "And here's my penance." He mock salutes and downs his shot in one gulp, grimacing at the burn.

James picks a name next. He snickers at the slip of paper in his hand. "Steven."

Steven shrugs and draws a name. "Charles. Come on, dude, let's go talk about our joint venture in the dark." Charles bemoans about his bad fortune and why he can't be paired with one of the hot ladies in the house but follows Steven into the closet.

I escape the lottery for a few more rounds as Melanie gets paired with Steven, and when they emerge from the closet Melanie is asking questions about stock investments. Emily ends up with Jess and they both giggle about God knows what after their seven minutes. I twiddle my fingers and bounce my knees against the plush rug, wondering how long my luck will hold out.

"Liz, finally! Your turn." Emily gives me a wink as she passes me the bowl. My fingers tremble as I reach inside to pick a slip of paper.

"Hey, don't worry. If the name you see isn't who you want, you can always just say my name," Charles whispers loudly as I feel the heat rise to my face, my lips curving into a smile at his blatant, harmless flirtation. My eyes automatically flicker to Parker, only to find him glaring at us, a muscle twitching in his cheek. I quickly glance away, flustered for no apparent reason.

My fingers feel around the glass bowl, my eyes looking up at the ceiling. I grasp the first piece of paper touching my hand. My pulse starts galloping as my palms grow sweaty. Taking a deep breath, I open the slip and read the name.

"Parker," I whisper, unable to look up at the man across from me.

The room falls silent, or perhaps the thudding of my heart eclipses all the noise in the background. I clutch the paper in my hand and bite my lip, waiting for his signal. *Does he want to take the shot? Should I just drink to avoid the embarrassment?*

"Are you a coward, Liz?" the gravelly voice haunting me in my dreams asks from beside me. I slowly look up, my gaze sweeping from his muscular calves, to his tan shorts sitting low on his waist, to the slim-fitting T-shirt clinging to his flexing muscles, finally reaching his face. Those soulful, green eyes stare down at me, the small gold flecks of his irises reflecting in the lamplight.

A taunt.

A challenge.

A dare.

I slowly get up, emboldened by the fire in his eyes.

"I can always take his place, Liz," Charles pipes up on the other side of me with a smirk on his face. He gives me a wink and arches his eyebrows. I laugh, shaking my head in amusement.

Parker growls. The rumble in his chest sounds loud to my ears, but perhaps it's only in my head. He clenches his hands, his corded forearms flexing with the movement. Then, he unceremoniously hauls me up with one hand and drags me to the closet as the crowd goes wild, hooting and jeering behind us.

"What was that?" I exclaim as he all but tosses me into the dark closet and shuts the door behind him. The burning heat of anger rises in my body at his rough manhandling. The room is sealed tightly except for a small sliver of light peeping through the gap between the door and the marble tiles.

"Is that what you want? To come in here with him?" His voice is low and quiet.

"You're impossible! I don't see how this is any of your business." I push a few articles of clothing away from my face.

"He's the perfect man you're looking for, right?" His voice comes closer as I feel his heated presence. "Handsome, rich, successful..." I feel his chest brushing up on mine as my nerves come alive. "Uncomplicated."

We are less than a hair's breadth apart. I see the shadow of his face before me, feel his minty breath on my cheeks, and hear his ragged breathing in my ear. His scent surrounds us, cloaking us in a bubble where everything is him and only him.

"W-what do you mean?"

His large palm coasts up my arm, eliciting goosebumps in its wake as he snakes his other arm around my waist, tugging me flush against him. I gasp at his proximity, my emotions warring between anger and desire.

"Charles. He's your type, right? Your fairytale prince on his fucking, shiny white steed," he spits out, his voice mocking, his breath tickling my ear. He continues trailing his fingers up and down my back. My heart pounds against my rib cage as the burn of anger slowly morphs into something else, something more intoxicating. I struggle to catch my breath.

"It's none of your business," I reply, trying to sound cool and indifferent, but a tremor betrays the rising heat inside me, my skin becoming sensitive to the touch.

Parker growls as he grips my waist with both hands and flips us around. My hands struggle for purchase and I grasp at his shoulders as he hauls me up against him, his hands a brand against my ass. I gasp at the heat pooling in my core, the sharp sensations overriding my senses and my emotions. He slams my back against the closed door with a *thud*.

"You don't want him," he hisses, his voice strained in the dark room.

I struggle against his hold, but he grips me harder, his palms kneading into my butt as I tilt my hips automatically toward him. I bite back a moan at the shards of pleasure gathering between my legs.

"Stop telling me who or what I want. You don't know me. You hate me, remember?" I fling my words that Saturday night against him, anything I can do to disentangle myself from this cobweb of madness. Pushing against him with my hands, I attempt to escape from his hold, only to find him pulling me tighter against him until not an inch of air separates us. Emboldened, I taunt back, my voice shaking, "And Charles *is* a great catch, and it's *absolutely* none of your business."

"Oh yeah?" he grunts, fury bleeding through his voice, "I bet he can't make you feel like *this*." The invisible cord between us finally snaps.

Parker slams his mouth against mine. I hit his chest and struggle halfheartedly, my resistance futile as he ravages my lips, his kiss feral. Wild. Unrestrained. Wetness seeps through my panties as I melt against him, chasing each nip of his lips with mine. He retreats, I parry, he conquers, I surrender. My legs curl around his waist and he moves against me. His body pins me to the wall as he grinds on me, the unmistakable bulge in the front of his pants hitting the bundle of nerves through my thin, cotton pants.

"Parker..." I moan as I writhe against him, wrapping my legs tighter around his waist, chasing each thrust with a tilt of my own. My nipples bead into hard points as he trails his lips down my neck, nipping and sucking at pulse points. My mind blanks, as nothing matters except for the man before me.

He snakes one hand between my legs over the thin pants and groans at the dampness he finds there. "Fuck. This pussy is aching for me, isn't it?"

I whimper as he slides his hand inside my waistline and his fingers brush against the thin lace underwear.

"Tell me, can Charles make you feel like this?" he growls against my ear as he tugs an earlobe between his teeth and swirls his tongue around the delicate flesh. His fingers push aside my wet underwear and delve into my slick folds. I cry in desperation as I grip his shoulders tightly.

"Parker, please..."

"Tell me, who's making your pussy wet?" He slides one long finger inside me as my walls clench around him. His thumb rubs circles around my clit, and I moan in pleasure. I arch my back, my tender breasts thrusting against him, my nipples calling to his attention.

His lips trail down my neck again, across my collarbone, and he drags down the loose neck of my shirt with his teeth, exposing one breast to the cool air. He sucks hard at a sensitive spot near the tops of my breasts as my cries turn into mewls and he adds another finger down below and proceeds to finger fuck me in earnest.

"Tell me or else I'll stop." His hands still as I move against him, my juices leaking down my thighs. The aching pressure builds between my legs.

"You," I gasp, my body a blazing inferno, ready to burst.

"Who gets to touch this pussy?" he rasps against my breast, his tongue soothing the ache from his suction moments before.

"You," I moan. "Please, Parker...I need..."

"What do you need? Do you want to come all over my fingers? Are you a good teacher on the outside with horny thoughts on the inside just for me?"

I pull at his hair, my sharp tug eliciting a groan of pleasure from him as my hips chase his fingers, the slurping sounds mixing with our erratic breathing in an erotic soundtrack that'll forever be burned into my memories.

"I need to come, Parker. Please..."

"No one gets to touch this pussy. No one..." He thrusts three fingers inside me now, the unfamiliar fullness bordering between pleasure and pain. "Fuck, your pussy is sucking my fingers in like a good slut. Come for me, Liz. Let me hear those cries."

With that, he clamps his teeth over my swollen nipple as he rubs circles on my clit, his fingers hammering inside me, and the pleasure reaches a breaking point. I fall apart with a scream, which he captures with another drugging kiss.

My legs spasm against his as he hoists me against him, his breathing ragged in my ears. My body melts against him as my mind turns to mush, the euphoria rendering me speechless. The closet is silent except for the loud heartbeats in my ears and the heavy sounds of our breathing.

Thump. Thump. Thump. "Hey, guys, the seven minutes are up. You can come out now." Melanie's voice travels across the door. His arms are still against my butt as he slowly lets go, sliding me down to the floor.

Thump. Thump. Thump. "Liz? Parker? You guys okay in there? Haven't killed each other yet, right?" No, this is something worse than death. Or something infinitely better than life. *What the fuck did we just do?*

Mustering a calming breath, I reply, "G-got it. We'll be right out."

I straighten my shirt and hair as best as I can in the dark as my racing heartbeats attempt to return to normal. If there even is a normal after this.

"P-Parker?" I whisper to the dark, warm shadow before me.

"You go outside first. I need a minute." His clipped reply sends renewed flutters inside my belly.

I turn the doorknob slowly, the hallway light slowly flooding the dark closet, and I gingerly step out onto the marble tiles. I turn around to beckon him to come out, but the look on his face stops me in my tracks.

Feverish hunger. Dilated eyes. Clenched jaw. Mussed hair. Light scratches on his neck. I slap a hand across my mouth. *I did this to him?* He pins me with a hard stare, the corded muscles of his arms flexing as he leans against the doorframe. His cock salutes in attention, creating a large tent in his cargo shorts. He struggles to take in ragged breaths as our gazes collide. He slowly brings his fingers, glistening wet with my essence, up to his mouth as he licks the juices off them, never tearing his eyes away from mine.

"I...I..." I stutter, my skin feeling feverish again.

"Go. Before I drag you back in here. People be damned," he barks.

I flee.

And I have a feeling nothing will ever be the same again.

CHAPTER 12

Parker

"There's animals?" Lucy exclaims from her car seat in the middle row of my SUV.

"Yes, sweetie. A lot of cute animals and you get to pet them too," Liz replies from the passenger seat as we drive down south to the Orange County Fair for a little summer excursion. Not my choice of activity to do in my free time, but Lucy has been looking forward to it for so long. The sunny SoCal weather remains unchanged, the dry heat thankfully buffered by a small breeze today. Jazz music plays from the speakers. Liz's favorite.

Liz.

I stare at the woman beside me, her golden-brown hair tied up in a high ponytail, her sparkling blue eyes looking out the window. Her silhouette so familiar and yet infinitely different. The familiarity drew me to her in the first place, yet her uniqueness ensnares my attention and awakens my heart. Clad in a gray cotton tank top and cutoff shorts, she kept her attire and makeup simple, unassuming, and natural.

But no one has ever looked more stunning than her.

Her beauty shines from within and bleeds out of her pores with every smile on her face, every twinkle in her eyes, every laugh from those luscious lips. Lips I've imagined wrapping around my cock more than once. Lips tasting like honey, so sweet and addictive.

I crave more.

My thoughts stray back to last week, to the most erotic seven minutes of my life. Her moans. Her gasps. The way she melts in my hands. The way she surrenders her control to me. The way she reacts to my touch. How her pussy feels against my fingers. Her cries when she's in the throes of orgasm. I must have fucked my hand raw every night since then, thinking how it'll feel to be inside her. To be with her.

But we can't. She doesn't know the truth. And if she ever finds out, it'll all be over.

After we came out of the closet the other night, we got a few curious stares from the girls and Liz avoided me for the rest of the evening. Then, for the rest of the week, she pretended nothing happened between us. As if she can wipe the memory from our minds.

"Daddy! Daddy!"

I flick on a turn signal as I prepare to exit from the freeway. "Yes, pumpkin?"

"Lizzy said I can eat a fried Oreo today. I've never had one before. Can I? Can I?"

I chuckle, and stare in my rearview mirror into my daughter's impossibly large eyes. "Yes, one fried Oreo. That's it."

More screeches of happiness sound from the backseat as I navigate the car toward the fairgrounds. Fifteen minutes later, we park at a lot a short walking distance from the entrance and I gather our belongings—a backpack with water bottles for the three of us, a light jacket for Lucy in case it gets cold, some snacks, wipes, and other essentials. Lucy stands between Liz and me and holds our hands. She happily skips toward the fair, with its large Ferris wheel looming in the distance and tents which no doubt hold a lot of fun activities for her to experience. We reach the ticket booth where a middle-aged woman is scanning our e-tickets.

"You have a beautiful family there," she comments, smiling warmly at Lucy and Liz.

My heart skips a beat as I glance at Liz out of the corner of my eye.

Family.

Something I don't deserve to have. Something not guaranteed to last. And yet, something I've recently started yearning for again.

Liz's face flushes pink as she shakes her head. "Actually, we're not—"

"Thank you, that's kind of you," I respond, not wanting to hear the rest of Liz's sentence. Perhaps today, we can just pretend.

"So, pumpkin, do you want to see the animals first, or do you want to play some games?" I give Lucy's hand a little squeeze.

"Animals!"

I glance over at Liz, who is eyeing the crowd with an excitement mirroring my daughter. "You okay with that, Liz?"

She nods vigorously. "Yes, petting zoo it is. I looove those little animals." Liz and Lucy trot over in the direction of the petting zoo, hand-in-hand. Liz's golden hair shines against the sun and Lucy's pigtails bounce with every step she takes. My two rays of light. My two embers of life.

Mine.

I trudge after them, committing every detail of the beautiful image before me to my memory. So that one day, when the darkness comes and overtakes me again, and it will, I'll be able to revisit this over and over, and remember a time when I almost felt happy again.

Lucy and Liz chase after the baby goats and lambs in the small enclosure, gushing over how adorable the little furballs are. They take turns feeding the animals with the plants provided by the venue. Lucy peppers Liz with questions about the creatures and Liz never falters, always answering her patiently with a smile on her face.

"Come on, Daddy! Take a picture of Lizzy and me with this little lamb. We're calling her Mary, just like the song."

Lucy and Liz crowd against a poor tiny white lamb, who honestly looks like she'd rather be anywhere else but here. I fish out my phone and aim the camera at my two giggling princesses.

"Ready? Sing 'Mary had a Little Lamb' for me."

Lucy shrieks in laughter while Liz sings at top of her lungs, not a care in the world, earning a few curious glances our way.

"Come on, Parker, sing with us!" She cackles as she tucks a stray lock around her ear, inadvertently snagging a large piece of hay on her head.

I reach out and gently retrieve the errant grass from her hair, and her body stills as she stares at me with those gorgeous blue eyes. Eyes, in another lifetime, I could spend forever swimming in it, basking in their warmth. She blinks slowly as my fingers skim over her cheeks, the skin pinkening as her lips part. I ache to pull her to me, to capture those enticing lips with mine.

"A piece of hay," I whisper, showing her the dried grass, my rapid pulse showing no signs of abating. I muster a smile and take a stunning photo of them. Backing away, I bump into an elderly man standing next to me who is watching a few little kids run around the pen. I apologize to him.

"Your girls are so beautiful," he compliments.

I swallow the lump in my throat. "That's my daughter and her nanny."

He hums in approval. "Really? Well, you got a good one there. She loves your child." He glances over at me and nods at my empty left hand. "Young lad, your face tells me another story. Don't let her get away."

He calls out to the little kids to finish their playtime. "My grandkids. My wife and daughter are taking the day off, leaving me with these little munchkins. It's funny where life takes you, son. I met my wife right before I was to be deployed to Vietnam. Wrong place, wrong time, but right person. I took a chance and won the lottery with her. We got married when I came back home, and the rest is history."

"What if it's the wrong person for you? For too many reasons?" Liz is now hoisting Lucy up in the air as they scamper around the enclosure, running after the little animals.

"You better be damn sure she's the wrong person. Sometimes, you may think she's the wrong person, but you lack the objectivity to see past your assumptions. If your gut is telling you something else, perhaps you should listen to it."

Liz leads Lucy out of the petting zoo and reaches us. "Hi!" She smiles warmly at the man before turning to me. "We just washed up and are ready for all the unhealthy foods we can get our hands on." She rubs her hands together excitedly and Lucy imitates her. Two peas in a pod.

"All right, let's go." I tip my head toward the man, who winks at me before turning back toward his grandchildren.

"What were you guys talking about?" Liz asks.

"Nothing of importance." I take Lucy's hand again and she resumes her favorite position between the two of us. "So, what are we having for lunch today?"

Liz holds up her free hand. "Okay, I have some ground rules for today."

I arch my brow at her, waiting for her to respond.

"First of all, we all get to take turns picking a food to eat and *everyone* must take at least three bites of it, no vetoes, no complaints."

"What if it's unhealth—"

"Nope, none of that today." She glares at me and continues, "Second of all, we can't waste food. So, if you try three bites and decide it's disgusting and not for you, you need to convince someone else to finish it. Or else, you'll need to finish it yourself."

Lucy frowns. "But I'm a kid. I can't finish everything. I'll be too full."

"You get to have an exception, sweetie. If you can't finish something after three bites, you can ask your daddy to finish it for you." Liz smiles at her sweetly as she gives me a side-eye.

"This is total bullsh—" Lucy looks up at me and I quickly amend, "crap. Complete bull crap. The odds are stacked against me."

"Lucy sweetie, you get to pick first today. What do you want?" Liz smirks at me and she ruffles Lucy's pigtails.

"Fried Oreos!"

"All right, Oreos it is."

A few minutes later, I polish down two fried Oreos, because, as expected, Lucy ate three bites of it and decided her belly was completely full. The creamy goodness melts in my mouth. *Maybe this game isn't so bad after all.*

Then, Lucy says she gets to pick again, which completely breaks the rules, but she gives us the cutest little pout and we relent, letting her choose again.

"Lizzy likes to eat those fishy things."

"What fishy things?" I ask.

"The fish on top of the rice things." She frowns, as if mad I'm not understanding her.

Liz interjects, "Do you mean sushi?"

Lucy nods vigorously. "I remember you telling me that the other day we were looking at photos of food from around the world. I saw the fishy, I mean, sue-sheee here too. I want to pick it for you."

Liz and I glance at each other and we take a stroll around the food carts. Sure enough, there's a cart for fried sushi.

"What in the blazes is fried sushi?" I mutter, my stomach protesting.

Liz grins, clearly excited. "I guess we'll find out." She slaps me on the shoulder. "Come on, Parker. Live a little!"

To be alive, something I haven't felt in a long time as a little sprig of hope blossoms inside me.

We purchase a small order of what looks like crispy rice and tempura, and she takes a bite.

"This is seriously the bomb." She closes her eyes and moans as she stuffs her mouth with a large piece of salmon sushi.

I chuckle. The simplest things bring such joy to her face. I wish I could put this smile on her face every day. "Someday, you should visit Japan. The food there is even better."

Her eyes snap open. "Have you been? I've always wanted to go!"

"I got a scholarship and studied in Tokyo for a semester in college."

"No way! You did? How was it over there?"

I polish off the sushi on my plate, surprised it actually tasted pretty good. "It's amazing. Completely different from the US. Different areas of the city have their own unique cultures and vibes. Everything is in technicolor. People are very polite. The food is to die for."

"It's on my list of places to go visit before I die."

My heart skips a beat at her mention of death as a pounding panic grips me.

She can't die. No, not before me.

Fuck. I'm in too deep.

"Someday..." I look at the plate before me and murmur, "Perhaps someday I can take you." I sneak a sideways glance at her.

Liz flushes prettily, glancing at me underneath her lashes, her eyes quickly darting away. My heart thumps loudly in my chest. Soon, it's time to choose another food.

I choose the jumbo turkey leg, because, who can say no to that? Lucy munches happily on the strips of lean meat as Liz devours her portion of the drumstick. I smile, watching the two of them eat with overt joy on their faces.

After the turkey, Liz chooses a crazy concoction called a "pickled fruit punch fried chicken sandwich."

"What the fuc—fudge is this?" I stare at the monstrosity in my hand. This fried chicken sandwich is stained red with what I presume is the fruit punch, stacked with tri-colored cheeses, sliced pickles, another thin layer of what looks to be ham or some sort of meat, topped with a bun and a giant dill pickle speared onto the sandwich with a long toothpick.

Liz licks her lips, temporarily drawing my attention away from this walking heart attack. She grins and replies, "I've read all about this infamous sandwich on the foodie websites. It's new to the fair this year. They say it's an explosion of flavors in your mouth."

"An explosion of something, all right," I mutter under my breath. We walk over to a small table with an umbrella and I slice the "sandwich" into three pieces, a smaller one for Lucy, who is making a face at the crazy colors in the mystery meat, and two larger slices for Liz and myself.

Lucy nibbles on a small piece before smacking her lips. "This is actually pretty yummy, Lizzy."

Liz arches her brow at me as she takes a bite of her sandwich and moans obscenely while swiping her tongue across her lips to lick off the errant crumbs. The sound sends blood rushing straight to my cock as I recall those same moans in the dark closet and her tongue tangling with mine. I clench my jaw, attempting to rein in my lewd thoughts.

"The last time I ate something questionable, I had food poisoning, which left me bedridden for three days. Completely traumatizing," I grunt, still staring at the explosion of colors in front of me.

"Man up, Parker. You need to face your fears in order to move past your trauma. Let a new memory replace the old one," Liz quips, grinning at me.

I take a bite of the sandwich and nearly spit its contents out. Everything is overwhelming and clashing together; the sweetness of the fruit punch, the sourness of the pickles, the greasiness of the cheese, and the saltiness of the ham. I don't think this is a heart attack waiting to happen. This is definitely food poisoning waiting to happen.

"Daddy, I had three bites, but I'm too full to eat anymore. Can you finish this for me?" Lucy bats her lashes at me and rubs her belly. Who did she learn these things from?

I groan and take her sandwich and plop it into my mouth, doing my best to chew and swallow at record speed. I wash down the contents with a few swigs of water.

"Parker, I'm full too." Liz looks at me from under her lashes, her face appearing a tad green.

"No. No way. You reap what you sow."

"Come on, please? I could barely squeeze into these jeans this morning and any more of this, I'll need to unbutton my shorts."

My brain short circuits at a vision of her with her shorts unbuttoned, easy access for me to just slip my hands in there and—

She inches her fingers over and walks them up my hands, to my forearms, to my biceps. The hairs on my arms stand at attention. "Come on, Parker. You're a big, strapping man. What's a *teeny* tiny piece of sandwich to you, anyway?" She lowers her voice to a whisper. "I'll owe you one."

"Oh yeah? And what will I get?" Filthy images of what I want to do to her flash through my mind as my brain lands firmly in the gutter.

"Anything you want..." her face flushes as she catches herself, "within reason."

I snag the sandwich off her plate and polish it down within three bites, my stomach protesting with a loud gurgle. I place my hand on top of hers on the table and give it a quick squeeze. "You absolutely owe me one...and I'll definitely collect." Her eyes widen as her breath quickens, and she looks away with pinkened cheeks.

The day passes by in a blur of laughter, nauseating food, and—I hate to admit it—fun. We're sitting in a small carriage on the enormous Ferris wheel as the sun sets around us, illuminating the sky in a watercolor of warm reds and brilliant pink hues. Lucy is curled up on my lap, her head leaning against my chest as she snores lightly, the day's worth of activities catching up to her. I look over at Liz, who is peering out the window, observing the fairgrounds below, bustling with activity, the noise and ruckus dulling to a quiet thrum in the confines of the compartment. She looks so happy and content as she twirls a lock of hair around her fingers.

Her eyes flick to mine as her lips tip up in a grin. "You should smile more often. You have beautiful dimples." Her gaze falls to her lap as she continues, "I've never seen you as relaxed as today."

My shoulders stiffen as the smile I was apparently wearing on my face slips away. I didn't realize I was smiling again. A real one. One which wasn't purposely engineered by me. How long has it been since this happened? Her eyebrows furrow and I itch to smooth away the frown marring her face.

I fall helpless to those ocean-blue pools staring back at me, her eyes reflecting the pink watercolors from the sky. Wordlessly, I tilt my head toward her as she leans in, her eyes fluttering shut. The sounds of our quiet breathing fill the air as the atmosphere becomes charged with tension.

Ding. Ding. My cell phone blares to life, the incoming jingle indicating a reminder from my calendar which needs to be turned off. I fumble around in my pocket and pull out my phone, swiping my thumb across the screen in haste so I can get back to the kissable lips of the goddess before me. My finger pauses as I notice the date on the screen.

Tomorrow is the anniversary of Abby's death.

The dark emotions which have taken a hiatus today come rushing back like a tidal wave. The twisting guilt mixes with the burning anger and I physically recoil, pulling away from her. I ball my hands into tight fists as nausea churns in my gut. Liz's eyes snap open in confusion and I struggle to rein in my emotions. It used to be easy. To lash out. To be angry at her. To be angry at myself. But now, that has been completely taken away from me, and I find I can no longer be angry at Liz. Perhaps the only anger coursing through my body is and always has been toward the same person.

Me.

I unclench my hands and crack my knuckles, each snap familiar to my ears as I grit my teeth to avoid castigating the person next to me. Someone who isn't even aware of the role she played in my tragedy.

"Parker, are you okay?" she asks softly.

I bounce my knees on the floor, desperate to escape this space, which a moment ago felt like an oasis but now feels like a prison.

"No...I'm not."

The dark clouds herald an unusual summer storm. The air smells musty and feels sticky as unease coils in my body. I don't know if I believe human beings innately have a sixth sense, but in times like these, I wonder if there's some truth to it. I stare out the floor-to-ceiling windows in my bedroom to the world in grayscale and bite my lip, feeling unsettled.

After we left the Ferris wheel last night, Parker became cold and distant. As if something happened in the compartment, flipping the switch on for the silent and mercurial version of him. Someone I haven't seen in a while now. The car ride back home was equally quiet as he stared broodily out the windshield, his hands gripping the steering wheel as if it were his worst enemy. After he said goodnight to Lucy, he locked himself in his room and didn't come out for the rest of the night. This morning, he left for work at the crack of dawn. The house was eerily quiet when Lucy and I came down for breakfast.

"Lizzy, what are we going to do today?"

I turn around and smile at Lucy, standing there in a yellow-and-blue sunflower dress she picked for herself, her wavy hair tied in the French braid she requested because she wants to resemble a certain fairytale princess.

"See those dark clouds outside? I think it'll probably rain today. So, let's stay inside. Do you want to have a Princess Day? We can eat lunch and watch *The Ice Queen*, then make paper crowns and pretend to be princesses in our kingdoms. We can then practice our letters and you can help me make pizza for dinner. What do you think?"

Lucy purses her lips as if deep in thought before giving a terse nod. "I like that."

We walk back downstairs, and I cue up the movie and position a few placemats on the coffee table. Lucy snuggles under the throw blankets, and I carry two plates of macaroni and cheese as the movie begins. We dig into our food and immerse ourselves in the magical world of trolls, ice magic, and the love of two sisters.

"Lizzy, do you think Daddy will find another mommy for me?"

My stomach flips at the thought of Parker with another woman. Someone who'll sleep next to him at night and tuck Lucy into bed. Someone who'll capture his attention. Someone who will enjoy his scorching kisses and tantalizing touches. A burning sensation unfurls in my gut. *No, Liz. You have no hold on him. He's complicated—everything you don't want.*

"Maybe, honey." I take a sip of water to wash away the sour taste in my mouth.

Lucy nods as she continues watching the movie. "Do you think I can have a sister someday, like how Queen Miranda has Princess Breanna?"

"I-I don't know. That'll be up to your daddy and if he gets married again. And even then, these things aren't for certain."

"I wish I have a mommy, Lizzy. A lot of mommies pick up their kids from school and take them to fun places."

I cuddle her to my side and rub tiny circles on her shoulder, my heart clenching for this little girl next to me. This little child who'll never get to cuddle with her mom again. She won't be able to do all the things I used to do with my mom. Going shopping and trying on clothes, partaking in afternoon tea at fancy hotels, talking about friend or guy problems at school. My eyes water up as I look at this pint-size human who's so sweet and adorable but will never experience her mother's love. *I wish I could love her as my own.* The thought is sudden, surprising, and yet, I don't feel afraid. I really love Lucy and want to give her a love which hopefully comes close to her mother's love.

"How about this? If you ever want to have someone to take you to fun places, you can ask your daddy to call me. Even after the summer, when he finds a new nanny."

"I don't want you to leave!" she cries. "I love you, Lizzy."

Tears spring into my eyes for reasons I don't want to decipher. My time is running out here. What first started as a favor to help this little girl has become so much more. How will I ever leave them?

"I love you too, Lucy." I kiss the top of her head and close my eyes, inhaling the sweet scent of her shampoo.

After lunch and a game of pretend play where Lucy is the princess and I'm a frog, because in her logic, she's always the princess, we spend the next few hours practicing her capital and lowercase letters and completing other activities. I continue to teach her how to add and subtract small numbers, and we also read five books from her bookshelf, because it is a five-book kind of day when the outside is so gloomy. We then spent a few hours watching her favorite movies and TV shows and even fit in a mini dance and wiggle party.

The day flies by and soon it's time to prepare for dinner. Rain pelts against the window in earnest now. I pull up a stool and tie an apron around Lucy and we take out the ingredients for our ham and arugula pizza.

"Lucy, go wash your hands and you can help me mix up the ingredients for the dough. You'll be able to practice your math. You see...cooking is like math. You add and subtract things just like I taught you."

"Yay! Wait for me, Lizzy. Don't start without me!"

I parse out the ingredients into separate bowls as she scurries to the bathroom to wash her hands. A few minutes later, she returns with a big smile on her face, eager to play chef with me.

"Okay, pour this cup in here...that's the flour." I watch from next to her, resisting the urge to help her. "The water next. Fill it up to the line and add it in here too." Lucy's hands shake as she fills up the measuring cup and pours it into the mixture. I teach her how to mix the ingredients thoroughly and we put the dough in the refrigerator for a little bit while we prep the other ingredients. Lucy stuffs her face with pieces of ham and cheese, giggling when I admonish her. Soon, we roll out the dough and scatter the ingredients on top.

"Lucy, you have so much flour on your face." I laugh, using my thumb to swipe the white dust on her cheeks, only succeeding in smearing it even more. "Oh no, I think I made it worse."

"You have some too, Lizzy! I'll help you." I bend down and close my eyes, grimacing as Lucy wipes her grubby hands on my face, no doubt creating a mess.

Just as we're both bowling over in laughter, I hear the jingling of keys and the quiet creak of the door opening.

"Daddy's home!" Lucy shrieks and jumps off the stool, bounding over to the noise.

"Lucy! Wash your hands first or else you'll ruin Daddy's clothes." I chuckle as she stops in her tracks and grins at her father.

Parker strolls in wordlessly, his eyes bloodshot, dark circles apparent, his scruff longer than usual, as if he didn't have time to shave last night. His strained smile doesn't reach his eyes and his shoulders harden. He is clad in a slim navy-blue suit, white shirt, and emerald tie today. He ruffles Lucy's hair as she darts past him for the bathroom.

The kitchen falls silent except for the soft hum of the refrigerator. Parker shudders, letting out a deep breath as he prowls closer to me.

"Parker?" My heart kicks hard against my rib cage. I smell a faint whiff of alcohol under his breath. *Something is wrong. Very wrong.* "Did you drink? Did you drink and drive?"

His glittering eyes are intense on mine, his lips pressing into a thin line as he stops a few inches before me. Brushing his thumb across my cheek, he swipes off the flour Lucy has deposited there. He tugs me against him and buries his head in my hair.

"I had a beer two hours ago. I waited before I drove back."

I push against his shoulders, wanting to see him, wanting to know what happened, but he only tightens his arms around me, rendering me immobile.

"Please. Just let me hold you. Just for a minute," he whispers.

My heartbeat thuds loudly in my ears as I slowly bring my hands to his back, rubbing his tense muscles. My chest spasms from pain, even though I don't know what I'm sad about, but my heart is bleeding out for this striking man before me, who is holding so much inside of him. I close my eyes and relish in the warmth of his embrace, even though I wish this were happening under different circumstances. He trembles slightly beneath my touch and my heart slices open, wetness tipping my eyelashes as I try to blink away the tears gathering there. I turn my head and press a soft kiss on his golden-brown hair.

Loud footsteps sound from the distance, and he slowly disentangles himself from me. I stare at his forest-green eyes through my blurry ones. His bloodshot eyes darken at what he finds on my face, and he gently brushes an errant tear with his fingers. He slowly steps away, his Adam's apple bobbing as he swallows. Biting down on his bottom lip, he tears his gaze from mine.

"Daddy! We're making pizza for you today," Lucy exclaims as she reenters the kitchen.

Another forced smile. This time with dimples showing. "I see that, pumpkin. Daddy is starving, and pizza is just the thing I want to eat. How did you know?"

"Did you hear that, Lizzy? Daddy wants pizza today. We're so smart!" I drag my gaze from Parker to Lucy, who is staring up at me expectantly with pride in her face.

I wink at her, doing my best to appear happy, as my chest is still heavy with concern. "I did hear that. Come on, let's put the pizzas in the oven while your daddy washes up and changes." Lucy scrunches her eyebrows and carefully slides the pizzas onto the baking sheet. My eyes flicker back to where Parker was standing a moment ago, desperate to ascertain if he's okay, but he has already disappeared.

Dinner is a quiet affair. A charged atmosphere fills the air but Lucy prattles on, oblivious to the disquiet tension in the room. She regales Parker with the adventures of the day, and he hums noncommittally in return. His pizza is barely touched as his hands clench the cup of water in front of him, his knuckles white against the glass. I try to catch his eyes throughout the meal, but he refuses to look at me.

"Daddy, will you give me a new mommy?"

My fork clatters on top of the plate with a loud ping. Parker's head whips up, his eyes flashing at me, then softening when returning to Lucy. "What's that, pumpkin?"

"I asked Lizzy today, and she said that depends on if you get married again. Will you get married again?"

Parker swallows as his shoulders stiffen. A muscle twitches in his cheek as he attempts, and fails, at procuring a smile for Lucy. "No, pumpkin. Daddy won't get married again." His eyes flick to mine as unidentifiable emotions swirl inside the emerald pools.

My heart drops to my stomach at his declaration. *Stupid Liz, why is this any of your business? Even if he gets married, it won't be to you.* I look away, staring at the rivulets of water running down the windows, blurring the world beyond us, trapping us inside this house, which suddenly feels stifling.

"But I want a mommy, Daddy." Lucy bursts into tears, each wail causing Parker to visibly flinch. He balls his hands into fists as his nose flares. His bloodshot eyes gleam with a wet sheen as he sits there, silent, unable to respond.

I take a tissue and blot Lucy's face with it. "Come on, sweetheart, you can ask your daddy another day. He had a long day at work today, so he's tired. Why don't we let him rest? Let's go upstairs and take a bath. Then I'll read you my favorite storybook and off to bed we go, okay?"

Lucy sniffles and nods as she follows me out of the kitchen. I turn back before we round the corner to the staircase. Parker sits silently at the table, his face buried in his hands, his back muscles flexing under his crisp, white shirt. His frame shudders once. Twice. His lonely silhouette splinters my soul.

I stop in my tracks, my body beginning to turn toward him even before my mind can catch up.

So much pain.

So much anguish.

I want to curl my body around his, if only to soften the harsh blows he is inflicting deep within himself. To halt his self-flagellation. To release him from whatever is shackling him to the hell he is trapped in. Lucy tugs at my hands, her large, sapphire eyes blinking in confusion. I slowly drag myself away from him and take Lucy upstairs to her room, leaving my heart behind.

With him.

• • •

Crash.

I jolt awake at the sound of glass shattering. My mind fuzzy from the beginnings of slumber, I clamber out of bed in my sleep shirt and put on my slippers. The agonizing howl of the wind and the pitter-patter of the rain hitting the windows let me know the storm is still in full force.

After I put Lucy to bed last night, I returned downstairs in search of him. But he was gone. Locked himself away in his office this time. I stood outside the closed door for the longest time, wanting to go inside to comfort him, but also finding myself unable to move. *I'm just the nanny. I'm just his best friend's sister. I'm a nobody.* I dragged myself back upstairs and attempted to fall asleep, tossing and turning as the storm raged outside until I drifted off into a light sleep. The last thing I saw in my mind was the pain in his eyes. His soulful, jewel-toned eyes.

Crash.

More glass shatters on a hard surface.

I sprint down the stairs in search of the noise, my heart at my throat.

I know it's him.

Parker stands by the sliding glass doors, looking out at the backyard. Two beer bottles lie broken at his feet, the glass shards sparkling under the hazy, storm-ridden moonlight shining in from the outside. He is shirtless, clad only in a pair of dark sweatpants hanging low on his waist. His striking frame wavers as he takes a swig of beer from the bottle he is gripping in his hand. A few gulps later, he mutters a curse and throws the bottle to the ground, smashing it to pieces on the hardwood floor, his corded muscles flexing from the exertion. He sways unsteadily on his feet before stepping on the broken shards in an audible crunch.

"Be careful!" I hurry toward him as he flinches, whether it's from the pain or from my voice, I don't know. He slowly turns around and the expression on his face sucks the wind out of my lungs and immobilizes me a mere few feet away from him.

Lightning flashes, illuminating his tousled hair, sharp jawline, and his wild, fevered eyes. His feral gaze is now pinned on me. His chest rises and falls with each harsh breath, drawing attention to every hard, defined slab of muscle, the dips and valleys of his abs and pecs. He prowls toward me as I remain frozen in place, my pulse wild in my veins as an invisible tension crackles in the air between us.

"You."

One step. A smear of dark liquid on the floor.

My heart thumps in fear or something else.

Two steps. Another smear. A slight limp.

Three steps. Untamed green eyes. Clenched jaw.

My body wakes up as if sensing the incoming threat and I turn around and flee, running away from him even though my heart is tugging me back.

Thump. Thump. Thump.

A few pounding footsteps sound behind me and a muscular arm snakes around my waist, pinning my back to a hot, hard body, cloaking us in a mist of amber and bergamot, and frying my senses. His fingers slide over my shirt, between my breasts, and encircle my throat as he leans down, his breath warm against my ear.

"You shouldn't have come down here," he murmurs, his gravelly voice sending shivers throughout my body. "And now, you can't leave."

My skin sensitizes as liquid heat pools between my legs. I feel hot, bothered—every article of clothing abrasive to my delicate skin. I hunger for him, for more, for this madness to overtake both of us. His hand arches my neck to the side, exposing my fluttering pulse to him, and he bends his head down, his teeth nipping at the tender spot where my neck meets my ears. His palm gently squeezes, restricting part of my airflow.

I gasp at the barrage of sensations hitting my body simultaneously. The sharp pain from his teeth. The soothing suction of the kiss afterward. The lightheadedness from the hand at my throat. The intensity of the ache between my legs.

"You're mine," he whispers, trailing kisses along the column of my neck as he releases his grip, sending the blood and air rushing back into my system, further inflaming my senses. His other hand slides down my body and clasps my swollen breast, twisting his fingers around the hardened nipple. I moan and lean my head back, my legs turning to jelly as I'm supported only by the strong arm now curling around my waist.

"Fuck. I tried to stay away." He nips my jawline as he pinches and tugs at my nipple, sending fire down to my core. "But I can't... I'm not strong enough."

"Parker..." I whimper, arching my back against him. I slide my hand to cup my other breast, the tender globes swollen as nerve endings send rioting signals to my brain.

Spinning me around, he wraps his hand around my hair, giving it a hard tug, the pain bordering on pleasure as he slams his mouth against mine in a ravaging kiss. He tastes of sweetness and alcohol as his tongue thrusts inside, conquering my mouth, devouring me. My mind blanks as I collapse upon him. He groans with pleasure, and I rub my body against him, my softness against his hardness. My brightness against his darkness.

He backs us toward the staircase and lays me down on the bottom step. He crowds above me, supported only by his strong forearms. The darkness of his pupils overtakes the green of his eyes as he stares down at me, his breathing rough and ragged. My lips are swollen, my scalp tender, and my neck is warm to the touch.

I want more.

He may be everything I don't need but is everything I currently desire, and I don't want to make sense of this anymore. I wrap my legs around his waist and gyrate against the outline of his hard cock. He groans, his eyes closing in pleasure.

"Fuck. Your pussy is aching for it, right? You want my cock inside you? Fill you up? Come all over you?"

Wetness seeps out of me at his dirty words. I moan as he hits the bundle of nerves between my thighs. Pushing my shirt up, he exposes my lace underwear, which is now soaked. With a rough yank, he rips the damp cloth from my body. The burn mixes with the heady pleasure of his movements against me.

He pulls back and spreads my legs wide, staring at me splayed before him. He leans in and bites my inner thighs.

"Look at this beautiful pussy. All pink and dripping wet for me." He licks his lips as the gaze in his eyes turn savage. "Only for me."

He dives in and he feasts like it's his last meal, his last chance at salvation. I scream before clamping a hand over my mouth as he unleashes his fury on my clit. His tongue circles the sensitive nub before sucking it in his mouth, the harsh drag sending a torrent of pleasure through my body. The sounds of his slurps mingle with my whimpers as I surrender my body to this virile man before me.

"Fucking delicious," he grunts as he slams two fingers inside me, wrenching a moan from me and I see stars behind my eyes. "Look at this pussy, so greedy for me. Fuck, I can't wait to see you take my cock. You'd take it so well."

Warm liquid gushes out as he curls his fingers deep inside, hitting a spot I didn't even know existed. Sharp pleasure spears through me. He slurps it all in before he goes in for the kill.

"Oh God," I mewl, the words sounding foreign to my ears. The pressure between my legs climbs rapidly as I thrash on the steps, my body about to combust.

"Come for me, baby. Give me all your juices," he growls, his voice raspy as he bites down on my clit.

My mouth falls open in a silent scream as I burst into flames, the flinch of pain from his teeth sending my body into a tailspin. My legs shake uncontrollably around his head as my juices overflow in a wet spurt. My core throbs with aftershocks as I writhe underneath him.

Parker groans at the sight. "Fuck, that's so sexy." He crawls up my body and ensnares my lips with his in another drugging kiss.

"Parker...I..." I gasp, wanting to say nothing yet everything at the same time.

He clasps my hands over my head as he drives his tongue between my lips, his hips whipping against me in a frenzy. The pressure between my legs renews, my need for him insatiable.

"Damn you, Abby," he grunts out as he grinds against me.

Abby.

I still beneath him, his words a bucket of icy-cold water effectively dousing the embers of passion inside me. *He thinks I'm his dead wife.*

Tears spring to my eyes as I shove at him, his large mass unmoving as he realizes his mistake. "Get off of me!" I shove him with my fists as he absorbs each strike without so much as a grunt. "Get the fuck off of me!"

Parker pulls himself up, his chest heaving as I clamber to a sitting position, tugging my sleep shirt down to my waist. Scrambling to get up, my legs nearly give out from the sudden movement. His hand reaches out to steady me, but I slap him away. Spinning around, I flee to my room, locking the door behind me before sliding into a puddle on the floor, the stickiness between my thighs and my swollen lips a constant reminder of what we had done.

My heart, which was thundering in passionate ardor moments ago, now spasms with excruciating pain. The tears come down in earnest as a sob escapes my throat. This time, I don't hold back as I bury my head between my knees, lamenting at the world, despising myself.

Hating him.

My head feels like it has battled with an anvil and lost. Horribly. Painfully. I groan as the sunlight streams in from the windows, which, in my alcohol-induced haze from last night, I must have forgotten to shut the shades. I slap my forearm across my eyes, blotting out the bright light as the events from the prior evening come to the forefront.

Liz.

Writhing underneath me, her legs splayed wide.

Her screams when she came on my lips, her juices tasting as sweet as the rest of her.

Her gasps when I choked her, how it inflamed her instead of turning her off.

My cock hardens at the memory, still unsatisfied even after the hand job I gave myself when I stumbled back into my room last night. Fuck, I'm eager for a rematch. Then, a heavy weight settles in my stomach as the missing piece of memory settles into place.

Her reaction when I said Abby's name.

The tears in her eyes as she glares at me, no doubt feeling betrayed.

Little did she know, I didn't mistake her for Abby. While they bear a passing similarity in appearance, if anyone spent more than five minutes with Liz, they'd know she is nothing like Abby. Her sweetness and steadfastness to Abby's flighty and sarcastic personality. Those voluptuous curves to Abby's athletic, model physique.

Liz's heart—an absolute one-of-a-kind.

During the anniversary of the night that changed my life forever, I succumbed to my desires for an inappropriate woman. A woman who is quickly taking over every waking thought during the day and chasing away the demons in my dreams at night. In the throes of passion, the burning guilt pierced my defenses as Abby's face flashed before my eyes, haunting me, asking me how I can move on when I'm the reason she's gone. I cursed her internally, not knowing I spoke the sentiment aloud.

I fucking hate myself.

I sigh as I swing my legs off the bed, wincing in pain when the shallow cut on my heel touches the floor. Perhaps this is for the best. Our relationship is doomed from the start. Too many secrets between us. I always hurt the people who love me. Perhaps it's best for this to end before it even begins. If only I can quit my craving for her.

The house is quiet aside from the birds chirping in the backyard. The sun shines a warm glow and the skies are clear as the smog is washed away by the torrent of rain in the last two days. The greenery is especially vibrant as water quenches the dry soil, reawakening the dull leaves, which are used to the scorching sun and relentless heat.

I wander around the house, finding no signs of Lucy or Liz. My heart begins to pound as a million scenarios run through my mind. None of them logical. A scrap of paper on the coffee table catches my attention.

Parker,

Last night was a terrible mistake, and I don't want to talk about it. There's a glass of water, two ibuprofens, and a BLT sandwich on the dining table. Eat something. I'm sure you'll feel better afterward. I replenished the first aid kit in the main bathroom. You should disinfect and wrap up the wound on your feet. The weather is great, so I'm taking

Lucy out to the park. We should talk about your nanny search when I get back.

Liz

My fists clench the note into a ball as I contemplate the near future when Liz leaves us. When she takes the brightness and joy from this household. When life will once again slow to a crawl and every hour is mundane, dull, and tortuous. I whip out my phone from the pocket of my sweatpants and text her.

Parker: Liz, I'm sorry for hurting you last night. It's not what you think it is. I'll explain tonight after I come home. I'll pick up dinner on the way home, so don't worry about cooking. Please don't make any rash decisions about the job.

A few seconds later, my phone chimes with a reply.

Liz: I made a promise to Lucy and I'll keep it. But I hope you've started lining up interviews for a nanny.

I mutter some curses under my breath as I text my secretary, letting her know I'll be in for only a few hours this afternoon and I make my way to the main bathroom, grabbing the first aid kit from under the sink before trudging back to my room to get ready for the day.

• • •

"You look tired, Parker. What has been going on?" Marybeth inquires as she sets her pen on top of her notebook and stares at me with concern in her brown eyes. Her hair is tied back in a sleek bun today.

I sit across from her in the trusty leather chair once again for our monthly meeting. My headache and churning stomach feel much better after the painkillers and sandwich Liz prepared for me in the morning.

"I...I haven't been sleeping well."

Her eyes soften and she nods in encouragement. "And why is that?"

"Is there always a reason why?" I cross one ankle on top of my other knee as I tap my fingers on the armrest.

Tap. Tap. Tap.

She leans back, mirroring my position. "In my experience, the quality of sleep is sometimes indicative of someone's mental health. Not always, of course. But when we have things on our minds, we tend not to sleep well."

I bite my bottom lip, debating how much I should reveal. Taking a deep breath, I respond, "Last night was the anniversary of Abby's death."

She presses her lips together and keeps her face neutral as she waits for me to continue.

"It... It's always a tough day for me. So, I didn't sleep well."

Marybeth murmurs, "Of course. That must've been difficult for you." She uncrosses her legs and leans forward. "Can you tell me a little bit about your day?"

I close my eyes, not wanting to see her face. "I woke up early, went to work. Couldn't focus at work. Came home early. Had dinner. Got drunk. The rain..."

"What about the rain?"

I grip the armrest tightly, the cool leather warming under my fingers. "It was pouring last night. Just like that night."

"Abby, you come back home right now! I can't believe you just walked out that door while we were in the middle of a conversation," I yell into the phone that's currently on speaker mode on top of the coffee table.

I hear static on the other line before she responds, "That wasn't a conversation! That was an argument. It's always about you and never about me. I'm not going to stay there and listen to you berate me about how awful of a mother and wife I am to the two of you." The clicking of the turn signal makes its way through the speakers.

"What on earth are you talking about? I've bent over backward to accommodate your lifestyle. You like to go out and spend weekends in bars. I drag myself out to be with you when I want nothing more than to spend it at home with Lucy and you. You

miss painting, so I ask you to sign up for art classes at the nearby college. I've been so supportive of you searching for your biological family. You wanted to spend a lot of money to hire the private investigators, I didn't blink at that. You spend all of your extra hours scouring the internet for information...I try to be supportive and try my damned best to take care of Lucy even though she clearly wants you. What more do you want!" I pace around the floor as anger boils within me.

"Parker, I feel like I'm suffocating. I want to be able to take control of my life. To live for myself and not for anyone else."

Lightning flashes through windows as the rain hammers loudly against the walls. "Well, reality check. You can't just live only for yourself anymore. You're a mom. We have an innocent child who depends on us. We are both adults and have responsibilities. We aren't in our twenties anymore."

"I don't care. All I know is I'm dying inside and I. Can't. Breathe," she sobs.

"Grow up, Abby. Why the fuck did you even agree to marry me in the first place? You know a stable family life is what I was looking for from the get-go."

"Because I got pregnant. Because you wanted to keep her!" she screeches, her voice a weapon piercing my chest.

I tug my hair in frustration. "It wasn't my decision alone. I asked you. We talked about it. You told me you wanted to keep her too. We made this decision together!"

The rumble of thunder overtakes the sound of the blood rushing in my ears. She never wanted us. It was always a mistake between us. Instead of growing closer throughout the years, the rift has widened, the gap between us insurmountable. But I can never, ever regret Lucy.

"Fuck you, Abby. Maybe you should just leave and not come back if you don't even care about us anymore. I won't have you resent—"

I hear the loud sound of a car horn.

"Oh shit—"

Click.

The line cuts off.

My heart kicks against my rib cage as my vision grows hazy. "Abby? Abby!"

Silence. She hung up on me. This is so typical of her.

"And you feel like you're responsible for her death?" Marybeth's gentle voice pulls me back to the present. My eyes flutter open. Bright fluorescent lights. The ticking of the watch on my wrist. I didn't even realize I had spoken aloud. I don't want to talk about that day anymore. I've already relived the moment more times than I'd care to count.

You need to face your fears in order to move past your trauma. Let a new memory replace the old one. Liz's reminder echoes in my brain.

My fingers tap the armrest as my legs bounce on the ground. "It's not a feeling. It's a fact. I *am* responsible. I killed her."

"Parker, look at me." My eyes flit toward hers and she continues, "Sometimes, the guilt we carry in our hearts is not telling us the truth. Sometimes, it's our brain's mechanism to try to make sense of something, like a tragic event, when these things can't be predicted or avoided."

I shake my head. *No. It's a fact.*

"It's not your fault, Parker." Her soothing voice reverberates in my mind.

No.

I bite my lip and stand. "I can't do this. Sorry, Marybeth. I'll see you next time." I stride to the door as she calls out to me. I keep walking away from the suffocating room as I work to stuff the memory back into the deepest recesses of my heart. If I don't think about it, perhaps one day it'll just fade away, finally freeing me from its shackles.

. . .

I set the bag with the gourmet sushi on top of the dining table. I recall Liz liking the restaurant when we went the other week. I pad down the hallway to the playroom, hearing their voices well before I'm close to the door. Anticipation and dread war with each other, fighting for dominance inside me. Taking a deep breath, I push open the door.

Liz looks up first, the wide smile on her face slipping as the sparkle in her sapphire eyes dulls. I hate myself for putting this expression on her face. Lucy looks up at me and she hops off the couch where they were reading books moments before.

"Daddy! You're home." She leaps into my open arms, and I smother her with kisses, never once looking away from the beguiling woman before me.

Liz's face softens as anguish still tinges in her features. "You're home early."

"Can't really focus at work today. Might as well come home to be with *my* girls." I implore for her forgiveness with my eyes. She flinches at my endearment and looks away.

Swallowing the lump in my throat, I turn to Lucy. "Daddy got Lizzy's favorite sushi today for dinner and I got you the yakisoba noodles you like."

Lucy licks her lips and pats her tummy. "Yummy! I love the noodles. I'm hungry, Daddy. Let's go." She tugs me out of the playroom as Liz trails behind us.

I pull out the plates and dipping dishes from the kitchen cabinets as Liz fills our cups with water for Lucy and hot green tea for the two of us. The two of us work in sync, quiet with our movements. The familiarity brings a warmth to my chest. Hints of vanilla mingle in the air. Her scent. I wish I could bottle this smell and carry it with me always.

Lucy sits in her chair, happily waiting for us to return as she stares at the dishes on the table. Liz portions out our food, distributes the soy sauce and wasabi, and we begin eating.

The atmosphere is stilted and awkward, but Lucy doesn't notice. She prattles on about how she wants to eat this noodle every day and I hum along, encouraging her to eat more and talk less. Liz laughs at Lucy's jokes, but the smile doesn't quite reach her eyes. I try to catch her attention throughout dinner, but she avoids my gaze. My heart pounds as worries float through me. *What if she just ups and leaves us?* My pulse races at the horrible thought. *What if she doesn't believe me when I explain it to her and she leaves, anyway?* I take a sip of hot green tea, trying to calm my nerves. It's all my fault. My royal fuck up.

The rest of dinner passes by uneventfully as we keep our conversation to the surface, both of us skirting the big elephant in the room. Lucy describes in great detail every little thing she did with Liz today, what she did at the park, who she saw on the playground. I clean up the table and wash the dishes while Liz puts Lucy to bed, a sense of contentment washing over me, despite the underlying tension. The mundane life. Work, kids, home. That's all I ever wanted, and this is the closest I've ever come to experiencing it. Even though I know it'll all fall apart soon.

The soft footsteps alert me to Liz's presence as she enters the kitchen and takes a seat on a barstool at the marble island.

"You want to talk to me?" she asks softly. I bite back a half smile. Even in these circumstances, she's never one to avoid a difficult topic. Her honesty is always so refreshing and admirable.

The complete antithesis to me.

I wipe my hands on a towel as I lean on the marble counter for support. Taking a deep breath, I reply, "Look at me, Liz."

She stares at her hands in front of her, refusing to look up.

I tap the counter next to her, afraid to touch and spook her. "Liz...look at me, please."

Her beautiful ocean-blue eyes gaze into mine, the flecks of gold shining under the pendant light. She bites her plump bottom lip.

"It really wasn't what you think it was." I let out a shaky breath. "I knew who you were last night, Liz. I wasn't thinking about Abby."

Tears gather in her eyes as she looks away, blinking rapidly. "You c-called me Abby."

Flinching at her tears, I shake my head and reach out to take her hands. She starts pulling away, but I grip her tighter. "No, I...I have issues." Taking one deep breath and another, I finally confess, "Liz, I...I killed her, and she haunts me every day." Lead settles in my stomach as I await her judgment.

"What? No, you didn't kill her."

"How do you know?" I look at our interlinked hands. I whisper, "You don't know many things about me."

She grips my hand tightly and responds resolutely, "You listen, Parker Wellington. I don't know what's going on in that brain of yours, but I know for a fact you're not a murderer. Maybe you're trying to scare me, but it's *not* working."

"It was raining that night...we got into an argument before she ran out of the house for an appointment." I toy with her fingers, the gentle motions completely at odds with the nausea roiling in my gut. "I was so pissed. So upset she left us in the middle of our fight to see someone who I thought was inconsequential. I called her to give her a piece of my mind. We fought over the phone and the next thing I knew, she got into an accident on the road. And I didn't even know it at the time. I just thought she hung up on me and I was so pissed afterward."

"Oh, Parker..."

My nostrils flare as I swallow the pins and needles in my throat. "They said she died on impact. I guess, in a way, I was there with her until the very end. Until the life was snuffed out of her. Just like that. Because I couldn't keep my shit together, I took Lucy's mom away from her. She'll never have her mom next to her for all her milestones." Moisture gathers in my eyes as I choke on the last words, "A-and it's all my fault."

Liz pulls her hands from beneath mine and gets off her stool, disappearing from view. *That's right. Now you see the monster. Leave while you still have a chance.* I close my eyes as I grip the countertop, the darkness already creeping back in now that I'm not basking in Liz's presence.

A few moments later, gentle arms encircle my waist from behind me as the scent of vanilla fills the air.

Liz. She didn't leave.

She curls her body around mine and places her head on my back. "Parker, it's an accident. It wasn't your fault. Don't kill yourself over it. You lost your wife and life partner too, not just Lucy. It must've been devastating."

"You know what's the worst part?" I whisper, my eyes unfocused in front of me as I grip her hands around my waist, needing her energy in order to say the next words. "I felt sad for Lucy and the fact a young life was cut short that day, but not...not really for me. In a way, it was a relief she was no longer here, so we didn't have to argue every day any more. I was free...or so I thought."

I crouch down, my forehead touching the cold marble as I confess my sins to the woman behind me. "What kind of monster am I?"

Liz hugs me tighter as I feel wet spots on my back. I slowly turn around and find Liz looking at the ground, her body shaking. My hand trembles as I reach out to tip her face up. Wetness coats her cheeks as she blinks her watery eyes at me.

She's crying. For me.

"You're a good man. You're someone who loves so much, you're actively trying to hold back all the negativity in your life to shield those people around you. You're someone who's working on giving back to the community while asking for little to no recognition. You're someone who doesn't require a lot in life, only the simple pleasures, but have been a victim of life's many tragedies. You're someone who, despite everything that has happened to you, still gets up every morning and refuses to give up," she replies shakily. "And it hurts me to see you like this. To watch you beat yourself up for the misfortunes in your past, things you have absolutely no control over." She places her hands on my shoulders as she rises to her tiptoes, the blues in her eyes burning hot. "You. Are. Not. A. Monster."

My shoulders crumble as a sob breaks out from my throat. I wrap her in my arms and bury my head in her hair, surrounding myself with her sweet scent. Silent tears flow out like an uncontrollable flood and she shushes me as I shake in her embrace, feeling protected by her love.

Receiving an absolution I don't deserve.

"L-last night was the anniversary of her passing," I choke out in a whisper, "but I was so overcome and taken away by you I forgot about everything...and then she finally made an appearance in my mind, cursing me for moving on when the chance was taken from her. That's why I said what I said. I-I didn't mean to say it out loud or to hurt you."

She presses a soft kiss on my ear as she smooths her hands down my back, calming my shudders. "I forgive you."

Her three words are a balm to my ragged soul. A drop of fresh water in the murky ocean. My breathing slows down as the rioting pulse quiets into a steady rhythm. I don't know how long this calmness will last, but I'll take it. I'm selfish and I'll take every ounce of this peace until I can't anymore. I'll keep her with me until she leaves me.

And I know she will because she still doesn't know everything.

CHAPTER 15

Parker

There is something about confessing your sins that is mentally draining and physically exhausting. It's as if somehow, by sharing your secrets, even if it's only the tip of the iceberg, you're somehow lightening the load on your shoulders. Albeit temporarily. I know I shouldn't drag Liz into this. I should keep her safe and protected from afar. If she goes down this road with me, she *will* get hurt. There's no doubt about it.

Liz sits next to me on the sofa as we watch *The Italian Holiday*, a classic movie from the fifties about a starlet who escapes to Rome for a much-needed vacation, only to lose her belongings on the streets but is thankfully rescued by an American reporter. I'm careful to keep the volume down as to not wake Lucy. Both of us are deep in thought, not really paying attention to the screen. There are a few inches of space between us, but not so much I can't feel the warmth from her body.

The last vestiges of willpower are holding me back from hauling her into my arms, from kissing her senseless, from taking her, and making her mine. The urge is so strong, to say hell with it, to be with someone my soul has probably recognized from the beginning but vehemently denied for the longest time. I want to tell myself things aren't as dire as I think they are, that perhaps she'll never find out, perhaps we can exist in the simple world of just Parker and Liz. But I don't want to ensnare her in my web of lies, ultimately pulling her down to drown with me.

"You might call me naïve, but I've always believed in having a soulmate. In finding someone who loves you for who you are, just like the movies. Then you live happily ever after," she murmurs to me, her eyes still glued to the screen.

I grip my knees. "Life is not like the movies. Trust me."

"I know...I think I'm beginning to realize." Her lilting voice is mesmerizing in the dimness of the living room. "I just want something uncomplicated. A simple love story. Like my parents' relationship. They met in high school, fell in love, got married, had us, and are still as in love with each other as they were all those years ago. Such a steadfast love. That's what I want."

My stomach flips at her idyllic description of her ideal relationship. Something I'll never ever be able to give her. I clutch the blanket next to me and force myself to relax the rest of my body. Even though I can't give her what I want, I still want to listen to her, to be part of her story, albeit briefly.

"I think that's why I've never really...dated anyone seriously. I haven't found anyone who's looking for the simple life I'm searching for. I may like to watch movies or read books where all types of dramatic upheavals occur, but I never want any of that in my real life." She glances at me but seeing how I appear to be focused on the movie in front of me, she continues, "But maybe it's too much to ask. Maybe this soulmate I'm searching for doesn't exist anywhere in the world except in my mind. And perhaps...I've just been holding back from trying to let anyone in because I'm afraid of disappointment."

My head leans back on the headrest and I close my eyes. "Abby and I met in grad school at Cornell. I was a scholarship student, and her family was well-off. All my life, I've scrimped and saved because my mom worked several jobs to put me through school after my dad died when I was a kid. When we met, I was enthralled by her carefree attitude and wry humor, such polar opposite of me. We burned fast, and it was an inferno which overtook us."

Hearing no response other than her soft breathing, I continue, wanting her to understand a little bit about me, even though nothing will ever come out of it. *Nothing can ever come out of it.* "Naturally, a relationship based on the surface fizzles out over time and we broke up two years later, parting ways on good terms. She wanted to travel and be a citizen of the world. I wanted to plant my roots and start my firm."

"How did you guys get back together, then?"

"Six years ago, she stopped in LA to see her parents before she was to hop back on the plane to go to Paris. We met up, had a few drinks. I just celebrated winning a large bid for a design contract. The few drinks became many more drinks and one thing led to another and we got together." I open my eyes and turn to her, leaving no room for interpretation in what I meant by those words. "That night, the condom broke and Lucy was conceived."

Liz sits up, her legs crossed on the sofa as she faces me, a frown on her face. "That must've been very stressful." Sweet, beautiful Liz. Always so empathetic.

I shrug and reply, "It was straightforward for me. I wanted to keep the baby and get married. She didn't. But ultimately, we decided to give marriage a try and to raise Lucy together." I shake my head and chuckle mirthlessly to myself. "Deep down, I think she resented me ever since. I was her jailor, and she was the prisoner, a little bird who wanted to escape her gilded cage."

"Lucy is such a sweetheart though," she murmurs as she places her hand on my knee, a gentle touch of reassurance.

"She is. I love her more than life itself. Our life wasn't all bad. We had love for a while there, but the novelty of marriage quickly faded for Abby and, well, you know how our story ended." I rub the back of my head and sigh. "I don't even know why I'm telling you this. I don't usually talk to anyone about her."

Liz smiles softly, her blue eyes warm. "It's lonely not to have anyone to talk to. I'm glad you're able to open up to me."

"Trust me, Liz." I hold her gaze intently. "One day, you'll find the fairytale prince you're searching for. He'll be able to give you the happily ever after you're seeking. Any man with you in his arms is the luckiest person alive."

And the man will never be me. She deserves much more than someone with a damaged soul with no hope of recovery.

She returns my sentiment with a sad smile, the blues of her eyes reflecting sorrow and anguish. She blinks as she shifts in her seat.

"Parker, I've been meaning to tell you. Lucy told me she misses her mother again yesterday. This time, she was a bit distraught over it."

I clench my shirt. No matter how hard I try, I can't replace Abby in Lucy's life. I'll never be able to make up for that loss.

"Do you think it's serious enough for professional help?"

"I think we can continue monitoring. I also think it was triggered because..." She takes a deep breath and murmurs, "Because we talked about me leaving at the end of summer. She may have grown very attached to me."

My hands still on my shirt as my heart twists at the thought of her moving out of this house in two months. *I've grown attached to you too, Liz. Perhaps too much for my own good.*

"I think we can try easing her into the idea of me leaving and telling her how I'll visit her and how she'll always see me at school, so it doesn't seem as big of a change when the time comes. That may help."

I nod, staring at the screen, but not really watching the movie. My heart clenches in pain and we quietly resume our movie night.

• • •

"Daddy, what is this place?" Lucy looks around in wonder as she climbs out of the SUV.

I crouch down and point at the large building in front of us. "This is a building your daddy helped designed. It's called the Regina McDonald New Beginnings Center. This is a place that'll help people with no home and no place to stay. There are other buildings like this one throughout the city."

"So, you drew a picture of this building and the construction people made it for you?" Lucy gasps at the sheer scope of the structure.

Laughing, I stand back up and ruffle her hair, something she doesn't like me doing ever since Liz has been braiding it each morning. Today it is in something complicated looking, which Lucy educates me is called a "fishtail."

"Daddy!" she growls, crossing her hands.

"Sorry, pumpkin. But Lizzy is here, so if anything were to happen to your braid, she'll be able to fix it." I glance back at Liz, who is catching up to us in the parking lot.

"Wow," she exclaims, slightly out of breath, "this is the homeless shelter you've been working on for so long?"

"Yes. This one has been opened the longest. A few others are wrapping up construction now." There's already a line forming at the entrance of the building, which, by all appearances does not resemble a shelter, with the smooth, reclaimed-wood exterior, light-green awning, carefully manicured lawns, and shrubbery; it's modeled to resemble more of a community center instead.

Liz nods. "It holds a special meaning to you, right? Regina McDonald..." She reads the plaque aloud. "Is this someone you know?"

"That's my mother's name. She took my stepdad's last name after she remarried. After my dad passed away from cancer, he left us with a pile of medical debt, and for a period of time, we had to utilize shelter services while Mom got back on her feet." I rub the soreness on my shoulders. "It's my way of giving back, I guess."

"That's commendable."

"Nah—something anyone would've done in my shoes."

Liz places her hand on my forearm, her touch like a brand I can feel through the cotton of my dress shirt. "Parker, that's not what anyone would do." She grips me tighter, causing me to look at her. "You are a good man. *Not* a monster." Her bright smile sears into my soul as my heart thuds in response. If I hear it enough, will I believe it someday?

Biting my cheek, I look away as we approach the receptionist's desk. "Hi, we're here to volunteer for tonight's dinner service."

The old lady with soft eyes behind the counter signs us in and directs us to the kitchen and the serving line. I'm relegated to being a busboy, carrying platters of hot food and cartons of beverages from the kitchen to the serving station. Liz and Lucy are in charge of serving the entrée and distributing the water bottles, respectively.

Sweat prickles my forehead as I lift a twenty-four pack of water from the storage room to stack next to the beverage station, which Lucy is proudly manning. I wink at her as she gives me a toothy grin and return to the kitchen where organized chaos is transpiring.

"The food smells great, Bob," I comment, my stomach growling from the aroma of stewed chicken with gravy, mashed potatoes, and collard greens.

The main chef, a burly man with a faded sleeve of tattoos and a white curly mustache, walks over, his harsh face breaking into a smile. "Parker, my son. Nice to see you here again. You're one of our frequent customers who come here not for the food or the payroll."

"Ha. Well, someone has to show up to make sure you're not trashing my creation."

He gives me a hearty slap on my back and guffaws, the jovial appearance completely at odds with his motorcycle club-esque appearance. He peers outside the large pane of glass to the serving stations. "So, who are those girls you brought with you today?"

My chest warms as I observe Liz throwing her head back in laughter at something a middle-aged man with a child is saying. Her expression is contagious and draws a few chuckles from other folks in the line. Lucy is gesturing animatedly at an elderly man in line who is carrying a tray loaded with food. My heart is bursting with an emotion I don't dare name.

"The little pipsqueak is my daughter, Lucy. Next to her is her nanny, Liz."

"Just the nanny, huh? The smile on your face tells me otherwise."

I blink my eyes and whip my head toward Bob, who is giving me a shit-eating grin. "What are you talking about?" I roll up my sleeves in an attempt to appear nonchalant, whatever smile he noticed before is wiped off my face.

"It's good, son. Real good. I haven't seen you like this in a long time." He nudges me and whispers conspiratorially, "Whatever the *nanny* is doing, tell her to keep doing it." He wags his bushy brows and walks away.

Visions of Liz "doing things" to me flash before my eyes and my cock stiffens in response. Fuck. It's as if my body is making up for three years of no sex. It's getting more and more difficult to control my response to her whenever I'm around her. And now, just hearing about her gets me hard. I grit my teeth and carry another heavy platter of food to the front, hoping the physical labor will dull the burning need I have for her.

"Wow, so you think you're related to George Washington?" Liz's question stops me midstride.

The current person in front of her, a middle-aged woman with brown hair and glasses, nods enthusiastically. "That's what my ma told me before she passed. Now whether or not that's true, that's anyone's guess."

Liz scoops some mashed potatoes onto her plate as she considers her response seriously. "You never know, Molly. Maybe one day when you get back on your feet, you can do some research. There may be some truth to it. I'm looking into my roots too and the things I've found are definitely surprising."

"Oh yeah? To be honest, I always thought it was gibberish, but it's an interesting idea, right?" Molly murmurs before moving to Lucy, who proudly hands her a bottle of water. "Maybe I'll look into it when I get outta here."

Liz is now flashing her million-dollar smile at the next individual in line as she bewitches yet another person. I shake my head, biting my bottom lip before approaching the table and setting down the extra platter of food.

"How's it going over here?" I whisper behind her.

She jumps at my intrusion, having been so engrossed in her conversation with the person in front of her. "Parker! Gosh, you scared me." She places her hand over her chest and laughs. "Things are going great here. We definitely should do this again. This has been fun, right Lucy?" She pokes my daughter's arm.

"Yep! This is so much fun! Everyone is saying how I'm such a great helper."

I pat her head again, earning myself another pout. "That you are. Thank you." I glance back at Liz, who is staring at the two of us with what I can only describe as adoration in her eyes. "Thank you for being here...with me."

Liz blinks, her smile softening as the blues in her eyes darken. "Always. Anytime."

My hands itch to pull her against me, but I restrain myself. Stuffing my hands into my pockets, I nod at her and return to the kitchen. In another life, perhaps, things will be simple, and I can be her fairytale prince.

A few hours later, the dinner service concludes and the residents who are fortunate enough to secure overnight quarters retire to their rooms. The three of us share a quick meal with the kitchen staff.

"Liz, you must come back here more often. Parker, my boy here, actually gives us real smiles these days. None of that fake shi—" Bob coughs, looking at Lucy, who is happily slurping her lime jelly, "stuff he used to pull on us. Do you know how I know him?"

Liz laughs, her eyes twinkling. "You noticed those fake smiles too? I thought I was the only one." She squints her eyes and twists her lips to the side. "Hmm... You seem to know him quite well... Are you family friends?"

"Naw. Well, I guess now you can say we are, even though I haven't met this little pipsqueak until today." He gestures at Lucy with his thumb. "I actually met him when he was a bit older than lil' Lucy over here. You see, I've spent most of my years working at shelters, sometimes as a chef, other times running them. Parker here was one of the boys who had stayed with us before. Always a bright one...a stubborn person at that." He gives me a wink, my face heating up at his accolades. I take a sip of water and shake my head. "He never forgot his roots...always coming by to help out whenever he can. And look at him now, designing this place, making somethin' of himself."

Now this is just too much. I roll my eyes. "Come on, I'm no boy scout."

Liz smiles slyly, tugging at her bottom lip in the process. "Now, I happen to think boy scouts are no fun...men who like to get themselves dirty are so much more interesting." She arches her right brow at me, her eyes taking on a teasing glint.

Blood rushes straight to my cock. I'd like to show her how dirty I can get. She doesn't want a clean-cut boy scout. Fuck. She doesn't even know what she's asking for. Her smile slips off her face and her breath catches when she sees my expression. Her face pinkens as she realizes the double entendre. She quickly looks away, the tip of her tongue swiping her plump lips.

"I don't like dirty anybody. They smell," Lucy quips from beside me, oblivious to the awkward moment at the table.

Everyone bursts into laughter. Kindergarten comic timing gold.

This is one of the best nights of my life.

• • •

"She's asleep?" I ask as Liz emerges from Lucy's room.

She puts her fingers to her lips, shushing me, and nods. "Let's go downstairs," she whispers.

We go to the kitchen where I hold up a bottle of merlot in question. She grins and dips her head in acknowledgment. I pour the wine and carry the two glasses to the dining table. We sit down, listening to the soft pitter-patter of the rain, another random summer shower, which is a rare phenomenon but is welcomed all the same, cooling the temperature by at least ten degrees.

"Thank you," she murmurs as she takes the glass from me and takes a healthy sip.

I swirl the glass in front of me, watching the red liquid slosh around and debate my next words. "Liz...I know we haven't started on the best terms. But I want to thank you for giving us a chance. For...giving me, I mean, Lucy, a chance. You've been a lifesaver in so many ways, bringing us so much joy and laughter...all the things missing in his house for too long." My eyes flicker to hers as my voice chokes up and I clear my throat. "Thank you."

Liz's mouth parts, as if speechless. She blinks slowly, her blue eyes pulling me in, so mesmerizing and captivating. She breaks into a wide smile and my stomach does a flip. "My pleasure, Parker. I'm glad things have...worked out."

I slowly reach out to her, taking her delicate, small hand in mine, the touch sending a live wire through my body. I swallow, staring at our interlinked hands as I circle my thumb over the smooth flesh. She shivers. The room warms as my entire body is focused on the small area of contact. My mind wars with my heart, one telling me to come clean and tell the truth, the other telling me to throw caution to the wind and let the chips fall where they may.

Ding.

Liz's phone chimes with an incoming notification. She bites her lip again, apparently flustered as she swipes the screen. She giggles at whatever she sees there. I arch my brow in question as she looks up.

"I just found a distant relative, Kim. She apparently lives in Orange County. So, we may meet up too."

"Hm. Small world. Where did you find her?" My fingers are still on her hand. A sudden chill runs through my body.

She smiles and types out a response. "I'm on this app called the Genetic Genie. It's a surprise project for my parents' upcoming anniversary. I'm creating a family tree of epic proportions. It has taken years of my time to get this far."

My hand slips from hers, and I pick up my wineglass, staring at its contents. Blood-red liquid. My heartbeats thud loudly in my ears as the warmth of my earlier good mood dissipates into a chill of something resembling fear. "So...are you done with your project?" I take a sip and swallow the acidic juices.

Liz looks up and tilts her head to the side. "Almost. There are a few people who haven't responded and some who have but ended up ghosting me. I'll probably try a last-ditch attempt to contact them or to look them up some other way. There are a few folks I want to circle back and check in on. Maybe I'll have James hire someone to look into them."

"Maybe you should let sleeping dogs lie. Maybe they don't want to be contacted."

She frowns. "Why?"

I shrug, staring at the dark living room. "Just a suggestion." My heart thumps as the alcohol burns through my veins, softening my inhibitions. *Is this my third glass?*

"You're being weird."

"Just saying, this project sounds like it takes up a lot of your time. If you use the time to date, maybe you'll find your fairytale prince and will be well on your way to your mythical castle, living your happily ever after." I scoff, setting down my glass, my fingers gripping the stem. *She can't continue to do this. Stop, Liz. Stop before you get hurt.*

"What? That's completely uncalled for." She sets her drink down, pushes her chair away from the table, and stands.

I look at her, taking in her fiery stance. *I know she thinks I'm insane.* I slowly stand and crowd over her. "I'm just telling the truth." A muscle twitches in my jaw as I ball up my fists. *This is for the best.* I repeat to myself. *This is for the best.*

She flinches, her eyes blazing fire, and she retorts, "What on earth is *wrong* with you?"

My nostrils flare as I mirror her posture. "What? You know I'm an asshole. I run hot and cold, right? That's what you told me before. This is nothing new."

"What the fuck? You know what? I'm so done with this." She spins around and starts walking away from me.

My body acts before my mind can catch up. I reach her in a few long strides and stand in front of her.

She glares at me and growls, "Get out of my way."

"No." She steps forward as I mirror her movements, desperation flooding my system.

"What do you want from me?" she grinds out.

"I don't know!" I bellow. *I must look like a lunatic. The whiplash moods. She doesn't know. She can't know.*

Liz flings her hands free from mine as she backs away. "I don't know what has gotten into you tonight. I-I thought we were doing fine. Good even. We were getting along...or even more..."

I chuckle humorlessly, the laughter sounding hollow to my ears. "What? You just thought because we made out a few times we're close now? I was just pissed, and you were someone convenient for me to take my anger out on. You thought what? That we'll be together because of that?" The lies pour out of my mouth like bullets from a gun, each sentence a self-inflicted wound.

I hate myself.

But this is for the best. This way, she won't ever find out. And she won't ever hold out hope for you. The impossible dream that is doomed from the start.

Tears gather in Liz's eyes and her lips wobble, her anguish a blade across my wrist, her tears are my blood, falling freely with no hope of stopping.

"I hate you." I recoil at the well-deserved words. *I hate myself for hurting her.*

She whips around to run toward the staircase but pivots at the last second and races toward the front door instead.

I chase after her, my steps echoing in the marble foyer. "Where are you going?"

"Out! I need to get some fresh air and get away from *you!*"

She grabs her keys from the hook on the wall and flings open the door, darting into the night, oblivious to the light rain.

Plop. Plop. Plop.

The water forms small puddles on the ground. Her steps echo on the wet pathway as she sprints away from the house. I stare at her retreating backside and take a deep breath, hitting my chest with my fist, hoping the pain will take away the ache inside. Nothing does. The ache only deepens in a pain far more tortuous than superficial wounds. Minutes pass by and she doesn't come back. I dial her cell and it rings on the dining table, the sound loud and jarring in the quiet house.

This is for the best.

And that's when I hear the crash.

CHAPTER 16

Liz

I stomp aimlessly down the quiet residential street, the raindrops hitting my face, but I pay no notice, my body too heated from my random fight with Parker just now. Who does he think he is? Why does he think he can just flip a switch on me and expect me to take it? If it wasn't for Lucy, I'd pack my bags and move out right now. *Well, except you have no place to live. You sublet your studio for the entire summer, remember?* I curse under my breath as a splash of water soaks my feet, indicating I just stepped in a large puddle. Damn it, I wasn't thinking...storming out like this in flip-flops and without an umbrella.

A slight chill sets in and I shiver, my body finally catching up to the fact I'm clad in a thin T-shirt and leggings, which are quickly becoming sopping wet. *Now what, Liz? You've made a dramatic exit...what will that accomplish?* I shake my head as the bright lights ahead indicate I'm approaching the intersection to the busy main street. I don't want to go back yet and I'm in no condition to drive, having drank wine a short while ago. As mad as I am, being a responsible adult is still my top priority.

My mind runs through the events of the day, searching for where things went south. I can't be wrong. We shared something last night. He opened up to me. He cried in front of me. We've changed, and not just on the physical attraction front, but on an emotional level too. And today at the shelter, he was so happy. He may have been sweaty and disheveled from the manual labor, but I've never seen him so relaxed. The usual rigidness in his shoulders softened. The dimples were deeper when he smiled. The crinkles in the corner of his eyes natural and not forced when he laughed. The sparkle in his emerald-green gaze when he smiled at me.

Everything was wonderful even after we came back home and put Lucy to bed. Things only went south when I started talking about my family tree project. A thread of unease makes its way to my chest, but I can't figure out the source. I stomp my feet on the ground, creating yet another splash. *What the heck, I'm wet already, anyway.* Parker Wellington is the most infuriating man I've ever come across, and yet I can't bring myself to leave him. It's like there's a masochistic streak in me I didn't know was there before.

It's okay, Liz. You're doing this for Lucy. Two months left and you can be out of his hair. And we can go back to what we were before. Cordial if not slightly cold. Avoiding each other in social situations. Somehow, the thought causes a deep ache in my chest. I don't want to go back to icy Parker and timid Liz. I want the man from the shelter today. I want—

I hear the loud screech of tires before I see the swivel of glaring headlights. My heart jumps to my throat as time slows and I witness a disaster happening in slow motion in front of me. A dark minivan barreling through the intersection T-bones a silver sedan making a left turn at the light.

The crunch of glass shards on the pavement.

The sedan careens toward the curb, stopped by the lamppost three feet from me.

The smell of burning metal and charred rubber.

The screams of passersby.

The slamming of car doors as folks jump out of their vehicles and come running to help.

The shock wears off quickly and my emergency training, part of my schooling as a teacher, kicks into gear. I quickly survey the scene to identify which car seems like it needs more urgent help. A couple climbs out of the minivan, which is now stopped in the middle of the intersection. Their hands cover their mouths as they stare in my direction. I dart toward the sedan, which is wrapped around the lamppost in what could be described as a horrible modern art exhibit. Smoke is coming from under the hood of the wrecked car.

"I've already called the cops. They're nearby and should be here soon," exclaims a teenage boy who appears next to me, a cell phone in his hand. "The operator is still on the line."

I nod and carefully approach the smoking wreck, which looks like it's about to combust at any minute. "Can you give me the phone?" The smoke is now billowing from what I can only assume is the engine or radiator.

He hands it over to me without question.

"Hi, I'm CPR certified and I just happened to see the accident. This sedan has a ton of smoke coming from under the hood. I smell something burning and it seems to be getting worse. There's a sweet smell in the air too." I bite my lip as I walk around the vehicle, my pulse beating wildly as adrenaline courses through me. "There's a lot of smoke, but I see a lady inside the vehicle, and she isn't moving."

"Okay, ma'am. First responders are on their way and should be there shortly. Are there other people around?" a calm voice asks.

"Yes, there are a few people here."

"According to your description, there may be imminent danger. Please stand far away from the scene until the first responders arrive. We don't want to put you or others at risk."

"Okay. I'll hand the phone back to its owner." I toss the phone back to the teenage boy behind me. "Keep her on the line, will you?"

The smoke is getting worse and there are sparks from the hood of the car. Crackling and popping sounds fill the air. Dread coils my stomach. Suddenly, a whooshing sound fills the air followed by a sudden blast of heat. The front of the vehicle bursts into flames, and the fire makes its way to the windshield.

Shit. I look around and still don't see the first responders or hear the shrill sounds of the sirens.

Making a decision, I hurry to the car and pull on the driver's door. It doesn't budge.

Two young men hurry over to me. "Let us help."

One of the men pries open the door and gives it a hard kick, and the door falls to the pavement with a clang. The rain pelts down in a gush, but we hardly notice as the other man takes a pocketknife from the back of his pants and cuts through the seatbelt. Sweat beads down my neck as the heat of the fire creeps close.

We don't have too much time left before it engulfs the car altogether.

"Okay, on the count of three. Keep her steady. Stabilize the head if you can. I'll take her feet." I take a deep breath, coughing from the smoke. "One. Two. Three." We hoist the woman up as the other man joins us and helps support her midsection. We walk ten feet away from the mangled metal and place her on the sidewalk, careful not to move her any more than necessary.

A loud whooshing sound fills the air.

We whip our head toward the sound just in time to see the fire engulfing the driver's seat, making its way to the passenger compartment, where it quickly takes over the car.

"Holy shit," we gasp collectively as the piercing sirens and flashing red and blue lights alert us to the first responders arriving on the scene.

Firefighters, in their yellow uniforms and helmets, come running over with their hose, spraying the fireball with a large torrent of water. Two medics carry a stretcher and the taller one calls out, "Anyone else injured over there?"

We all shake our heads and back away, making room for the professionals to handle the situation. My hands start to tremble and my heart kicks against my rib cage as the severity of the situation finally hits me in the face. *If you walked a few more feet, you could've been hit. You could've died.* Suddenly all my issues cease to matter and all I feel is the bone-chilling fear of losing my family, my friends.

Losing him.

"Get out of my way! Liz!" A desperate voice pierces through my inner chaos. "Liz! Where are you? Oh fuck. Oh fuck."

Parker.

I step out of the shadows as I search for the person behind the deep, gravelly voice I've come to love. My eyes scan the large crowd, my vision impeded by the falling rain.

He stands at the far edge of the crowd, his hands cupping his mouth as he screams, "Liz! Where are you?" He whips his head around, his eyes frantic as he pulls at his hair.

"Parker! Over here!" I yell, waving my hands above my head. My feet begin to move as I push against the people standing between me and the man who has become so important to me, a man who makes me feel things I don't dare name. A thousand emotions flood through me and my heart pounds against my chest, threatening to give out. I need to be by his side this very moment.

His head whips toward me, and he freezes. His hand clenches his sodden shirt, which is sticking to him like a second skin. He breathes harshly as he takes me in, his eyes roving down my body, as if checking to see if I'm fine. Snapping out of his trance, he moves toward me with the desperation of someone lost in the desert, only to see an oasis on the horizon.

The chatter and chaos around us fade into the background.

The flashing lights melt into the darkness.

The crowds blend into the surroundings.

All I see is him.

"Liz!" he hollers, but I don't hear him. The only sounds are the racing heartbeats in my ears; my heart, which now only beats for him. I run toward him, my legs not carrying me fast enough.

Parker reaches me in a few strides and sweeps me up into a crushing embrace. His arms curl tightly around me as he buries his face in my hair. He shakes and shudders, apparently overcome with emotions. I close my eyes, savoring the warmth emanating from his body through the wet cotton. My heart bursts free as half of my soul finally recognizes its other half in him.

"Liz, I thought I lost you," he rasps in my ears as he lifts his head up and cradles my face with tenderness.

I blink rapidly, my blurry vision meeting his mesmerizing green eyes, now smoldering hotter than the fire being put out by the first responders.

Words are unnecessary.

Whatever he sees in my eyes must have been enough for him.

He grips the back of my neck and crashes his mouth against mine in a scorching kiss. I claw at his back as I deepen the kiss. His tongue sweeps into my mouth and sparks fire in my nerves. I can't get enough. I can't get close enough. I moan against his lips as he kisses me with wild abandon like a man who's starving and is finally feasting on his first meal before him. He kisses like a brand, like a man marking his territory. He kisses like he is about to drown underwater and I'm his oxygen tank.

He kisses as if he needs me to live.

Parker sweeps me up in a fireman's carry, and tucks me against him as he strides toward home. Somehow, his house feels like home to me now.

My skin is on fire, the throbbing ache between my legs intensifying with each step he takes. We don't speak, but the loud thumping in his chest tells me everything I need to know. His fingers grip my thighs forcefully, his arms trembling, most likely not from my weight, but from the tightly leashed emotions I can feel inside of him.

Moments later, he slides me to the floor as he shuts the door behind him. The house is quiet except for the sounds of raindrops against the ground outside and the sounds of our harsh breathing. I flatten my back against the wall in the foyer, the coolness behind me doing nothing to douse the burning fire inside me.

He stands a few feet before me, his forest-green eyes darkening with intensity, staring at me, peering into my soul. His hand rakes his tousled, wet hair, and his thumb slides across his lips, now pressed in a firm line. With every breath he takes, his hard muscles ripple, translucent against the white shirt plastered to him. His hands clench and release as his nostrils flare. Seemingly making a decision, he prowls toward me, his steps silent against the marble floor, yet resounding at the same time.

Parker steps up to me, the muscles in his body tightly coiled as he drags his large palm over my stomach, sliding over the wet shirt. He dips his forehead toward mine and my eyes flutter close. His hand travels to my neck as he thumbs the wild pulse there.

"I'm sorry. I tried to stay away...but I can't."

With that, he seals his lips on mine as his grip tightens on the back of my neck. I let out a breathy moan as wetness gathers between my legs and my body melts against his. Taking advantage of my parted lips, he slides his tongue in as he sucks on my swollen lips. His tongue duels with mine as he thrusts in a motion akin to sex. He devours my lips in a desperate, punishing kiss, setting us both on fire. His hands grip my swollen breasts and the hard nipples prickle to attention. He groans as he cups the weight and flattens himself on me, his steel shaft pressing against my stomach.

I curl one leg against him, desperate to rub his erection against me. I need him. More than anything else. Muttering a curse as we come up for air, he hoists me against him and carries me upstairs to his room. I writhe against him, my skin a live wire as I grind on him, trying to relieve the ache.

"Fuck," he groans as he opens the door to his bedroom.

He drops me onto the bed, and I stare at him. The room is dark except for the moonlight streaming in from the windows. Tugging the edge of his shirt with one hand, he peels off the wet garment, his eyes never leaving mine. The moonlight lovingly caresses every dip and valley of his hard, corded muscles. His golden-brown hair gleams silver in the low light. His chest moves with exertion, with each ragged breath.

My pussy involuntarily clenches as he drags his sweatpants and briefs off in one motion and he stands naked proudly before me, his rigid cock, so thick and long, curling against his stomach. I bite my bottom lip as my hands involuntarily snake up to cup my heavy breasts. I pluck at my nipples, my legs parting on the bed and arching up, wanting him to fill the space, my body asking for something I have no experience in and yet desperately need. A necessity akin to oxygen and sustenance.

His nostrils flare as he stares at my fingers, which are eagerly twisting the sensitive nubs. I let out a whimper, and he grunts, his hand fisting his hard cock, which is red and angry-looking.

"Take it off," he commands, his low voice sending shivers down my body.

Biting my bottom lip, I tug my shirt off me, my breasts springing free in a bounce. His molten eyes latch on to the movement as he closes his hands around his cock in a punishing grip.

"Keep the panties on," he instructs next, his eyes hooded as he stalks toward me.

His terse commands send bolts of heat to my core. I slide my leggings off, leaving me clad in a thin scrap of white lace, which I'm sure is translucent with my juices.

He climbs on top of the bed and hovers above me, his biceps flexing with effort. "You're so beautiful, Liz. You're killing me," he groans as he trails his nose up my neck.

"Parker. I need...I need..." I babble incoherently as I'm swept away by the tides of pleasure.

He brings my hands above my head and locks them there in a death grip. "I know. I'll give you what you need."

I wiggle on the bed, thrusting my breasts in the air, desperate for him to touch me, to do anything other than stare at me. As if he hears my prayers, he settles his weight on top of me, his hardness against my softness, our bodies moving against each other like flint stones sparking fire. With one hand still keeping my hands pinned above my head, he slips his other hand between our bodies, trailing over my belly button piercing, before dipping his finger in my wet heat and mewling sounds fill the air. Sounds apparently made by me.

"So fucking wet. All for me," he grunts as he slides two fingers in, and I whimper at the pleasurable intrusion.

"Yes. Oh God. Please..." I thrash on the bed as the pressure builds between my legs.

"Look at that greedy pussy sucking my fingers in." He swirls his thumb around my swollen clit, and I arch off the bed with a keening cry. He adds a third finger and I flinch from the pain, which only serves to heighten the pleasure. "Yes, take what you need, Liz. Fuck my fingers," he rasps as he sucks hard on my neck and nips on a tender spot, the sharp pinch of pain sending me over the edge. The dam bursts and I come with a scream, my juices gushing out in a torrent.

"Fuck, a screamer and a squirter," he grunts, "all mine." His fingers slow, the sounds of the slurping loud and obscene in the dark room, but I don't care as my body turns to mush in the aftermath.

He grinds against me, his hard shaft teasing the over-sensitized nerves, and I struggle to shift away, but his grip on me holds. I part my mouth in a gasp as his lips move from the tender spot in my neck to capture my lips once again. He plunders my mouth like a pirate raiding a vessel full of treasures. I don't know where he begins and where I end.

Parker reaches to his nightstand and pulls out a condom, the metal foil glinting in the moonlight. Tearing off the wrapper with his mouth, he slides it onto his turgid length. He spreads my legs wide and hoists me against him, his swollen tip poised at my entrance.

"You sure?" he asks, his deep voice breathless with exertion, as if the question is taking every ounce of energy left in him.

My eyes find his, searching for an answer to a question on the tip of my tongue, a question I don't want to confront yet. The stormy greens are overtaken by the dilated pupils. He stares back at me, his face intense as a muscle twitches in his cheek. I nod, knowing I'm agreeing to something far more than just sex.

His eyes flare as he captures my lips in another drugging kiss. "I'm sorry," he whispers as he slams in one full thrust, groaning in what appears to be pleasure or agony. Tears spring to my eyes at the sharp pain as I clench my legs tightly around his back. "I'm sorry...I'll make it better." He kisses my tears away, his gentle touch at odds with the coiled tension in his muscles.

The ache dulls, and he lets go of my hands, his kisses gentle as he plays with my nipples. Sparks of pleasure begin anew inside me, and I stroke his back, reassuring him as he trembles on top of me, holding back, struggling to leash the beast within him. Parker slips his hands between my legs and finds my hard nub. He twirls the bud in his fingers as sharp pleasure courses through me, combining with the fullness of him inside me in a heady sensation. I moan as more wetness seeps out of me and I arch my hips, needing to relieve the building pressure.

"Oh fuck. I can't hold on, Liz. I can't be gentle."

I shush him, gripping him hard and tilt my body back as much as I can, and impale myself back on him, the sensation drawing a whimper from me.

"Take me, Parker. Fuck me hard." *Fuck me like you love me.* The unbidden thought rises to the surface of my mind as I wiggle against him, each movement pouring gasoline on the fire. It's not enough. I need more.

With a roar, his restraint snaps and he plunges inside me, hammering me in earnest. The rapid slaps of skin against skin reverberate in the room as I cry with pleasure at each thrust.

He intertwines his hands with mine and presses them into the bed as he moves at a punishing pace, his eyes closed, his face taut.

"This is so good. You take me so well, just like I thought you would," he groans as he pistons himself inside me, his thick cock bottoming out with each thrust. He bends his mouth toward my chest and captures a hardened nipple between his teeth, the sharp twinge adding to the liquid fire between my legs. I arch up as he sucks my nipple in forcefully, his cock relentless inside me. I feel so full. The best type of feeling there ever was.

The burning pleasure climbs up rapidly as he throws my legs across his shoulders, sliding in even deeper, the tip of his hard cock hitting a sensitive region inside, eliciting a scream from me.

"Yes, scream for me, Liz. Let the world know who you belong to."

I open my mouth in a silent gasp, the fire gathering between my legs and my muscles tense as I balance on the precipice.

"Who do you belong to? Who is fucking up this pussy real good right now?" he rasps against my breast, his pace unrelenting.

"You, Parker! Only you," I scream as I combust and fall into the abyss of passion and pleasure. The walls of my pussy throb against his hard cock and, with a few more punishing thrusts, he shudders against me, coming with a loud groan. Capturing my lips once again, his teeth tug at my bottom lip as I drink in his essence. He squeezes his fingers around mine as we slowly come down from the high.

My enigma. Baggage, complications, and everything coming along with him. The rush of feelings nearly floors me as I suddenly realize, what others may find premature, but I know is true in the core of my body. In my gut.

Parker is the prince in my fairytale.

Logic—what I should want, what I thought I wanted all cease to matter.

I never stood a chance.

CHAPTER 17

Parker

Liz burrows her head against my chest as we lay on my bed in the aftermath of what I can only describe as the most transcendent sex of my life. I smooth my hands on the silky skin of her shoulders as we lay there in peaceful silence, listening to the soft rain outside our windows.

"I'm sorry for yelling at you earlier," I murmur against her hair.

She snuggles closer, curling her leg over my stomach. "Can you tell me what happened?"

I hesitate. I know I can't tell her the truth, but she deserves more than an apology. "Our conversation triggered an unhappy memory for me, and I overreacted irrationally." I press a soft kiss into her hair, hoping she doesn't ask me to elaborate.

Seconds pass as her fingers draw circles on my pecs. She props her head up with her arm and stares into my eyes. "I'll be honest with you. It wasn't okay what you did back there. I don't know what's causing your abrupt mood swings but I hope...in the future, you'll communicate with me instead."

Swallowing the lump in my throat, I nod. That's fair. Her expectations are completely reasonable.

She sighs as she lays her head back on my chest. "Maybe someday you can tell me more." She doesn't push me. Liz is considerate that way.

Turning over so I'm leaning above her, I stare into the blue pools of her eyes, dark in the moonlight. I brush a strand of golden hair off her face and smile. Cradling her cheeks with my hands, I whisper, "I know what we did means a lot to you, and I don't take any of it lightly. This means a lot to me as well." I press a soft kiss on her inviting lips. "This is serious for me." *For as long as you'll have me...and longer.*

Liz's eyes shine with intense emotions as she lifts her hands to caress the roughness of my jaw, her touch eliciting shivers inside me. The three special words, a phrase I've only told one woman in my life before her, are on the tip of my tongue, the emotion overriding everything else. I swallow the lump in my throat as I stare at this woman before me. This woman who's brought me back to life. This woman breathed oxygen into me when I was drowning in full view of everyone. This woman who's seen past all of my facades, who's seen my ugliness, and not only does not shirk away but instead gives me her all.

She smiles as moisture gathers in her eyes. "Is it always like this?"

She doesn't need to tell me what she's referring to.

"No, it's never like this for me. Ever," I murmur, staring intently into the bottomless blue of her gaze. And it's true, I've never connected with anyone as much as I have with her. It's as if our souls have joined together, forming a new entity which is unlike its individual parts. It's as if my heart has finally found its missing pieces, and now I'm finally made whole. "It's only ever been like this with you."

Her eyes flutter shut as I lean in and press my lips against an errant tear wetting her cheek.

A kiss on her eye to represent my gratitude to her for seeing through my armor.

A kiss on her lips for her words of encouragement and understanding in my dark moments.

A kiss on her ear for her keen ability to understand what I'm not saying with words.

A kiss on her heart for her loving soul, her generosity, for her existence in my life.

My lips trail back up from her chest to her mouth as I pour the words I cannot say in a deep kiss. My heart feels raw, my soul reawakened. She clutches the back of my head as my hands tenderly cradle her face. I drink in her moans, her sighs, her breaths as her scent mingles with mine in an irresistible combination. Her softness yields to my hardness. My cock stiffens, but I hold myself back, knowing she must be sore from her first time.

Disentangling myself, I pull back and smile at her, a deep warmth spreading from the deepest depths of my soul to my entire body. Liz returns the smile with tenderness.

Words are unnecessary.

I curl her body against mine—her being the small spoon to my big spoon, and her breathing slowly evens out as she falls asleep in my arms. My eyelids grow heavy, and I soon drift off in the deepest sleep I've had in years.

• • •

"Daddy, why do you and Lizzy look so tired?" Lucy takes a sip of milk as she spears a sliced strawberry with her fork at breakfast. Liz chokes on a mouthful of ice water as her face turns dark red. I bite my cheek to keep from laughing as I hand her a tissue. I may have woken her up once or twice last night as I went down on her, eager to explore every inch of her body, to give this woman all the pleasure she deserves, even if it didn't end with my cock in her tight heat.

Struggling to keep a straight face, I reply, "Well, Lizzy and Daddy are adults...and sometimes, we're busy doing...adult things." I glance at Liz, who has recovered from her choking fit but is currently staring at the plate in front of her, her skin still dark pink. "And sometimes, because of these things we must do, we don't get to sleep as much at night. So that's why we look tired today."

Lucy nods, seemingly appeased with my vague response, as she munches on the strawberry. "So, when I go to Skylar's today, you and Lizzy can rest. Poor Daddy. Poor Lizzy."

I pat her hand. How am I so lucky to have such a sweet, considerate little girl to call my own? "Right. We'll definitely be resting for sure." I sneak another sly glance at Liz, who is as mute as ever. I think the pink will permanently remain on her skin.

Lucy finishes the fruit on her plate and turns toward Liz. "Aren't you hot today, Lizzy? Why are you wearing that?"

I burst out laughing as I sit back in my chair, smirking, waiting for Liz to gather her composure to respond. She shoots daggers at me, and I give her a wink. *Nope, not going to help you out of that one.* Liz is wearing a gray turtleneck in eighty-degree weather while Lucy and I are in short-sleeves and shorts. She berated me earlier for the love bites and hickeys I left all over her smooth skin.

My dick hardens at the memories of the best twelve hours of my life.

I didn't escape unscathed, as I have pink scratch marks all over my chest and neck, but I wear my battle wounds with pride. I cross my arms and stare at her flustered face.

"Um...Lucy, I'm just feeling a little bit cold this morning."

"But you're sweating. I see it on your forehead."

Liz places a hand on her damp forehead in mock horror. "Oh my! You're right! Maybe I'm coming down with something. I do need to rest today, then." If looks could kill, I think I would've died a thousand times just now.

"Okay. I hope you feel better, Lizzy." Lucy smiles, her dimples showing as she hops off her chair, and runs up to her room to change for her playdate with her best friend. Liz begins clearing the table.

Once she is out of sight, I sidle up to Liz, who's currently washing the plates. I curl myself around her, relishing in the scent of vanilla and the warmth of her body. Bending down, I whisper in her ear, "I'll take Lucy to Skylar's..." I press a kiss against her ear, eliciting a soft moan from her. She's so responsive to me. "So you don't need to show up looking ridiculous in a turtleneck."

She elbows me hard as she turns around. I laugh at the out-raged expression on her face, the sound seemingly foreign to my years. How long has it been since I've laughed like this?

"I hope you're very proud of yourself." She wipes her hands on a white dishtowel and crosses her arms, glaring at me.

"Oh trust me, I definitely am." Another hard shove.

"Ugh! You're impossible!"

I tug her close against me as I lean in for a kiss. "Only for you, baby. Only for you."

Liz melts against me as her eyes flutter shut. Lucy comes skipping, her footfalls quick and light against the hardwood floor. We quickly spring apart and I nudge Liz out of the way to finish rinsing the dishes.

"I'm ready, Lizzy!"

Putting the last of the dishes on the drying rack, I respond, "Lucy, Daddy will be taking you to Skylar's today so Lizzy can rest."

"Okay!"

I move to grab my keys but pause before I round the corner. Turning toward Liz, I murmur, "We should talk about this tonight." She gives me a firm nod, her tongue wetting her lips. I return a reassuring smile before I follow Lucy to the door.

The drive to Skylar's house is quick and cheerful, with Lucy prattling on about the many things they'll do when she gets there. The sun is warm against my face, the weather is balmy and comfortable, and the birds are chirping, whistling dulcet melodies as they congregate on trees. I drum my fingers on the steering wheel, suddenly overcome with an urge to start singing myself.

What the fuck is happening to me?

We ring the doorbell and moments later, a little girl with brown hair and a ponytail welcomes us with her dad in tow. The girls greet each other with a shriek as they disappear into the large, two-story colonial home.

"Thanks, Chris. I'll pick up Lucy after dinner tonight. Call me if anything comes up."

Chris smiles and shakes my hand. "Sure thing, man. So, it's a day of freedom for you today. You got any plans? Please don't tell me you're going into the office like the last few times again?"

I shake my head. The office is the last thing on my mind right now. "Nope, not the office today. Just going to chill and relax."

He arches a brow. "Wait a second. You? Chill and relax? Where's Parker Wellington, and what did you do to him?"

I shrug. "Got to let loose sometimes."

Chris narrows his eyes at me. "You found a woman, didn't you?"

"What? No."

"Dude, congrats, man! The glow on your face totally gives you away." He slaps a hand on my shoulder. "We dads gotta look out for each other. I'll be your wingman anytime. Just say the word and Lucy can come and hang with us." He gives me a wink. Fatherhood solidarity right there.

Shaking my head, I say goodbye to him and head back to my car, whistling under my breath. My phone pings with a few text alerts from my "Asshole Friends" group.

James: Jess wants me to remind you dinner is on Friday night at six thirty. Get off work on time, guys. And by that, I mean you, Parker. Be there or be square.

Steven: Wish I could be there, but it looks like I won't be able to make it down today. Still up in SF with Charles. Unfortunately, because this SF trip is taking longer than expected, we're changing our flight to fly straight back to NYC.

Parker: We'll be there. You sure you don't need us to bring anything?

Steven: Btw, Charles says hi.

I roll my eyes at the Charles's comment, but I'm feeling very forgiving today.

Parker: Tell Charles hi as well. He's welcome to visit anytime.

Steven: You sure? *Insert skeptical face*

James: The guy is a punk, right? And no, we got the food covered.

Parker: Stop being so jealous, James. Green is definitely not your color.

Steven: Pot calling the kettle black, Parker. Btw, Charles is petitioning to join this chat group. He says we're having too much fun.

I smirk and pocket the phone before driving as fast as I can under the speed limit to go back home.

Back to her.

Liz is lounging on the egg-shaped recliner on the backyard deck, completely engrossed in her book. Her caramel strands are arranged in a loose top bun, and she has changed into more warm-weather-appropriate attire consisting of a white ribbed tank top and a pair of rainbow-striped cotton shorts. Three strawberry-colored love bites mar the smooth column of her neck. Satisfaction floods me at seeing my marks on her. Her mouth quirks to the side as she flips a page. My breath catches in my throat as I take in every detail of this image before me to file away for safekeeping so I can revisit it later.

Maybe I can play a game of pretend. A game where we're just simple Parker and Liz. A world where there's no past, no future, just the present. A world where we can simply exist and be together. No secrets. No drama. No baggage. We can live in my castle, be in our own little bubble, and forget everything else.

If only.

My eyes burn and I clear the pins and needles in my throat. Liz looks up and bestows upon me a glorious smile, causing my heart to skip a few beats. My chest warms and I smile back as I walk toward her. Climbing into the large lounger big enough to fit two people, I gather her in my arms. The scent of vanilla mixes with the floral perfume from the flowers currently in bloom. She tucks her head against my chest as she looks up.

"Is Lucy happy?"

"Definitely. She and Skylar act like they haven't seen each other in years, when it's only been a week or so."

Liz chuckles softly before looking down at her book and flipping another page.

"Did you get to the happily ever after yet?"

"No, I'm at the seventy to eighty percent mark. That means things are about to happen and the lovers will break up."

"Why do you read these books if you already know the 'formula'?" I ask, my fingers in air quotes.

She snuggles closer to me and takes a whiff of my shirt. She sighs in contentment. "I like to see how people overcome obstacles. As idealistic as I am, I know life will throw us some curveballs. But I think true love can conquer them all."

Love.

Something I haven't thought possible for me anymore. And yet, here she is, in my arms. The feelings from last night come back in a resurgence, the wave stronger than before.

"I love you, Liz." I guess I'm throwing caution to the wind. I'm tired of fighting my feelings toward her.

She sits up, her deep-blue eyes sparkling with the tiny flecks of gold glinting in the sun. Blinking away the moisture gathering on her long lashes, she reaches out and cradles my face in her palm. I close my eyes and lean into her gentle touch. "Don't say it back. I know this is an important thing for you. Don't rush through it. Think it through. I...I just want to be true to myself once and for all and to let you know."

"Parker..." She swallows, her voice thick with emotion. She seals her lips on mine and curls her arms around my neck. Her fingers clutch my hair as she pours herself into the embrace. Tangling her lips with mine, she fervently kisses me, answering my question without words. I grip her tightly against me as I return her ardor, my heart beating in sync with hers. Pulling back slightly, her breaths coming in quick gasps, she stares into my eyes and murmurs, "I know you hold a lot of things inside of you. I wish... I wish one day you'll want to share them with me." She smiles softly, her eyes warm as she leans in and once again presses her lips to mine.

I can't. If I do, you'll get hurt. And you'll leave me.

Unable to respond without telling her more lies, I cradle her face in my palms and kiss her like there's no tomorrow. Every day with her is a beautiful gift. One I'll treasure always. I'm not naïve.

I know one day, things will implode. But until then, I'll love her as long as she'll have me. I'll love her because I know I won't let myself love anyone else after her.

Breaking our kiss, she lays her head back on my chest, her fingers drawing circles on my abs. She looks at the ink on my biceps.

"*Memento mori*. What does your tattoo mean?"

I kiss her hair and reply, "It's Latin for 'remember you must die.' I got it when I was eighteen to commemorate my dad. It was a reminder death may be around the corner and I mustn't waste my life. It was also the reason I decided to start my firm with my partner. To try and make something of myself because our time on earth has no guarantees. I want to leave my mark on it before I go."

"Hm. I see. I guess that's true, if not a bit morbid."

I laugh as I twist a lock of her hair around my fingers. "What about you? What's the story with your piercing?"

She sits up and looks at me sheepishly. "It's not as deep of a meaning as your tattoo." Biting her lip, she continues, "Everyone just expects me to be miss good girl or miss nice girl. I guess it was my little act of rebellion when I was in college. And plus, I thought it looked hot."

I guffaw and draw her close. "Damn straight, it's very hot."

"So...you wanted to talk about us?"

I smile into her hair. Straightforward Liz, never one to beat around the bush. I sit up straight and cradle her face in my palms. "Liz, I know I told you this last night, but I want to tell you again. I don't take what we did lightly. I know this means a lot to you and it's the same way for me."

She stares at me mutely, her entire body stilling as if waiting for me to continue.

"If you'll have me..." *And until you don't want me...* "I want to be yours. In public. You're not any secret I want to hide from the world," I say as I clasp her hands in mine.

Liz breaks into a watery smile and nods. "I'd love that, Parker." She squeezes my palms excitedly but sobers up and adds, "I'm okay with us telling friends, but I think maybe we should be more careful around Lucy? She's so little...may be better to wait and tell her later."

"I agree." She took the words out of my mouth. So responsible and thoughtful, my sweet Liz. Leaning over her, I press a soft kiss on her lips. She releases a sigh of pleasure as she wraps her hands around me. I tease the seam of her lips with my tongue before seeking entrance, our mouths moving against each other in an ancient dance.

Our kiss turns heated, and I trail kisses down her throat, suckling at her fluttering pulse. She moans and climbs on top of my lap, the oval recliner swinging softly under our weight. She whips off her shirt and her full breasts bounce with the movement, her pinkish-brown nipples perking up under the open air. I groan, my cock stiffening in a matter of seconds. It's as if my body is finally waking up after over three years of slumber. Her tongue darts out to lick her fingers before she swirls them around her nipples, tugging at the hard nubs, her eyes seducing as she holds my gaze.

"Fuck, where did you learn that?"

She leans back, basking in the sunlight as she plays with her breasts and gyrates against the hard bulge in front of my shorts. "I may have been a virgin, but I do read things..." She opens her eyes and looks at me, biting down on her lip. "And watch things."

My cock stiffens at the thought of her playing with herself while watching "things." I grit my teeth and grunt, "You sure you're up for this?" My voice ghosts over her ear as she trembles. She understands my question. My lovemaking is rough even for someone experienced, and she was a virgin.

Was.

My cock hardens even more when I remember the smidge of blood on the condom last night. The caveman in me roars with pride.

Liz moves faster against me, our chair swinging more intensely, but none of us pays any attention. She nods and tilts her head back, her eyes fluttering close. "Y-yes. I need you, Parker. I need you right now." She writhes against my body like she can't get enough of me. She whimpers, her mewls driving me insane.

I'm going to blow without being inside her.

"Shorts off, now. Show me how much you want my cock."

She moans as she drags off her shorts and panties. I quickly pull down my pants to my knees, too impatient to undress fully. The silver stud in her bellybutton shines under the sun. She settles back on top of me, as naked as the day she was born while I'm still dressed. This is more erotic than any wet dream I've ever had.

Poising herself at my entrance, she rocks against the turgid tip. With each grind of her hips, the purple tip slips into her soaking wet heat, but she withdraws, leaving me on edge, before repeating the motion over and over again. I grip her waist tightly as I grit my teeth, trying to hold back, trying to let her run the show.

She leans in and whispers, "I'm on birth control for my periods."

I freeze. My patience is held on by a thread.

"I'm clean. Haven't been with anyone since Abby."

Her eyes widen at the implication, and I slam her hips down on me, impaling her in one firm stroke. She moans at the intrusion, and I nearly die from the pleasure of being inside her bare.

She moves on top of me, her rhythm sporadic, hinting at her inexperience. I take over, keeping her hips still as I thrust into her from below. Her slick heat grips every inch of me and without the condom, the sensations are one hundred times more intense. Her breasts jiggle with each movement and I bring my face to one of her large nipples and suck the swollen bud.

So sweet. So fucking fantastic.

Liz mewls, her erotic cries loud in the garden. I hope none of my neighbors are around, but if they are, they'll know she is mine.

Mine to fuck. Mine to love. Mine to possess.

"Fuck me, fuck me, oh fuck me," she chants as she tosses her head back, her hands playing with her beautiful tits.

Our movements quicken as we both chase the pinnacle. Her dripping, wet heat grips my thick cock with each thrust. I spread her ass cheeks as I angle her differently, hitting a deeper spot. She starts panting, her eyes rolling back, and I bring my hand to the front and tease her clit.

"Parker!" she cries as her juices squirt out of her and she comes, her entire body shaking with pleasure. Her throbbing heat strangles my cock and I release a guttural moan, emptying myself inside her, filling her up, each squirt of cum eliciting shivers in both of us.

Madness. Our love is madness. And I never, ever want to be sane again.

"**R**eady, baby?" I wrap my fingers around hers as we walk up to James and Jess's condo in Manhattan Beach. The temperature is always ten degrees cooler and it's a tad more humid down by the coast. The skies are clear tonight and still glow bluish purple from the remnants of the sunset. The air smells of the ocean, salty and brisk. Lucy is with Skylar again today. Chris gave me the slyest of side-eyes known to man when I dropped her off earlier. I don't even bother denying my newfound relationship status. It's been a few days since we got together, and every day feels better than the last and I finally feel like I can breathe again.

Liz grips my fingers tightly, her hand a little clammy. "You think they'll be okay with us?"

"Why wouldn't they be?"

"I have no idea. I'm just very nervous." She glues herself by my side as we stand in front of the door, ready to ring the doorbell. "I've never brought a guy home as my boyfriend to family and friends before."

My heart warms at her declaration, and I want to shout to the rooftops. *This woman is mine, Parker Wellington's, and I'll be the only man she'll bring home to her family and friends from now on.* If only life works the way I want it to.

I pat her hand in reassurance. "We'll be fine. You'll see." I ring the doorbell.

"Come in, the door's unlocked!" Melanie screeches from inside. It appears we aren't the first to arrive.

My pulse speeds up for some unknown reason. It's been years since I've brought anyone special to meet my friends and family too. Somehow, with Liz, this feels even more significant. I give her a gentle squeeze and push open the door.

"Hey, guys, we brought dessert." Liz swings the bag in her other hand as we walk inside the dim, soothing living room of white and turquoise colors. Her hand grips mine tightly as she smiles at our friends.

"You guys didn't need to, we have enou—" James strides out of the kitchen, wearing an apron over a simple V-neck shirt and jeans, with Jess right behind him, and stops mid-step when he takes in our interlocked hands.

Click.

A small flash illuminates James's shocked face as Jess shakes with laughter.

"You're welcome," chirps Emily, who is leaning over the back of the sofa with her phone pointed at James. She looks down at her photo, apparently pleased with her work, and starts typing away. "Sending this to Steven."

Melanie shrieks as she comes flying over to us in a flash of bright pink from her summer dress. Her long ponytail nearly whips Liz in the face as she comes to a stop a foot away. "You guys are *together*, together?"

I turn to look at Liz, whose cheeks are flushed red as I bite down on my lip to keep from smiling too much. "Yes," I respond on her behalf. "It's pretty new."

James apparently unfreezes himself and furrows his brows. "Ems, why are you sending a picture of me to Steven?"

Emily looks up, a teasing glint in her eyes. "It's not every day when you see the man your wife has dated before you, who is now your best friend, come to your house, now holding your sister's hand in an apparent display of romantic affiliation." She exhales.

"Whew, that's a mouthful." Melanie snorts and gives her an air high-five.

I roll my eyes. "Guys, it was one date and one dance. How long will you hold this over my head?"

"Forever!" Melanie and Emily chorus.

My phone chimes with a text from a newly created chat group.

Emily: Steven, this is what the five bucks was for. Exhibit A: James looking flabbergasted at Parker and Liz's new relationship.

A few seconds later, the phone dings again. Steven is attached to his phone, as always.

Steven: Dude, Melanie should've bet more. It took me fifteen minutes at Parker's place to figure out the dude's obsessed with Liz.

Melanie groans out loud and types a reply.

Melanie: Steven! We spent seven minutes in the closet talking about investments. You couldn't have told me this little observation then? I would've raised the stakes right then and there!

Emily: My bro, between this and my birthday party, you're now back in my good graces.

Steven: Cue eye-roll.

Jess walks up and smiles warmly at us. "I'm so happy for you guys. Two of my most favorite people in the world together."

Liz grins shyly back at her as I let go of her hand to take the desserts to the kitchen. The girls giggle behind me as they gather together, no doubt to interrogate Liz about how we ended up together. I hope Liz tells them the PG version of events.

I walk into the clean, bright kitchen, which used to be mainly white when it was James's bachelor pad. Now, the space has Jess's colorful touches in it, from the bright terrycloth dishtowels to the rainbow-colored pots and pans, of which a few are on the stove with a fire burning brightly underneath them. I open the stainless-steel refrigerator and put the freshly made fruit tart inside. Shutting the door, I find myself face-to-face with a serious-looking James.

"Shit. What are you doing standing there like that? Save the glowering alpha male for Jess."

James crosses his arms, narrowing his piercing blue eyes. "So, you and my sister, huh?"

I lean back on the countertop and mirror his stance. "Yes."

"Didn't think to run it by me?"

I arch my brow. "What are we, in the nineteenth century? We're dating, not getting married." My heart skips a beat at the mention of marriage. Where did the thought come from?

His eyes widen as if the same thing crossed his mind. "So, are you two serious?"

My jaw clenches tightly as I slowly exhale. "Yes, it is. As long as she'll have me."

James relaxes a smidge at my answer and stands next to me, leaning against the counter as we stare at the food cooking on the stove. The smell of beef stew and some aromatic soup fill the kitchen and my stomach growls.

"You know, my sister is a hopeless romantic. She's been holding out for her ideal relationship. She has had it in her mind since we were little she wants what our parents have. In her mind, things are simple. Man meets woman. They fall in love. They get married and live happily ever after."

I nod, understanding where James is coming from and dreading what he's going to say next.

"As you probably know, she's a sweet soul and a simple person. She deserves to find someone who loves her and puts her in the forefront."

I kick my heel out and roll the tense muscles in my shoulders.

James turns to me, his baritone voice laced with warning. "Parker, both you and I know you're not a simple person. You may appear to be the charming, successful man on the outside. But we both know you have something more going on inside of you."

He pauses and grabs two bottles of water from the counter and tosses one to me. He continues, "I'll be honest with you since we're good friends. You know Jess and I never want to push you to talk to us about anything. We want to respect your privacy and we figure you'll open up to us when you're ready...if you're ever ready. But if you're with Liz, please make sure you tell her what you're holding back from us. Relationships can't be based on secrets. I don't want her to get hurt later on when she bites off more than she can chew."

An icy chill settles in my stomach as James's words hit home. What he's saying is true, of course, but something I don't want to think about. To protect her, I won't ever tell her the truth. I can't. But where does that leave us? She deserves so much more than me. She should be with someone who doesn't carry darkness inside of him. What if I suck up all of her light?

The sound of blood rushing in my ears distracts me from my thoughts and I grip the cool marble counter behind me for support. No, Liz knows you better than anyone else, even if she doesn't know everything. She still chose you. Things can work out somehow...and if they don't, at least you'll have this time period for your memories.

I twist the lid off the bottle and take a sip, the cool liquid wetting my suddenly parched throat. "I understand what you mean, James. I can't guarantee what will happen in the future, but I'll tell you this..." I turn to him, so he can see the sincerity in my eyes, "I'll protect Liz as much as I can. As long as I can. The last thing I want is for her to get hurt, least of all by me."

James holds my gaze, his eyes scrutinizing something before he nods, apparently appeased by what he saw there. He slaps his hand on my shoulder. "Love you, man. Just know I'll always be here for you, no matter what happens."

My eyes prickle at the sentiment. I don't deserve the Chapmans. I nod and pat his hand in acknowledgment, my heart suddenly full, so full I don't know what to do with this feeling.

"Come on, let's grab some refreshments for the ladies. And you may want to interrupt them before Liz shares any embarrassing stories of you." James grins at me, breaking the solemn atmosphere in the kitchen.

Chuckling under my breath, I grab a few more bottles of water and head back out to the living room to rejoin the group. The girls are giggling in hushed voices, leaving no doubt as to who they're talking about. I walk behind Liz, who's sitting on the sofa, her legs curled up underneath her, and hand her a bottle of water over her shoulder. I dip my head down and kiss her lightly on her cheek. She shivers.

"Awww...you two are so sweet. It's nauseating," Emily comments, her sardonic tone betrayed by the bright smile on her face.

Melanie sighs. "True love. I'm still waiting for my turn."

"Not for me." Emily shakes her head as she clutches the bottle in her hands. "Nope, not for me," she murmurs quietly.

"So, where's Lucy tonight?" James inquires.

"She's with her best friend from school. Her parents offered to watch her so I can have some 'adult only' time. That's why we can't stay late tonight because we have to swing by to pick her up at a reasonable hour."

Melanie exhales loudly. "Ah, to be a kid again. Summer vacation, sleepovers, and playdates. Sign me up."

Liz asks, "So, how's the bookstore gig, Melanie? Any hot men fall for your bookish charms, yet?

"Ugh. Unfortunately, no." Melanie's face takes on a dreamy look. "But working at a bookstore is so much fun. Every day when I step into the place, I'm hit with the smell of freshly printed books. It's an instant high. We also have a staff book club, so that has been fun."

"That sounds pretty awesome! Thanks, by the way, for the employee discount last month. I filled my bookshelves with these gorgeous hardcovers I've been eyeing for the longest time," Jess says.

James stands behind Jess and massages her shoulders. "My office is filled with books with covers of half-naked men. I don't know what to think about this." Melanie and Emily snicker in the background.

Leaning forward in her temporary seat on a bright-blue ottoman, Jess turns her attention to me. "So, we heard *the story* from Liz's side. But now we want to hear it from you, Parker. How did you guys get together?"

I laugh, trailing my hands on Liz's arms, smoothing over the goosebumps appearing there. "That's for me to know and you to find out."

"Come on, that's no fun. Please tell us! I'm in need of some real-life romantic stories, as the men I'm finding online are no good," Melanie chimes in.

"Fine, fine, fine. Long story short is, Liz and I got into a fight because I'm an asshole, and she left the house in the rain. Then I heard a car crash outside and went racing after her. It was then I realized how important she was to me. Thankfully, she was fine. Then we got together. The end."

Emily points both of her thumbs down. "Booo. Even though I'm not a hopeless romantic, that has got to be the most boring rendition of what surely must've been a romantic moment...ever."

My lips twist up in a grin. "That's all you're going to get."

"Thanks, Parker. That's all I need to know. Don't need to know anything more about my sister's love life." James tips his water bottle at me.

Emily guffaws. "Dude, that's what Liz said when you and Jess got together!"

Soon, it was time for dinner. Jess and James whipped up a curried beef stew with potatoes and carrots to be served with a side of white rice. There's also *xiao long bao*, or soup dumplings from Jess's and Emily's Chinese heritage, and hot and sour soup. Melanie hums in approval as platters of food are placed on the rectangular dining room table.

"This looks so good, Jess," Melanie exclaims. "My mom makes these at home too."

Jess smiles and replies, "Thank you. It's comfort food for me. Hope the taste is on par too."

We dig into the food and for a moment, everyone is quietly enjoying the delicious meal in front of them. The savory beef stew has the perfect amount of creaminess to cut the acidity of the onions and vegetables and the soup dumplings melt in your mouth, the pork inside flavorful without being overpowering. The hot and sour soup, something I haven't tried before, has the right balance of pepper and vinegar, and really whets the appetite, making you want to go back for more. I can't help but have a few servings of the mouthwatering soup.

"That's it. I need you to teach me all of this, especially the soup dumplings," Liz announces. She turns to me and says, "I think Lucy will love the dumplings, don't you think?"

I clasp her hand in mine. I can't seem to stop touching her when I'm around her. She's already thinking of Lucy wherever we go. A deep-seated warmth spreads from what used to be a hollow in my chest.

"Yes, baby. I think she will," I respond softly.

Emily groans. "Excuse me while I puke." She throws a napkin at us.

We all laugh at her dramatic response.

Liz takes my hand in hers as she leans into my side, filling my senses with her sweet vanilla smell. She glances up at me, her pretty, plump lips beckoning me to kiss her. Her blue eyes darken at my expression and her face pinkens. "I'll make the hot and sour soup for you too. You had three bowls tonight, so I take it you liked it."

I lean down as my hand trails light circles at the tender pulse point on her inner wrist. Interlacing my fingers with her, I lift and place a soft kiss on the back of her hand. Her face reddens even further. "How will I repay you for being so considerate?" I murmur. "Actually, I know just how to repay you later tonight for being such a good girl...and such a thoughtful...nanny," I rasp under my breath and I smirk, enjoying her apparent embarrassment. She's so adorable as she sits there looking flustered, the pink on her face spreading to her neck and chest. Her hand gives me a squeeze as we turn our attention back to the group, which has already turned their attention to other matters.

My heart is so full, it could burst. Contentment I don't think I've ever felt before settles inside me. But in a dark corner of my mind, a thread of fear begins to form, slowly stitching its own tapestry. They say the higher you fly, the harder you fall. And God I hope I can reside in the skies for a little while longer.

· · ·

"Relax your throat, yes...just like that," I groan as Liz kneels before me in the double spa shower in my master bathroom. Despite our previous rounds of lovemaking, it's almost as if once we've had our taste of each other, we can't stop. We picked up Lucy on the way home from dinner and quickly put her to bed. Liz left the bathroom door ajar when she took her shower, all but inviting me to join her. Now she's giving me the best fucking blow job I've ever had in my entire life.

I grab fistfuls of her long hair, wrapping it around my hand and she attempts to swallow my turgid cock. Warm water sluices over us as she closes her eyes and sucks my dick like it's the best thing she's ever tasted.

My goody two shoes teacher is a secret slut.

Just for me.

All for me.

Only for me.

And fuck if that doesn't turn me on.

Liz slurps loudly as she teases the slit on the tip with her tongue. I grit my teeth and grasp the glass wall for purchase. Liquid heat races up my cock. My balls start to constrict and I tighten my hold on her hair, eliciting a whimper. I thrust into her, hitting the back of her throat over and over again as she moans and gags around me. She opens her eyes and stares up at me with those beautiful sapphire pools, which are currently clouded over in a sheen of lust.

I pull out of her, drag her up my body, before pushing her body against the glass. The steam mists around us as citrus, her shampoo, permeates the air. She tilts out her round ass cheeks at me as her breathing grows ragged. I lock her hands behind her, my tongue swiping the top of my teeth as I stare at the two enticing globes beckoning me to mark them up, something I've always craved with her.

Gripping her hands so she can't move, I bring a palm up and smack one butt cheek, the slap reverberating in the enclosed space.

Liz gasps, "Parker!"

"Yeah, baby, look how your skin turns pink. Only for me." I rub my palm around the red mark, soothing the sting as Liz wiggles her butt against my hand. "You want more?" I ask huskily, my mouth kissing her ear before nipping at the lobe.

She moans, apparently incapable of speech. She's perfect. In every way. *Except she doesn't know everything, Parker.* I shove the thought away and bring my palm down for another audible smack, mesmerized by the way her ass cheek jiggles against my hand. She screams and the sound turns into a mewl as I capture her lips with mine, smothering her sounds with a ravishing kiss.

"I never punished you. For darting out of the house without an umbrella or your cell phone late at night." I release her plump lips, allowing her to take a few deep breaths as she melts against me. "Don't ever do that again." I suddenly choke up, my voice thick. "I don't know what I would do if anything were to happen to you," I whisper against her lips.

Liz's eyes flicker open as she meets my blurry stare with hers. Her pupils dilate at what she sees there, and she leans back and brings her lips to me, tangling her tongue with mine, communicating everything we want to say with the deep kiss. A mind-blowing kiss.

I've never had this. With anyone.

The tender kiss quickly turns dirty, as nothing exists in the world other than the two of us in this shower, worshipping each other's bodies, purging the madness within us.

"Put your hands on the glass and don't move them."

She follows my instructions. Such a good girl.

"Spread your legs and don't move an inch."

I kneel and tilt my head up between her legs, bringing my mouth to her beautiful, thick lips below. She emits a lusty shriek at the contact and starts to close her legs. I grip her thighs tightly and pause my ministrations. She whimpers at the action...or the inaction.

"I said. Don't. Move," I growl as I bite her sensitive inner thigh, soothing the bite mark with gentle suction.

Liz gasps, "P-Parker. Please. I need you..." She stills against me, and I resume feasting on her juices, my tongue tracing the lips before circling her entrance. Then I go in for the kill, sucking her clit like it's the answer to all of my problems.

She screams as she pounds her hands on the glass. Fuck, I love her screams. Her legs start to shake as I insert a finger inside her tight canal. She's so close, I can tell. I climb back up her body, trailing kisses over every pink and red mark I've made on her pale skin as she whimpers against me, babbling incoherently. Interlacing my hands over hers on the glass, I crowd behind her, flattening her body against the wall. I rub my thick cock, currently leaking precum at the tip against her buttocks, every slide the most exquisite torture for the both of us.

Linking her hands tightly with mine, I line myself up at her entrance and slide in with one full thrust. She gasps as I nearly burst at the pleasure of being inside her tight, wet heat. Moving slowly against her, I let her adjust to my size, each slow glide torture to us both.

With each thrust, I forget all the reasons why we shouldn't be together.

With each moan, I meld our souls together.

With each whimper, I walk down a path I can no longer return from.

Liz arches her butt against me as she snakes one hand between her legs. She whimpers with frustration.

"You want more?" I grunt, my voice hoarse and low. "This isn't enough for you?"

She shakes her head and says, "More. Harder, Parker."

"Your wish is my command."

I start hammering in her as my vision grows blurry. My body is on fire as all my nerves send signals of red-hot pleasure to my brain. I look beyond the glass wall to the full-body mirror across from us.

Biting on her earlobe, my hips never stop thrusting against her, I rasp, "Look, baby. Look at us in the mirror. Look at how your tits slap against the glass. Look at how you're writhing on me, so fucking desperate, loving my cock inside of you."

Liz snaps her eyes open and attempts to focus on our reflection. I feel a gush of liquid inside her as she grows impossibly wetter, hotter. Fuck. My balls tighten as all the blood in my body rushes to the point of our connection below. Her legs start shaking uncontrollably. The lurid sounds of skin slapping against skin echo in the bathroom.

I love you. I kiss her, conveying my emotions in a demanding kiss as she approaches the pinnacle. She has burrowed herself inside me without me noticing and I don't ever want her to come back out. Liz freezes before her breathing quickens.

With a few more punishing thrusts, I pinch her clit, and she screams my name as she comes. Her clenching walls trigger my release and I capture her open mouth with mine. *I'm sorry I can't stay away from you.* I swallow her moans, wanting to prolong the connection, wanting to stay in this fairytale where I'm the prince in her happily ever after.

I stare at the deep-navy-blue, one-shoulder chiffon gown hanging in my closet, lovingly tracing my fingers over the lace and sequin applique, which makes up the single shoulder and long sleeve of the gown, ending at the waist, seamlessly blending with the long and smooth chiffon skirt. The gown has a low sweetheart neckline and tightens at the waist before draping over the hips to the floor. Two thigh-high slits, one on each side, add a bit of a sexy flair to the otherwise formal dress. Even though I'm sleeping in Parker's room most nights, waking up early in the morning to go back to my room before Lucy wakes, I still keep most of my clothes in the guest bedroom.

Tonight, Parker has invited me to accompany him to a charity gala to celebrate the success of the new homeless shelters his firm helped design. There are rumors of a special recognition award for him and he's in his office working on the final touches of the speech for tonight, should the award come to fruition. The bedroom door opens softly and closes with a click. Amber and bergamot waft to my nose as muscular arms wrap around my waist.

I smile, my heart skipping a beat at his presence. "You done with your speech?"

Parker trails his lips over the whorl of my ear, lightly nipping the lobe. Molten heat gathers between my legs as my eyes flutter shut. "Yes. I have five minutes before I need to head out to the airport to pick up Mom and Rick," he replies, his low, rough voice eliciting goosebumps over my body.

I gasp, leaning back against him as he kisses his way down my neck, sucking at sensitive areas he's become very familiar with recently. "You better not give me a hickey, Parker. We're going to a gala tonight."

He chuckles and lightens his kisses. His tongue slowly dips out to trace my fluttering pulse. My core clenches as it becomes wet. He always does this to me at the most inconvenient moments.

"Parker! Stop it. Where's Lucy?" I move to turn around, but he holds me in place.

"She's downstairs, putting on her shoes. She's excited to see her grandparents." His hands trail to my breasts, cupping their weight. My nipples slowly bead to hard nubs, poking through the thin lace bra I have on under my cotton T-shirt. Parker groans as he kneads the mounds. "Fuck, I'm addicted to you. I can't get enough," he rasps and pulls me flush against him, letting me feel his hard length on my back.

I bite my lip and tear myself away from him, my breathing heavy. Turning around, I look at him, the man who ensnared me the moment I met him, even though for the longest time, I thought the feelings were dislike and hatred. But I guess there's some truth to the saying, "There's a fine line between love and hate." Parker stares back at me, his chest moving with every breath he takes. His mesmerizing green eyes hold so much love and tenderness, I can hardly breathe.

"Go, don't be so horny. You just got some last night. Don't make your daughter wait for you." I shoo him with my arms.

He grins, his dimples making an appearance. "I'm famished. Always starving for you. I think you broke my cock."

"What do you mean 'broke it'? It looks just fine." I gesture to the tent in his slacks.

"That's what I mean. It was nonfunctional for three years, then you appeared, and now it always looks like this whenever you're around."

My face heats up as I push him out of the bedroom. "Go, Parker. Let me prepare dinner for Lucy. Then I'll need to get ready for the gala. Stop distracting me."

His laughter, so rich and deep, echoes outside of the bedroom, fading away as he makes his way down the stairs to the front door. I'll never get sick of hearing the sound. Lately, the darkness within him seems to have abated, and I think I'm getting a peek at who Parker used to be before Abby's death. I turn around to my closet and pull out a simple, light-orange sundress to change into. Nervousness threads through me as I think about meeting his parents soon.

After a quick change of outfits, I pad downstairs to whip up a fresh batch of meatballs and tomato sauce. I place spaghetti in boiling water and take out my phone to confirm with the temporary sitter for tonight. Playing some jazz music on the smart home speakers, I work efficiently, setting aside two plates of spaghetti and meatballs for Lucy and her sitter before packing the excess in glass containers and storing them in the refrigerator.

I'm wiping down the counters as the front door opens. Laughter travels from the foyer. I set the towel down and wipe my clammy hands on my dress. Smoothing my hair out, I take a deep breath before walking to the living room to greet the McDonalds. *You got this, Liz.*

A tall, lanky man with gray hair carries a suitcase into the living room, followed by an elegant woman with golden-brown hair streaked with gray whom I recognize from the photos Parker showed me once. His mom, Regina. She's looking at Lucy, who is laughing and gesturing at something, clearly thrilled to see her grandparents again.

"Hi, I'm Liz," I announce as I tuck a few strands of hair behind my ears.

Regina and Rick glance in my direction. Rick walks over and clasps me in a tight hug. "Hello! Parker, my boy, told us about you, but he never sent us any photos. It's good to put a face to a name, and I can see why he's so head over heels for you." I laugh at his exuberance and relax slightly in his presence. Rick is very approachable. I look beyond him at Regina, who is staring at me with a strange expression on her face.

Turning her head back toward her son, she asks, "Parker? Didn't you say your girlfriend is Lucy's kindergarten teacher?"

"She is." Parker walks in, carrying his parents' jackets and a duffel bag.

"B-but, she—"

"Is also Lucy's nanny. They get along very well. She's a wonderful person." His voice takes on a clipped edge as he stares at his mom. Silent messages pass between them. A curl of unease gathers in my stomach.

Regina whips her head back at me and slaps a hand on her forehead. "Where are my manners? Forgive me. Old people, sometimes we don't know what we're doing." She breaks into a smile and now I know who Parker got his dimples from. She comes up to me and pulls me into a light hug. "Hi, my dear. Thank you for taking care of our Parker and Lucy."

I let out a deep breath as my muscles slowly relax. "It's my pleasure." I glance at Parker and Lucy, who are smiling warmly at us, even though Parker's shoulders are still a bit rigid. "They're both easy to love."

Regina freezes briefly, so quickly I almost didn't notice it. She pulls out of my embrace and gives me the warmest of motherly smiles. "Of course, those two are pieces of my heart, out there in the world. I tell you, once you're a mother, you never stop worrying about them."

I lead them to the playroom, which we've repurposed into a guest room, and they begin unpacking their luggage. Lucy insists on staying behind to "help" her grandparents. Leaving the merry trio to themselves, Parker and I step out of the room and head upstairs.

"Parker?"

He turns, his hand curled around the doorknob to his room. "Hmm?"

"Is everything...okay? Your mom seemed like she had some reservations about me just now." I twist my hands as the unease from earlier prickles to the surface.

Parker walks up to me and cups my face with his hands. "Everything is fine, baby. Mom is probably just a little bit tired from the flight. She loves you or she wouldn't have hugged you otherwise. Trust me, I put in a lot of good words for you."

He winks and smiles, but the smile doesn't quite reach his eyes. Before I can ask him any more questions, he pulls me in for a deep kiss, which short-circuits my brain, as usual. Warmth spreads through me, chasing away the dull ache in my chest.

Pulling away, he murmurs, adoration in his eyes, "Let's get ready for the gala. If you need any help with getting undressed, just let me know." He wags his brows and chuckles at my eye-roll. I shove him, my lips tipping up in a smile, the earlier tension slowly melting away.

I take a quick shower and shave all over, saving a special surprise for Parker to find out later. My face flushes, thinking about how I went from being a virgin not long ago to this new vixen who apparently has been hiding inside all along. I slip on the dress, careful not to pull on the delicate lace too hard. For makeup, I opt for a simple liner and maroon lip color, a perfect contrast to the dark dress. Then, I blow dry my hair into loose, voluminous curls, a la Hollywood starlets in the sixties. I snap a photo of myself and text it to the girls.

Liz: This teacher is all glammed up and going to the gala. Thanks to Emily for picking out this dress for me.

Emily is the unofficial stylist of our group as she works on image makeovers on a daily basis, even if it's her team doing the actual work.

Jess: You look so gorgeous, Liz! Enjoy the gala. Can't wait to hear all the details.

Emily: I shouldn't be surprised by now, but I'm good. I'm excellent at what I do.

Melanie: Dang, friend. The blue dress is perfectly draped over your figure. Whew! Has Parker seen you yet?

Emily: Pssh. I'm sure he hasn't or she wouldn't be texting right now. IYKYK.

My face heats up as I anticipate showing off this beautified version of myself to Parker. He has never ever seen me in formal eveningwear before, except for the one time when I was in a bridesmaid dress for Jess and James's wedding.

Liz: Oh please, we can keep our hands to ourselves. We're all adults here.

Emily: If you can only see my face right now. My eyebrows are all the way up to my hairline.

I snicker before turning the screen off and sliding the phone into a small silver clutch. Taking a deep breath, I step into the hallway, where I hear the sounds of Parker speaking with the babysitter downstairs near the entrance to the kitchen. God, he looks good in a tux. The slim cut of the black material fits him like a glove, highlighting his fit and tall physique. Definitely cover model material. My pulse races as I take him in. How did I get so lucky? Gliding down the wooden steps, I feel like the princess I'd always yearned to be as a little girl.

"Daddy! Look at Lizzy! She looks like a princess," Lucy exclaims beside Parker.

Parker stops mid-sentence and freezes. His emerald eyes darken with intensity as he swipes his lips with his tongue and swallows hard.

"Excuse me," he murmurs to the babysitter as he walks to the bottom of the steps and I feel very much like the main character in a fairytale, with my prince waiting to escort me to the dance floor.

He holds out his hand as I descend the last few steps. I clasp my hand in his as he pulls me against him, leaving a few inches of space between us, mindful of our audience. He wraps his arm around my waist and leans in, his mouth near my ear. "You look stunning, Liz. If there weren't so many people around, I'd peel that dress off and worship every inch of you."

He steps away, his eyes smoldering. My fair skin feels feverish as my breathing quickens. We stare at each other for what feels like forever. His hands clench before he slides them into the pockets of his pants.

Lucy bounds over, clapping cheerfully. "Lizzy, you look so pretty today!" Her small fingers touch the sequins on the bodice with reverence.

I ruffle her hair and crouch down. "Someday when you grow up, you'll get to wear a pretty dress too. But in the meantime, you focus on eating your food and having fun with Jamie over there." I acknowledge the babysitter, who is standing, patiently waiting for us.

"I wish I can go too."

"I know, sweetheart. Unfortunately, the gala is for adults only. How about this? If you behave tonight and listen to Jamie, we can have our own dress-up party later on and invite Skylar too. What do you say?"

Lucy shrieks with happiness and Jamie leads her to the living room, while listening to Lucy describing everything she wants to do at her party.

"You always know just what to say to her," Parker murmurs as I stand back up.

I walk my fingers up his lapels and look at him from underneath my lashes. "You're talking to a professional here. I never do anything by half measures."

He wraps his arm around me, pulling me flush against him this time. "Oh yeah? Does this include taking care of the daddy of your charge?"

My hand makes a slide down south, to the broken appendage that is very happy to see me. I rise to my tiptoes and whisper in his ear, "Oh yeah, I have full services for the daddy. Especially the daddy."

Parker's hand grips my butt as he groans, leaning his forehead against mine. "Fuck, what did I turn you into? Where's the sweet and innocent schoolteacher?"

"Don't they look beautiful together, Regina?" Rick exclaims, his jovial voice carrying across the large living room as he makes his way to us with Regina behind him, who is giving us a muted smile, her eyes somewhat solemn. *What's wrong?*

Parker and I spring apart like teenagers being caught making out in the car. It doesn't matter how old you get, somehow you always feel like you're doing something you aren't supposed to be doing when you're around your parents.

Smoothing my dress, I turn to them, cursing my fair skin, which is no doubt pink right now. "Thank you, Rick. You and Regina look beautiful too."

He tugs his wife next to him. "I'm glad you invited us today. It's been a long time since these old bones got a workout on the dance floor."

"Come on, the town cars are waiting outside." Parker leads us to the front door.

Sure enough, two elegant black town cars, longer than the average sedan but smaller than a limo, await us outside.

"Mom and Rick, you guys can take the second one. Liz and I will take the first one."

He waves the driver away and opens the door for me, waiting for me to carefully slide into the car before climbing inside. The interior of the car is more spacious than I expected, with supple tan leather and various refreshments on the side compartments.

"This car is huge. They could've shared one with us. Why two?"

Parker tips up a secretive smile as he speaks to the driver. "We're ready to go. Please knock when we arrive." He presses a button and a partition comes up, effectively separating our space from the driver's side.

He crowds me against the corner of the seat, my back flat against the window. "So I can do this to you."

Gripping my neck, he brings his lips to mine. My eyes flutter shut as I'm seduced by the sensations, the tingles appearing throughout my body. His kiss quickly turns hungry as he nips at my bottom lip, sucking it before plunging his tongue inside my mouth. Heat rises rapidly in me and I moan, eager to meet his tongue with mine.

"God, I wanted to do this to you since I saw you on the stairs." His lips trail down my neck, suckling my collarbone as his hands move to the back of my dress and slowly ease down the zipper, his fingers lingering over the sensitive skin of my back.

"Parker," I moan as I bite down on his lip, earning a hiss of pleasure from him.

"Shh...the driver may not see us, but he can definitely hear us. Don't scream unless you want him to know what we're doing."

I bite my lip to refrain from emitting more noises as Parker slowly peels off the top half of the dress, exposing my swollen breasts.

"Fuck, no bra?" He grips one heavy globe in his hand, kneading the softness, spreading fire over my body.

I gasp. "Don't want the lines to show through."

Parker's lips close over one nipple and shards of pleasure shoot straight in between my legs. Clamping his hand over my mouth to muffle my moan, he lavishes his attention to the distended tip, laving it with his tongue before moving to the other side. He twists the sensitive nub, the pleasurable pain setting my skin on fire and dampness seeps through my thong.

"I wish you could see what you look like right now, arching your tits up to me like my personal whore." His dirty words elicit another moan from me. He slaps one globe and soothes the sting with another soul-sucking kiss, and my legs turn to jelly.

"Please...I need you." I twist in my seat, my breathing heavy, eager to relieve the aching pressure between my legs.

Parker kneels on the floor of the car and spreads my legs. "Love this dress. Remind me to send a note to the designer, such easy access." He slides his hands up the two slits of the dress and trails kisses up my thighs. Pushing the skirt up to my waist, he sinks his teeth into my inner thigh as he brushes his fingers on my soaked thong. His other hand slides to his pants and he pulls down his zipper and takes out his swollen cock.

Gripping his shaft, he leans back and admires his handiwork, no doubt another pink mark on my fair skin. He reaches up to slide the thong off of my legs, tossing it to the side.

"If I wasn't afraid you'll flash everyone at the gala, I'd have torn off that scrap of underwear from you so you'd be bare underneath your dress," he grunts as I widen my legs so he can see my surprise from the shower earlier.

"Fuuuck me. You're completely bare." He groans as he pumps his cock, which is deep red and swollen with white pre-cum dripping from the tip. I twist my nipples as I tilt my legs up at him, eager for him to give me what my body needs.

"This pussy needs you," I breathe.

Parker dives in, his lips sucking my juices, his tongue twirling around my entrance. I let out a keening moan at the acute pleasure and I slap my hand over my mouth.

"Look at this pink pussy, flooding me with her juices," he rasps as his lips move to my clit, suckling the hard bud in. He inserts two fingers inside me, curling at just the right angle, and I nearly slide off the seat as the throbbing intensifies.

I grasp at his hair, not knowing whether to push him away or pull him closer as he continues his torture. The heat reaches an unbearable point, and he inserts the tip of his pinkie into the puckered rosebud of my ass.

"This hole is mine, too. Someday, you'll take my cock here."

The added pressure sends sparks to my clit and I pant heavily. "Parker...please." I tug at his head, not caring if I'm being too forceful.

"Please what? Use your words, Liz," he parrots my phrase back to me.

"F-Fuck me, please," I whisper as my legs start to spasm around his head.

His fingers still against me. "What did you say? I can't hear you."

"Fuck me, Parker. Fuck me with your big hard cock!" I arch my back off the seat.

He climbs up over me and slams inside me with one firm stroke. "Shit, I love your dirty mouth," he grunts while he pistons against me, each slap of skin against skin reverberating in the compartment. My eyes roll back as he hits my clit over and over again, torturing the sensitive region with his ardor.

I moan with each thrust, and he captures my sounds with his mouth as we chase the pleasure. Some people make slow and sweet love. Parker and I are water and oil, hot and cold, and when we make love, we burn down the house. I'm the light to his darkness. He's my dark knight, whisking me away from my tower, showing me all parts of the world, the beautiful and the ugly, and I adore him for it.

His lips tangle with mine in a fervor matching the punishing rhythm down below. The two halves of our souls merge into one, burning brightly as we leap into the flames together. I scream into his mouth as I come, my legs clasp tightly around his back. He follows seconds later with a harsh groan and he floods my womb with his seed, his tremors mirroring mine.

Our heavy panting fills the compartment as the world spins around me. Parker drops his forehead against mine and rasps, "I love you so much, Liz. You have no idea how much."

Moments pass by, the car quiet other than the sound of our breathing and the blood rushing in my ears. I take a deep breath and say the words I've been holding inside for so long.

"Parker, I...I love you too." My heart pounds in agreement. Yes, I love this man, his idiosyncrasies, his moods, his baggage. Him.

Lifting his head up, his green eyes stare into mine, his gaze intense with love. He trembles and clears his throat as if recognizing the significance of my statement. I give him a watery smile and nod. *Yes, it's true.* He lets out a ragged breath, as if he can't believe I'd love someone like him, before breaking into the most glorious smile I've ever seen from him, his dimples deep in his cheeks. Parker leans in and places a soft kiss on my lips, his mouth slowly moving against mine in a tender embrace.

He slowly disentangles himself from me as he pulls out his pocket square and cleans us up before tidying my dress and his clothes. My heart is full, overflowing with love for the man before me, the man who used to hide his true self away from the world, but has finally let me in. A nagging kernel of doubt remains, but I quickly shove the thought away, not wanting paranoia to make an appearance. He glances up, his eyes bright, his flushed face returning to his normal color, and he takes my hand in his, giving it a soft kiss.

"I guess he probably knows what we're doing back here," he chuckles, his thumb pointing to the fogged-up windows and the partition.

My face heats up and I bite my lip. *God, I'm so embarrassed. I never thought I'd be like this.*

He sits back down next to me and tucks me to his side. "Don't worry, your secret's safe with me." He smooths my hair as best as he can, his lips quirking to the side.

I snuggle next to him, and my eyes feel heavy, drowsy from happiness and love.

I wish I could freeze time and stay cocooned in this moment forever.

CHAPTER 20

Liz

The gala is held at a beautiful historic hotel in the heart of downtown LA. The gothic architecture, with its soaring arches, flying buttresses, and high ceilings, transport you back in time. The theme is floral and greenery, signifying a fresh start and new beginnings, a nod to the name of the shelters. Strands of lavender, pale pink and white wisteria hang from the arches around the room and the columns are twined with dark-green vines. Large centerpieces of towering fragrant bouquets decorate each table. The practical person in me automatically thinks this must have cost a fortune. Then again, I guess it's all for charity. I don't dare ask what the cost per plate is.

"Parker, the man of the hour. I've been looking for you everywhere." A tall, striking man with black hair and slate-gray eyes walks up to us, his lips tilting up in a smirk.

Parker laughs and hugs the man in question, giving him a big, hearty slap on the back. He turns to me and says, "Liz, this is Dylan, my partner in crime."

Dylan shakes my hand and flashes a megawatt smile at me, highlighting his excellent facial structures. I grin back—perhaps all architects have a minor in modeling. "So, this is Liz. I've heard so much about you, finally happy to meet you in person." He cocks his head to the side, a slight furrow appearing between his eyebrows. "I swear you look familiar, but I can't place you. We haven't met before, have we?"

"No, we haven't. I don't hang out with many architects in my line of work. I'm a school teacher." I laugh. I must have one of those faces.

"And you've met my parents before." Parker gestures to Rick and Regina, who've appeared next to us.

"Mr. and Mrs. McDonald, lovely to see you here."

Regina swats his arm. "Oh hush. It's Regina and Rick to you. Still can't break the habit from college?"

Dylan winks. "I'm a man of good breeding. Always respect my elders."

Rick laughs and pulls his wife to the side. "Come on, honey, let the young kids have fun. Let's go find our table with the older folks." Nodding at us, they walk away to find their seats.

Parker asks, "You're staying for a week this time?"

Dylan rubs the back of his head. "I was going to, but the museum project is kind of blowing up, so I'll be heading back tomorrow." He shrugs. "Perks of being the big man in the house, I suppose. Putting out fires."

"I get it, but better you than me this time. Come on, let's mingle and do some obligatory schmoozing."

Parker wraps his hands around my waist as he introduces me to all of his coworkers, who all seem friendly and happy to see both of their young managing partners in one location. We say hello to a few local politicians, and I think I even spot an actress or two. We take a seat at one of the three tables reserved for the employees of their architectural and design firm. Dinner consists of pan-seared halibut with lemon caper sauce, a side of broccolini and fingerling potatoes. The flaky fish falls apart in my mouth, and I close my eyes and savor the buttery and tart flavors.

"Not too bad for a charity dinner, right?" Parker murmurs beside me.

"Much better than expected, but I don't have anything to compare this to."

"You'll have more of these dinners to go to in the future. Don't think I'm letting you off the hook that easily."

I smile, my chest warming at the implications of a future beyond the summer with Parker and Lucy. Maybe dreams do come true.

I take a sip of chardonnay and dab my mouth with a napkin. Pushing my chair back, I whisper to him, "Excuse me, I'm going to go to the restroom for a minute."

He glances over and starts to stand.

"Don't, I'll be back soon. Talk to your coworkers." I grin and add, "Don't worry about me. This isn't a dark club with drunk people. I'll be fine."

Chuckling at the reminder of our night at Ambrosia, Parker then turns to the person next to him and begins a discussion filled with words like "BIM" and "spatiality." I grab my clutch and walk to the nearby restroom right outside the ballroom.

Finding an empty stall thankfully, since you never know with these public events, I sit down and complete my business as I hear the door opening and two ladies walking in.

"So, I guess Parker is taken now?" a higher-pitched voice asks. I peek in the gap between the door and the partitions of the stalls. This is one of the brunettes at the table next to us.

"Yeah, bummer for us single ladies," the blonde next to her replies as she freshens her makeup.

"Did you see his girlfriend? I guess he has a type, huh?"

"Yeah, I mean, the resemblance is just..." The blonde finishes what she's doing and leaves the bathroom with her friend in tow.

What resemblance? What type?

A weight settles in my gut as the unease from earlier creeps back in. Something doesn't feel right, but I can't place it. It feels like I have all the puzzle pieces, but I'm somehow not putting it together correctly.

Never mind them, Liz. Parker loves you and that's all that matters.

Mind firmly made up, I exit the stall and wash my hands. I catalog my appearance. My hair is a bit flatter—no doubt the tryst in the car didn't help, but it still looks good. No obvious hickeys or scratches, always a plus. I blot my face and leave the bathroom.

Parker stands as I reach the table. His eyes rove over my face. "That took you a while. Everything okay?"

I nod. "There was a line," I fib. No use in worrying him. Nor do I want him to go on some weird witch hunt over seemingly innocent comments.

He holds out his hand and leans in. "May I have this dance?"

I place my hand in his and he leads me to the dance floor, where a string quartet is playing nearby. He swings me around and dips me in a flourish before pulling me back up against him.

I laugh. "So, is this what happened with Jess at the gala? Did you try wooing her with your mad skills?"

He wags his brows. "Is it working? Are you wooed?"

"I was forewarned, so this is to be expected." I lean in, my lips close to his ear, and murmur, "But lucky for you, I already fell under your spell a long time ago."

We sway to the romantic music as the crowd blurs around us, locking ourselves in our sphere of happiness and love.

"I was never very nice to you before. I'm sorry." His temple touches mine, and I close my eyes, relishing in the warmth of his body and the deep timbre of his voice.

"Let bygones be bygones. You weren't exactly mean to me until those few times earlier this summer. You were a bit standoffish, but now I've learned what you were dealing with, and I completely understand. You were handling a lot. And plus, you did buy me a wonderful stack of books from Pendleton."

He laughs as his hand tightens on my waist. "I don't deserve you," he murmurs in my ear.

"You deserve so much more than you give yourself credit for."

He places a kiss on my forehead and whispers, "I hope you'll feel this way about me always."

A sense of melancholy emanates from him and my heart twists, wishing one day Parker would be completely free of whatever is haunting him. He's a good man who is too tough on himself.

I pull back and look into his eyes, which are intense in the dim light. I smile, seeing my small reflection in his pupils. "I love you, Parker. You're a good person."

His jeweled-green gaze tears up and he blinks away the moisture. Cradling my face tenderly with his palm, he places a light kiss on my lips, not caring we are in the middle of the dance floor. Squeezing my hand, he pulls away and leads me back to the table as the music quiets down and an emcee takes the stage.

"Ladies and gentlemen, thank you for coming tonight to the Los Angeles Charity of Fresh Starts Gala. I hope you've enjoyed the food, the music, and the dancing. I'm here to remind everyone of some housekeeping items. A silent auction will take place in the next room later this evening and all proceeds will go to the maintenance and upkeep costs of our homeless and battered women shelters. I'm also happy to announce we've raised one million dollars tonight from everyone's attendance here. Please give yourselves a round of applause."

The room erupts in cheers and applause. Wow, I guess I was right about the per plate costs. A moment later, the emcee continues, "There'll be more music and dancing later, but let me first introduce you to Philip Fleischmann, the President of the Los Angeles Charity of Fresh Starts, for a brief message."

A middle-aged man with curly dark brown hair walks up to the stage and takes the microphone. "Thank you. I'd like to thank everyone for your support in this important endeavor and before we resume our festivities, there's a special award I'd like to present, to recognize someone here who's been instrumental in the design and construction of the New Beginnings shelters. Someone who has not only achieved a pinnacle in his career at a young age, but someone who's always humble and has also supported our charity since day one. As a special thank you, I'd like to present the first Parker Wellington Charitable Award to…well, Mr. Parker Wellington."

I wipe a tear from the corner of my eye and cheer as the world recognizes the goodness in the man beside me, something he's unwilling to acknowledge in himself. Standing up, I give him a big hug, followed by a chaste kiss as he smiles at the crowd, his face flushing pink. He rakes his hand over his hair as he makes his way to the stage, stopping to give his mom a brief hug. I clap loudly, unable to stop smiling.

Parker shakes Philip's hand and takes a small plaque from him. Turning to the microphone, he squints a little at the bright spotlight shining on his face. Rubbing his palm over his mouth and jaw, he takes a deep breath.

"Thank you, Philip, for those kind words. If I ever need someone to boost my image, you'll be the first person I'll call." He flashes a dimple-showing smile, his teeth dazzling up on stage. The audience chuckles at his lighthearted humor.

He stares at the plaque in his hand and begins his speech, something he has kept private until now. "When I heard I may be getting an award of some sort, I was genuinely surprised, because the amount of effort and time I've dedicated to this project is so minuscule compared to all the employees and workers who have, and are, working every day at New Beginnings. So, this award is really for all of you." He shifts his stance on the floor and stares out into the crowd.

"The Regina McDonald New Beginnings Centers holds a very personal importance in my heart. Most of you probably don't know this, but I come from very humble beginnings. My father passed away from cancer when I was a little kid and my mom, Regina, who these shelters are named after...I love you, Mom." He points to his mother and clasps his hand over his heart.

"My mom worked so hard, too hard, to put food on the table and to keep the electricity on. For a short while after my father passed, we were inundated with medical bills and were evicted from our home. I remember the first day I arrived at the homeless shelter. I was scared shitless. Forgive my colorful language." He coughs into his hand, his voice taking on a rougher edge.

"The folks there did everything they could to make a little boy and his tired, grieving mother feel welcomed. They helped me with my homework and kept encouraging me, saying one day, things would get better. Even after we were able to leave the shelter, I never forgot the days I spent there."

He looks up and wets his lips. "So, I vowed to myself one day, if I make something of myself, I'll give back. I'll do what I can to help folks who are in my situation, or worse circumstances."

Parker raises his plaque and stares at Regina. "Mom, thank you for all you did for me. I wouldn't be here without you. Rick, thank you for taking care of my mom since I'm not by her side." Rick nods, rubbing his hand on the shoulder of a weeping Regina.

Parker's gaze searches the room until he finds me. His eyes are intense with heavy emotions. He swallows, and says, "Liz, thank you for loving me. I know our journey has just begun but do know you're my heart. Thank you for loving the very imperfect me." My eyes tear up as I clasp my hands over my lips, my fingers trembling at the huskiness and sincerity in his voice.

"My daughter, Lucy, is at home complaining about not being able to go to a dress-up party." The crowd laughs. "But I'd like to thank her too, for I wouldn't be who I am without this little angel in my life." He points to our tables. "Thank you to the best colleagues a man can have. And most importantly, thank you to all of you for supporting this very important cause."

He thumps his hand over his heart, and walks down the stage, his knuckles quickly swiping at the moisture in the corners of his eyes. The room erupts in cheers and applause as he makes his way back to our table.

I open my arms and he wraps me up against him. Pulling back, he looks into my eyes, his penetrating eyes telling me things I already know deep down inside. I curl my arms around his neck and pull him in for a deep kiss, responding to the question in his gaze. "I'm so proud of you," I whisper as we pull apart and take a seat back at the table. He swallows and presses his lips into a flat line, his body trembling. I give him a watery smile and he turns to acknowledge the rest of the folks at the table who are congratulating him.

A perfect night with my perfect man.

He's perfect, even with all of his imperfections.

The rest of the evening is full of laughter as I get swept up by Parker in a few more dances. His parents and I chat about Lucy and my work at school. I experience my first ever silent auction, where Parker wins the bid on...surprise, yet another black-and-white photograph. I'll make it my personal mission to add some colorful decorations to his home.

The ride back home is quiet as I lean my head against his shoulder. He intertwines our fingers together, his thumb rubbing circles on my inner wrist. I close my eyes and surround myself with my new favorite scent—the rich fragrance of amber interlacing with hints of vanilla.

When we arrive at home, Lucy is already fast asleep. Parker pays and thanks the babysitter, and his parents head off to bed. I quickly change into my sleep shirt and wash the makeup off my face while he takes a shower. My heart feels raw and vulnerable somehow, as if I'm afraid this happiness will slip out of my fingers. When we retire for the night, Parker curls me against his body in his bed and my heart settles into a steady rhythm, beating next to the man who has held me captive since the day I met him. I press a soft kiss on his forearm as he snuggles me closer, our breathing in sync.

"I love you, Liz." Those are the last words I hear before sleep overtakes me.

• • •

"Liz, over here!" Emily waves her hands at me from her seat at the table outside of a trendy coffee shop featuring espresso and drip coffee from coffee beans sourced around the world. Melanie and Jess grin as I make my way to their table.

Sliding my sunglasses off my face, I take a seat in the remaining open chair. My eyes squint as I adjust to the bright sunlight, the day already warm despite being ten in the morning. I stifle a yawn and grab the menu. "Boy do I need a coffee this morning. Maybe a double shot."

"Someone keeping you up at night, eh?" Emily teases, her eyes sparkling with mirth.

My face warms as I reply, "We stayed out pretty late last night because of the charity gala. Didn't get to bed until well past midnight. Get your mind out of the gutter, Ems."

"Ha. Well, maybe not last night then...but your face isn't flushing pink for no reason."

Melanie sighs. "Man, everyone is getting some. I feel like I'm growing moldy down there."

Jess snorts as Emily leans over. "You know, I can share my ways with you, lil' grasshopper. There are plenty of fish in the sea if you just know where to look."

"Don't mind her, Melanie. I'm with you. Better to find someone you like than to casually date around just for the sake of it," Jess murmurs.

"It's fun to date around. Why stick around for the shit to hit the fan? I still don't understand that."

"But isn't the point to find someone to ride life's ups and downs with you?" Melanie swirls her ice coffee with her straw before taking a sip.

"Says who?" Emily retorts before adding, "Sometimes, it's easier to have fun and end things on a high note than to stick around and see if someone you're depending on will stay with you for those so-called downturns of life." Her voice quiets to a near murmur. I frown and glance at Jess, who's looking at her sister with the same concerned expression on her face.

"Enough about all this philosophical relationship talk. So, Liz, how are things going with you and Parker?" Melanie leans forward with the enthusiasm of the students in our class as they wait for us to read them a book at story time.

I smile, thinking of the alluring, enigmatic man who complained about me leaving him behind with his parents and his daughter this morning, something I know he clearly enjoys. "Things are going well, I think. Parker...he's not at all what I expected."

"What do you mean?" Jess asks, her hazel eyes serious as she takes in my question.

"All my life, I thought the person I'd end up with would be simple and uncomplicated, and our love would be equally effortless." I take a sip of the double-shot espresso the server just placed in front of me. "But he's anything but simple...there are so many layers to him, I don't think I've gotten to the core of him yet. But somehow, I can't seem to stay away."

"How do you feel about that? About him not being an open book, which is what I assume you're saying?" Jess is always the inquisitive one in the group.

I glance up and find three pairs of eyes staring at me expectantly. I cock my head to the side and reply, "Perhaps that's love. He may not be who I've imagined for myself, but now that I'm with him, I can't imagine being with anyone else. As complicated as he is, I feel like his soul calls out to me, and mine the same to him." I bite my bottom lip, feeling a little vulnerable with sharing these feelings, but wanting to let them know all the same. "I guess it's true what they say, a heart can't help what it wants. To love, perhaps you do need to take some risks."

Melanie sighs, her heart in her eyes. "That sounds so epic." She turns to Emily and explains, "See? This is what I want. Romance novel levels of epicness in my love story."

Emily shakes her head as she takes another sip of coffee. "Epicness is overrated."

Jess reaches out and places her hand on mine. "But you're happy with him, right?"

I nod. "Yes, I am. I can't imagine anyone else beside me. I know it's still very new, but I feel this deep down in my core."

She smiles. "Then that's all that matters."

"How was the gala last night?" Emily inquires, her earlier uncharacteristic sullen mood seemingly forgotten.

"It was so beautiful, and they presented him with an award for his work with the shelters. I totally got teary-eyed at the speech."

Jess nods. "James did mention Parker has spent a lot of time designing and overseeing the shelter project. It meant a lot to him. I'm happy he got recognized."

"I really want to do something with my hands to commemorate yesterday. Give him a little something of my own creation. I think the artist in him will appreciate it." An idea strikes me and I continue, "I think I'll present him with a detailed framed drawing of my rendition of gothic architectural motifs and the image of him on the stage. A nod to our evening in the historic hotel. What do you think?"

"I think that sounds lovely. A gift you create from scratch is worth more than anything you can buy him, I'm sure. Especially since he can pretty much buy anything he wants," Jess replies.

I smile, imagining his face when I reveal the completed artwork to him. A burst of energy courses through me as I think about the project I'll begin when I get back home later today. He'll be so happy, I'm sure of it.

"You have the look on your face," Melanie comments.

"What look?"

"The one you get when you come up with new projects for the kids in our class."

"I love coming up with new projects! They're fun, and..." I twist the napkin in front of me. "This is fun too."

Melanie looks up at the sky and sighs. "Ah, true love. When will it be my turn?"

We all laugh at her dramatic expression and our conversation moves to other topics for the rest of our meetup.

Later in the day, I quietly creep into Parker's office, eager to collect the supplies I need for my project while he's with Lucy and his parents in Lucy's room. Pulling a sheet of blank paper from the printer in his masculine office of dark woods and leather furniture, I scan the floor-to-ceiling bookshelves filled to the brim with books, awards, and other decorations. I'm searching for a book with gothic architectural designs for me to browse through to get some inspiration. Finding a few album-looking volumes on the middle of the shelf resembling architectural photography books, I decide to pull them down. Maybe I'll find inspiration there. I rise to my tiptoes to retrieve the volumes.

Clang.

The books knock something behind them down. Setting the volumes on the leather sofa, I reach up to pull the object which has fallen over. It's a photo frame.

My heart drops to my stomach when I see what's in the photo.

Dirty-blonde hair. Large, sapphire eyes. Heart-shaped face. The woman next to Parker is laughing, holding a little bundle in her arms. Memories assault me—his mother's reaction when she first saw me, Dylan's frown when he met me, the woman in the bathroom earlier...

The woman in the photo is svelte and twiggy. Her hair is lighter and her face is thinner, but the resemblance is unmistakable.

I look like her.

Abby.

I clasp my hand over my mouth as I grip the picture frame. My heart thumps a mile a minute as the beginning of nausea roils in my stomach.

Is Parker with me because of Abby?

CHAPTER 21

Parker

Liz sits quietly in the SUV, her face pensive as she stares out the window. The warm glow of the sun shines through the tinted windows, caressing every inch of her face. She closes her eyes as if she's basking in its warmth. She's been a bit more subdued since the night at the gala three days ago, and I don't know why. Whenever I ask her, she insists everything is fine. My parents finally flew back home last night. I think Liz won them over.

"Honey, I want to talk to you about Liz," Mom says as she pokes her head into my office where I'm wrapping up a few project reviews after Lucy goes to bed. I've always tried to be more present with Lucy after Abby's death, but ever since Liz has joined our lives, I make an extra effort to go home early and enjoy a few hours with them before I finish my work later on at night.

My family. That's who Liz has become to me.

"Sure, come on in."

Mom takes a seat on the leather chair on the other side of my oak desk. I hold my breath, knowing what she'll probably say next.

She purses her lips, staring at me for a few seconds before opening her mouth. "She's a sweetheart. I really like her...but don't you think she deserves to know?"

I shake my head. "No, she can't know. I can't bring myself to tell her. It'll devastate her." I let out a deep breath, which doesn't alleviate the heaviness creeping back into my chest of late.

She frowns and leans forward. "You know, when I first saw her a few days ago, I was worried. I know you told me she's not a replacement for Abby—"

"Liz is nobody's replacement!" I pound my fist on the table and take a ragged breath. "She's one-of-a-kind. They're nothing alike, only a passing resemblance at first glance—"

She arches her brows. "You know you can't hide that forever—"

"I don't want her to think I'm with her because she looks like Abby, because that's the last thing on my mind. I know her. She'll go down the deep end and draw incorrect conclusions. I know it's unrealistic to think I can keep everything from her forever...but for now—"

Mom raises her hand, giving me a stern glare. "Let me finish. I was originally worried, but then over these past few days, I've gotten to know her better and I agree, she's nothing like Abby. I may even go as far as to say they're almost polar opposites. But son, your past is part of who you are. Abby is an important part of your past. You can't hide the truth forever."

The blood rushing in my ears calms down as my breathing evens out.

Mom continues, "I've never seen you so happy before, Parker. Ever. The joy and love in your eyes. Your laughter. As a mother, this is everything I ever wished for you. But, son, you can't base a relationship on a lie, and you know it's a very big lie of omission and not just because of their resemblance to each other. One day, the truth will come out and what'll happen then?"

I rub my temples, a dull ache forming. "I don't know," I admit. "I-I just can't tell her. It'll devastate her and I'd rather hurt myself than hurt her."

She places her hand on top of mine. "Son, be brave. Maybe she'll react differently. Maybe things aren't as dire as you think they are. If you love her, tell her the truth and let her decide." With the parting wisdom, she gets up and leaves me in the office with my thoughts.

I can't lose Liz.

The love of my life.

Someone I wasn't even looking for but is now an indelible part of me.

Lucy's snoring in the backseat drags me back into the present. We're going to a small town up in the mountains a few hours away for a get together with friends. I'll teach Lucy how to fish and we'll ride our bikes together. It's something I remembered doing with my dad when I was little, and I want to continue the tradition as a way of remembering him. My memories of my dad are fuzzy now, but I still remember the feeling when I was with him, his laughter, and the warmth of his body.

"Liz, is something on your mind? You know you can tell me, right?" I reach out and clasp her hand in mine.

She turns her head and gives me a wistful smile. She squeezes my hand softly. "I'm fine. Just thinking through some things lately."

"Anything I can help you with?"

"Can you tell me why you love me?"

My heart warms at her question. There are so many things I love about her. Where do I begin? "You, Liz, are the other half of my soul I've been searching for. Your kindness, your zest for life, your positivity, and so, so much more." I sneak a glance at her. "Why this question?"

"Just wondering," she murmurs and curls a loose lock of hair behind her ear. "Can you tell me more about Abby?"

My heart sinks. The earlier warmth is replaced with a sense of foreboding. Why is she suddenly asking these questions? "I told you about her the night in the kitchen. What else would you like to know?"

"What did she look like?" Liz fidgets in her seat, adjusting the hem of her shirt. "Lucy has your dimples, but I'm guessing her eyes must take after her mom."

My heart skips a beat. I frown, not liking the direction this line of questioning is going. "Abby had blue eyes, dirty-blonde hair, average height and physique. I guess Lucy does take after her mom." I chuckle nervously, my pulse fluttering rapidly in my veins. "You curious?"

"Of course I am. She was Lucy's mom after all, and the woman who held your heart before me. I know you said your marriage was tough toward the end, but I know you loved her at one point...or maybe..."

"Maybe what?" I turn on the signal to prepare to exit the freeway. I grip the steering wheel tightly as a million scenarios run through my head, all trying to explain Liz's uncharacteristic solemn moods and her current line of questioning.

Liz shakes her head and chuckles. "Ignore me. I don't know what I'm asking, anyway." She reaches out to the control panel and flips on the radio. "Let's listen to something."

The news station switches on, my default. She cocks her eyebrow at me and I grin, thinking back to the day when she first got into my car and was utterly unimpressed with my radio station choices.

"Breaking new for today: If you're in the downtown vicinity, stay safe and avoid going to the hospitals. Local area hospitals are reporting a large influx of patients from the Laurel Gas Refinery explosion this morning, which decimated almost five city blocks and toxic fumes are affecting homes and areas miles away from the site. There was a National Gas Union meeting on site today, leading to a high number of victims from the tragedy. The exact cause of the wide-scale gas pipeline and refinery explosion is unknown and officials have declined to speculate, but local hospitals are reporting blood shortages and are requesting extra units to be flown in from blood banks and other hospitals in the state..."

Liz clasps her hand over her mouth. "Oh my gosh. How terrible! Let me send a few messages to friends who live in the area."

I place my hand on her thigh as she whips out her phone and begins texting, a worried expression on her face. Hitting a few buttons on the control panel, I find the jazz station Liz loves.

A flurry of chimes and texting later, Liz relaxes back in her seat.

"They're okay?"

"Yeah, thankfully. The air quality is horrible, but my friends are fine." She exhales.

I squeeze her thigh in reassurance. "Good, I'm glad to hear that." I run my fingers on her soft inner thigh, soothing the goosebumps appearing there. "Come on, let's think about all the fun things we'll do later. It'll be fun to see the gang, right?"

Liz lights up and nods. "Yes, it's been a while since we all went on a trip."

Soon, we arrive at the RV rental site next to the village. There are no hotels nearby, but there is one glamping site with luxury RV rentals. Perfect for city dwellers who are looking for a more rustic experience but unwilling to give up modern comforts.

"Come on, Lucy. Time to wake up. We're here!" Liz exclaims in a singsong voice, hopping out of the car, her usual energy returning. I breathe a sigh of relief. *Perhaps I'm overthinking things.*

Lucy yawns and stretches her hands above her head while Liz unbuckles her from the car seat. "Where are we going to stay, Daddy?"

"See the big cars over there on top of that little hill? They look like large vans? We're going to stay in one of them tonight."

Lucy's eyes grow wide. "We're sleeping in a car tonight?"

"Yep! It'll be an adventure! So much fun." Liz winks at Lucy, then closes her eyes and takes a deep breath. Turning to me, she says, "Smell this fresh air, Parker. It's just different up here, away from the smog and the traffic. Give me a book and a bed and I'll be happy forever."

The temperatures here are cooler due to the higher elevation and the skies are an expanse of baby blue, not a single cloud in sight. Birds fly from tree to tree, filling the air with joyful melodies. The air smells crisp and clean and I automatically feel some weight lifted from my shoulders.

I exit the car and carry our luggage to the check-in counter, while Lucy and Liz explore the central lodge where explorers gather. We booked adjacent RVs to Jess, James, Emily, and Melanie. Looking at my watch, I see it's half past two. They should already be here.

"My princesses, let's go to our luxury home for the next two nights." I wave the key cards in front of them, smiling at the joy on their faces.

I drag a small cart with our luggage to a trail leading up to our luxury rental and open the door to peek inside. "Wow, who found this place? I've heard about glamping but haven't done it before. This is a pretty impressive setup."

Lucy runs in and squeals, "Daddy, this is like a very tiny home!"

"It sure is, pumpkin."

Liz's gaze roves around the space. "Jess and James picked this spot. Jess is a good trip planner. She usually likes to do something nature-related once a year to decompress."

The RV is fully furnished with a small kitchen complete with granite countertops, sea glass-colored tiles for backsplash, an electric stove, a small stainless-steel refrigerator, and a microwave. There's a little breakfast nook which can be converted into a long sofa facing a flatscreen. Two bunk beds with privacy curtains are situated near the bathroom and there's one bedroom with a queen-sized bed and two modern nightstands, complete with two small wrought-iron sconces. The entire space has the furnishings of a luxury house, but at a miniature size. A knock on the door interrupts our perusal. Liz opens the door and breaks into a big smile.

"Ems! Melanie! You're here."

Emily ducks in and pulls Liz into one of her well-known koala hugs. "Melanie and I are staying at the RV over there. James and Jess are next to us. We got here midmorning and are fully rested from the best nap ever." She glances over and grins. "Hey, Parker. Looking good these days." I laugh and shake my head.

"Pretty neat, right?" Melanie points to the room as Liz nods, still admiring the craftsmanship of the vehicle.

"Auntie Emily!" Lucy careens into Emily, wrapping her little arms around her waist.

"Hey, pipsqueak!" Emily glances at us and smirks. "Want to come hang out with me and Auntie Melanie? Daddy and Lizzy are probably exhausted from all that driving. Why don't we give them a little break so they can take a small nap?"

"A nap? Even I don't take naps anymore. Naps are for *little* kids and I'm not little anymore. I'm almost six," she proudly announces.

"I know...they're getting old and don't have as much energy as us." Emily snickers as Melanie snorts. She takes Lucy's hand and they exit the RV. Before closing the door, Emily pops her head back in. "Enjoy your *nap*, guys. Don't do anything I wouldn't do. Toodles!" With that parting thought, she bangs the door shut, leaving Liz and me alone in quiet peace.

"I knew I liked her," I murmur as I pull Liz flush against me. I dip my nose along the slender column of her neck, loving the involuntary trembles in her body. She's so fucking responsive to me. Such a fucking turn on. I back her into the bedroom and push her onto the bed. The sight of her lying there, her chest heaving, her golden hair spread across the pristine white sheets nearly unravels me. I can't believe she's mine. *I can't believe she loves you back.* The nagging voice inside of me interjects. Her plump lips part as she stares at me with those mesmerizing eyes.

Her eyes. Every fleck of gold in the irises. The precise blue mirroring the most flawless of sapphires.

Uniquely hers. I can't believe I ever thought so otherwise.

"Parker." She stares at me, her gaze suddenly intense.

My heart starts thudding at the serious expression on her face. "Yes, baby?"

"I-I..." She blinks at me, her eyes suddenly taking on a wet sheen. "I-I love you."

I swallow the lump in my throat. Something is wrong and I don't know how to make her feel better. A sense of foreboding comes over me. I gently cradle her face in my hands as I place a gentle kiss on her parted lips, conveying all my emotions in the deep embrace. *You're my love. My all.* "I love you, Liz," I rasp against her mouth.

She gasps as I draw her shirt up, my fingers caressing every inch of exposed skin. She's wearing another skimpy lace bra. My girl loves all things lace. I want to fill her closets with them, then rip them off her one by one.

I want to worship every inch of her forever.

Clasping my lips over one erect nipple, her back arches up into my kiss, her hands grasping my hair in a soft tug. I lave my tongue over the areola before flicking the hardened tip, a move which never fails to make her squirm.

"C-Clothes off," she moans, writhing under me as she tries to claw up my T-shirt. The earlier heaviness has seemingly slipped away from her as she succumbs to the sensations I'm inflicting upon her.

"Patience, baby." I bite her nipple, the sharp sting eliciting a cry from her. "Good things come to those who wait."

Moving to the other side, I suck her other nipple as if my life depends on it and drag my hands down her body, slipping them under the waistband of her shorts. I trail kisses down her body as she moans and wiggles on the bed. I pinch her clit and she shrieks, her body thrashing, then I sooth the sting with a gentle suck on the swollen nub. Moisture coats my fingers as I continue my gentle ministrations.

"I need you, Parker. I need you now." She kicks her shorts and panties off and spreads her legs, her hips chasing my fingers.

There's something extremely erotic about her gyrating on the bed, her eyes hazy with lust, clamoring for me.

"Fuck. Look at you, your cunt dripping all over the place." I insert two fingers inside her, curling them as I unzip my pants. Gripping my erection in one hand, I finger her, watching her arch off the bed as if she's beside herself with desire. Her pale skin flushes pink as she starts panting.

Her juices gush out of her pussy, drenching my fingers, and she whimpers. She starts throbbing around me and I know she's close. I withdraw my fingers and she moans in complaint. Peeling off my clothes, I climb above her and slide into her in one smooth stroke, both of us groaning from the pleasure. Clasping her face with my hands, I kiss her parted lips as I move against her, my motions picking up in speed. The bed rocks against the wall with each thrust and she widens her legs and curls them tightly around my waist.

"Liz, Liz, Liz..." I pant, each drive of my cock deeper than the last. I feel like I'm leaving a part of me behind with each thrust. "You're my end all, be all. You're my fairytale," I murmur against her lips as my balls tighten.

Her eyes flutter open, her hazy gaze suddenly clear. She grips me tightly around my back, her nails scoring the skin, but I don't really notice. I only see her. I arch my hips at the end of each stroke, and her lips part in a silent scream. Her legs tense around me as my cock twitches in warning.

"Come, Liz. Come for me, baby," I grunt as I slip my hand between us and rub circles around her clit.

She flies apart as juices gush out of her, her inner walls clamping and throbbing around me. I tumble into oblivion with her, white dots appearing behind my eyes.

Panting against her, I kiss her once more, telling her I love her with each suction, each nip, each swipe of tongue, and that's when I feel it.

Wetness on my cheek.

Opening my eyes, I find her staring at me, an errant tear escaping from the corner of her eyes. "I love you, Parker." She pulls me close before I can ask any questions and she sniffles against my neck, apparently overcome with emotions.

"Silly baby. I'm here." I shush her, not wanting to ask her what she's thinking.

I don't want to know.

I'm afraid to know.

Liz's shudders slow as she burrows herself against my chest. I look over at her and find her fast asleep. Pulling the blankets over us, I wrap my arm around her and stare at the ceiling feeling unsettled as unease tangles with fear inside me. Something is wrong, and I'm scared I'll soon find myself tumbling down from the skies.

"It's really frustrating they won't tell me who this 'mysterious' client is." Emily kicks the rocks by the campfire we started near a small stream by the campsite. It's late afternoon, and the area is relatively quiet, which is a stroke of good luck since the summer season is usually one of their busiest times of the year.

"Is it normal for them to keep it a secret from you?" Melanie asks.

"No, definitely not. If anything, I'm usually involved with the deal negotiations and am one of the first to know when we bring on new clients. So, this is definitely unusual."

Jess muses, "Maybe it's one of those secretive individuals who is very sensitive about their privacy."

Emily shrugs. "I don't know. Maybe. It's all very strange. They said I'll find out soon enough when the ink is dried."

After Liz's nap, we rejoin the broader group for some outdoor activities. To unplug and reconnect with nature, as Jess says. I'm finagling with the buckle of Lucy's princess helmet as she stands there, clearly impatient with this entire process.

"Can we go riding yet? This is taking too long."

I finally snap shut the annoying buckle. "Yes, pumpkin, now you can ride the bike. Safety first."

Lucy takes off, ringing the little bell on her handlebars. Her giggles travel through the air and I chuckle, my heart full. Right now, at this moment, I have everything I want, everything I ever wished for in my life.

"Don't go too far," I holler at her shrinking backside, shaking my head.

James sidles up next to me as I walk toward Lucy's direction, keeping my eyes on the tiny speck that is her. "So, things are going well with you and Liz?"

I look back at the girls gathered by the campfire. Liz is leaning forward, her eyebrows scrunching up as she listens to Emily complain about her work. "I think so. I sure hope so."

James hums in acknowledgement. "That's good. You're happier, Parker. I'm glad to see that."

I smile. I couldn't agree more. "Your sister is a really special person, but I'm sure you already know that."

"She definitely is. For a long time, I was afraid she'd never find anyone, with her idealistic expectations of princes and fairytales and her obsessions with those romantic TV dramas and novels. But I'm glad she found you. Even though..." He pulls me to a stop and stares at me, his eyes narrowing in assessment. "What does she see in you? You're far from 'perfection,'" he deadpans.

I shove him hard, laughing at his harsh assessment.

Trust me, I have no idea.

"You always ask me why we're friends. Now I'm beginning to wonder the very same," I tease back, my lips quirking into a grin.

"So how are things going with you at Brighton?" James is the Chief Data Honcho at the investment firm.

He shrugs. "Can't complain. Even though it may be time for me to jump—"

A shriek travels across the air.

The hairs on my arms stand up.

My heart jumps to my throat as I whip my head toward Lucy.

The moving speck in the distance is a now lump on the ground.

"Lucy!" I run toward her as fast as I can, my heart kicking against my rib cage. "Lucy!"

She doesn't respond.

No. No. No. Please don't.

Flashbacks of me standing on the doorstep when the cops came hit me. *I can't lose her too. I'd rather die than lose any more people I love.* Scurrying up to the unmoving figure on the ground, I kneel beside her, my hands trembling as I shake her gently on the shoulders.

"Lucy, can you hear me, pumpkin? It's Daddy." I struggle to keep a calm voice as I take in her appearance.

She whimpers as she clutches her stomach, her face pale. Way too pale. "It hurts, Daddy," she whispers, her face wet with tears. Her helmet is loose on her head and her face is scratched up and bleeding.

"Shhh...Daddy is here. Let's take a look at your tummy." I gingerly peel up her shirt and the air is sucked out of my lungs when

I see the large red welts across her abdomen. I survey the area, seeing no large objects when my eyes finally snag on a thick, raised tree root on the dirt behind us. She must've tripped over the root on her bike and smashed herself against the handlebars or something. I gently touch the redness and she cries out in pain, her tears hitting me in the deepest recesses of my chest.

"Oh sweetie, are you okay?" a warm, familiar voice filters past the roaring sound of the blood in my ears. Liz crouches beside me, holding Lucy's hand. Her eyes are red as she tries to hold back her tears. Lucy whimpers as her face turns paler, sweat beading on her forehead. "Don't worry, sweetie, we're getting you to the doctor and they'll fix you right up." Liz's voices wobbles at the very end, betraying her fears.

Turning to me, she murmurs, "I asked James to call the ambulance and go to the receptionist to see if they have medical staff here. I think we need to take her in."

I nod as I grip Lucy's small hands tightly. Her fingers are so cold. *This is my fault. I should've kept my eyes on her. I should've told her to ride beside me and not go too fast. What kind of a father am I?* I beat myself up internally as the burn of self-hatred and the clawing guilt joins the panic inside me.

Jess and Melanie reach us. "Emily is returning to the camp. She's going to knock on doors and see if anyone is a medical professional," Melanie says.

Jess places her hand on my rigid shoulder as I stare helplessly at my flesh and blood, lying on the ground all bloodied up, in such excruciating pain. "Don't think of the worst, Parker. Trust me, whatever you're thinking right now isn't true."

Lucy's eyes start to roll to the back of her head as she spasms. "Lucy!" I scream as I grip her hand tighter, tears welling up in my eyes. She shakes in my arms as I hug her as gently as I can. "Please, Lucy. Please be okay, pumpkin. Daddy can't live without you," I sob into her shirt.

Liz curls her arms around my back, her voice choked up with emotions. "She's going into shock, but we're getting help. She'll be okay, Parker. We must believe that."

After what seems like forever, paramedics arrive with James, Emily, and on-site staff in tow. The male paramedic pries me off of Lucy, whose body is still other than the rise and fall of her chest as she breathes. I grip his forearm tightly, reflexively wanting to punch him in the face for preventing me from being with my little girl. "Sir! Sir, I need you to focus and take deep breaths in order for me to help your daughter."

His words pierce through the chaotic whirl of my mind and I look at him, his face blurry in my gaze. "Please help her. She's not moving. She was talking earlier and now she's not responding." I put my hands on his shoulders as I stare at the ground, my breath coming in harsh gasps. "Please save my little girl," I plea.

"Tell me what happened."

I bite my fist, my pulse frantic. "She was riding her b-bike, and I was just walking behind her. I turned around for a few minutes and heard a scream. I think she tripped over the root there and smashed herself against the handlebars or something. Her stomach is all red and hurt when I touched her earlier."

"Marcus, ready for transport!" The female paramedic finishes strapping Lucy to the stretcher with Liz's help.

Marcus turns away from me and sprints toward them. "Greta, on the count of three. One. Two. Three." They hoist the stretcher up and slide it in the back of the ambulance as I climb in behind them.

Liz moves to get in, but Greta stops her. "Sorry, only one person can accompany the patient. We're going to the local hospital. There's only one here."

Liz grabs my hand, giving me a squeeze. "I'll drive there with the others. Things *will* be okay, Parker. The doctors will help her. Stay strong."

The paramedics give her a terse nod before they shut the doors and Greta fiddles with various monitors next to Lucy as Marcus climbs into the driver's seat. The swirling sounds of the sirens are loud in my ears as we speed toward the nearest hospital. Panic grips me tight in its clasp. I grip Lucy's small, limp hand and chant under my breath, praying to anything or anyone who'll listen.

"Please, Lucy. Please hang in there." I bring her hand to my lips as I stare at my little girl. The beeping of the heartbeat monitor echoes in my mind, both reassuring and traumatizing at the same time.

How could you, Parker? How could you let this happen? What type of father are you? A million regrets float through my mind as I drown in a sea of guilt. Sweat beads on my forehead and drips down to my neck as my breathing quickens.

"Sir, take deep breaths. You need to be strong for your little girl," Greta instructs beside me, her calm voice something I'm latching on to...a last lifeline.

The hospital quickly comes into view. It's a tiny building with two stories, its exterior yellowing with age. Marcus parks the ambulance at the emergency entrance, and they wheel Lucy inside, past metal double doors, into a room with a small waiting area.

"Sir, you need to stay out here," an orderly in blue scrubs intercepts me as a doctor and a nurse wheel Lucy through another set of double doors.

"That's my daughter!" I push past her, desperate to be by my little girl's side.

"I understand. We'll do everything we can. Let us do our work. Please wait out here. We'll come get you when we have news." Her voice is sympathetic but firm, leaving no room for discussion.

I watch the double doors swing shut, the swishing sound reverberating in my ears. My legs shake as I stagger back, collapsing in an open chair in the waiting room. My heart threatens to give out as it kicks hard in my rib cage.

It's all your fault, Parker. You can't protect those you love. You're toxic. You don't deserve happiness.

I crouch over in the chair, my head buried in my hands, nausea churning in my gut.

Nothing will ever be the same again.

CHAPTER 22

Liz

I twist the tissue I used to dry my tears earlier on my lap, my knees bounce against the seat in a nervous rhythm. Jess is sitting in the backseat with me while James is driving up front. He looks in the rearview mirror, his gaze meeting mine.

"Liz, things will be okay. They're medical professionals. We need to have faith right now." His baritone voice is calm and soothing even though a vein pulses on his forehead.

Pieces of tissue fall onto the floor of the car as I rip the paper into shreds. My eyes blur as wetness gathers there again. *Parker must be panicking right now. He must be blaming himself.* I really want to be by his side.

Jess stills my fidgeting fingers with hers. Her signature scent of strawberries and cream wafts over to me and she murmurs, "We'll be by your side every step of the way. Stay strong for Parker, Liz. He needs you right now."

I sniffle, swallowing the lump in my throat as I swipe the tears away with my hands. Blinking rapidly, I look outside the window, seeing a tiny building with a hospital sign on the horizon. *I need to be strong for Parker. I need to be the calm to his storm. I need to be his shelter.* I repeat the mantra to myself as I take deep, ragged breaths.

James slows down in front of the entrance, and I jump out before the car makes a complete stop, my pulse rioting inside me. Darting down the various corridors and rooms, I scan the area, looking for a distraught man who is most likely beside himself with fear and panic right now. My eyes roam around the waiting room, past the blurry faces of strangers, all united in the worried expressions on their faces.

That's when I see him.

A man crouching over his chair, his head hanging low, supported by two strong arms on his knees. His golden hair is in disarray as his tense, rigid shoulders shudder with each harsh breath. His lonely profile. Heartbreaking.

A thousand arrows hit me in the chest at once, the pain searing as I rush toward him. I curl my arms around his head, tugging his face to my chest as I rub soothing motions on his coiled back.

"Liz," he rasps without looking up.

I bite my lip to keep from crying. *I need to stay strong for him and little Lucy.* "I know. I know. Let's not jump to any worst-case scenarios yet. Things will be okay. They must be okay," I murmur, using every ounce of energy to keep my voice steady and calm. *He needs me. He needs this strength and faith.*

He finally looks up, his eyes red-rimmed and bloodshot. "What if?" His voice cracks at the last word, as if he can't contemplate the rest of the question.

"No what ifs." I shake my head firmly as I take a seat next to him. "No what ifs. In a few weeks, when she's all recovered, we'll take her out to celebrate with ice cream. She'll go to school and tell her friends all about her visit to the hospital. Things will be okay," I respond resolutely as I take his hands in mine.

He grips my hands tightly and I lay my head on his shoulder, providing him with my presence and my warmth as we sit there in the agonizing wait. His feet tap nervously on the ground and his eyes are vacant, staring into space. I rub one hand over his, soothing his white knuckles, which are clenching my other hand in a death grip.

I don't notice the pain. All I notice is the fear pouring out of his being. The harsh thuds of my heart as I worry for little Lucy in this freak accident. *What if something happens? What will Parker do? He can't take any more of this suffering. No, Liz, don't think about that. We're not there yet.*

"Family of Lucy Wellington?" a man in a white coat holding a clipboard strides through the doors, his eyes surveying the room.

Parker leaps out of the seat, and we hurry over to the doctor. Panic flashes in his eyes, and I grip his hand in mine. Whatever happens, we'll deal with it together.

"I'm her dad. How is she?" His body stills, as if bracing himself for bad news.

"I'm Dr. Kreswick, the attending physician here today. The good news is, we have stabilized your daughter's condition."

Parker relaxes marginally and releases a breath, but the expression on the doctor's face gives me pause.

"So, she's okay for now, but she has severe internal bleeding, most likely from the handle bars hitting and rupturing her spleen during her accident. We already did a CT scan, and it shows blood pooling in her abdomen and that's why she was in so much pain. She fainted, most likely from shock. Because of the bleeding, she needs to have surgery as soon as possible for us to not only stop the bleeding, but also to assess the damage and see if the surgeon can repair it. Worst-case scenario, we'll need to remove it."

Parker physically recoils as the doctor describes the details of the procedures and the consents to be filled out. "I'll sign anything. Please, just take care of her."

Dr. Kreswick nods as he hands over the clipboard with all types of legal releases. "One more thing, we tested Lucy's blood and unfortunately she has one of the rarest blood types, AB negative." He rubs his hands over his hair and continues, "This is a very unusual situation, as blood shortages rarely happen. But there was a huge incident in Los Angeles today—"

"Yes, we know about that. The refinery explosion. We're from LA," Parker interrupts.

"So, due to the accident, a lot of our reserves for AB negative blood have been diverted to help the hospitals there. We still have some here and have made the request to some blood banks farther away to see if they can airlift some more to us. But as Lucy has severe internal bleeding, we'd like to make sure we cover our bases. Are you AB negative? Or does she have any other relatives here who may have the same blood type? We'll like to draw some blood just in case it's needed later and we need time to test it beforehand."

Parker freezes next to me, his nostrils flaring. He looks at our intertwined hands and slowly lets go, the movement feeling significant somehow.

Hold on, I'm AB negative, I can offer—

"I don't have that blood type," he whispers and pauses before exhaling a deep breath, "but her aunt is here." His head slowly lifts and he looks me in the eye, his face pained.

I frown, not understanding the expression on his face. Parker stares at me as a wet sheen gathers in his bloodshot eyes. My hand flies to my lips and I gasp. Both Lucy and I have the same blood type. Our blue eyes. Abby's resemblance. The final pieces of the puzzle slide into place. My hands are clammy as I clutch my chest.

"Liz, please. D-Do you know your blood type? If not, can we get you tested?" Parker murmurs, his eyes filled with sadness and the unidentified emotion I've never been able to pinpoint but can now see as clear as day...guilt. "I'm s-so sorry."

"You're the aunt?" Dr. Kreswick asks, interrupting the revelation. "Do you know your blood type?"

I tear my gaze from Parker, staring at the doctor, who's waiting for my answer.

Because we need extra blood.

For Lucy.

My niece.

"Y-Yes," I whisper, hardly believing the words coming out of my mouth, "and I'm a match. I'm AB negative."

The final nail in the coffin. Why Parker always seems like he's keeping secrets from me. Why everyone in his life is cagey around me.

Why he is with me.

I can't think about this right now. Lucy comes first. I swallow the glass shards in my throat and calmly reply, my firm voice belying the flurry of emotions inside me. "Yes, I have the same blood type. Draw what you need. I'll sign anything."

Dr. Kreswick nods and beckons me to follow him. As I pass the double doors, I turn around, looking at Parker. The man who has lied to me since day one.

Parker stands where we left him, his hands clenching fists, a muscle twitching in his jaw. His eyes are closed, his face twisting in a grimace.

The liar.

My prince.

My fairytale ending.

What irony.

• • •

Beep. Beep. Beep. Beep.

The steady sounds from the heart rate monitor echoes in the small room. Lucy's surgery went well and thankfully, they were able to repair the spleen and stop the internal bleeding. Lucy will be fine. She'll be at the hospital for one to two days, then she can go home. Recovery will take a few weeks, but she'll be up and running in no time. *"Things should be normal again," the doctor said.*

What's normal anymore? You can't put the genie back into the bottle.

Jess and the others are gathered in the waiting area while Parker and I sit in the room in silence. I smooth my hand over Lucy's hair, the golden curls I've brushed so many times during these last few months. How did I not notice? Those unique blue eyes, just like mine.

I'm numb. Perhaps still in shock. I don't know how to face him.

"We should talk," he murmurs, staring at his hands on his lap. A vein pulses on his forehead.

"How long have you known?" I think I already know the answer to this one.

"Since the day I met you at the Greek restaurant. When I saw you for the first time. I suspected, then I went through Abby's files and accounts and confirmed my suspicions when I got home." He lifts his gaze to mine and he takes a deep breath.

"What files and accounts? What do you mean?"

"Genetic Genie. You were chatting with her for a long time. Do you remember how you said some folks ghosted you on the app?"

Frowning, I say, "Yes, I had a few people ghost me, but I didn't really talk to them...well except..." I gasp, realization dawning. "Gail. I talked to her for the longest time, and we were supposed to meet up, but I had some scheduling issues and had to reschedule a few times but she didn't show up that day. I waited for an hour..." My hand flies to my mouth as realization dawns on me. I whisper, "Gail is short for Abigail, isn't it?"

He nods. "She used her maiden name on the app. She wanted to meet you. It was raining hard that day..." Parker begins, his eyes full of sorrow.

"S-She died that day, didn't she?" Tears prickle my eyes as I stare at him. "She died on her way to see me?"

Parker rakes his hands through his hair as he swallows hard. "Yes."

"She died because of me?"

His green eyes flash with ire. "No! Don't you dare put this on yourself. You didn't know. If anyone killed her, it's me. I was the one who called her because I couldn't swallow my anger. Because my pride got in the way. Because I wanted to win an argument. Even though there was a storm outside, I didn't care. I was just furious and because I couldn't control myself, Lucy doesn't have a mom anymore and you lost your half-sister before you even met her."

"H-half?" How much more do I not know? How much more can I take?

"Abby was adopted when she was a baby. It was a closed adoption. But she did a lot of digging and spent a good amount of money trying to find her biological family. She wanted to know where she came from. When you two were matched on Genetic Genie, she looked you up. It became an obsession for her. She hired a private investigator to research everyone in your family. She researched your parents, their lives. Ultimately, she figured out she was your half-sister from your mother's side."

Nausea churns in my gut. I feel sick. My tongue feels furry, disgusting. I pour a cup of ice water, my hands shaking as I take a sip. Abby is not my full sister? My mom had another kid, but the father is not my dad? But they were high school sweethearts and didn't have me until they graduated from college. How is this possible?

This can't be. There has to be a mistake.

The air feels thick, and I can't breathe.

Thump. Thump.

"Liz? Parker? How's Lucy doing? Can we come in?" Jess's voice travels across the closed door. I've never loved her voice more before now.

Swinging the door open, I try my best to put on a brave smile. "Y-yes, you guys can come in now. I'll step out so you have room."

Jess frowns when she sees my face. Putting her hand on my arm, she asks softly, "Are you okay, Liz? Is it Lucy? I thought the doctor said everything went well—"

"No, Lucy is fine." I shake my head as I bite on my lip. Anything to stop me from becoming a bawling mess on the hospital floor. "I'll tell you later." My voice chokes up as I dart out of the room. The tears start to fall from my eyes. *Damn it, why can't I stop crying? Stop it, Liz.* I flee from the waiting room as footsteps pound after me.

"Liz! Wait up. Liz!" a familiar baritone voice hollers at me.

James.

I turn around and see my brother's blurry figure running toward me. With a cry, I collapse into his arms, burying myself in his warm chest.

"What happened?"

Oh God. He doesn't know either. Or does he?

"So, that's it. That's all I know." I stare into the firepit in front of our RV. The crackle of the fire and the occasional hoot of an owl keep us company on this clear night. Thousands of stars sparkle in the dark sky, a view we usually can't see in the city, but something I don't even appreciate anymore. I slowly raise my head and look at the people around me.

James, his face grim, an expression that hasn't changed since I told him the truth at the hospital. It turns out, he was kept in the dark by his best friend too.

Emily, Jess, and Melanie all stare at me, apparently dumbfounded.

"He never told you *anything* before?" Melanie asks, apparently as confounded as I am about this turn of events.

I shake my head. "I had no clue. I'm so stupid."

Emily scoots her chair next to me and puts her hand on top of mine. "Hey, hey." She snaps her fingers in front of my face. "None of that. Who the fuck can imagine this? I mean, this is the stuff of TV dramas. I can't believe he never told you anything." She narrows her eyes and snarls. "I'll kill him when I see him next time."

"Not if I kill him first," James mutters, glaring at the blazing fire.

"Come on, you don't mean that," Jess, the voice of reason, interjects, stopping us before we do something drastic...or continue to think about doing something drastic.

"Liz, it's been a long day. Don't make any rash decisions right now. Maybe he had his reasons for not telling you," Jess murmurs, her hazel eyes glowing gold in the firelight.

Melanie harrumphs. "I don't care what his reasons are. He should've told her." Perhaps we teachers are more black and white. Shades of gray don't exist in our eyes except in the color worksheets we give to our students.

"What if he was with me all along because I remind him of Abby? Who the fuck gets together secretly with their late wife's half-sister? What kind of twisted joke is this?" I may like to read taboo romances, but I sure as hell don't enjoy starring in one.

I kick the dirt in front of me. "What about our parents? I thought they were high school sweethearts, got married, had James and me, and are living their happily ever after." My nose twitches as I feel my eyes burn again. I don't want to cry anymore. I think I ran out of tears. "How did I have a half-sister? What does this say about them?" *What does this say about the fairytale I was holding out for? The simple, uncomplicated relationship. The happily ever after.*

Maybe everything is a lie.

"As much as I want to punch him in the face on your behalf," Melanie says, "I agree with Jess. I think you're too wired up to think clearly right now. Go to sleep, and tomorrow we'll figure out what to do next."

"You're not alone," Jess chimes in, her eyes fierce with protectiveness.

Emily nods. "We'll figure this out. One step at a time."

My eyes prickle again. My girls. How lucky am I to have them?

James gets up and wraps his arms around me. "I'm here as well, sis. I-I just need to take a walk to clear my head and think through some things. But call me if you need anything." He nods to Jess before striding away, his gait heavy and his shoulders tense.

"You're right, girls. I-I think I just need to rest. Maybe things will seem better tomorrow." I try my best to muster a smile.

"Do you need me to stay with you tonight?" Emily asks.

"I totally don't mind having the whole RV to myself. Maybe I'll meet a rugged mountain man who'll ravish me in my sleep." Melanie wags her brows at me.

I snort and shake my head. I love them so much. "I'll be fine. I probably need some time alone as well." I get up and reach for the shovel, ready to pile some dirt on the burning fire to put it out for the night.

"We got it. Go rest, Liz," Jess says as she shoos me away with her hands.

"Thank you, girls. Goodnight."

I walk to the RV, which earlier in the day seemed warm and small, but now seems cold and vacant, too large for one person. I wash my face and brush my teeth, going through the motions. Staring at the mirror, I notice the dark hollows under my eyes, my pale skin, which is porcelain on a good day but now looks lifeless. I change into my nightshirt and crawl under the covers, the cotton sheets feeling cold against my body.

Hints of amber and bergamot linger on the pillow. Parker's pillow when we made love earlier today. I close my eyes, gathering his pillow against me, trying to pretend the events of today didn't happen. A sharp pain pierces my chest as sobs wrench out from my throat. It's useless. The nightmare is a reality. The tears I've been holding on to just now slide down my face, wetting the pillow in my arms. I wrap my body around the softness and cry myself to sleep.

I wish this was all a hallucination.

I wish I could go back in time.

I wish I had never met him.

CHAPTER 23

Parker

T*hump. Thump.*

I stir awake at the sound of the knock on the door. I slowly sit up, the muscles in my back spasming from the uncomfortable position I was in for a prolonged period of time in the cheap faux-leather hospital chair.

Thump. Thump.

Rubbing my eyes, still heavy from fatigue, I make my way to the door of the hospital room. I haven't slept much since the accident. Maybe one to two hours, tops. Opening the door, I find myself staring at the angry face of my best friend. James stands there, his jaw clenched tightly, his hair in disarray, as if he has been tugging it for a while. His nostrils flare and he takes a deep breath.

"Is she doing okay?" he asks gruffly, nodding toward Lucy.

Lucy is sleeping soundly after eating a small meal of chicken noodle soup and lime gelatin. The nurses turned down the volume of the heart rate and pulse monitor, but the stats are still showing on the screen. Lucy whimpers as she shifts in her sleep. My heart clenches at the sight of my little girl all bandaged up on the hospital bed.

I nod and step out of the room. I knew this was coming. Clicking the door shut behind me, I walk past a small group of people in the waiting area toward the hospital entrance. I take out the phone from my pocket and check the time. Six forty-five p.m. Time is an abstract concept to me as the events of the day all blur together, my emotions getting a thorough workout. I'm physically and mentally exhausted, my mind barely keeping up as my body crashes from the adrenaline rush from earlier in the day. As we step through the double doors, the cool air hits me in the face, a shock to the system. The sky is still dim with the remnants of daylight.

"The doctors say she will recover just fine. She should be up and about in a few weeks, but we need to make sure to keep her wound clean to avoid infection."

I walk over to a wooden bench by the entrance and sit down, watching the cars drive by on the main street, folks moving on with their lives while mine has ground to a sudden halt. James strides over and sits next to me. He clenches his hands into tight fists and places them on his knees. I brace myself for what's coming.

"How could you?"

I hang my head at his question. There isn't a suitable answer, no acceptable reason for lying. It always sounds like an excuse to the victim.

James cracks his knuckles as fury bleeds into his voice. "I warned you, Parker. I warned you when you showed up at my place, holding my sister's hand, you better not hurt her. And guess what? She's fucking hurt. She's miserable. She's been crying all day and my guess, all night last night. I've never seen her like this before. Ever!"

I flinch. My heart breaks at the thought of strong Liz crying because of me.

It's all my fault.

Your best is still not enough. People you love still get hurt.

You should've stayed away.

James paces in front of me, tugging at his dark hair as a flush spreads up his neck onto his face. "If you didn't look like shit already, I would've punched you in the face." He whirls toward me and spits out, "What type of sicko gets together with his late wife's sister and doesn't think to tell her about the connection before-hand? What's wrong with you!"

Cars honk in the distance, flashing red taillights of cars stopping and going on the road. I stare at the traffic, unable to find adequate words to address his questions. Nothing I say will matter at this point. It was all a mistake, a collision of "should haves" and regrets. I gambled with fate, and I lost.

"And what about me? I thought I was your so-called best friend. You were the best man at my wedding, for goodness' sake. You didn't think to tell me, 'Hey, by the way, my late wife was your half-sister and my daughter is really your niece?'"

He scoffs and continues, "'Oh, and your mom actually had another child whose father isn't your dad.' You didn't think this is something your best friend would be interested in knowing? You didn't think this would be pertinent to my life?"

A bus parks by the curb and people disembark at the street corner. I don't know what to say to him. I don't know what I can do to take away the pain I've caused to everyone around me.

"Say something, dammit!"

Exhaling forcefully, I glance up as James stares down at me, his arms crossed against his chest. A vein pulses on his forehead as his sapphire eyes flash in anger.

"There's nothing I can say that'll make this better. I-I'm so sorry, James. I thought I was protecting you guys by not telling you. Abby's no longer here, anyway. I didn't see the point in opening up old wounds for your parents or creating new ones for you and Liz."

"It wasn't your secret to keep, dammit. Especially the moment you decided to get involved with Liz."

"I'm sorry. That's all I can say at this point, whether or not you believe me. The last thing I wanted to happen was to hurt the two of you."

James tilts his head up to stare at the sky as he rakes his hair again. He resumes pacing back and forth in front of me. "All these years...I had another sister out there..." He trails off, apparently overwrought with emotions.

Minutes pass by and we fall silent, the sounds of cars driving by and birds chirping in the trees keeping us company. I grip my knees tightly and bow my head as I struggle to breathe deeply. My head flashes in pain—the beginnings of a headache or a migraine. The heaviness of guilt sits on my chest like a forty-pound dumbbell.

"Is she doing better now? I tried calling and texting her, but she didn't pick up or answer me." I stare at my shoes as I let out a deep breath.

He sighs before sitting down next to me once again. "The girls are with her right now. I honestly don't know how she'll process all of this and frankly, while I appreciate your intention and your misguided attempts to not hurt us, I still can't wrap my brain around how you've kept this from us all this time. Maybe one day, when the dust settles, I'll be able to understand your position more clearly and will be able to forgive you, but that day isn't today."

I nod. "I get it. I don't blame you for being angry at me. I deserve it." I clear my throat and attempt to take another breath. Pain and regret filter through my veins, the darkness once again making its home inside me. I wonder, when Icarus plummeted from the sky, did he ever regret flying so close to the sun?

I can't bring myself to regret Liz. Not ever.

"Can you tell me about her?" James clasps his hands on his lap and stares into the distance, his shoulders slumped, resignation in his body language.

I rub my face with my palm and wet my parched lips. This I can do. The least I can do for him. "Abby was a free-spirit..."

And so, I tell him everything he wants to know about his late half-sister.

CHAPTER 24

Liz

“**M**y bandages are itchy,” Lucy complains in her car seat. “Everything hurts, Lizzy.”

I take her hand in mine and give it a squeeze. “I know, sweetie. Your boo boos will get better over time. The doctors fixed you up. You just need to continue to be a brave little girl.”

Looking at the rearview mirror from the backseat, I catch Parker’s piercing green eyes staring at me. My eyes dart away, not wanting to face him. Well, as much as I can. I’m an adult and Lucy’s aunt. Her wellbeing must come first. Even though I want to pack my things and escape with James and Jess, I don’t want to disrupt Lucy’s life or routine, especially after she’s been through such a traumatic event.

“The seatbelt hurts my boo boo too. How long until we get home?”

I take out the tablet from my bag. Desperate times call for desperate measures. “We still have an hour or so left. Since you’ve been such a brave little girl at the hospital, I think I’ll make an exception and let you play with your tablet in the car...just this once though.”

Lucy claps as she takes the device from me, her earlier pain seemingly forgotten. The cheerful sounds of *Fruit Bandit* fill the

SUV and I close my eyes, feigning sleep. I don't want to look at him or talk to him, but I know he won't be able to help himself if I appear awake. Lucy ended up staying two nights at the hospital, with Parker never leaving her side. James had a talk with him at some point and he looked more resigned than angry when we left for home this morning.

"Give him some time, Liz," James murmurs as he watches me pack my belongings into the suitcase. Parker and Lucy's things are barely touched, so it doesn't take much time to get their things in order.

"I just don't know how to face him."

"Aside from the anger, which you very much have a right to feel, what are you most afraid of?"

My hands falter at the zipper, and I look up at him. He furrows his brows, his perceptive blue eyes staring back at me. Swallowing the lump in my throat, I continue zipping up the suitcase. "Too many things, James. If I can't trust him, how can I believe he actually loves me for me? What if this grand love I'm holding out for is fake? I thought I wanted what our parents have, but..." I chuckle humorlessly. "What they have apparently is a lie too."

He takes the suitcase from me as we exit the RV and wraps his free arm around my shoulder.

"What kind of twisted love story is this? Falling in love with your late wife's half-sister, when she was the one who rescheduled the meeting with your late wife, causing her to be out in the rain... and dying from a freak accident?" My voice turns hysterical, and I cover my mouth with my hand. "How can I believe in anything anymore?"

James walks next to me, his presence making me feel less alone in this swirl of craziness. "You know, I had a chat with him last night. I was so pissed off. Not only because of what he did to you, but also for holding out on me, his supposed 'best friend.'"

He clears his throat and continues, "He didn't try to justify his actions. He just sat there and took every insult I hurled at him. I couldn't remain mad at him when he's obviously in his own personal hell. My gut tells me he's so far gone in his mind, he hasn't been making the right decisions for a very long time. I should've forced him to talk to me sooner. Jess and I knew he was shouldering a lot as a widowed, single dad, but we didn't want to push him into doing something he wasn't comfortable with. I should've done more. Maybe then, he would've felt like he could've confided in me. Maybe his mind wouldn't be so muddled."

James glances over. "Liz, I know we don't have all the answers right now, and I definitely think you guys should talk things through, but our eyes can't be wrong. How he was with you these last couple months, the smiles on his face lately. The man loves you. Other things I can't be sure about, but this, I'm pretty damn sure of."

I shake my head as we approach the parking lot, my chest heavy with sadness. If only I can be sure of it myself.

"Liz? Wake up, baby, we're home." I feel a gentle shake as my eyes flutter open. A pair of emerald eyes stare at me. My favorite eyes. The deep, gravelly voice. I smile. Parker.

His eyes flash at my expression, jolting me back to the present as the cobwebs clear from my brain. The memories of the last two days flood my mind, and my smile slips off my face. My chest clenches in pain as I stare at the man I love, with his golden-brown hair poking out at different angles on his head, no doubt from his abuse, his strong jaw currently covered with two days' worth of scruff, and those beautiful, soulful eyes. I glance away and unbuckle my seatbelt.

"Parker, honey?" The door connecting the garage with the house opens, and Regina steps out. "I was able to catch an earlier flight. I used your spare key."

She crouches down to Lucy, who is walking very slowly to avoid touching her "boo boo." She frowns as she says, "Oh my sweetheart, how are you feeling? Grandma is so worried about you." She nods at me and takes Lucy's hand, helping her into the house.

"I'm going to put our things back in the bedrooms." I move past Parker, wanting to escape.

"Liz, we need to talk—"

I hold my hand out. "No!" Taking a deep breath, I lower my voice. "Not now, please. Tonight, after Lucy is asleep. She just got home, and your mom is here. I don't want to have this conversation right now."

He nods as he backs away, his hands clenching and releasing. I hurry to my room and lock the door behind me. The curtains are closed, cloaking the room in darkness. I slide down to the floor, my hands shaking as I ponder my next steps. *What should I do now?* My phone pings with an incoming message.

Mom: Sweetheart, Jess told me Lucy got into an accident. How horrible! Is she okay?

I stare at her message and, with trembling fingers, I dial her number.

"Sweetheart? How's everything going on over there? Are Lucy and Parker okay?" Mom asks, her sweet voice carrying a tinge of concern.

"They are fine, but...I am not."

Rustling sounds filter through from the background. "What happened?"

I take one deep breath, then another, and another, my hands gripping the phone tightly.

"Liz, are you still there?"

"Mom, how come James and I have a half-sister we don't know about?" With one simple question, I flip open the lid to Pandora's box.

Loud clanging sounds come across the line as mom most likely drops something. My heart sinks. Deep down inside, I was still holding out hope somehow this is all a ridiculous mix up, that none of this is real.

"H-How did you find out?"

"Please, just tell me."

"God, I never thought I'd tell you this," she mutters under her breath. "But since you asked, I won't lie to you." I hear her shaky breath. "Your father and I broke up in college. We were together since high school, you know? We were each other's first in everything. Liz, how did you find out?"

I lean my head against the wall behind me, a headache forming. "Mom, please..." I know she'll find out her daughter is dead eventually and it'll be painful.

"Your father and I decided to separate. We were arguing a lot, and frankly, our relationship was in a lull. We were both young and thought maybe there's something better out there. So, we broke up. I dated a string of men, and I'm sure he had his share of girlfriends. I wasn't too careful or smart one time and I got pregnant. I was in no position to raise a baby, Liz. I was so young and scared. You have to understand. I just...couldn't keep her. So, your grandparents and I decided putting her up for adoption was the best thing for us. It was a closed adoption. All I know was she went to a good home...but not a day goes by when I don't think about her and wonder if things were different..." Her voice trails off as she's probably contemplating an alternate future where we'll be one happy family together.

"Does Dad know?"

"He does. Your dad and I reconnected a few years after college, and we fell back in love. I eventually told him about the baby when I was pregnant with you. He was so angry at me, even though he technically didn't have any right to be, since this all occurred when we were apart."

I let out a deep breath as a million thoughts whirl in my mind. How does one move on from something like this? How did my dad move on after learning such a secret?

"Liz, sweetheart, how did you find out about this?"

Dread snakes up my body and curls itself around my throat. This will devastate her, but there's no way around it.

"Parker's late wife was my half-sister."

• • •

I sit on one of the benches in the gardens after dinner, holding a glass of wine in my hands. The sky is clear tonight; the stars sparkling against a black backdrop, but still not a match to the millions of tiny fireballs which were visible back up in the mountains. I close my eyes and smell the light scent of wildflowers, the heaviness easing slightly in my chest.

"May I sit with you?" a deep voice asks. Parker.

I make room for him as he sits down, his familiar fragrance still sending warmth throughout my body, although the comfort is now laced with pain.

"Is this why you were an ass to me for so long? Because of my role in Abby's death?"

He sighs loudly and takes a sip of something from his glass. "The first time I met you, I was shocked. I thought I recognized you from the files Abby had. I didn't know how to react, so I left the restaurant as fast as I could. Then over time, yes, I think I avoided you because I was furious she dashed off that night to meet you. If you hadn't rescheduled your meeting, maybe things would've turned out differently. So yes, for the longest time, I was angry at you."

My heart drops at his confession. Things make so much sense now.

He continues, "Then I got to know you better...and even from afar, I couldn't help but fall under your spell. Then you moved in because of the nanny situation and well...I just couldn't stay mad at you for something which really wasn't your fault to begin with. Like I told you earlier, if anything, it was my fault."

He gulps audibly. "I tried to stay away from you because I know how complicated everything is. You're the *last* person I should fall for, with your relationship to Abby, and especially after knowing how much you idolized your parents' relationship. I didn't want to take your dream away from you. I knew it would devastate you if you found out, and the last thing I want to do is to hurt you." He sighs heavily. "But it seems like all I do is hurt the people around me."

My nose twitches as my eyes get blurry. *I still got hurt in the end.* "Did you ever love me? Or was it because I look like her?" I whisper.

There. My deepest, darkest fear, out in the open.

"Liz, it was *never* about her. My feelings toward you are all real."

"But how could you keep this from me? How could you lie for so long?" I gasp as my lips tremble. "How can I even believe *anything* out of your mouth right now?"

"I was trying to protect you." He laughs mirthlessly. "I can *never* protect the people I love. I fail everyone. If anything, I hurt the people I love. Abby. Lucy. You. I don't deserve to be happy. I just drag everyone else down with me."

We fall silent, the gardens quiet except for the chirping of crickets. I take a deep breath, memorizing the tantalizing notes of amber and bergamot, a scent combination that'll forever remind me of him.

"Parker..." I begin, my fingers gripping the stem of the wineglass. "I-I can't do this anymore. I don't know how to face you. To face the lies or the so-called truths. I don't know what to believe in anymore. Your mom is here. Lucy will be well taken care of. I-I'm going to stay with James and Jess until my sublease is up." I stand, my mind made, and walk back toward the house.

He stays silent.

So much for loving me.

Maybe my story isn't a romance. After all, it doesn't end happily ever after.

Parker

"Daddy, do you have to go to work today?"

I groan, rolling over in my bed, a bed that is cold and lonely without her. *What day is it? What time is it?* The pain in my chest is the first thing I notice. An empty hole where my heart used to be. At least a week has passed by since Liz left, but I can't keep track anymore. Everything just blurs together. Life is a continuum of tedious agony, pain, and regret.

I miss her. I miss her so fucking much.

But I don't have any right to drag her down into hell with me. I can't be so selfish anymore. I'll just end up hurting her more, like how I hurt everyone I love around me. I need to let her go, for her own good.

Grabbing my phone, I glance at the home screen. Tuesday. Eight a.m. Shit. I'm late for work. "Yes, pumpkin, Daddy is silly and overslept."

Lucy giggles, her dimples showing, and she reaches up to hug me from the side of the bed. Kids are so resilient. While she has talked about her big accident, the nice doctor, and the funny nurses at the hospital from time to time, her wounds are improving, and aside from being a bit more careful with her movements, she's bounding about the house like her old self. If only adults could be like that too.

I swing my legs off the bed and quickly get ready for work, grabbing the nearest suit and shirt I can find. Staring at my face in the mirror, I'm amazed by how my appearance remains relatively the same as a week ago, albeit a little more haggard, as if a life-changing event didn't occur and tear up my heart which has only recently started beating again. Brushing my hair back, I splash my face with cold water. *Smile, Parker. Everything is fine. Everything will be fine.* I head downstairs, my eyes squinting from the bright sunlight streaming in from the windows. I'm greeted with the smell of freshly cooked bacon and eggs.

"Honey, do you want some breakfast before you head out?" Mom asks.

I shake my head. The sight of food nauseates me. "I'm late, so I should get going." Twisting my face into a smile—a habit I've stopped doing for the last month or so—the muscles protest at the forced action.

Mom stares at me, her face grim. She isn't buying any of my bullshit anymore. "You need to eat something, Parker. You look so gaunt and unhealthy lately."

More guilt claws through my gut as I reach out and give her a brief kiss on her cheek. "Don't worry about me, Mom. I'll be fine. I'm Lucy's dad." I wince as a flash of pain hits my head. Migraines are apparently on the menu today. "I must be fine...for her," I mutter.

"Oh, honey...don't do this to yourself. Go after her, make her underst—"

"Daddy, why is Lizzy with Uncle James and Auntie Jess? Is she going to come back soon?" a cheerful voice interrupts us. Lucy stares at me, her doll-like blue eyes blinking in confusion.

Those beautiful blue eyes.

The ones that used to haunt me in my sleep are now the ones I want more than anything to see again.

Liz's eyes.

Swallowing the pins and needles in my throat, my eyes burn as I ruffle her head and lean down to talk to her. "Lizzy needs to go home. She needs to spend time with Uncle James because he's her brother. She can't always be here with us. We can't be so selfish." *What a fucking hypocrite you are, Parker. You shouldn't have gotten together with her either. Look what your selfishness has done to her.* "Daddy will find a new nanny for you, okay, pumpkin?"

"But I want Lizzy!" Her pouty lips wobble and the loud sound of blood rushes in my ears. Lucy starts crying, her tears streaming down her face. I flinch and grit my teeth.

A vein pulses on my forehead.

The tie chokes my windpipe.

I need to get out of here.

"Daddy needs to go to work. Be good for Grandma." I spin around, ignoring her sobbing as she cries against my mom's waist. Sadness and failure cloak my entire being.

Will things ever return to normal post-Liz? Can it ever return to normal?

The hollow in my chest grows, threatening to swallow me whole. *We all know the answer to that question.* Starting my car, I back out of the garage, the motions automatic. The world is gray and dull, as if she took the colors with her when she left. The jazz station turns on, filling the vehicle with soothing music, music she loves. I listen to the soft melodies and wetness prickles in my eyes. I hold on to the last vestiges of my life with her as I drive on into a future of loneliness. A future where she'll only be with me in my dreams.

• • •

My muscles burn as I haul a large crate of beverages from the loading dock to the pantry at New Beginnings. The air is thick, and the heat is sweltering. Sweat drips off my forehead as I breathe heavily from the exertion. A flashing pain pounds in my head. The bright lights in the room make it worse. The damn migraine, which ibuprofen haven't helped. Groaning, I unload the crate in the pantry as a wave of nausea hits me. Even my body is working against me. Just then, a large shadow appears in the doorway.

"Son, you look like hell," Bob mutters, giving me a water bottle.

I wave him away. "No, I'm fine. I can do this."

"You're obviously not fine. You look sick...with something. What's going on?"

I collapse in a chair right outside the pantry door as the nausea abates. I open the bottle and take a sip of water. I close my eyes and attempt deep breathing. *I need to keep going. Do what I did before. Pretend everything is fine.*

I take another big gulp and reply, "Just busy with work. That's all." I grin, hoping it's enough to stop his line of questioning.

He frowns. "No, I don't think that's it. You're doing the face again. The fake shit."

The smile slips off my face. Somehow, Liz has rendered me unable to hide my emotions anymore. I grip the water bottle tightly in my hands, the cracking sound loud to my ears.

"Where's Liz?"

I freeze. The kitchen clock ticks noisily in the background.

"She moved on. Summer vacation is ending in a few weeks anyway."

"But she's still with you, right? Don't bother denying it. I saw how you two were the last time you were here."

I hang my head low, not wanting to meet his gaze. My chest spasms in pain as another bout of nausea rises up. "We broke up. I fucked up. We shouldn't have ever gotten together in the first place."

A beefy hand slides into my vision as he pats me on my knee. "Son, look at me." I tilt my head slightly and gaze warily at him. "I don't know what's going on with the two of you and you don't need to tell me. But if being apart is making you so miserable, then think about whether or not you should be apart in the first place. Whatever obstacles there are, that's life. Overcome it together."

I turn my head back, staring mutely at the checkered floor as another stab of pain hits me in my head. Wiping my hand over my forehead, I get up slowly. I walk toward the exit to the serving stations and glance back at Bob, who's sitting there, his brow furrowing.

"Thanks, Bob. Don't worry about me. I'll be fine."

Turning around, I stride toward to the dining area to the front exit, weaving through the patrons who are walking around or carrying trays of food to the tables. I need to get some air away from the questioning glances and concerned expressions.

That's when I see her. The back of a young woman with caramel-colored hair.

Liz.

I dart toward the woman who's currently helping someone in the dinner line and grab her by the shoulder. "Liz!"

"Excuse me?" The woman turns around, confusion in her chocolate-colored eyes. Not Liz. *Pathetic, Parker. Why would she show up here, anyway?*

"S-Sorry, I thought you were someone else." I stagger back, the hollow in my chest widening, the ache deepens.

I turn around and look at the dining hall until my eyes rest at the table we sat at last time. I can hear her laughing at Bob's jokes. I can see her teasing glances and beautiful smiles as if it were yesterday. Everywhere is her. Memories of her. Thoughts of her. Life will never be the same, and deep down inside, I don't think I ever want it to be the same. Even if I can't be with her, at least this way, she's with me always. Taking another deep breath, which does little to relieve the pain in my chest, I change my mind about going outside. Instead, I hurry back into the kitchen. More manual labor, tire myself out, and perhaps one day the pain will be forgotten, leaving me with only the beautiful memories.

Four hours later, my headache has finally abated and Lucy is already asleep by the time I arrive home. I fit in a kickboxing session in my home gym, punching the heavy bag as if it were my worst enemy, as if it were...me. Every punch, a throw I wish she would inflict upon me herself. Every jab, my muscles scream in agony. Punishment. I pay my penance in the price of pain. White dots appear behind my eyes as the punching bag blurs in front of me. I clasp the bag with both hands, sweat dripping down my forehead, and the floor swirls around me. My hands and feet hurt, but nothing compares to the pain in my chest. I wait until the dizziness subsides before finishing my workout. My body is tired but my mind is unfortunately still awake. I towel off my sweat and make my way to the kitchen.

I grab a six-pack of beer from the refrigerator then retreat to the backyard, to the oval recliner Liz loves, the one we made love in. The cushions still smell faintly of her. Her sweet vanilla scent. I pop open a can and take a huge sip, the cool liquid tasting dull as I relive the last few months, the happiest time of my life. She and Lucy shrieking about a volcano in the living room. Her smiles when she saw the little lamb at the county fair. Her sweet body when she takes over the bed at night, pushing me to the far edge of the mattress. Her tears when I told her about my role in Abby's death. Her lips. Her eyes. Her voice. I toss an empty can to the ground and grab another one, drinking the liquid as if it were my last lifeline. I close my eyes and think about her once again.

"Honey... Honey!" Mom's gentle voice wakes me up. Apparently, I drifted off to sleep on the recliner.

I blink my eyes, trying to focus on the blurry image of the woman before me. "M-mom," I slur. "W-why are you u-up? Go to bed." Swinging my legs off the chair, I attempt to get up, but only succeeded in swaying unsteadily as the ground moves beneath me. I pitch forward before her arms grab me and hold on tightly.

"Parker. Don't do this to yourself, please," she pleads, her voice desperate.

I wave her away, my arms gripping the recliner. "I-I'm fine. Go to sleep. Let me be."

"She won't want you to be like this!"

Collapsing back on the chair, I reply, "I'll only hurt her. I can't protect the people I lo-ove." My voice cracks at the last word as the heaviness settles in my chest. "I can't be the prince in her fairytale. I'm the villain."

Everything hurts.

Mom wraps her arms around me as she shushes me. "Honey, don't blame yourself anymore. Everything that happened wasn't your fault. Don't punish yourself."

My eyes burn with tears. "I m-miss her so much. So damn much." The wetness slides down my face, and I'm helpless to stop it. The alcohol didn't numb the pain. Nothing ever can.

"Oh honey. Please, please call Marybeth, I beg you. I-I don't know how to help you any more than what I'm doing right now." Her voice chokes up as she continues, "I can't see you kill yourself like this...and that's what you're doing slowly but surely. You're like a walking corpse. Please...do this for me." She grips my back tighter as her petite body shakes against mine, her pained sobs slashing me from within. My body trembles against hers as tears roll down my face. I'm toxic, a failure.

Yet another person I love who's hurting because of me.

"Thanks for doing this, Jess." I carry one suitcase through the door with Jess tugging the other one in behind me.

My apartment still looks the same. The cheerful art prints and photos. The linen sofa and bright bean bags. The subletter moved out two days ago. The place is clean, and the renter told me she washed and dried everything before she left. So considerate of her. I can't, in my conscience, stay at Jess and James's place anymore. So, I'm finally moving back home.

Home.

Somehow, this place doesn't feel like home anymore. My heart yearns for a beautiful two-story house with amazing gardens, a little girl full of energy, and a man.

A man I can't forget, no matter how hard I try.

A flash of pain spreads across my body. The ache comes and goes, some moments better than others. In the good moments, I can *almost* forget about him and focus on other things. In the bad moments, I feel like curling up in a ball and hiding away from the world, not wanting to see anyone or do anything. In the deepest recesses of my soul, I often wonder, *Am I making a mistake by walking away? How can something that feels like this be the right thing to do?*

James has kept in touch with Parker and would sometimes let me know how Lucy is doing, how she's recovering. Sometimes, he'd use his phone to video chat with me while he was at their place so I could see the little girl myself. I never expected this when I started this job. I didn't expect to miss her so much either. Lucy would tell me she misses me too, and as if she's wise beyond her years, she wouldn't bring up her daddy to me. Instead, she'd tell me about her day, her friends at school, and how her boo boo was feeling much better. Her sweet voice would always bring me to tears after we hung up. James also never talks about the man himself. I think he knows it'll unmoor me. I'm barely hanging on as is.

"Of course, Liz. Don't worry about it." Jess dusts her hands off as she enters the apartment. She opens the window, letting in some sunlight and fresh air into the space.

I take out a bottle of water from my tote and hand it to her. "Sorry, I'll have to treat you to something better next time. Water is all I have."

She waves me away and takes the bottle from me. Plopping down on the linen couch, I slowly refamiliarize myself with my apartment, a place which used to be warm and cozy for me, but now feels cold. I close my eyes, finding myself wishing he was next to me, his warm arms tucking me against him. His heartbeats. His scent. It's as if I left half of my soul with him the night I packed my bags and left his place.

Jess sits down next to me and a few minutes pass by before she says, "Liz, I'm not going to bother asking you how you're doing, because I can only imagine how much pain you're in. I've seen it in the last few days." She shifts closer to me. "I just don't want you to make the same mistake I did and let go of someone who loves you because you're afraid. I got lucky with James, but life isn't certain that way. Are you sure you're making the right choice?"

"I-I don't know," I whisper. The funny thing about time is, the longer it passes by, the hazier the memories become. While it's only been a few days since I left him, the burn of betrayal has lessened its sting. In my weaker moments, I wonder why I left him in the first place. Why can't I just forgive him and move on? I'll then think about Lucy, the little girl who has wormed her way into my heart. I miss the little games we play, her shrieks of laughter, the way she eats most of the food I prepare for her with unmatched enthusiasm. But more importantly, I miss him. Even though he's all sorts of wrong for me.

I stare at one of the group photos on the wall, all of us together at Jess and James's wedding. Parker smiles at the camera, his dimples deep, his shoulders relaxed. A genuine smile. Me smiling at him. I don't remember what I was thinking of at the moment or why I was smiling at him. Perhaps our relationship started then. My heart clenches in pain as my tears threaten to make a resurgence. Things are so muddled.

"Deep down, I don't know what to believe in anymore. Everything I've built up in my mind about my ideal relationship is false. His lies—how can I get over that? How will I ever be sure the one he loves now is really me and I'm not some replacement for who he's lost?" I glance at Jess from the side of my eye. "I-I also feel guilty. I know it's stupid. But if Abby didn't die, I wouldn't have experienced what it was like to be loved by him. In some sick way, I feel like I took him from her, and he wasn't mine to take." I shake my head. "I know it makes no sense."

She smiles sadly at me. "No, don't be too hard on yourself. What you went through is not for the faint of heart. I can understand where you're coming from. But you know what I've learned from my therapist? Guilt and fear make you think and feel things that aren't real sometimes. What happened to her was a freak accident, something none of us could've foreseen or prevented. You know this, and it's not your fault. Keep telling yourself that when you have these doubts." She sits up and places her hands on her lap. "I also think sometimes love requires you to take a leap of faith...so you don't leave any regrets. Life is too short to live in fear, don't you think?"

My eyes burn as wetness tips my lashes. Another sharp flash of pain in my chest as I think about him. The flawed man. The man who feels too deeply. The man who has had so many people unjustly taken from him. The man who is too hard on himself. The man who let me experience what it feels like to be loved.

"How's James doing?" I blink my eyes rapidly as I change the subject. My brother didn't talk much about Parker or Abby during the days I stayed with them, but I know he's still reeling from it all.

Jess sits back. She doesn't force me to respond to her advice. She's considerate that way. "He's doing better. You know how it is. Men don't think the same way we do. I think he's sad he never got to meet a sister he didn't know he had, but she's abstract to him in a way she never was to you. You two actually chatted and got to know each other. There's grief to that. You both are going through a lot, but don't ever compare your experience with James's. There's no timeline to process everything."

Swallowing the lump in my throat, I smile at her, so proud of how much she has grown since her anxiety breakdown a few years ago. My brother is so lucky.

"Come on, let's do something fun. Let's watch a movie." She picks up the remote and turns on the television. *The Italian Holiday* plays on the screen and my eyes immediately water up again as I think back to the last time I watched this movie with Parker by my side.

Liz glances over and frowns. "What's wrong, Liz?"

I grab a tissue and dab away my tears. "I watched this with him," I whisper.

"Let me find something else." She picks up the remote again and I stop her, my hands clutching her wrist.

"Don't. I want to watch this."

Jess asks softly, "Are you sure?"

I nod. If I can't be with him, at least I can do the same things I used to do with him. Maybe that way, it'll be like we never broke up and he's still by my side. The heaviness in my chest mingles with the warmth from my memories of him, whether it's watching movies together at night in the living room after Lucy sleeps, making love in his beautiful gardens, or him wrapping his arms around me when I cook us dinner at night. Everywhere is him and I can't escape it. Deep down, I don't want to escape it. I miss him like a mermaid misses the ocean. It feels like I can't breathe properly because it hurts so badly.

Jess sits quietly as we watch the entire movie, laughing at the happy parts, crying at the sad parts. In a way, it's helping me process my emotions by letting it out. I'm sure the reprieve is only temporary, but I'll take what I can get. Soon enough, the sky darkens as the day bleeds into the night.

Her phone rings and she grabs it, looking at the caller ID. "It's James. He's coming by to pick me up for the work function I told you about. Are you sure you're okay being here alone? I can stay with you if you like. I'm sure he won't mind."

Shaking my head, I reply, "No, that won't be necessary. You've done more than enough for me. Thank you. Go and have fun at your event."

"Do you want me to order you some food? You have nothing in the refrigerator."

I shake my head and muster up a smile. "Don't worry about me. I'll order something later."

She stands and walks to the door. Wrapping her arms around me in a tight hug, she murmurs, "Call me if you need me. Night or day. I'll come straightaway."

My eyes tear up again. Sniffling, I nod, closing the door behind her. I open the drawer in my kitchen, where I keep my takeout menus. Italian. Mexican. Chinese. Nothing looks good. I stare at the photos of food with distaste, my appetite nonexistent. I walk toward the door, my footfalls sounding loud in the empty apartment, and I pick up one of the suitcases and haul it into the center of the living room.

Opening it up, I begin unpacking, taking out my clothes one by one and stacking them on the floor to put back into the closet later. I pull out the paper drawings Lucy drew for me in the last few months. My eyes burn at the colorful renditions of rainbows, butterflies, and unicorns. The last sheet of paper is a stick person family: the tall man being Parker, the long, wavy-haired woman being me, and the short girl in a dress with a ponytail and a crown being her, because she's always a princess. A sob escapes my mouth as I trace my fingers on the drawing. How will I ever move on from this? Then, I take out the one thing I stole from his house. His white T-shirt. The one he wore when he found me on the street that night.

Clasping it in my arms, I carry it to my bed in the corner of the room. I crawl under the white covers and hold his shirt close to me, the scent of amber and bergamot filling my heart with warmth and with pain. But I can't make myself let go. I clutch it closer to my chest as I pretend he's here with me. Maybe he's in the bathroom or going downstairs to pick up food. Maybe he's taking Lucy to the park across the street. Maybe he's missing me as much as I miss him. Tears spill out of my eyes, and I close them, crying softly into his shirt and the pillow. I don't know if I'll ever be able to move on. My chest spasms in agony as I try and fail to bite back my tears. Heartbreak is so much more than a simple word. It's a condition. One I don't see myself recovering from. Clenching his shirt tighter against my chest, I surround myself with his scent, wishing things were different.

Wishing I could be in a world where things were simpler, and we could be happy.

Together.

Parker

"I'm so proud of you for reaching out to me. I know it must have taken a lot of courage." Marybeth sits in her usual chair as she faces me, her eyes soft behind her horn-rimmed glasses. I contacted her after the night my mom held me in her arms as she cried with me. There's something extremely humbling and devastating when your mother is in tears because of you. It's a wake-up call.

"Thank you...for making the time to see me on a Saturday. I know you're usually off today." My feet tap against the carpeted floor as I grip the armrest of the leather chair. A position I've been in many times before, yet somehow this time it feels different.

My watch ticks in the quiet room, the sound prodding me along. Pushing me to do something, to say something. Marybeth sits quietly in her chair as she waits for me to continue. I used to find this behavior of hers extremely annoying, but now I think I finally understand. She can't help me unless I make the first move.

And I need to take that first step. It's not just about Lucy anymore, it's also about Mom. And me. I can't forget about myself and pretend everything is fine because if I don't help myself, the remaining people in my life will be hurt by it. And I can't hurt anyone anymore. Not if I can help it.

Taking a deep breath, I begin, "The reason I came to see you the first time was because my mom found Lucy crying by my bed after I got piss-assed drunk, punched a hole in the wall of my bedroom, and passed out cold afterward."

To her credit, she didn't flinch. She just sits there, her gaze unwavering, as she waits for me to proceed.

"I didn't want to come. What good was it to talk about it? How would talking change anything? But I didn't want to lie to Mom, so I made myself call you. I made myself show up month after month when I felt nothing but resentment toward the idea of talk therapy."

She nods as she jots down some quick notes. "I can understand that. Life has thrown you some hard curveballs. It may seem like talking won't do anything to change that. And you're right. It doesn't change the past, but it can help you change your future, by allowing you to process the tragedies in a healthier manner," she says softly, "but everyone's path is different. You can't force someone to open up when they don't want to. Nor should you. All that matters is you're here today and you want things to change. That's the bravest first step you can take."

My lips arch up in a half smile. I twist open the cap of the water bottle she gave me earlier, a motion I've done many times before, but this time, I'm not doing this to hide my emotions anymore. Inhaling deeply, I pause to gather my courage in order to continue. I take a sip of water, and explain, "For the longest time, I hated myself. I'm angry. So angry it's hard to function at times. I blame myself for Abby's death, for taking Lucy's mom away from her because I couldn't control my emotions that night. Then I met Liz..."

The words spill from my lips as I pour my sins out to her as if I'm in a confessional at church. I told her how I was barely hanging on by a thread before Liz burst into our lives. I told her how I was so angry at her in the beginning, but soon realized I was furious at myself this entire time. I confessed my lies, the secrets I kept hidden from Liz, the secrets that ultimately devastated her. I told her about Lucy's accident and my role in it. And finally, I told her about our breakup, and how I couldn't go back to hiding behind a façade of fake smiles and charm, how I ended up drunk once again a few nights ago, barely surviving.

"And I haven't spoken to her because I know if I do, I won't be able to hold myself back from her. I'm selfish that way. But she has never really left my side...not really. Everywhere I go contains memories of her." I chuckle sadly as the burning sensation returns to my eyes. Looking down, I stare at the empty water bottle in my hand as I await her judgment.

Sounds of pen scratching against paper reach my ears. Finally, she puts her pen down and says, "I don't think it's selfish to want to be with someone you love."

Of all the things out of her mouth, I didn't expect acknowledgement and acceptance of my flaws. I stare mutely at her.

"God forbid, if something like this ever happens to Lucy, what will you tell her?"

My response is automatic. "Don't beat yourself up over a series of unfortunate accidents. Don't let the mistakes of the past affect your future." I shake my head, chuckling humorlessly at myself. "Don't let fear ruin something good in the present. Shit, it's easier said than done, isn't it?"

Marybeth smiles, her eyes soft and kind. "You know why that's the case? It's easier to be rational and logical when we analyze other people's problems and much harder to be objective when it comes to our own issues. Our emotions, fear, guilt, and anger are all powerful motivators for us and often interfere with the rational side of our brains. But sometimes, even though we feel these emotions, we need to acknowledge what we feel isn't reality, even if we don't believe it at the time."

"But what if it's actually true? What if the people I love always get hurt because of me? What if I open up and get hurt once again?" I whisper, my blood rushing in my ears.

Perhaps that's the deepest fear inside the darkest recesses of my traumatized soul all this time.

"Well, let's check the facts then. The facts don't lie. Did you have any direct control over Abby getting into an accident?"

"Not directly, but I didn't help—"

She holds her hand up. "Let's focus on direct control because the world is filled with too many what ifs, which may or may not be relevant. Even if you weren't in a fight with her, the result could've been the same."

"Did you have any direct control over Lucy getting into her bike accident?"

"No, but if I had watched her—"

"What would you have done? Could you have been faster than a kid barreling down the path on a bike? Chances are, probably not. Did you do your job by making sure she had on a helmet? Yes, you did. In fact, because you did that, you most likely saved her from suffering a traumatic head injury."

Marybeth waits for me to contemplate her answer before continuing, "Do you love your daughter and try your best to be a good father to her?"

I nod. I may not be meeting my internal standards, but I know I'm trying my hardest for her. The weight on my shoulders lessens slightly as a little bird of hope whispers in my ear, *Perhaps you shouldn't be so hard on yourself.*

"So now, let's talk about Liz. Do you love her still? And what have you done that's directly hurting her?"

I bite my cheek and grip the armrest. Liz, perhaps my biggest victim in this entire ordeal. Looking down at my hands, I murmur, "I do love her, with all my heart. I feel like I can't breathe without her. But I was an asshole to her. I took out my anger on her...I lied to her."

Marybeth's voice is calm and soothing as she responds, "And what will you tell Lucy if she has hurt someone else emotionally?"

"To apologize and to do better next time."

"So, by taking your own advice, we must make amends, right? If those actions are directly controlled by you, then the next steps are also in your control. If you really love her, perhaps working on yourself, rewiring your brain to think differently, teaching yourself ways of coping with these strong emotions in a healthier manner may be a way to make something out of a series of difficult situations. Then, do what your heart tells you to do...apologize and try to win her back or apologize and move forward. Those are both options for you to consider when you get to that point."

"But what if I hurt her again or hurt others around me?"

"In psychology, we call this fortune telling. At the end of the day, it's a cognitive distortion, because no one really knows what'll happen in the future. You've dealt with a lot of difficult situations, Parker, and that's a fact. You'll be able to deal with whatever happens in the future. If you catch yourself thinking 'what if' in the future, remind yourself it's fortune telling and may very well not happen." She leans back. "As for your other question, whether or not you'll get hurt again, no one can tell you, but perhaps the question to ask yourself is whether your life is better with Liz in it or without her in it. And if it's better with her in it, is she worth the risk of opening yourself back up to vulnerability? That's something for you to think about and decide."

I roll out the tense muscles in my shoulders as I think about what she's saying. It all sounds so logical right now.

"I'm not going to lie and tell you this will all be easy. We can set our expectations and know you may default back to your old way of thinking, but recognizing those unhealthy patterns is the first step for you to do something about them. We're rewiring neural pathways, and that takes time and practice. If you go in with these expectations, we can do this over time together."

"How do I reconcile with all those accidents? Just damn bad luck?"

Marybeth walks over to her desk to pull out a printout. She hands it to me. "Radical acceptance. This is a worksheet explaining this distress tolerance skill. I want you to read it and try using it when these thoughts come up. The theory is simple, but it takes practice. It boils down to accepting there are things outside of your control and we can't change the present facts. This doesn't mean we approve of the situation. We just accept things as they are. You know the saying 'it is what it is'? That's radical acceptance. Then, allow yourself to feel all the emotions that come up and process them in a healthy manner."

My mind whirls with the possibilities, the various scenarios which can come up and sidetrack me. I sigh heavily as doubt creeps back in, trying to take root in my chest.

She leans forward. "Parker, this will take time. But I'll be with you every step of the way. There's hope, and that's what you need to hold on to right now. You already took the first step. Keep moving forward, one step at a time, and focus on the next step, and not too far in the future."

The rest of the session passes by in a blur and we make an appointment to increase our frequency to meeting weekly. When I walk out of her office, for the first time in a very long time, I feel something deep inside my soul...hope. I'm no stranger to hard work and perseverance and if doing this work with Marybeth will help me get back on track and be a better father to Lucy, a better son to Mom, and a better man to Liz, if she'll have me back, I'll die trying.

I'm too stubborn to lose.

DING DONG.

I look at my phone. Eight a.m. on a Sunday morning. Who's here so early on a weekend? I don't think I have any events this morning. It has been a month since I moved back to my apartment, but then again, my life has been a haze of going through the motions of attempting to put together some lessons for the new school year beginning next week and trying not to think about him. About Lucy. About the gaping hole in my heart.

"Coming!"

Rolling out of bed, I look at the rest of my apartment. Old takeout boxes are on the table, papers scattered over the sofa and the floor, freshly washed clothes strewn about everywhere. I sigh. Hopefully, whoever is out there won't mind this mess. Peering through the peephole, I find myself staring at the serious face of my brother, and it appears he has brought other people with him. I swing open the door and am greeted with James, Jess, and my parents.

This is an intervention.

"Mom? Dad? What are you doing here?" I step aside and allow them to enter the apartment.

"Oh my, this is worse than I thought," Mom mutters as she starts picking up the papers from the floor and stacking them into neat piles.

Jess starts retrieving clothing from all over the apartment and putting it onto my bed for folding later. James walks to my kitchen and takes out a few glasses, pouring water, and starting coffee, the whirring sound of the machine breaking past the initial shock of having my entire family here in one place.

"What's going on, guys?"

My dad walks up to me and puts his hand on my back, ushering me to take a seat on the sofa. "Sweetheart, we're worried about you...and your mom and I thought it's best to talk to you in person about what you found out recently." He smiles softly at me, his kind eyes crinkling at the corners.

"When did you get in? Please don't tell me you took the red-eye from Boston and came straight here. You should've rested—"

"No, no, no we didn't, honey. We came in last night and stayed with your brother."

Nodding, I feel relieved. My dad can't sleep well on flights and every time he takes a red-eye, he always ends up getting sick afterward. I grab a hair tie from the coffee table and put my hair up in a messy bun. Rubbing my hand over my face, I ask, "So, what do you guys want to talk about?"

Mom finishes stacking the papers on the table and sits on the other side of me. "Sweetheart, I can't imagine what you've been through...experiencing so much and learning about...Abby." She chokes up at her late daughter's name. I can't imagine how it must feel to know your flesh and blood has passed away, even if it was your choice to give her up as a baby. My eyes prickle at my mom's anguish and also at my loss. She was someone I could've grown close to.

I nod as Jess and James sit down on the bean bags, their faces concerned. "I-I'm just so confused and feeling too much. She was my sister, and I didn't even know it. I didn't even get a chance to know her better. I know it's stupid, but I also feel like I took her place with Parker. He never would've been mine if she didn't go out to meet me that night. I still can't reconcile that." My heart twists as the ache settles in my chest. I clasp my hand to my chest. "There's so much guilt and sadness here and I can't seem to move through this."

My mom takes a tissue for herself and hands one to me. "It's okay to grieve, sweetie. It's a loss for everyone and you already know it's not your fault. The feelings will fade in time." I dab my wet eyes and hang my head down.

"Have you talked to him?" my dad asks. I don't need to ask who he's referring to.

I shake my head. "I-I can't."

"Why, sweetie?"

"I'm afraid I'll just go back to him if I see him," I whisper, the floor blurry as tears gather in my eyes.

"And would that be so bad?" Jess asks softly.

"What if he hurts me again? What if I'm just a replacement? I know he said I'm not, but I don't know if I really believe him. What if one day, he just lets me walk away again?" I don't know if my heart can take the heartbreak. My gaze flickers to my parents. "I always thought I wanted a relationship like yours, the idealistic fairytale. The 'first love, then marriage and kids,' but with every-thing recently, I don't know what I believe in anymore."

The room is silent as everyone ponders my questions. My dad speaks up first. "They say life is short, but I think it's not so short where there won't be any ups and downs. Love is the same way. When your mom told me she had a daughter when we were apart, I felt betrayed, even though I had no right to. I think I was more up-set she kept it from me until we were pregnant with you. At the end of the day, the trust or lack thereof was the biggest issue for me."

He takes a sip of water. "But in time, I came to realize I'm not perfect, just like how life isn't perfect. We all have our issues and our own baggage. If we truly love someone, we need to accept them for who they really are and accept the risks of getting hurt. After all, love in and of itself is a risk. You're joining your heart with some-one you have no control over and that's always scary. But where there are risks, there are rewards as well. I decided I love your mother too much to lose her over issues in her past. We worked hard to rebuild our trust and here we are, almost forty years later, still deeply in love."

"Only you can decide whether or not Parker is worth taking a risk for. And he can't read your mind, sweetheart. If you're afraid you're a replacement, ask yourself how you felt when you were with him. Trust your gut. Also, ask him. Communicate with him. If you decide your life is better with him in it, take the risk and find out for yourself. Don't live your life with regrets." Mom grabs my hand and gives it a quick squeeze.

"Liz, I'm here for you. You haven't asked, so I haven't told you, but Parker had a bit of a breakdown earlier on. He's taking your breakup really hard," James volunteers.

My heart skips a beat and my head snaps up. "Is he okay? What about Lucy?"

"He's fine. His mom intervened, and he's meeting with his therapist more regularly now. I don't think he'd feel that way about someone who is merely a 'replacement.' I know you need to find out from the source if you choose to do so, but from my perspective, he loves you...even the blind can see that."

"Sweetheart, we're staying in LA for a week. Let me know if you want me to come over and stay with you. We just worry so much about you," Mom says as she pulls me in for a hug, her warmth comforting. "Whatever you decide, we'll support you the whole way."

I return her hug as questions linger in my mind. Whatever I end up deciding, I'm so thankful for having such a wonderful family.

. . .

"Hi, Ms. Chapman!" Marcus waves to me in the playground at lunchtime. He's a proud first grader now. There's always an innate sense of pride at seeing my kids move up to different grades in school each year, to see them become more independent, surer of themselves. The blistering heat of summer is slowly fading into the cooler weather of fall, or whatever can be considered as fall in LA. The temperatures are in the mid-seventies, perfect weather for the first day of school. I wave back as I cut through the cafeteria toward the staff lunchroom. Work is an excellent distraction for me, allowing me to take a break from thinking about him and what I should do.

"Hey, Liz, wait up!"

I turn around and see Melanie walking toward me, her perfect ponytail swaying side to side. I smile sheepishly at her. "Hi, Melanie." I know what she's going to say next.

She gives me a once-over. "I just want to make sure you're doing okay after everything that went on. You were a hard person to get ahold of, missy. I even stopped by your place the other day and you weren't home."

I pull her in a brief hug. "Sorry. I just needed time to process through some things. Thank you for trying to check in on me. That's very sweet of you."

We begin walking next to the lunch tables, which are now filled with rowdy kids eating their food, laughing, and chatting with friends they haven't seen for a few months.

"So, how are you?"

I sigh. "I don't know. I think the initial wave of shock and emotions has settled down. I'm just trying to figure out the next steps."

"To see him or not?"

I nod.

She links her arm with mine. "Follow your gut, Liz. What's the worst that could happen, right?" Suddenly, she slaps her hand on her forehead. "Oh shit. I forgot I need to meet with Sandra for lunch today. We'll talk later, okay?" She hurries off in the opposite direction.

My phone buzzes in my pocket.

Jess: Hey, hoping the first day of school is not too busy for you. Fyi, Charles is on a business trip in LA and he stopped by our place the other day to say hi. He mentioned he was going to Pasadena soon to meet with one of their local partners and was going to connect with you to say hi. Just wanted to let you know so you won't be surprised.

I smile as I type a response.

Liz: Sure, that's nice of him. Thanks for letting me know. So, what does James have to say about him dropping by?

Jess: Technically, he dropped by to see him, not me. They were laughing after dinner. I think he's finally over it. Your brother can be so...

Liz: Possessive? Demanding? All the above?

Jess: *winks*

"Lizzy!"

I freeze. I'd recognize the sweet little voice anywhere, and only one person calls me by that name. Turning around, I spot Lucy running toward me, her hair in a low ponytail again. I'm guessing Parker did her hair this morning.

"Lucy! I miss you. How are you doing?" I crouch down and wrap my arms around her.

She slaps her hands over her mouth and whispers loudly, "Oops! I forgot and called you Lizzy at school."

"Shhh... I won't tell." I look around surreptitiously. "I don't think anyone noticed."

She grins, but then her smile falls. "I miss you, Lizzy. Other than the times when Uncle James let me use his phone to talk to you on video, you haven't come to visit me."

My heart twists. Other than missing Parker, the person I worry most about is her. "I know. Maybe someday I can visit you. Right now, Lizzy has some things going on and can't come to your house."

"You're too busy?" She hangs her head low, her shoulders drooping. "I get it. Adults are busy. That's what Grandma tells me. Daddy is busy too."

"Has he not been at home?"

"For a long time, he was really busy at work, and I didn't see him a lot, but now he's at home again." She leans in, beckoning with her arms as if to tell me a secret. "I think Daddy is sad."

The heavy ache returns to my chest as I think of him. His penetrating eyes, his tense shoulders, the profile always looking so lonely. I wish—What if I just go and talk to him? My heart kicks against my rib cage. "Is he still sad?"

She nods. "I think he's trying to be happy, but sometimes I see him with a sad face. But he'll smile when he sees me."

"Sometimes, adults get sad like little children too."

"Because they were mean to their friends and their friends don't want to play with them anymore?"

I laugh, ruffling her hair before tying it into a better ponytail. A little kid almost barrels into Lucy and I quickly pull her to the side. "Something like that."

"Why don't they just say sorry to their friend and play together again?"

The ruckus in the cafeteria fades to the background as I stare at Lucy, her hopeful blue eyes gazing back at me. Suddenly, things seem clear to me.

I know what to do.

The cemetery is quiet when I arrive after work. The dim glow of daylight as the sun sets illuminates the path before me. I walk past centuries-old tombstones, which depicted lives that ended too soon or lives that survived untold heartaches until old age. So many stories on these hallowed grounds. Birds chirp softly in the dense trees. A small breeze ruffles the freshly fallen leaves on the grass. The grounds are immaculately kept, as can be expected in this private resting place for the rich and famous.

Finally reaching my destination, a private family plot at the corner of the grounds, I stand in front of the grave I was searching for.

Abby Wellington, beloved wife, mother, and daughter.

She was laid to rest in her adopted family plot, next to her great-grandparents and her other ancestors. A fresh bouquet of lilies lies in front of the tombstone. Perhaps her parents were here before. I lay down my bouquet of daffodils, her favorite, and take a seat on the stone bench in front of her headstone.

"Abby," I begin, my voice rusty, "I...I hope, wherever you are, you're painting again. You always wanted to be free, to be a citizen of the world, and I hope you're up there doing just that. I hope you're looking down upon us and not too disappointed at how I'm raising Lucy. She's such a sweet little girl, a spitting image of you, really."

I wet my lips and let out a deep breath. "I'm sorry I haven't visited as often as I should. I think, deep down inside, I've never forgiven myself for that day when I called you when you were on the road. I-I just couldn't come and face you. But now, I'm learning sometimes tragic things happen for no reason, and there's little I could've done to prevent these things from occurring."

A small gray bird with a yellow beak flies from the trees to sit atop of her tombstone, its eyes keen as it stares at me.

"Thank you for giving us a chance, for giving me your love, however long it lasted. Thank you for bringing Lucy into this world. I know you loved her with all your heart, even if the way she came into the world wasn't planned. I hope as you look down on us in the future, you'll see her grow into a wonderful human being."

I wipe a stray tear from my cheek. "You'll always have a place inside me, but I want to let you know there's someone else occupying my heart now." I let out a ragged sigh. "I actually met Liz, your sister, the person you wanted to meet that day. You were right. She is wonderful. She's the best person I know and I...I love her. I love her so damn much. I'd like to think perhaps you're up there orchestrating this, probably laughing at how I've made a mess of the situation. Or perhaps you're irritated at how I've fucked this up. Liz loves Lucy too. I did some things to make her mad at me, but I intend to win her back."

Standing, I look at the bird still perched there. "T-Thank you, Abby, for everything. I want to tell you in person I'm moving on. I'll work on myself and be a better dad to Lucy, and hopefully one day Liz will take me back."

The bird coos at me, the soft sounds feeling significant somehow. As if Abby is letting me know she's listening. "You'll always be in our memories, Abby, and Lucy will know what a wonderful mom she had."

With those parting words, I walk slowly back to my car, each step feeling lighter than before. Perhaps the truest absolution I've been looking for actually comes from myself.

• • •

"Good to see you looking more like a human being and less like a zombie." Dylan smirks into the camera as I lean back in my leather chair in the office. We're wrapping up our biweekly catch-up call, which usually consists of us going over our latest financial statements and updates on our largest projects.

I shrug. "What can I say? I told you I'm working on myself, and I never undersell."

"Easy for you to say now. You don't know how worried I was a few weeks ago when you were looking like the husk of a man you used to be...and I mean the post-trauma Parker, not even the pre-trauma version of you. Any more moping from your side and I would've flown over there and kicked you in the ass."

"Geez, your concern is duly noted."

"You're welcome. Always glad to have your back. But really, how are things going with you?"

I take a deep breath. I've been going to therapy once a week, sometimes even twice a week, when I feel my control is slipping. Marybeth told me in one of our sessions the people who really care about me want to help me, even if it means just being a listener. *They don't need you to be perfect and happy all the time. They just need you to be you.* "It's touch and go, to be honest." I toy with my phone. "Some days are easier than others. But on the bad days, especially when I see Lucy staring at moms holding their daughters when we go out, the guilt is overwhelming. I know now it's not my fault, but those days are still pretty tough to deal with."

His slate eyes stare at me, his expression somber. "I can't imagine what you went through. But I do know this. You are a good man and a good father. Lucy is lucky to have you. And if you ever need someone to talk to, I'm always here for you. Time zones be damned."

Biting my inner cheek, I reply, "Thanks, man. That means a lot."

"Anytime, my brother from another mother."

I snort as I shake my head. "That's what you used to say in college."

"Some things age really well, just like—"

"Please don't say you. Please don't."

He grins at me as he arches his brow. I chuckle as I rub my forehead and smile.

Knock. Knock.

"Come in."

"Sir, your eleven o'clock is here." Betsy pops her head in.

"Sure, send him in." I look at Dylan. "Hey, I have to go. Meeting with Adrian—will keep you posted."

"Sure thing. Say hi to him for me."

A few minutes later, Betsy opens the door again and in steps a person I haven't seen in years.

"Parker Wellington, haven't seen you in ages," a deep voice greets me. Adrian walks in and I'm momentarily stunned. He's not the quiet, serious kid I mentored at Cornell when I was in grad school and he was in college anymore. Instead, he strides in, confident in his tall bearing, and his dark-brown hair is carefully tousled. He's in a dark, high-quality three-piece suit even I'm envious of, and I own a closet full of bespoke suits. His lips tip in a small grin.

I walk around my desk and bring him in for a brief hug, slapping him hard on his back. "The infamous Adrian Scott. It's been... what? At least ten years? You dropped off the face of the earth soon after you graduated and I don't hear from you until now. The only info I ever learn is through newspaper articles and gossip rags, and they don't even print photos of you in those things. 'The reclusive billionaire investor strikes again.'" I raise my fingers in air quotes at his moniker. "Should I be worried now that you're here?"

"I'm not the grim reaper." His light-blue eyes shine with mirth as he takes a seat across from my desk. I sit down in my chair and clasp my hands in front of me.

"Depends on who you ask, I suppose." I cock my head to the side as I study him. His face, all sharp angles, is serious. If I didn't know him any better, I really would think he's the grim reaper. "So, what brings you to my office today?"

"Catching up...and business. I'd like to hire your firm to construct my new offices here, among other things."

"Relocating from New York?"

He nods. "I am. I still have an office there, but I want to move back and revamp our businesses here. I already bought the land and the building. Ready to tear it down and rebuild, and I thought of you. I've been following the news and achievements of your firm for a while now and do admire your designs, the elegance of modern architecture with the usage of environmentally friendly materials."

"You came prepared. I don't know if I should be pleased or worried."

"Definitely pleased. I'm not here to acquire you. If I were, trust me, you wouldn't see it coming."

I bark out a laugh and shake my head. "Still a dickhead. Some things never change."

He lets out a low chuckle, the smile instantly transforming his face. "I need to run to another meeting, but I'll have my secretary contact yours and we should meet again to finalize some details." He gets up and walks toward the door.

"And to catch up," I holler after him, arching my brow.

Adrian laughs, waving his hand in the air as he walks out the door, leaving as swiftly as he came.

Just then, my phone rings. *James.*

"Hey, thanks for calling me back," I say in the way of a greeting. I set the phone on speaker.

Paper rustles in the background. Tapping of keyboard strokes. James murmurs something to his coworker before speaking. "Sorry there. What's up?"

My pulse picks up in speed as flutters gather in my stomach. Taking a deep breath, I say, "Consider this your heads-up. I intend to win Liz back."

The tapping stops, and for a few moments, it's silent. James clears his throat. "Are you sure that's what you want?"

"Yes. I love her, James. It was always real between us. I fucked up and I need to make things better. I need to show her we belong together." I drum my fingers on the table, feeling like I'm waiting for a verdict from a judge.

"She's not a rebound, right?"

"No." I pound my fist on my desk. "Never. If anything, she's the last person I should fall for, and yet I did...hard. And I don't regret it, ever." I swallow the lump in my throat. "I love her, James. I really do. Everything between us is real. I-I need her...she's the other half of me."

More silence. Finally, he takes a deep breath and says, "I've always felt like I owed you something for helping get Jess and me together. This is me repaying you." He walks me through Liz's life these days, her schedule, and slowly, a plan comes to fruition.

• • •

Parking my car in front of her school, I wait for her. The crowds of children are thinning out as parents come by to pick them up from the front lawn or the courtyard inside of the school. I grip my steering wheel, rehearsing in my mind what I plan to tell her, preparing to bare my soul to her and receive the consequences, whatever they may be. *She's afraid she's a replacement for you.* James's words echo in my brain. *No, Liz, you were never a replacement. You're the other half of me I've been searching for without realizing it.*

Swallowing the lump in my throat, I reach for the door handle. Just then, I see the unmistakable silhouette of Liz walking out of the gates, her beautiful hair shining like a halo under the sun. She raises her arms and waves, her smile so blinding my heart stops for a few beats. My lips tip up in a smile as I pull the lever.

"Liz! You look great. It's nice to see you in your element." A familiar blond Adonis walks into view, his gray suit draped over him like second skin, like he's a model for a major Parisian fashion house. I grit my teeth as I let go of the lever, debating whether or not I should exit the car.

"Thank you. I didn't expect you to be here so soon. Already done with your meeting?"

"Yeah. It was a quick one. Where do you want to go?"

Liz shrugs, her hair swaying over her shoulders. "I know a few places nearby."

"Sure, let's take my car. I parked over there."

I fall back into my seat, the burst of hope inside me deflating, as I watch the woman I love get into the car of another man. *Charles is better for her, Parker. Successful, uncomplicated, not dealing with so much. He'd treat her well. He wouldn't hurt her like you did.* The nagging voice deep inside me makes an appearance. The blood rushes in my ears and I grip the steering wheel.

No.

The past is in the past and you're doing the work now. She loves you and you love her. Don't let fears and fortune telling rule your future. I slowly take three deep breaths, releasing the coiled muscles in my neck and shoulders and close my eyes. What will I tell Lucy if she runs into obstacles in the future? Regroup and try again.

Try. Again.

Turning the key in the ignition, the car purrs to life. I slowly back out of my spot and merge onto the main street.

This time, I'm not giving up.

CHAPTER 30

Liz

Standing in front of my bathroom mirror, I stare at my reflection. I let out a shuddering breath as I smooth my wavy hair. I'm wearing my favorite blue sundress today, the one that brings out my eyes. My hands feel clammy and I wet my lips. I can do this.

I'm going to see him.

I'm going to tell him how I feel and what I'm afraid of. Then I'll wait and see what he says. At least, this way, I've tried my best and have given it my all. I'll be able to say I have lived with no regrets.

With that, I give myself a nod and stride to the sofa, picking up the leather tote. I grab my keys from the dining table and walk to my door.

Ding Dong.

I jump a little, my hand flying to my chest. The sudden sound of the doorbell jolts me to a halt.

Ding Dong.

"Liz! I know you're in there. I see your car parked outside. Please...please open up. I know you probably hate me and want nothing to do with me—"

Parker.

I swing the door open and come face-to-face with the man I love, the person I haven't been able to forget or let go of, despite wanting to so many times. He stands before me, his chest heaving as if he ran up several flights of steps to get to me. He's wearing a thin gray Henley, which clings to his sculpted body, the shirt tucking partially into his dark jeans. Amber and bergamot permeate the air. My heart skips a beat. My pulse races. My body finally wakes up after a month and a half of slumber.

Parker stares into my eyes with his piercing green gaze. The seconds bleed into minutes as we stand in front of each other, neither of us knowing where to begin, what to say, or what to do next. Finally, he lets out a ragged breath.

"Liz. Please, hear me out. Just five minutes of your time. Then, if you want me to leave, I'll go, and you won't ever have to see me again."

I nod, still speechless at seeing him on my doorstep. I grip the fabric of my dress as I wait for him to continue.

"I-I love you. Everything between us has been real and it still is." He swallows audibly. "I'm stupid for letting you walk out the door that night. I thought what I was doing was the best thing for you, and you deserved better than me, someone who is damaged goods. I blamed myself for hurting everyone around me, including you…and the last thing I wanted to do was to hurt you. But…I can't live without you. I tried, and I failed. You are my air, my sunshine, the reason I smile each day. You're the first person I think of when I wake up in the morning and the last person on my mind before I drift off to sleep."

My eyes sting with tears as I stare at him. I wet my lips and I let out a ragged breath, my heart thumping loudly in my chest. Parker's eyes take on a wet sheen as he reaches down to pick up a pink gift bag from the floor. His fingers tremble as he hands it to me. I pull out a small hardcover album and smooth my hands over the supple lavender leather cover, engraved with the words, "The Best Parts of Me." I flip open to the first page and gasp. A photo of me laughing in the backyard.

Parker recites, apparently having memorized the contents of the album, "There are so many reasons I love you, too many to name, but I thought I could share a few with you in this album.

I love your smile, the way your eyes crinkle at the corners, the way your cheeks pinken up when you laugh, without a care in the world."

I flip to the next page. A photo of me volunteering at the shelter, talking to someone in the food line. He murmurs, "I love your heart, the way you have room for everyone. The way you see the best in people around you, even people who've hurt you in the past. The way you treat everyone, regardless of their station in life, with the utmost respect."

A drop of liquid splashes onto the matte pages. I swipe it off before realizing those were my tears. On the next page, a photo of me sleeping, my arms curled around a muscular torso. "I love the little sounds you make in your sleep. The way you use me as your body pillow. The way you wake up a little disgruntled, as if someone dared to interrupt you in your dreams."

The next page is a photo of the atrocious sandwich at the county fair. He continues, "I love your zest for life, the way you always want to try something new. The way you don't back down from a challenge. The way you'd bat your lashes at me whenever you want me to do something I don't want to do."

I wipe my wet cheeks and caress the pages, flipping to the next one, a photo of me and him at a table, eating sushi at my favorite Japanese restaurant. He's looking down at me, his gaze full of love, while I'm grinning at the camera. "I love how you challenge me, how you call me out on my bullshit. I love how you see past the fake mask I put on in front of others, but you're compassionate at the same time, giving me parts of you I have no right to take."

His voice chokes up, and my gaze flickers to his, staring into his eyes. A vein pulses in his forehead as he clenches his hands. His lips tip up in a shaky smile. "I love how you love Lucy and me, giving us your all, even when I have nothing to offer you in return." I look down at the next photo, a photo of the three of us when we got on the Ferris wheel, Lucy laughing as she stares at me. "You love so fiercely, so bravely, so unapologetically...and I love you for it." My lips tremble as my eyes return to his intense emerald gaze, my pulse racing.

Parker takes a deep breath. "There are one hundred pages in the book, each with an inscription of why I love you and only you, Liz. You're never anyone's replacement. You shine too brightly to be in anyone's shadows. You're the other half of my soul, the yin to my yang. You got it all wrong. You were looking for a fairytale and a prince to whisk you off to a castle, but you're a queen all along and I hope you'll let me stand behind you at the throne, to live in *your* fairytale with you."

He looks down at my fingers currently clenching the photo album in a death grip. "You have every right to not give me another chance. I've hurt you, I've lied to you, and I'm so sorry for my actions. I'm working on myself and seeing my therapist regularly. I can't promise you there won't be any more moments of guilt and self-doubt in the future, but I can promise you I'll try to face them in a healthier manner. Even if you decide you can't take me back, I just want to tell you, I love you all the same."

He lifts his eyes to mine as I swipe my hand over my cheeks again. The tears won't stop falling, but these are tears of joy, not sorrow.

"Liz, please forgive me. Please—"

I slip the album into the bag and drop it behind me, the *thump* of the bag hitting the floor sounding loud in the hallway. Pulling his head down, I press my lips to his, my heart thudding rapidly. He freezes, his body coiling with tension, and I bury myself in him. I kiss his closed lips, the lips I've missed every day since we were apart. I communicate my forgiveness with each suction. I declare my love with each swipe of my tongue, each tease of the seam of his lips.

Groaning, he shudders against me for a brief second before his mouth parts and he returns my embrace fervently, as if I'm the air and sustenance he needs to keep on living. Parker consumes me as he wraps his arms around me, pulling me tightly against him. His lips capture mine as our kiss turns frantic. His tongue slips in, each swipe melting my insides. We breathe each other in, kissing each other as if our lives depend on it. I climb him, wrapping my legs around his waist, and he hoists me up, his hands palming my butt. Warmth and heady pleasure spreads throughout my body and soul.

I'm home. I'm finally where I belong.

"I love you, Parker, and I always will," I manage to whisper against his lips as we break apart to take a breath. The first real breath I've taken since we were apart.

"I love you," he rasps, his voice husky and thick with emotion, before tugging my lips with his again. He carries me into my apartment and kicks the door shut behind us. Slamming me against my door, he kneads my ass and he kisses me as if he's ravenous. As if I'm the reason his heart beats every day. Each suck from him draws a moan from me. Each nip from his teeth, a shiver from me. I clutch his hair and part my lips as he trails kisses down the column of my neck, his teeth grazing the sensitive pulse points.

He tugs the straps of my sundress off my shoulders as he buries his head against my cleavage. His hips grind against me and the unmistakable hardness in his jeans hits me right at the bundle of nerves between my legs. Shards of heat gather there as wetness dampens my underwear. I writhe against him and claw his back, desperate for these layers of clothes to be gone between us. He hisses as my nails dig deeply into his muscles, his kissing turning feral as he bites down on the tops of my breasts.

"Parker!" I gasp at the sharp pain, which he follows with a hard suction and a swipe of his tongue to soothe the burn. Liquid heat flows through my body as I arch my back against the door, thrusting my chest at him, needing more. So much more.

"Fuck me. These tits have haunted me every night these last few weeks," he grunts, his voice hoarse as he spins us around and strides to the bed, depositing me onto the blankets.

I lay there, my mind in a mush as I breathe heavily, my lungs aching for more air, my heart aching for more of him. My chest rises and falls, and his emerald eyes darken in intensity. He zeroes in on my heaving breasts and I look down, realizing one side of my dress has slipped off in our passionate embrace, baring one full breast and the pebbled nipple to the cold air. "I can't wait to taste them, to suck them until you're going mad for me."

Parker swipes his tongue across his lips and he draws his Henley over his head, tossing the shirt to the ground. His chest flexes with each motion, the morning light illuminating every contour of his shredded physique. I bite on my bottom lip as wetness coats my mouth and the throbbing between my legs intensifies. He prowls toward me, shedding his jeans and boxer briefs as he goes, until he stands before me naked, his long, hard cock jutting out, the vein on the underside pulsing, the tip dark red and wet with pre-cum. He grips his erection, giving it a rough pump, and a groan emits from his chest.

"Take your dress off," his voice commands, an octave deeper than usual.

His domineering words send a gush of wetness out of my pussy, the juices leaking through my panties. My core clenches in anticipation as I wiggle my body on the bed, sliding the dress and underwear down my legs.

My heavy breasts shake with each movement, and his eyes flare at the motion. "Fuck me," he whispers under his breath. He bends over and captures one hard nipple between his teeth, nibbling at it before drawing it into his mouth with a hard suction. He repeats the process until I'm moaning beneath him, grasping his hair, needing him to relieve the deep ache between my legs. He slowly unpeels himself off me and I whimper at the cold air.

"Open your legs. Let me see that wet pussy." He grips his cock tightly, the tip now looking angry and purple.

My legs fall open as he pulls me to the edge of the bed. His fiery gaze stays on me as he kneels on the floor. "My queen," he growls, trailing kisses up my inner thighs, "let me worship you." He sucks the edge of my thigh, where my leg meets the corner of my core. My body trembles as each suction pulls me deeper and deeper into this lustful haze.

"Look at your juices leaking out of these pretty lips." His breath ghosts over the folds of my pussy as I clench, my hips tilting up as he presses me against the bed with a firm grip. "Don't move."

My head twists on the bed as I whimper, desperate for him to do something, anything other than this torture he's inflicting on me. He trails his fingers lightly over the folds as he rubs my juices all over me.

I gasp and tug his hair. "Please, Parker. I-I need more."

"You want me to lick you? To suck you? To eat you up like it's the last meal I'll ever have? Does this soaked cunt want me?"

I nod mindlessly, my eyes fluttering close as my entire focus sharpens to the area between my legs.

"Whose cunt does this belong to? Who are you a filthy slut for?"

"You," I mumble, my hand gripping the blanket next to me.

"Say it again." His finger teases the hardened nub as I arch off the bed in a moan.

"You, Parker! I'm your filthy slut!" I wail desperately.

I feel his smile on my pussy as he growls, "Good girl." His mouth sucks hard on my clit and I scream, seeing stars behind my eyes. I mewl as I gyrate my hips against his face. Gripping my thighs, he doubles down, his suction more intense as his tongue flicks the nub in between kisses. He slams two fingers in and curls at just the right angle, hitting me in a sensitive spot, and I cry out, my juices gushing, coating his fingers in wetness.

"That's so fucking hot," he growls. "Look at you sucking me in like a good slut." He grunts as he finger fucks me in earnest, each wet slurp loud in the quiet studio. I pant hard as the pressure builds at an astonishing speed and within moments, I feel like I'm standing at the edge of a cliff, ready to take the leap into the abyss below. My legs start to tremble around him as he pulls his face away.

He wipes the juices off his face and slowly licks his fingers clean, as if my taste is a dessert he hasn't had enough of. He climbs on top of me, his muscles flexing with each movement. "You don't get to come until you're strangling my cock." The green of his eyes is eclipsed by his blown pupils, and he leans down and bites a hard nipple between his teeth, pain mixing with rising pleasure in an erotic cocktail. I claw at his back, earning me another hiss as I whimper, my legs attempting to coil around his back to bring him flush against me.

Parker hovers before me, the tip of his cock poised at my entrance. His face is flushed, his golden hair in disarray. He breathes hard against my face. "I'm yours, Liz," he whispers, his voice rusty. "And you're mine. I love you."

With that, he slams himself inside me in one full stroke and I cry at the pleasure, not caring if the walls of my apartment are paper thin or if the windows are open. I'm too delirious with pleasure and love to care.

He captures my screams with his mouth as he thrusts hard against me, each stroke filling my emptiness. The sounds of skin against skin echo in the small space as he picks up his pace. I grip his back, my fingernails digging into his muscles, the pain spurring him on. He hoists my legs over his shoulders as he slams back in, the angle deeper and fuller.

"Fuck, I'm so deep inside you, I can flood your womb with my cum, mark you up, and make you mine inside and out." He grunts against me as his cock hits a sensitive region inside, and I arch back in a silent scream. My legs begin to tremble around him as his pace quickens.

"You're going to come soon. I can feel that pussy strangling my dick, wanting all of my cum. Fuck, you take me so well." He brings my hands to my legs, clasping them around my ankles. "Hold on tight and don't move."

I hold on to my ankles with trembling hands as the pleasure builds up, the burning fire coursing through my veins. Suddenly, I feel the tip of his pinkie enter the puckered rosebud of my ass as his thumb swipes my clit and that does it for me.

"Parker!" I scream as I shake around him, my orgasm tearing through my body as he hammers hard inside me. He captures my lips with his in a desperate kiss and my body spasms around him, my juices flowing out in rapid spurts. The orgasm goes on and on as he flicks my clit and pistons hard inside me.

"Fuck. Fuck. I'm going to come," he pants gutturally as he shakes on top of me, his throbbing cock sending spurts of cum deep inside my pussy, the warm liquid prolonging my high. He gradually slows down his movements, his body collapsing on top of me as our harsh breathing fills the air.

"I love you, Liz Chapman," he whispers in my hair as we slowly come down from our fucking. Our lovemaking. Our promises to each other.

"I love you too," I mumble against his skin as I lay there in a daze. He lifts himself off of me and chuckles as he takes in my state. Leaning over to the nightstand, he grabs a tissue and cleans himself up.

He wipes me down gently and I flinch against his caress, the area too sensitive. "The sight of you lying there with my cum dripping out of you," he describes hoarsely, "makes me want to go again." Moaning, I turn my body around, my face buried on my pillow, too tired to move.

"You know, if you think giving me your butt is going to deter me, that's backfiring."

Mustering up my strength, I turn my head around and give him an unconvincing glare, earning myself another deep laugh from him.

I love the sound. I want to hear it all day, every day.

He throws the tissues in the trash can and curls his body around mine, his hot heat lulling me into a deep relaxation.

He murmurs, "I'm sorry for hurting you, Liz. I'll do better, I really will. Please forgive me."

I tighten his arms around me and give him the only reply I've ever had. "I forgive you, Parker. The truth is, I don't think I can ever stay mad at you."

He presses a soft kiss into my hair. "I'll use the rest of my life to make it up to you, so you'll never question my love for you."

With the parting thought, exhaustion overtakes me, and I fall into a deep, dreamless sleep.

My prince is by my side again.

"I can't tell you, it's a secret."

I twist my lips to the side. "What secret? You can tell Auntie Lizzy. I won't tell anyone."

Lucy blinks, her large eyes bright with excitement, and she shakes her head firmly. "Nope. I promised Daddy. I can't break promises. That's bad." Laughing hard, I help her into her thick jacket and put on her shoes.

Two months ago, Parker finally told Lucy about my relationship with her mom. It was a tough conversation to have with a young child, to explain the circumstances in a way she'd understand. Lucy reacted as we thought she would, pelting us with question after question, surprised at the sudden appearance of an aunt, who used to be her teacher and her nanny. Ultimately, after a few weeks, she came around to the idea and has been calling me Auntie Lizzy ever since. She also said she was so happy, much to Parker's and my relief. Parker also told her he really likes Auntie Lizzy and we're special friends now.

"Like a prince and a princess?" she asks, her eyes wide.

Parker takes my hand and places a kiss on top of it. "Yes, just like a prince and a princess."

"Are you going to get married and live happily ever after?"

We laugh as we bring her closer for a group hug. "We hope so. We'll all live happily ever after. What do you say?"

A car honks, drawing my attention back to the present. We cross the street to the new park opened nearby. Some reclusive billionaire bought up huge plots of land throughout the city and has been slowly revamping the areas with new parks, playgrounds, and affordable housing. The press has been speculating about why this man, who never allows his photos to be printed, is playing a game of *Property Investor Tycoon* in the streets of Pasadena. The headlines on the front pages range from "Cold-Hearted Bastard Trying to Revamp His Image" to "City Gentrification a Smokescreen for Something Sinister." I know Parker's firm is working on this massive project, but he can't share more with me, as he is under a mountain pile of non-disclosure agreements. But he is excited. The joy in his eyes when he brings up the project in passing is unmistakable.

The new park, with its bright-orange-and-blue jungle gyms, slides, and swing sets, calls to Lucy's attention. She pulls me, mustering all her strength, as she makes her way to the playground. "Come on, Lizzy! I want to play on the tall squiggly slide."

I clomp after her, my shoes silent across the soft, green grass. "The spiral slide?"

"Yes, hurry up before someone takes it."

Shaking my head, I let go of her hand and watch her run toward the equipment, her two pigtails flying behind her as she shrieks with joy. My heart bursts with warmth. I love this little girl just as much as I love her dad.

Sitting on a bench next to the playground, I take in the scene before me. Happy kids running around the foam floor, some laughing on the swings, others enjoying the monkey bars or the other slides and equipment there. Parents chasing kids across the lawns, some playing with balls and other lawn games. Dogs of multiple breeds running across the grass, yipping and yapping in happiness. The crisp and cool December air finally heralds the holiday season in LA.

"Which one is yours?"

I turn my head toward the soft voice. A woman around my age smiles at me as her fingers point toward the playground. A newborn is snuggled against her chest, wearing the cutest little outfit with a knit cap.

My breath catches in my throat and my heart pangs. *Someday.* This time, I can imagine it clearly in my mind. Parker, Lucy, and me at the park, a small baby with caramel hair and jeweled eyes strapped to my chest.

"The little girl on the slide. The one with the pigtails. She's my niece." Lucy waves at me and I wave back. Niece. I say the word with ease now. *Abby, if you're looking down upon us, I hope you know Lucy is in great care. I'll protect and love her with all of my life.*

"She's really sweet. My oldest is the little guy on the monkey bars."

I smile and chitchat with her for a little bit while Lucy makes her way around every piece of equipment on the playground, her laughter carrying across the area in the light breeze. Before I know it, the sky turns warm pink and orange as the sun dips low on the horizon.

"Lucy! Time to go home. It's been an hour already."

"Five more minutes." Another giggle as she chases a little girl around the jungle gym.

The mom next to me says goodbye as she takes the hand of the little boy and heads toward the parking lot. I stand up and start packing our things for home. Their home for now, at least. I'm still living in my studio until the lease runs out in the summer. Parker has been asking me to move in with him afterward, and I'm inclined to say yes.

Finally, Lucy runs toward me, her chubby cheeks pink from exertion. "That was so much fun! Let's come back again."

"Sure thing, sweetie. Let's go home. I wonder what your daddy has planned for today."

"I can't tell you!" she reminds me.

"I know, I know. I'll find out myself when we get home."

A brisk ten-minute walk later through a neighborhood already fully decked in the bright green and reds of Christmas decorations, we arrive at the beautiful two-story oasis, a place which is already the home in my heart.

Walking up the steps to the front of the house, I pull out the keys from my purse, only to find the entrance already unlocked. Frowning, I push the door open and walk into the dark and quiet foyer with Lucy in tow. Didn't he say he wanted us to be back by four p.m.?

"Parker? We're back!"

Bright lights suddenly flood the room and I take in a small crowd of people gathered in the living room. "Surprise! Happy birthday, Liz!"

"Happy birthday, Auntie Lizzy!"

I clasp my hands over my mouth as my eyes tear up at this surprise party. James grins with Jess by his side. Melanie gives me a peace sign while Emily whistles and cheers. Mom and Dad are standing in the back, having apparently flown in from Boston. Even Steven and Charles are here, with twin smirks on their faces. The living room is decorated with rainbow streamers and helium balloons and the coffee table is littered with presents of all shapes and sizes.

The house is brighter now after I insisted on bringing over some of my colorful art prints to contrast with the black and white photos he has on his walls. A new photo collage hangs on a wall in the foyer, full of colorful pictures of the three of us and friends. The large sofa has giant, soft pillows of blue and lavender, still blending in with the neutral surroundings but adding a pop of color to the barren palette. Small potted plants Lucy and I picked out at a nursery the other day now sit atop the marble counter in the kitchen.

Parker steps into view from around the corner and pulls me to him. Placing a gentle kiss on my lips, he whispers, "Happy birthday, baby. May this be the first birthday of many birthdays you'll spend with me by your side." He smiles, his dimples showing, his shoulders relaxed. A genuine smile, one I've seen in him more and more often these days.

My parents slowly walk up to the front and they crouch down at eye level to Lucy. I bring her over and murmur softly in her ear, "This is your other grandpa and grandma, Lucy. They're so happy to meet you." Mom's eyes are red-rimmed and Dad's eyes have a wet sheen over them. This is the first time they've met Lucy, the granddaughter they didn't know they had.

Lucy smiles shyly next to me. "Hi."

Mom returns a watery smile. "Hello, sweetheart. Can you give Grandma a hug?"

Lucy looks at my parents and thinks for a minute before responding with a nod. She walks over to the two of them and wraps her little arms around Mom's waist.

"Oh sweetie pie, Grandma is so happy to meet you. We'll have lots of fun together."

Dad wraps his arm over Mom's shoulder, giving her a soft squeeze in reassurance. The rest of us look on, no doubt thinking about the dramatic events which have led us to this moment. I wipe my wet cheeks with my sleeve as I lean against Parker, his warmth and strength holding me up.

Dinner is catered from the Greek bistro where I met him for the first time. As we dig into the fragrant food, Parker stands, proposing a toast with a glass of water. After his last drunken episode when his mom cried with him after we broke up, he decided not to keep alcohol in the house anymore. He still drinks when he is out and about but is especially mindful to drink in moderation.

"To the best person in my life, the person who makes me want to become better each day, and the person who has stood by me during my highs and my lows, happy birthday, Liz. You're the brightest star in the night sky, the warmest sunshine during the day. Thank you for being born."

Everyone cheers and I blink away the moisture in my eyes, my lips tipping up in a warm smile. My heart feels so full of love as I'm surrounded by the most important people in my life.

"Sweetheart, I'm so happy to see the smile on your face again," Mom says softly to me, with my dad nodding along.

"Like I said, just like the drama, true love conquers all," Emily chirps, still talking about *Fated for You,* the excellent TV show which has finally concluded with its happily ever after. I haven't finished the show yet with all the work at school and spending my extra time with family and friends. Oddly enough, I don't feel the strong urge to chase after fictional happily ever afters anymore because I'm living my version of happiness in real life.

James rolls his eyes as Jess chuckles next to him.

"So, Charles, why are you here this time?" Parker asks, arching his brow in his best sardonic look.

Steven coughs, choking back a laugh. Charles places his silverware down, completely unfazed. "Bro, you invited me."

"I was just asking an innocent question. No need to get your hackles up." Parker resumes cutting up his kebab, a smirk on his face.

Charles rolls his eyes. "You know, when I decided to join what I later learned is called the..." he looks at Lucy and clears his throat, "'A-hole friends chat group,' I didn't expect to be ribbed on at all times by these two." He points to James and Parker, who give each other a high-five.

"Better you than me," Steven murmurs. "It's a rite of passage."

Emily announces, "Men are like adult-sized children. Why can't they be friends and have normal conversations like us girls?"

"I have no idea, Ems. I have no idea. This is probably why I still haven't found a guy for me." Melanie shakes her head as she spears a grilled bell pepper with her fork.

"Still no fish out there?" I ask.

"Nope. The pond is dry. Dead. Even the lake moss has shriveled up. It's hopeless." She grimaces.

"So, Ems, how are things going with you? You mentioned work is picking up?"

At the mention of work, Emily slams her silverware to the table, the clanging noises drawing our attention to her. "Don't even get me started. They finally told me who my client will be. Have you guys ever heard of Adrian Scott?"

"Everyone knows of him in the business world. He rarely makes appearances in person, but when the shark is coming, everyone swims away." Steven takes a sip of water. "He's your client?"

"Apparently so. It's finally public knowledge now, but his firm will be working with ours on some sort of project I've yet been brought into, but apparently will be involved in when it starts next year. It's supposedly a big win for us."

"He's a billionaire. Deep pockets. I'm sure it's a win for you guys," Charles comments.

Parker looks up, his face puzzled. "You know, he's an old friend from Cornell. I used to mentor him."

Emily whips her head over to him. "Really? What's he like?"

"Hate to break it to you, but he's a good man, very smart, definitely loyal, but not the easiest guy to work with. You have your work cut out for you."

"Ugh." Emily groans as she mock bangs her forehead on the table. "Just my luck."

"Ahem, may I have everyone's attention?" James asks, clearing his throat as he hugs Jess tightly against him. Jess's face pinkens as we all stare at them.

"On this joyous occasion, we want to make an announcement as well. Pile onto the happiness, so to speak." He pauses and grins, his eyes sparkling with excitement. "Jess and I are expecting."

"Oh my gosh! Congratulations, you guys!" I leap out of my chair and hug my brother and Jess. "I'm so happy for you guys. I'll be an aunt again!"

I glance at Lucy and beckon her over. "Lucy, Auntie Jess's tummy has a baby inside. You'll have a cousin to play with soon."

Lucy shrieks and runs over, her little hand careful as she places it lightly on Jess's slightly rounded stomach. "A baby...in there?" she marvels, her eyes wide. She then frowns, as if remembering the conversation we had at the end of her kindergarten school year. "Auntie Lizzy, how did a baby get inside there?"

Melanie coughs. "Clump of cells, right?" Parker cackles at the table, his eyes shining with mirth.

Rolling my eyes, I pin her with a look. "You're no help whatsoever. Not then, and definitely not now."

Squatting down next to Lucy, I respond, "That's a great question, Lucy. Now, why don't you go and ask your daddy?"

Grinning smugly, I give the very flustered Parker a wink as I sit back down. Melanie tips her glass up at me and mouths, "Nicely done."

. . .

The air is chilly at night around the holidays, but I still like bundling up and sitting outside whenever I stay over. Lucy is sound asleep in her princess bedroom. I wrap my scarf tighter around my neck and curl up in the egg-shaped recliner, my favorite seating of choice. Leaning back, I stare at the stars in the sky. The scent of hot cocoa fills the air from my steaming mug on the side table next to me. A few months ago, my heart broke in half in this very garden, but now I sit here again, my heart complete and full to the brim with happiness.

It's funny how life works sometimes.

I reflect on the last few months. Parker is still seeing Marybeth, working on how to process the trauma in his life. He's smiling more, laughing often, his expressions no longer seeming forced to me. He has his tougher days, but who doesn't? On those days, we'd sit side by side on the sofa, watching some old movies. I'd lean on his shoulder as he curled his arm around me. Sometimes he'd share what's on his mind. Other times, we'd sit quietly watching the movie. He doesn't hide from me anymore and for that, I'm grateful.

"It's beautiful out tonight, right?" my favorite gravelly voice asks.

I smile. "Yes, very beautiful." I bring my gaze to his warm eyes, lit up by the ambient lighting in the garden. "Thank you for organizing this surprise birthday party. It's the best birthday I've ever had."

"My pleasure. Seeing you so happy makes all the preparations worth it."

I stare back at the skies, the stars twinkling brightly. The perfect night. My soul feels calm and content.

"Liz, I know we've only been together for a few months. But I think my soul recognized yours the moment we met. You've taught me it's okay to be vulnerable. You've shown me the grace of forgiveness. You've bestowed upon me the priceless gift of your love."

I turn my head toward him and find him kneeling, one knee on the ground in front of me. I gasp and sit up, my heartbeats reverberating in my ears.

"I wouldn't be who I am without you. I'm *nothing* without you. Liz, I love you so, so much. I wake up each day, wondering how I got so lucky to have you here with me, and that you chose me to walk alongside you." He takes a small blue box from his pocket and flips it open. A round, sparkling diamond sits on top of a simple platinum setting. "Liz, maybe it's only been a few months for you, but I can't wait any longer. When I saw this at the store last month, I immediately thought of you. I love you. Will you do me the greatest honor of marrying me?"

I find myself nodding before I can speak. Leaping off the recliner, I wrap my arms around his neck as I stare at his smoldering eyes. I say the only word that comes to mind. The only answer to his question.

"Yes."

Blinking the moisture away from my eyes, I murmur into his ear, "Yes, Parker. Yes, I'll marry you. I love you too."

He chokes up and laughs as he slides the ring onto my finger, pulling my lips toward him for a kiss. A shooting star appears in the nighttime sky, but I barely notice.

And so, the queen and her prince live happily ever after.

"**I** love the sounds you make when you're horny," I murmur against her neck as I slide my hand to her round ass, squeezing the firm flesh. "Is your pussy wet for me?"

Liz moans as her head tips back in pleasure. She's sitting on her stool in front of the vanity in her hotel room. "Parker, we don't have time for this. We need to be at the rehearsal dinner in half an hour."

We checked into the hotel earlier in the day and booked two separate rooms for us because of Liz's insistence the bride and the groom can't see each other after the rehearsal dinner until the ceremony. I stopped by to check in on her, but the sight of her in a white, silky negligee brings me to my knees.

"Why are you wearing that then? If not to tempt me?" My nose travels up to the tender place where her neck meets her ear. The vanilla scent is the strongest there. I want to drown myself in it. I give the area a gentle suction, careful not to overdo it because she'll kill me if I leave her with a hickey the night before the wedding.

"I didn't know you were going to come up. I was wearing this for my—ah," she whimpers as I squeeze her breasts, her nipples hard and showing through the thin material.

"You were saying?"

Liz pants, "Myself. I was wearing this for myself."

"Too bad. I saw you and I need you now." I peel off my clothes in record speed as she stares at me through the vanity mirror, her gaze foggy with arousal. "I'll be quick." Her eyes flare as she takes in my naked form. Her mouth parts.

"Stand up. Arms on the table. Show me that ass." She follows my instructions as if in a trance, and I move to stand behind her. I flip up her short slip and groan as I take in her round ass, clad in the thinnest thong. "Fuck, I'll never get enough of you."

She whimpers as I slide my dick in between her legs and hiss in pleasure. I look in the mirror and nearly come at the sight before me. Her neckline gapes open and her full tits sway as she moves against me. I crowd my arms around her as I cradle her breasts in my hands, thumbing the hard nipples.

"Parker, oh God," she moans and arches against me. I grip her tightly as I get ready to thrust into her wet cunt.

"Look at us in the mirror. Fuck, that's sexy."

Her head whips up as she stares at our reflection, her lips falling open at the erotic sight. Suddenly, her cloudy eyes sharpen as they focus on something in the mirror. "What's that on your arm?"

I smile and kiss the side of her neck. "I went to the tattoo parlor this morning to add this to my arm. *Memento vivere*. It means 'remember to live' in Latin." Twisting her nipples, I'm rewarded with another moan. "Before you, I was too focused on death, on trying to do so much because our time is limited in this world, but I forgot how to live. With you, I finally learned what I really want is to be alive...to enjoy every moment of my waking hours with you by my side." I press a soft kiss against her neck, and she shudders, apparently overcome with emotion.

"I love you, Parker. Take me, please," she pleads as she gyrates her ass at me, the tips of her eyelashes dotted with moisture.

Pulling her thong aside, I whisper, "I love you." I thrust myself inside her and nearly faint from the pleasure of her hot, wet heat gripping my cock.

She mewls at each drive, our movement shaking the table. Curling my hand around her throat, I give it a gentle squeeze. Her eyes snap open. I nip her ears and rasp, "Look at us in the mirror. Look at how I'm going to make you scream." I piston inside her, the heat building fast in my cock. My balls tighten as my muscles tense up. With my free hand, I slip between her legs to circle the hard nub. She whimpers, warm liquid gushing out of her and her eyes flutter closed, her breathing coming in sharp gasps.

"Come, Liz. Come all over my cock."

She lets out a loud scream as she shakes against me, my arm holding her up as I pound against her until I empty inside of her. Our breathing slows as we gradually come down from our high. I chuckle against her hair, beads of sweat gathering on my forehead. "It's always so good with you, fiancée." I lean down and whisper against her ear, "I can't wait to fuck you as my wife." Her face flushes, and she smiles at me.

As if suddenly realizing the time, she snaps up and pushes me away. "Ugh, you totally derailed my plans. Go, go, go. I need to finish getting ready."

Laughing hard, I get dressed and exit her room, feeling like the luckiest man on earth.

• • •

"So, the girls are late, huh?" James murmurs beside me as he looks at the empty chairs at the table for Liz and Jess.

"And so it would seem." I bite my cheek to hide a smile. I have a pretty good guess as to why Liz is late to our rehearsal dinner.

"You don't think she would've gotten cold feet, right? I mean, you're full of drama and shit."

I shoot him a glance. "No, of course not." *No way. Right?* The small voice inside me questions. *No, that's stupid.*

"I mean, marriage is a lifetime commitment, which you already know. But you know her, you're really her first boyfriend. It's common to question whether or not this is it for the rest of your life," he murmurs, his voice piercing in my ears.

My heart kicks against my rib cage and a chill creeps over me. *Irrational paranoia—this is what it is.*

James bursts out laughing, slapping his hand on my back. "You should look at your face. This is payback for what you said on my wedding day, dipshit."

My rioting pulse calms down as I growl, "Fucker. This is not over."

He throws his head back and wipes his eyes with the back of his hand. The asshole is laughing so hard he's actually crying. "Oh gosh, this is a classic. I've been waiting *years* for this moment. And don't you worry, my sister is head-over-heels in love with you."

Just then, as if on cue, Liz comes rushing in with Jess trailing behind her, holding a small wiggling bundle in her arms. My heart warms at the sight of Liz, clad in a classic white sheath dress, her hair carefully pinned up on her head. She mouths *sorry* to me, and I shake my head. Technically, I caused her delay. I sneak a glance at James, who is wearing his heart in his eyes as he stares at his wife and baby daughter, Violet.

Liz and Jess take a seat and Jess hands Violet off to James, who is making funny faces at the baby, completely at odds with his normally wry personality. I grab a flute of champagne and stand, facing the other tables in the room.

"Thank you, everyone, for being here tonight. Liz and I are so very thankful and grateful for your love, your support, and of course, your help in making this wedding happen so I can finally call this beautiful woman next to me my own."

"It's not too late to run away, Liz!" someone calls out from the back.

The room roars with laughter.

"Whoever said that can consider themselves uninvited to tomorrow's festivities." More chuckles sound from the crowd. "We have this room until ten tonight, so feel free to hang out after dinner, enjoy the bar over there, and relax before the big day tomorrow. Cheers everyone." Clinking of glass and excited murmurs fill the room. Since this is my second marriage, we've opted to forgo tradition and pay for everything ourselves. I move to sit down before inspiration strikes me and I stand back up. "Before I forget, James, my best man here, has offered to buy everyone drinks tonight. So, let's raise our glasses to James!"

The crowd breaks out in cheers as I mutter under my breath, "Payback's a bitch, huh?" I lift my brow and level him with a stare.

Amusement shines in his eyes as he grins. "Touché."

Dinner is a cheerful affair as we enjoy delicious food. Everyone has been working hard this past week with getting the details completed and now, it finally feels like we can rest a little. James and Jess make their best man and maid of honor speeches, respectively, and thankfully, their speeches are not too embarrassing.

Soon enough, the night comes to an end. I snake an arm around Liz's waist as we walk toward the door. The elevators open and out steps a tall, dark-haired man with sky-blue eyes. I smile, recognizing my old friend, who has recently become a regular presence in my life.

"Adrian! You didn't have to come. I told you not to worry about it."

He walks over with an ivory envelope in one hand and shakes my outstretched hand. "No, I insist. I feel bad for not being able to make it to the wedding, but with the family emergency, I have no choice." He hands me the envelope. "My wedding present to you and Liz." His normally cold eyes soften at Liz as she brings him in for a brief hug.

"Thank you, Adrian. You didn't have to." She steps back, frowning. "I hope your family is okay."

"I hope so too. I'll be flying out tonight. Thank you for your concern." He smiles softly.

"Adrian?" A shocked gasp sounds from behind us.

I turn around and see Emily frozen at the door, staring at the man in front of us. The color leeches out of her face.

"You know Adrian Scott?" Liz asks, her face clearly puzzled at Emily's expression.

"What?" Emily whispers, her face incredulous. "This is Adrian Callahan."

Adrian moves to step forward but stops himself at the very last second. Clenching his hands into tight fists, his blue eyes turn cold again. He swallows, his Adam's apple bobbing in his throat.

"I go by Adrian Scott now."

Ding. The elevator doors slide open.

Stepping back, he dips his head toward us. "Liz and Parker, congratulations again. May you both have a lifetime of love and happiness." With those words, he turns around and steps into the open elevator, the doors closing on his tensed face.

"Are you okay, Ems?" Liz asks, concerned at her friend, who is still standing there looking shell-shocked.

Emily shakes her head, as if waking herself up from a dream… or a nightmare. "I'm fine. Sorry about that. Ha. Blast from the past." Her face twists up in an unconvincing smile.

Liz nods but doesn't comment further, most likely because she doesn't want to question Emily in front of everyone. She curls her arm around mine as we wait for the next elevator. Melanie, Jess, James, and the others have gathered behind us now, with every-one talking about the festivities tomorrow. Lucy prattles on in the background, having wrapped Liz's parents around her fingers. Her voice sounds louder when she suddenly taps Liz on her waist.

Liz turns around, smiling at her cute little face. "Yes, Lucy?"

"Daddy told me tomorrow you'll be my new mama. Is that true? Can I call you Mama now?"

Liz's eyes tear up as she glances at me. I rub my hand over my jaw, my own eyes prickling as I look at my daughter. Liz faces Lucy again and responds, "Yes, I'll be your new mama, but I'm also your auntie, and you're one lucky girl because you have one mommy in heaven and one mama on earth. We both love you very much." She hugs Lucy tightly. "And yes, you can call me Mama now if you like."

"Mama," Lucy garbles in Liz's hair, "I love you."

"I love you too, sweetheart."

I blink away the moisture in my eyes as the heat of love and happiness spreads through me. Liz pulls away and Lucy sprints back toward her grandparents.

I take Liz's hand in mine, giving it a gentle squeeze, and she looks up at me, joy shining in her deep-blue eyes.

"I love you," I murmur, my eyes staring intently into hers.

"Go get a room, guys!" Melanie taunts behind us.

"Give her a kiss, Parker!" Charles hollers as the cheering continues.

Shaking my head in laughter, I clutch Liz tightly against me. Cupping her face in my hands, I ask, "Are you a coward, Liz?"

Liz throws her head back and laughs, no doubt remembering my question before we went into the closet for the seven minutes that changed everything. She rises to her tiptoes and replies, "Game on." Liz pulls my face down and plants her lips on mine.

The crowd goes wild.

• • •

Thank you for reading THE COLDEST PASSION. Hope you've enjoyed Liz and Parker's story as much as I did writing it. Please consider leaving a review on the retailer website and Goodreads (https://www.goodreads.com/book/show/123246787-the-coldest-passion). Your reviews will really help this author out and will allow for more readers to find this book.

Do you know Emily and Adrian are going to star in the next book, THE HARSHEST HOPE? Their story is filled with angst, steam, all types of swoon, and features a rags-to-riches, dirty-talking billionaire hero. Don't miss it. Order it here: https://geni. us/theharshesthope

Want to tag along with Parker and Liz on their three-year anniversary trip to New York City where Steven wines and dines them, then takes them to the exclusive establishment, Orchid, the pinnacle of Fleur Entertainment? Sign up for my newsletter to get THREE EXTRA BONUS CHAPTERS, new release alerts, exclusive bonus material, and more. Just click on the "The Coldest Passion Bonus Chapters" in the website: www.victorialum.com/bonus

Join my Facebook group, Victoria Lum's Luminaries (https://www.facebook.com/groups/576423100572205) for sneak peaks, exclusive giveaways, and to chat about all things book-related! You can also find me on Tiktok @victorialumwriter, Instagram @authorvictorialum , and other sites at this link (https://linktr.ee/authorvictorialum).

ACKNOWLEDGEMENTS

I can't believe I get to write an acknowledgements section again! I really loved writing Liz and Parker's story and hope it touched your hearts as it did mine. Many thanks to (and not in any order of importance):

My family: To my husband, thank you for putting up with all of my questions, re-reading chapters, and watch me go from a giggly person to a sad puddle in a span of minutes as I deal with plot problems. To my children, thank you for being your awesome selves and for being the light of my life.

My editors: Becca Mysoor, Grace Bradley, and Amy Briggs, thank you as always for all the wonderful feedback, criticism, and working with me as I level up in my skillset as an author. You are my teachers in this journey and I'm so grateful to have you on board.

Proofreader and Formatter: Thank you to Virginia Tesi Carey and Elaine York of Allusion Graphics for getting this baby to the finish line so I can share it with my readers.

My PAs: The awesome Stevie Schneider and Nikki Johnson for helping me with all the tasks associated with getting this book out to the public and also for your guidance on social media and marketing.

Cover designer: To the awesome LK Farlow of Y'All That Graphic, thank you for bearing with me as we try out different photos for Parker before landing on this one.

Beta readers: Malia, Jenn, Jess, Fiona, Suny, and Isha, your feedback is gold! Thank you for answering my many questions, chatting through your thoughts and reactions so I can make this story a better one! I truly appreciate your love and support from the bottom of my heart.

Fellow authors: So many authors have helped me on this journey—it is impossible to name everyone, but I appreciate each and every one of you.

PR Firms: Thank you to Greys Promo and Literally Yours PR for your promotional efforts and helping me get the word out.

My Fellow Readers: Thank you for your continuous support and encouragement. One of the best things to happen to me as an author is to meet you online, whether it is through Instagram or Tiktok DMs, Facebook comments or messages. Thank you for loving my stories and giving me a chance. Without you, I wouldn't be where I am now. I hope you'll continue to stay on the ride for my stories in the future. I love you all.

With love,
Victoria

ABOUT THE AUTHOR

Victoria is a lover of all things romance, including movies, books, and television shows. A hopeless romantic since childhood, she is always dreaming up stories and happily ever afters. Caramel lattes are her fuel in the morning and she can usually be found reading anything she can get her hands on. She lives with her family and a beautiful Siberian husky in sunny California.

Keep in touch!
Sign up for her newsletter below:
Newsletter
https://dashboard.mailerlite.com/
forms/289149/81041142820374109/share

Follow Victoria on social media:
Tiktok
https://www.tiktok.com/@victorialumwriter
Instagram
www.instagram.com/authorvictorialum
Facebook Group
www.facebook.com/groups/576423100572205